Numinous Fortune

His Name Was Augustin
Book VI

C.L. Carhart

NUMINOUS FORTUNE

Book 6 of *His Name Was Augustin* series

Copyright © C.L. Carhart 2022

First edition: June 2022

ISBN: 978-1-954807-11-2 (paperback)

ISBN: 978-1-954807-12-9 (eBook)

https://www.clcarhart.com

Edited by Elizabeth Johnson

Cover Design © J. L. Wilson Designs | https://jlwilsondesigns.com

For Daddy
the sole reason Teutonic magic
may have celestial origins after all

Other Books by C.L. Carhart

His Name Was Augustin [complete series]

Arcane Gateway, Book I
Mystic Passage, Book II
Astral Fantasia, Book III
Cryptic Pathway, Book IV
Lurid Curse, Book V
Numinous Fortune, Book VI
Veiled Magic, Bonus Short Story

Legacy of the Cursed [series in process]

Cursed Escape, Book I
Cursed Desire, Book II
Cursed Omen, Book III
Cursed Wraith, Book IV
Cursed Sorcery, Book V
Cursed Luster, Book VI

Brief Pronunciation Guide

Augustin – Au-GUS-tin
Bayerisch – BEYE-rish (eye is pronounced like eyeball)
Bayern – BEYE-urn (eye is pronounced like eyeball)
Eihalbe – EYE-hahl-buh (eye is pronounced like eyeball)
Freia/Freya – FREYE-yuh (eye is pronounced like eyeball)
Isar – EE-zahr
Jarvis – YAR-viss
Muniche – MYOO-nih-khuh
None – Nohn
Swanhilde – Swan-HIL-duh
Thaden – TODD-n
Torstein – TOR-stein (stein is pronounced like a beer stein)
Toteheri – TOH-tuh-hare-ee
Wuotan – VOH-tahn

You can find a full pronunciation guide and translations at the end of this book.

Table of Contents

Prologue

I prepared at last to compose the final installment of my life story, a portion rife with complexities that astound me to this day. Despite the sorrows hidden within the forthcoming pages, gratitude remained my overarching sentiment as I readied myself to confront the results of my final journey to the eleventh century. Augustin perused the last of Book V while I refilled my inkwell, his visage darkened with conflicting emotions.

"Part of me wishes I wielded the authority to punish those fiends who splintered your twenty-first century life," Augustin commented after I fashioned the title page in elegant calligraphy. "Their crimes tormented you more than I ever realized."

Looking up at him from where I sat upon the stool, I recognized grief and wrath simmering along his aura, his eyes reflecting the candlestick's blue flames. I sighed and admitted, "I think writing it out has helped me come to grips with it in some strange way. Putting the NVH's crimes on paper makes them seem more real, more heinous. Like my anguish is justified."

"No one ought to scorn your heartache," Augustin said. "It pains me to read how desperate you felt then, how Freya's death and Marga's betrayal convinced you that you had no recourse but to offer yourself as a sacrifice." He turned away from me with a groan, hiding his face beneath his left hand.

Augustin was not wrong. Guilt and betrayal scratched at my peace as those awful memories arose anew, how one of my closest friends kidnapped my daughter and used her as a scourge upon my maternal instincts. Marga's envy had inspired her to commit treason against her people. If I had taken more time to nurture a relationship with her, all of those innocent lives could have been spared. The *what ifs* haunted me more often than I preferred . . . and now I was about to write of my presaged reunion with a traitorous Prince.

"At least I never relinquished my grip on hope," I noted, having placed the pen in its inkwell, the fingers of my right hand drumming a staccato rhythm upon the writing desk. "And neither did my son." My lips formed an uneven smile as I recalled his vehemence at time's gateway, when he begged me to find a way to be with my one true love, not Prince Otto.

Augustin caught my eye, a smirk dispelling the tension that had tainted his face. "I would advise you not to prolong the man's suffering. Write, Swanhilde."

He headed for the stairwell and left me alone with my work. Grinning in an expectant fashion, I took up the pen.

Chapter One:
Unexpected Discord

When Joel and I leapt into time's tornadic currents, I prepared myself for the usual experience. Loss of control, my body and spirit shoved violently into a tide that rushed contrary to the direction I traveled. Ghostly whispers spoken by Wuotan's sirens, his inhuman worshippers who mocked time travelers in a dialect understood only by the ancients. Eldritch moans slinking upward from the depths, from an unreachable abyss, horrors to frighten humans who dared to wield magic dissimilar to nature's progression.

In other words, I expected uncanniness that meant nothing in the grand scheme of things. Frights that I could brush off once we reached the gateway at the far end—May 27th, 1074.

But the ordinary escaped me this time.

As soon as I passed through those labradorite gates, my right hand linked with Joel's left, I felt my body upended. My wide eyes caught sight of the gates as they closed behind us and dissolved, leaving nothing but a tangled web of sweltering colors and obscurity in their wake. The standard sensation of advancement against a tide grabbed hold of me—but there was something else there, too. Something more than the mere threads of history trying to block my path.

I heard a *scream*.

That should not have been possible. I recognized the voice as Joel's, and an instant later infernal blades sliced through my torso in a quest for my heart. Terror seized me, and I tried to move my arms to shield myself, to thrust my bag at the spectral entity that attacked me. In vain. The blades pressed deeper, and my eyes wheeled, my neck muscles refusing to shift my head's position. All I could see was the storm ripping at my braid, my clothing, my body.

"Swanie!"

Joel's tortured voice crying out my name snapped me from my confusion. I tried to answer him, but the sound my lips made was that of a dying animal. I *felt* my heart beating against the blades that held it—claws, I abruptly realized—my will infusing me with defiance. *The demon's trying to stop us both. He can't. I refuse to give him that power. We have to reach the past one last time!*

I sought the magic I claimed inside—my Teuton blood, my elemental ice, my eternal spirit. As my mortal lips screamed out in anguish, my soul recognized that it was time I take hold of the beliefs I had thrust at Augustin—a Black Priest bound in a demon's service. If Wuotan wanted to stop Joel and me from reaching the year 1074, only the divine Creator could defeat his plans.

"God!" I cried out, hardly able to force my lips to speak words in the midst of torment. "We belong to You! Bring us . . . to—"

Foolish mortal! Wuotan's sinister thoughts washed over me from the inside out, his claws dragging me toward an infinite void. *Your Deity has no power here! He relinquished his hold on these currents millennia ago.*

Even in my agony, I knew the demon lied, trying to corrupt my faith as his liege lord had corrupted Eve. And now I heard the sirens whispering in my ears, calling me false, traitorous, a disappointment, a Teutonic Lady who allowed her children to die without remorse, who could not prevail against a human antagonist, let alone a fallen angel. But I gritted my teeth and clung to my faith. In the sixty-two years I had walked in various timelines, God had not failed me yet.

"You're the one . . . with no power." I managed to shove the words between my teeth, the pain of the blades tapering off into the tossing of a storm, churning of the countless threads of time. A withering groan pricked my ears, and afterward Wuotan laughed, his scorn finding no purchase.

We shall see about that, Leitalra.

The light of day sliced through the darkness and I landed hard upon grass, Wuotan's frightening epithet ringing in my ears. I felt Joel's grip on my right hand, his fingers slick with sweat as he gave a choking gasp. Breaking my hold on him, I whirled to face the labradorite gates, poised behind us atop the hill where we stood. The violent currents within seemed to reach forward to grasp for me, and I raised my left arm in a silent command.

Be gone! Leave us to greet the past in peace.

A few threads of laughter trickled outward as the portal vanished. I breathed a huge sigh of relief, clutching my right hand to my throat. My leather bag bumped my hip as I shifted my feet and glanced down at the red fabric of my bodice. Had those invisible blades *actually* injured my body?

Before I found the wherewithal to slip a hand beneath my neckline to check, Joel yanked me into his arms, crushing me against his chest. His actions prompted my ice to freeze my blood, my eyes widening in shock as his fingers clutched me in a frantic hold. "Swanie? What . . . the hell . . . was that?"

Joel panted, and my own heartrate increased in the aftermath of what we had experienced. Despite the horrors I sensed breathing down my neck, I had no wish to seek comfort in my ex-husband's embrace. "Can you . . . let me go?"

He stepped away from me, his expression stricken. His graying blond hair appeared somewhat disheveled, and he placed a hand over his dark blue tunic. His hazel eyes shifted from my face to his hand, and he said, "I guess . . . we didn't really get stabbed in there? It sure *felt* like that's what happened!"

"I don't know what happened," I answered honestly, taking a few seconds to look around at the landscape. I recognized the Rhine's waters glinting gold in the sunlight opposite the village below us, farmland extending to the north while dense forests stretched to the south and west. This was indeed the hill beside the eastern trade route, with the medieval village of Eisenwald tucked away under the early morning mist. "It looks like we're in the right place," I remarked.

"Thank God," Joel murmured, sounding distressed. "I was praying the entire time we were caught in those currents. It felt like Wuotan tried to tear me apart."

"Same," I said, invoking my ice magic into my eyes to improve my vision. I saw no signs of stirring amid the houses below, so hopefully no villagers happened to notice the massive gates before they disappeared. "Did he say anything to you?" I shifted my attention to Joel, who stood with his hands on his hips, his chest still heaving.

"Wuotan *said* something to you?" His eyes widened.

"Mocked my faith, basically." Apparently the demon had not felt the need to do the same to Joel. I looked away, memories of my father's warning gnawing at my spirit: *Wuotan didn't say whether he wanted you dead . . . or something worse.*

"Pretty sure demons always do that," Joel said. He had set his things into the grass, bending down on one knee to sift through his quiver of arrows. "I read a story about some old preacher from the 1900s who called up a demon, and it told him he wasn't exuberant enough to keep the crowds entertained. After that, he went all fire and brimstone."

A snort escaped my nostrils. "A preacher who called up a demon. Hypocrisy much?" I laid my own bag onto the ground to give my left shoulder a rest, moving to situate myself upon it. "Did all your arrows come through?"

"Looks like it. There are twelve in here." Joel took in my position and knelt into a more comfortable posture. "It really felt like something was trying to hold us back from coming here. That wasn't anything like our other trip, when it was just the whispers and the laughter."

"Makes me wonder if there's more to my fate than meets the eye." I propped my chin up with one hand and gazed out at the river.

"You don't want to commit suicide with the Prince like Augustin's record said," Joel discerned.

"No. I don't. And I have only twenty-eight days to figure out why he'd write something so insane. Muniche's bonds or not, I *don't* feel some hopeless attraction to the man who cursed my city with his blood. Keyholder or not."

As soon as I spoke the words, though, Muniche's spirit awakened inside of me, her countless departed children wrapping their essence around my heart in an unbreakable grip. A strange sensation of nakedness came over me, as if all of creation saw and mocked my solitude. *Muniche is lost, crumbled, cursed, forgotten,* her city's spirit moaned within me. *Our master has forsaken us . . . the future holds no hope, no light . . . only heartbreak.*

Tears formed in the corners of my eyes, and I shook my head, struggling to reassert my willpower. *Prince Otto doesn't matter. Muniche doesn't matter. The city will be reborn in the next century. I'm here for Augustin—the Teuton priest who loves me for who I am.*

"Swanie, I need to apologize." Joel cleared his throat, distracting me from Muniche's reverie. His eyebrows curved upward as he said, "I shouldn't have grabbed you like that when we burst through the gates. I know you don't feel that way about me. I don't know what came over me."

"You were just in shock. It's okay," I said, still trying to pull my awareness away from Muniche's distress. Each heartbeat brought renewed discomfort.

"No. It's not. I felt you freeze, sensed your element coming to the fore. I'm sorry."

I sighed, my shoulders drooping a little. "I'm the one who should apologize to you," I confessed, guilt agitating my spirit. "I should have been honest when you tried to court me the first time we came here. I knew you weren't my type from the start, but I was too afraid to tell you."

"At least we both got to relish true love in the modern day," Joel said, his fingers running the length of his bowstring.

I managed a half smile in response, for I had not told Joel about the bomb Hans dropped on his deathbed. My true love was here, south of Eisenwald, hidden in a woodland cabin apart from civilization—apart from the living. But the dead city of Muniche wailed for Prince Otto, the Keyholder who rejected her.

"What made you fall for Augustin?"

Joel's question surprised me. "Is this the moment where we're supposed to spill our guts or something?" I raised an eyebrow at him, sensing the dew in the air around us. If we sat too long on this hill, we might need more than the spring's sun to dry our clothing. I took a deep breath, working to maintain my focus on the here and now.

"I'm just curious." Joel smiled and scratched at the slight growth on his cheek.

My gaze drifted toward the forests to our left as I replied, "It was mainly the fact that he treated me like a peer instead of like a brainless, emotional woman. You know we spent hours studying English and Ælte Teutonica before the Prince cursed him." I glanced at Joel, and he nodded.

"He was smart, experienced, and unashamed of who he was. He had a reason for everything he did, even the terrible sins. And he was honest. He taught me things about Teutonic magic that no other priest would dare to unveil."

"Gust told me you had the heart-bond with him."

That threw me for another loop. I should not have left Joel alone with my twenty-first century son, apparently. There seemed to be no point in denying it, so I said, "Augustin held my heart for twenty-three years. And he didn't need a city's influence to inspire his devotion. We loved and respected each other."

"I think I might agree with what your son said before we leaped through the gates," Joel admitted, his forehead wrinkled. "'Find a way to be with the man who loves you.' Screw the Prince. If I were you, I'd run off with the Cursed One."

I chuckled at how he phrased it. "That's my plan as soon as you've made the Rhine your grave. Assuming Muniche's bonds don't give me heart failure. We probably ought to decide how we're going to handle this . . . seeing our children again. Cammie and Max might recognize us."

Joel looked thoughtful. "Are you sure about that? Your hair was short back then." He nodded at my braid. "And you're in better shape now, for that matter."

I scowled at him. "Thanks a lot." It had taken a lot of effort to rein in my urge to overeat after the NVH targeted my family. I had gained only five kilograms as a result of stress.

"I'm not sure if they'd recognize me, either," Joel went on. "I had a full beard in the eleventh century, and my hair was longer then, too. I probably should have dyed it before we left your son's castle."

"Too late now. I'm not going back through those gates for a do-over. Besides, I didn't bring the Torstein."

"Yeah, I know. We need to come up with a story either way, for why we're here, who we are." Joel rubbed his forehead.

"Teuton adventurers seeking asylum from the Saxons," I supplied.

"What should our names be?"

That gave me pause. "Well, Heinrich and Freia will know who we are. But I guess if we want to keep our travels secret from our children, we'll have to ask them to call us something other than Swanie and Joel." I tried to think through the names of our noble peers from years past.

"I could be Otto. Or Paulus." Joel shot me a goofy look as he rose to his feet and stretched, shaking dew from his sleeves.

I scrunched my nose at him and stood up myself. "I'll be Hildegard and you can be Dominik." Those were the names of the husband and wife who had occupied a neighboring estate to ours, back in Muniche.

"So we're the Kueglers. Fantastic." Joel shouldered his bag and quiver, then nocked a single arrow. "I might try to hit a squirrel on our way into town. So we'll look like true adventurers."

"I'm surprised you remember so much about a time you claimed to 'forget,'" I said as we descended the hill toward the trade route.

"The dreams never stopped," he muttered, his wind evident in his eyes as he scoured the grasses for unsuspecting prey.

Eisenwald lay still and quiet below the hill, the dirt path marking the eastern trade route curling off toward the main street. Joel and I set out for that familiar path, and he voiced a few reminisces about the last time we had come. I remained silent as we progressed, my thoughts in many directions. Part of me followed Joel's recollections—the children frolicking upon the grassy knoll, running into Freia's old nanny on the street, getting to know Lord Edwin, Freia's gracious father.

But I also thought of meeting that phantom on the river, when I observed the Rhine snaking along its time-worn path. He had paddled us to his cottage, the bonds of the spirit loosened at last . . . the glory of our mutual love during that day we spent together . . . and the horror of the night, facing the demon who had long conquered my lover's sanity. Would I have to fear such a thing when I sought my immortal husband in several days? Wuotan had tried to slay me in time's currents. If he took charge of Augustin's hands, the demon could launch me back to my son in the twenty-first century—back to a place where Muniche's bonds lured me into a relationship I could never consummate.

I have to plant myself here in this timeline, whether Wuotan likes it or not, I told myself, shoving aside the past that haunted me. *I don't think he possesses his Black Priests very often, only when he's aroused their anger.*

And Augustin shouldn't be angry to see me again . . . I hope.

Joel shot an errant squirrel before we reached the edges of the village, his hands directing the arrow with ease. It struck the squirrel right through the nose, and Joel flopped its body over his shoulder with the remark that he could offer it to the cooking pot that afternoon. That reminded me that most people ate only two meals per day in this era—lunch and dinner. Lunch would be at Sext or noon, and dinner would be at Vespers or twilight. Eisenwald's church bells had not rung since our arrival; I judged the hour to be somewhere between Lauds and Terce.

I heard livestock stirring as we neared the first cottages, but overall the town appeared strangely quiet. We ran into no one on the road. When we reached the main street we saw just a few women headed for the well, a pair of boys herding a troop of goats. None of the townsfolk looked our way, and I noticed that the women all sported scarves tied about their noses—odd, for the weather was balmy for late May.

"So why is everyone scurrying around like they're expecting the apocalypse?" Joel muttered to me in English, casting doubtful glances toward those gathered at the main well.

The truth hit me in the face, for I realized that I had seen no boats moored at the wharf—an extremely rare occurrence at this Rhenisch town dependent on trade. "Augustin's record . . . mentioned a pestilence."

Chapter Two:
Pestilence

"You mean to tell me," Joel said in a flat voice, "that we've escaped one virus just to dig up another? Or is this one bacteria-related like the Black Plague?"

"What is it with you and the Black Plague?" I beckoned Joel to follow me into a shadowed alley between a pair of shuttered businesses. On our first journey to the past, he had attributed every sniffle to the plague, which would not hit Europe until the fourteenth century.

Joel paused at the street corner and glanced toward those gathering at the well. "Did you look up our children's lifespans? Are any of them going to die from whatever this is?" He leveled me with a grim stare and shifted his feet.

I shook my head and leaned my back against the log wall of what I judged to be a woodworker's shop—the scent of sawdust itched my nose. "I didn't dive too deeply into our children's lives, but they'll all survive this pestilence. Erika's the only one who dies young, in 1091." I shut my eyes to concentrate on my ice, extending its mysticism in a silent quest for other Teuton spirits.

"You could make a good living here as a fortune teller."

"Quiet. I'm trying to sense where everybody lives," I snapped at him. Joel's type of humor did not usually appeal to me; and it certainly did not now, when we had come for the sole purpose of dying. Offering our lives to the Rhine River. I felt the spirit of its waters weaving around me, inviting me to rejoice through dance. Gritting my teeth, I shoved its amity aside and quietly listed the pulses of Teutonic life that inhabited the Rhenisch town.

"Energy, light. Ice, whirlwind, yellow fire. Earth, metal, light . . . there! That's Freia and Heinrich, the light and metal together. There are other Teutons nearby, in the same house. Earth and air . . . another metal and fire."

I felt Joel's hand on my shoulder, jostling me slightly. "Enough is enough. I don't think we need an exhaustive list of all the Teutons in Eisenwald. Lead on."

Freia and Heinrich had taken residence in a sizeable dwelling adjacent to the local foundry. I remembered Augustin telling me that Heinrich worked there alongside his eldest son and mine—as of 1067, at least. Whether that was still the case seven years later, I could only speculate. While Joel murmured a few thoughts on the value of his old friend's metal in a foreign town, I considered the elements I detected earlier, trying to discern to whom each belonged.

The energy and light together would be Max and Katchen Denlinger; they probably married, like my son had hoped. Cammie would be ice, and whirlwind must be Alger Mohr, the knight who came here with Heinrich. I hope she's having a pleasant marriage, one built on love rather than necessity. There were a lot of elements in the Denlinger house. Earth would be Lorraine, air for Erika, metal for Freia's son Edwin, and fire might be one of the servant girls. I wonder if Jarvis and Ulka are still alive.

We soon reached their front porch, a wooden affair adorning the wall that faced the street, wide enough to serve as the stage for a modified dance. Hesitation gripped me as I climbed the three steps at Joel's side. The house appeared serene in the light of early morning, its shutters closed, not a servant or child in sight. Would Freia and

Heinrich be happy to see us? What would they say when they learned why we had come?

"Do you think they're all sick in there?" Joel asked, his brow wrinkling as he paused at the threshold. The house before us showed no sign of life, apart from the smoke rising from two of its chimneys.

"I hope not, but I'm starting to think we're breaking some local taboo, wandering the streets so boldly during an epidemic." I glanced back the way we had come; the road behind us remained deserted. The ironworks, which rose from the ground at the edge of the forest not forty meters from where we stood, appeared dark and silent, emitting no smoke into the sky.

Joel sighed and dumped his bow and quiver of arrows onto the porch along with his squirrel. "The longer we wait, the less time we'll have to see how our kids are doing. I had my flu shot, anyway. I'm not afraid of any pestilence." He knocked firmly, then stepped to the side with the declaration, "Ladies first."

I smacked him on the shoulder, irritated at his disjointed sense of humor. Joel had changed little over the years aside from growing more cynical. "I hope you catch the pestilence and die," I said, only half-joking. "Then you'll have to do this all over again."

"In my attempts to lower the fever, I'll conveniently bleed myself and jump into the Rhine." Joel knocked again and smirked at me.

I huffed, placing my hands onto my hips. "You still don't take anything seriously, do you?" I accused, recalling how he had shrugged off so many issues during our lengthy stint in the past.

His smirk wavered. "The one thing I can't laugh away is my family's fate. Some things are hard to forgive."

I lowered my eyes, ashamed for teasing him so harshly. I had no right to scorn Joel now, when we had come to Eisenwald with shattered lives behind us. Wuotan and his racist cronies should have left Joel's family alone. He had shunned Teutonic traditions entirely when he built his life in the U.S.

He frowned at the closed door, his irises taking on a grayish hue. "They really must be in there dying, since they won't come to the door," he commented, his wind brushing the locks of my hair that had escaped from its braid. "And they *are* in there. Even I can sense the elements. Light, metal, earth, air."

"Maybe their house is quarantined." I concentrated on my ice again, sending it beyond the door to call for Freia, my radiant friend. A moment later, I heard the sound of approaching footsteps, so I took a deep breath in an attempt to gather my courage, unsure what sort of welcome awaited us.

A latch clicked, and the door swung open to reveal a darkened parlor lit by a single candlestick poised atop the hearth across from the entrance. A weary woman stepped into the sunlight to greet us, clad in a simple tan dress and apron, her waist-length blond hair uncovered and flecked with threads of pure white. Her green eyes, ringed with wrinkles and circles of fatigue, locked with mine and widened, her pale lips parting into an *O* of shock.

I stared back at her without speaking, my words having gone out of me. And she whispered my name in evident disbelief, "*Swanie?*"

It took me a second to order my brain to switch from thinking in German or English to Teutonica, my people's dead language. Swallowing, I fashioned the first sentence and spoke it. "I apologize . . . for coming . . . at such a bad time."

Freia waved her left hand dismissively and stepped onto the porch, shutting the door behind her. "No, you need not apologize. When I sensed your ice out here, I feared you were Cammie bringing me a sick child. Lorraine has some skill with remedies, you see." She shook her head and leaned against her front door, offering Joel a belated and faltering smile.

"I read about the sickness," I told her, then clarified, when I saw her frown, "in Augustin's histories."

"Ah." Freia's features became unreadable. "He's trying to convince my brother-in-law to stop all trade until the illness has run its course. This disease came from the trading ships, naturally. But Reginald doesn't always take his advice, although the town does look barren this morning." She nodded toward the deserted streets.

"I read about that, too. Augustin's advice to halt commerce." Freia gave me a doubtful look, and I rushed to reassure her. "But don't worry. Only eighteen people will die of it; and afterward, life will go on." I had read through the 1074 tome from May to October, so I was confident of Eisenwald's recovery.

Freia's lips twitched, her gaze dropping from mine to the boards of the porch. "Unfortunately, my youngest child has already passed, and one of my grandchildren lies on her deathbed now."

The sorrow in her tone broke the barriers between us. I embraced her tightly, my eyes dampening as I felt her weeping upon my back. We stood like that for a long time, two mothers who shouldered the pain of loss, our spirits entwining with offerings of consolation and understanding. As my ice communed with her brilliant light, a small portion of the guilt that had hampered me since the NVH began murdering my loved ones slipped away.

This is enough, I thought to myself as a measure of peace calmed my heart. *Even if Augustin and I can't work out some way to subvert my recorded destiny, it's enough to be together with Freia. How I've missed her.*

Freia dried her eyes upon her apron when we parted. "Forgive me. I try not to cry in front of the children. I've been doing all of this talking and weeping, and I still don't know why you and Joel are here."

She sniffed, forcing a smile as I shuffled a bit, suddenly unsure whether I wanted to admit the morbid reasons for our visit. "If I'd known you were coming, I'd have arranged a celebration."

"We just got here today." Joel spoke up at last, standing off to the side with his hands thrust in the pockets of his trousers. "I doubt we could have sent you a message first, with a thousand years between our home and yours."

Freia laughed a little, brightening at his joke. Then Joel took on the role of chivalrous gentleman, gesturing toward the weapons and kill he had discarded by the porch's railing. "I shot this squirrel when we were coming down from the hill. If your family needs any fresh game, I could do some hunting."

Freia hesitated at first, but I mentioned that Augustin's writings claimed the pestilence would rage for over a month. Therefore, it might be best to stock up since some of the shops in town were closed. My friend gave a single nod and urged Joel to go, asking him to bring his kills around the back of the house to be cured. He departed, shouldering his bow and quiver while leaving his pack behind. Freia suggested that I make myself comfortable on one of the porch benches while she prepared tea.

In her absence, I set my own pack down beside Joel's and leaned my elbows upon the railing, my ice sharpening my vision to gaze toward the cluster of houses and shops with the Rhine River beyond. Joel and I were here now, on May 27th of 1074, having forsaken the tumult of the twenty-first century. I had left my cursed son, Max, in charge of exacting vengeance upon the Saxon extremists who murdered our friends and family in a mad effort to obtain the Torstein—the blood-red stone with the power to summon time's gateway.

Now it was up to Max to protect both the Torstein and the Teuton people. A dead man bound to Wuotan who had put his faith in God. Wuotan, the nefarious demon who tried to slay Joel and me less than an hour ago, when our bodies and souls writhed in time's currents. Joel and I came here with the intent to die, after catching up with Freia and Heinrich and seeing the lives our eleventh century children had built for themselves. But the demon who had haunted me since I first found the Torstein attempted to block us from reaching our goal.

In vain.

Why would he care if we're here to die? Shouldn't he be glad we won't be around to disrupt his evil schemes anymore?

Before I could work out Wuotan's motivations, Freia reappeared with two pewter cups of mint tea. As I took the one she offered to me, her husband slipped out of the house, his gait halting, though he carried naught but his own teacup. Heinrich favored me with a polite nod, his cheeks hollow beneath his gray beard. "It's good to see you again, Swanie. Can't say I ever expected you to return, though my wife has always believed." He and Freia settled themselves onto the bench that faced the road.

"I wish I had come at a better time," I said as I took a seat upon the chair to their right, the tea's warmth seeping into my fingers, a welcome feeling. Heinrich would be nearing sixty now, if I judged his age correctly. His tunic seemed to hang from his shoulders, unlike the robust man I remembered from medieval Muniche. "Have you been sick with the pestilence?"

Heinrich bowed his head, and Freia answered me in a quiet voice. "He only just regained the strength to get out of bed last night. When I told him you were here, he insisted upon greeting you himself, against Lorraine's advice."

I judged from Heinrich's body language that he did not wish to discuss his weakened state. But a morbid curiosity chewed at my insides. "Are there any others . . . who are sick in your house?" Freia had already lost one child and mentioned an afflicted granddaughter.

"Erika has it, but she's starting to improve," Heinrich replied, his gaze fixed upon the road. "Same with our grandson Otto." He cleared his throat and finished, "Baby Swanie has been listless since yesterday morning; Lorraine can't get milk or tonic into her. Jarvis likely won't last another day."

"Jarvis," I whispered, his status upsetting me more than the idea of a dying baby named after me. He had managed the Thaden estate so effectively over the years, his guidance directing my steps. I wondered whether I dared show myself to him, to wish him an easy crossing into eternity. If he was delirious, like Augustin's record described, he might imagine me a saint.

"It's been a difficult month, but we're doing well overall," Freia put in, her sunny countenance cheering me despite the situation. "Cammie married Alger of Freising just six years ago, and they have two young boys. They've established a grain farm on the northwestern edge of town, and our son Heino helps them run it, along with Emilie. They're married now; her first husband died in battle."

I sipped at the tea in my cup, ordering my brain to keep up with Freia's tales of our children. My oldest daughter, Cammie, was married with sons and a farm. Heino Denlinger set aside class differences to wed Jarvis' daughter, Emilie. Two new families whose Teutonic magic would remain strong. "Are Max and Katchen together?" I asked, remembering the energy and light I had sensed near the riverbank.

Freia nodded. "They married the year before Cammie did. Max directs the flow of goods along the Rhine. He has a talent for business."

"He was the first who caught the pestilence," Heinrich added, "but he's already pushed through it. Strong lad."

My son Helmut was apprenticed to the tanner and had married a Rhenisch girl just two years before. They lived in a garret of the tanner's cottage and were expecting their first child. I cringed at the notion of Helmut diluting his magic with an outsider, but Freia offered a kind explanation. "He fell in love with Holda, the tanner's daughter, because she sings almost as beautifully as you. Helmut always had an affinity for music, you remember."

I nodded, taking a sip of tea to conceal my disappointment in him. But then Freia said, "He gave his blood for her."

A trickle of tea slid down my windpipe. For a minute I coughed and gasped for breath, my hands clutching the arm of the chair where I sat. "*He* . . . gave his blood . . . for *her?*" I barely got the words out, but Heinrich and Freia both affirmed it. "It *worked?*" I had never heard of a successful cross-gender blood-transfer.

Freia managed a small smile and pointed out, "We trusted him."

I rubbed my temple, frightening images filling my mind. The gentle Helmut, howling in agony as a blue-fired demon tore his arteries from his body and burnt them in Wuotan's flames. "They didn't do it in public," I guessed, shuddering at the memory of the bloody river drowning my spiritual lungs.

"They went to his cottage," Heinrich said with a pained expression. After glancing at his wife, he finished, "They came back alive, and ninety-seven percent."

I barked out a hollow laugh, disturbed at how major a role Augustin seemed to play in this Rhenisch village inundated by Teuton refugees. Then Freia told me about Erika and Hansi—who went by Johann now. Erika was betrothed to Edwin Denlinger, who worked at the foundry alongside his father. Their wedding would be held in August, and they planned to build their own cottage near the ironworks as soon as they could afford it.

Johann, my youngest, had a talent for archery like his father. He currently had no love interests and spent most of his days in the forest, hunting game and trading it at the butcher's. That meant Joel might run into the kid during his own hunting expedition. I hoped he would handle himself wisely if they met.

By that time, the three of us had finished our tea, so Freia collected the cups and said that she would have Felda prepare a chamber for Joel and me. "Lorraine has isolated the sick upstairs, but there's a small room near the kitchen that you can use."

I studied Heinrich out of the corner of my eye as we waited for his wife to return. The war had aged him, but his back was as straight as ever, his hands still sturdy, although the pestilence had stolen some of his bulk. His hair retained no trace of its natural light brown; his gray eyes carried strains he might never express. Part of me longed to ask after his experiences in battle, but I knew not how.

He spoke again after a time, his gaze upon the roses ornamenting the bushes that lined the porch. "The last time I saw Joel, he led a group of soldiers on a hunt outside of Bamberg. Supplies were running low, and the ground was still frozen. I heard later that he died. It's peculiar sometimes, being friends with a time traveler." Heinrich managed a wan smile and turned his face toward me.

His story sent me into February of 1061, to that morning when I awoke to find the scar from our Teutonic marriage gone. I had assumed Joel died in battle, but upon our return to the future . . . .

"Did you get it too?" I heard myself asking the beaten warrior. "Dysentery?" I wrapped my arms around my torso.

"It ran through Count von Reuter's regiment, not the Prince's."

So Heinrich had been spared the dehydration, the terrible death. Grateful though I was for this news, Muniche's mournful spirit agitated my heart, unveiling a worse memory. Prince Otto and his knights poised upon the city wall as the Saxons and their inhuman allies ravaged her, casting their blood upon her stones, her avowed master abandoning his duty, cursing her to Wuotan.

"Did you . . . help the Prince . . . curse Muniche . . . with your blood?" I could not look at Heinrich as I asked the question. I tightened my arms around myself, trying to smother Muniche's anguish, to reassert my willpower.

"I did not," Heinrich answered, bitterness lacing his tone. When I met his eyes, I saw that his element had darkened them. "I could not betray my mother in such a way. On that night I questioned my loyalty to him, the Keyholder who dared relinquish his obligation to one of Satan's minions. Treason."

I could have hugged him, but instead I loosened my arms and smiled as a sense of validation washed over me. Heinrich knew the Prince had sinned, and he was brave enough to take a stand for our city's honor. Before I decided how to thank him, he asked what brought Joel and me back to the eleventh century. And I replied without thinking, my discernment evaporated. "We came to die."

A beat of silence, and then a bladed interjection. *"What?"*

Chapter Three

These Final Hours

Freia spared me from her husband's interrogation, but Heinrich grumbled a few phrases implying that Joel had better return for the noon meal. He seemed to view his suicidal intentions as a personal offense, and I wondered whether Joel would be able to keep up with whatever vitriol Heinrich wished to unleash. A practicing Catholic, he believed suicide barred the gates of heaven. Neither Joel nor I shared that belief, yet it would be instructive to learn whether his most trusted eleventh century friend could sway him.

Joel had nothing left to live for . . . but here in this era, five of his children lived in peace. Maybe there was more to his story, and more to my own.

Freia showed me around the yard after her husband went inside to rest. She listened while I finally told her what brought me back to her time. A widowed Lady who had lost everything at the hands of a demon and his human sycophants, her end described in her cursed husband's ancient volume. *Fate wished to smile upon the shamed Prince one final time, sending his Lady back to him as a comfort in his final days, a companion in death.*

Augustin had sealed my fate in blood. I was to die on the 27th of June.

My best friend's visage appeared distraught by such a prospect. She took my left hand in her right, clutching it as though she would never let go. We passed by a small collection of sheep and chickens, likely the same ones I had sent with my children in the spring of 1066 when they departed Muniche for good. Then we entered the barn to spend some time with the horses, several of which I recognized. While I stroked the tan-and-white-splotched mare Erika had treasured, Freia voiced her thoughts on my prophesied demise.

"I'm not comfortable with what your husband's record suggests," she said, her back turned to me while she ran a brush through the mane of a dark horse in another stall. "You've read many accounts of Prince Otto's suicide, I'm sure. It's sensible that Wolfgang would have witnessed and recorded an event like that. But he's the only chronicler who mentioned your involvement." She shot me a worried look and offered the dark horse some berries from her pocket.

"Augustin wouldn't have lied about something that momentous," I noted, unsure what Freia meant to imply. "A Keyholder and Lady dying together."

"Whether Prince Otto's faith will be enough to save him, I can hardly judge," Freia went on, not sounding especially concerned whether he would reach heaven or not. She had watched him curse his city just like I had; neither of us harbored a positive opinion of our people's Prince.

"But Swanie, what are you hoping to gain by ending your life with him? I've reminisced about how you and Wolfgang cherished each other on those final days often, over the years. I remember how your aura glowed with joy when you told me your heart-bond remained, even after we leaped to the future."

Her green eyes locked with mine as chills swept over me from head to toe. With time, Muniche's spirit had blurred my memories of Augustin, fixing my desire upon

Hans, my Keyholder . . . the man who preferred a woman long gone. Here, the throbbing bonds of a dead city cried out for the master who deserted her, Prince Otto von Bayern. The coward who cursed his brother to prove himself worthy of Wuotan's approval.

It nauseated me to sense Muniche's attempts to modify the yearnings of my heart, to convince me that I needed the Prince, not Augustin.

"I don't know what to think, or what to do," I confessed, my voice breaking over the words. I buried my face in the horse's tawny mane and mumbled, "I don't want Prince Otto that way, not at all. But Muniche does, and she's stronger than me. She's whittled away at me for twenty years, fueling my need to serve the Teuton people, to help them, to protect them, to lead them at my *Leitaeri's* side. And here in this place, Prince Otto is my *Leitaeri*. And he's destined to die in a month. Every historical account agrees on that."

I heard Freia sigh, and I lifted my forehead from the horse's neck, giving her a grateful pat. "We have no right to take away the life God has granted," my friend said, her back turned to me again. "In battle it can be justified, but no one seeks to harm you here. You left your enemies in the future. And yet you wish to play God over your own life, your own destiny. You can't be certain your path is complete if you take up the knife yourself."

"I know. I *know*," I groaned, stomping away from her to the far end of the barn's hallway and back. "I don't *want* to kill myself with Prince Otto. I want to go to Augustin's cabin, to bare my heart and stay with him for all of eternity, like we promised in our vows. But he's going to be on earth for another four hundred years, and it'd probably be worse for him to have me only to lose me again." I clenched and unclenched my hands as I paced, frustration simmering inside of me.

"Maybe there's some other way to interpret what your husband wrote in his record," Freia suggested. "I don't think he'd give up on you that easily. I remember how he acted after he broke your heart-bond."

Dread froze my feet in place, and I lifted my chin to meet her eyes. I chewed on my cheek for a second, then said, "Tell me." Part of me feared to know. I braced myself for the worst.

Freia's lips formed a sad smile. She reached back to stroke the dark horse's nose as she said, "He used to mention you from time to time, whenever we chanced to meet on the street or if I saw him with Reginald. But he has always drifted here and there, chasing the Saxons and the *Toteheri* until he desired a respite from the fray. Then he'd return to his cabin and make deals with my brother-in-law, always watching over the Teuton refugees, though most of them fear him. He was here six years ago, and when I ran into him at the port he said that he'd been seeking your Keyholder, that once he found the man, he would have to break your bond.

"He paddled back to his cottage a few days later, and no one saw him in town for nearly a year. Reginald assumed he stalked the *Toteheri*, but I feared otherwise. Several times that summer, I sat amid the flowers, my light embracing the sun. And when I blocked everything from my mind save that magnificent light, broadening my spirit to span the far reaches of the forest . . . ."

She broke off with a shudder, then admitted quietly, "I almost believed I could hear him screaming, a blue fire burning out, barely answering the brilliance of the fire that brightens me. When he finally visited Eisenwald, he was changed. More distant than ever, more reserved, conducting most of his business after dark . . . and he never spoke of you again." Freia's eyes were filled with sorrow.

"So you're saying he mourned me and then finally moved on," I translated, disappointment deepening my despair.

"No, I don't think he ever moved on." Freia crossed the floor to my side and gave me a supportive hug. "I think he hid from the world for a whole year after he lost you. Your husband won't let you escape him again without a fight."

My ice sensed my friend's light reaching out to me, trying to bolster what little hope I had left. So I did my best to claim her optimism as we headed back to her house, though I feared I could never regain the devotion Augustin and I once shared. Muniche would always stand in the way, closing my heart off from the man who sought it without reservation.

Lunch at the Denlinger house was an intriguing event, and not just because the stew included pieces of Joel's squirrel. My ex-husband returned from the forest right at Sext with a pair of hares. After handing those off to a servant around back, he found Freia and me in the kitchen and blabbed about our youngest son, without offering to help with the food.

"Johann's eyes look exactly like mine!" Joel groused in English, sprawled upon a stool before the cooking fire. "And he comes up past my shoulders. He's thirteen, right?"

I rolled my eyes as I helped Freia retrieve mugs for everyone. "Johann's birthday was on the 9th of this month, so he hasn't been thirteen for long. You didn't tell him you're his dad, did you?"

"We didn't say that much to each other. I've been stumbling a lot when I speak Teutonica. He asked me what it's like to be an adventurer, and I had to make something up. The kid has two geese already," Joel emphasized, holding up two fingers. "I think he said he stays out most of the day, but he'll be back at dinner."

I translated that for Freia, who said, "It's impossible to keep that boy indoors. We're never short on game, thanks to him."

"His element is snow," Joel declared.

"Like Beth's," I murmured, remembering how my cousin and I used to dance in winter, our elemental magic summoning the ice and snow to encircle us in mystique. Beth, like many of my loved ones, had fallen prey to the NVH, poisoned alongside her dear husband.

"Wait. Beth did the blood-transfer?" Joel lowered his voice and trailed Freia and me into the dining room, where some of the household had gathered around an expansive oaken table.

"That's a story for another time," I replied. "Remember, we're the Kueglers. Dominik and Hildegard," I added under my breath. I saw Heinrich glowering at us from the head of the table, and I noticed a few other familiar faces. Would any of them identify us?

Joel sat upon the bench to Heinrich's left, his countenance alight with joy as he greeted his friend of old. To Heinrich's credit, he conducted himself with the utmost decorum, making polite conversation rather than condemning our lethal plans. Freia sat on her husband's right with me at her side, and I concentrated on my food for much of the meal, listening while the others chattered.

Lorraine Denlinger sat directly across from me, her light brown hair tucked beneath a violet covering, the scents of medicinal herbs rising from her clothing. She was twenty-seven and had not married, though I noticed her casting glances toward Joel beside her. She gave him her full attention anytime he talked, curiosity seeming to shine in her hazel-green eyes. At first I feared that she recognized him from years past, but she did not pay me any special heed.

My daughter's fiancé, Edwin Denlinger, sat to my right, his build identical to his father's—an ironworker whose element reflected his vocation. Concern radiated off of him in strong waves; he asked Lorraine about his fiancée's health three times. Across from him was Beni, the last child Freia bore before Muniche's destruction. He seemed more interested in his brother's and father's duties at the foundry than in any of the adult conversations.

Servants occupied the far end of the table. I did my best to avoid looking toward them, for the majority were old enough to connect me with their former mistress. Felda and her husband were in their forties now, with three children of disparate ages between them. Along with her youngest, a boy, Felda was in charge of supervising Freia's little blond girl, Anna. The cute five-year-old insisted upon clambering all over Heinrich's lap after she finished her vegetables. This brought a gleam of delight into her father's eyes, and he encouraged her to recite a bunch of Bible verses in Latin.

Seeing the Denlingers interact with one another filled me with happiness. Although I had not been privileged to create a family with my one true love, Freia had reaped the glories that evaded me. Her faith remained strong, her contentment evident in her smile. *And yet she still wants to see me with Augustin, even though his record stated otherwise. The Black Priest's living consort, fated to leave the earth and him within a decade or two. Can I really ask that of him?*

When the meal ended, I asked Lorraine whether Joel and I could check on Jarvis, delirious or not. Her eyebrows arched downward as she inquired if the two of us had already recovered from the pestilence. "We haven't, but we meet all sorts of sicknesses on the road. It'll be fine," I assured her. She dithered for a minute but ultimately allowed it, advising us to make our visit brief.

Jarvis lay upon a thin mattress in a tight garret beside the staircase. I could not stifle a gasp of horror when I saw him, for he looked nothing like I remembered. A single candlestick stood upon a small table, along with a bowl of water with towels and a few potion bottles. The natural flames cast shadows upon Jarvis' sunken face. His skin resembled Hans' in his final weeks, his frame appearing emaciated beneath a single blanket, his fingers curled and still. His eyes were closed, his chest rising and falling in an erratic manner, saliva pooling around his chin. Clearly he had been unable to climb to the second floor; his personal chamber had become an anteroom to eternity.

As I drew closer, the heat of his fever seemed to scratch at my ice, prompting it to cool my blood in defense. Joel crept to my right side and whispered, "What . . . exactly . . . does this pestilence do to people?"

"Augustin mentioned fever, delirium, inability to take in food or water."

"He looks like he's about to die from dysentery," Joel uttered, the fingers of his left hand brushing my right, an unspoken request for support. I took his hand in mine, realizing that his past haunted him now. Even if Jarvis could not sense our presence, we must maintain our composure.

I reached for a towel with my free hand and dabbed the spittle from Jarvis' chin, something I had done regularly for Hans in his final days. Our former bailiff did not react to my touch, but I dipped the towel in water, cooling it before placing it upon his forehead. Only a few wisps of hair remained around his ears.

"Maybe I should be more worried about this since I'll be here for a month," I muttered to Joel as I stepped back from Jarvis' bed. My plan was to spend eighteen days with Augustin, seeking a way to unify our destinies. If the pestilence shackled me in its fever, we would hardly have time to accomplish anything.

Joel exhaled. "At least I'm gone tomorrow night." His hand twitched against mine, and he edged nearer to Jarvis, bending close to his left ear. He murmured something to him that I did not hear, and to my surprise, the elderly man's eyelids slid open. I felt Joel tense as he met Jarvis' clouded eyes.

The sick man's jaw quivered. "My . . . lord?" he said in a cracked voice.

Joel tugged me to his side, and Jarvis focused on me. I suspected that he believed us both to be apparitions on the brink of heaven. "You . . . came . . . for me." He wheezed, and his eyelids closed again.

A mad idea came over me, and I bent down to whisper in Jarvis' ear, "I need your help with the accounting. Keep track of all God's cattle."

Jarvis did not respond to this, and Lorraine ushered us out of the chamber seconds later. I looked toward the kitchen with the intent of finding the room Felda had readied for us, but Joel's grip on my hand halted me before the staircase.

"Now he's going to be looking for you the second he gets to heaven, wanting to help count all the cattle. What am I supposed to say if he asks me where to find you?"

Joel's brows were cockeyed, as though he was unsure whether to be annoyed with me or amused. "Tell him the time traveler will enter heaven when she wants to. Not a second before." I winked.

He smirked and released my hand. "Guess I'd better go find Heinrich. He said he wanted to talk to me alone." He flexed his fingers and turned for the front parlor.

"He's probably going to try to talk you out of dying. Prepare yourself."

Chapter Four:
Looming Strife

I spent the afternoon catching up with Freia. We sat together in the chamber Felda had prepared, its open window inviting spring's fresh breeze into its stillness. The room had one bed—something I did not appreciate, even though sleeping quarters were often shared in this era. A small wardrobe, washing table, chamber pot, and a single stool rounded out the room's other furnishings. Someone had laid my bag and Joel's at the foot of the bed, a blanket of dyed blue wool cloaking its straw-filled mattress.

Freia told me more of her private struggles as we lounged upon the bed, her gaze drifting regularly toward the window's view of the side yard and ironworks. Heinrich had taken over from the previous ironmaster who died in an accident. He faced some unrest at first, from locals who wanted their industry to remain under Rhenisch management. But the community gradually accepted him, his gift with metals working in his favor, along with his generosity. Heinrich was training Edwin to succeed him, since his oldest son chose to farm the earth.

Since her husband's return, Freia experienced three pregnancies. The first had given her Anna, and the second brought the child who succumbed to the pestilence. Freia had miscarried the third child early last year, an episode that terrified her. She nearly bled to death, and Heinrich went to Augustin in spirit form to beg for aid.

"He gave me some of his blood to restore me and counseled us not to try for any more children unless I want to leave them motherless." She wiped her index finger across her nose with a resigned look.

Leave it to Augustin to be blunt. "He's honest, even when it's something you don't want to hear," I observed, my longing for him clawing against the bonds upon my heart. That was not the first time he had saved my best friend's life. I would have to thank him when I sought him in the forest after Joel's suicide.

Though Freia and I had been apart just shy of eight years per her timeline, the twenty years I spent as *Leitalra* in the modern era made me feel as old as her husband appeared. I told Freia how frustrating it was whenever I learned of some atrocious tradition that Teuton priests practiced in secret.

"Every time I thought I'd actually made a difference, I'd find out priests in another city were breeding Teuton women in a wicked attempt to 'preserve' our magic. There were priests in my own city who mistreated their wives and used the heart-bond to keep them quiet. Then the NVH showed up and murdered everyone close to me. Maybe I should have just stayed here, never bothered to return to the future."

"Sometimes it's hard to understand where God is leading us," Freia agreed. "All we can do is pray for wisdom. It took me a while to accept that I shouldn't have any more children. But it's time for me to transition to crone, I suppose, even if my heart thinks otherwise."

She chuckled quietly and I placed an arm around her waist, thankful that she understood my turmoil, though our life experiences were far different. Her light reached out to blend with my ice, our blood-sisterhood rejuvenating the close friendship we cherished. And then the dark truth fell from my lips.

"Wuotan tried to stop Joel and me from getting here. Ever since we made it through the gates, there's been something foul addling my heart. Something more than just the sorrows of a fallen city. Prince Otto cursed Muniche with his blood, and it's like Wuotan's stalking me, trying to lure me away from the light."

That was the first time I gave words to the sensation that had prickled at my heart since my arrival. I had tried to brush it off as a mourning city, but it continued to stick in my mind, refusing to grant me reprieve. Muniche's master had cursed and forsaken her, her mortal stronghold ground to dust. But her distress should not make me feel raw and open for all to see.

"Did you ever feel that way in your time?" Freia queried after a pause. "That Wuotan held influence over Muniche's bonds?"

"No. He holds a grudge against me, but I never felt this . . . this weird tingling at my heart. It's not physical. But it's like something's trying to make me question myself, question my goals. I want to reunite with Augustin and figure out some way to stay with him. But my connection to Muniche is getting in the way."

"Maybe that's your path. To discover the method of breaking the bonds of a Teuton city," Freia mused.

Razors seemed to slice at my heart, and a groan broke from my lips. "I don't know, Freia. I just don't know."

My friend suggested that we pray together then and there, asking for divine wisdom and protection against Wuotan's deceits. We knelt upon the floor as Freia whispered a heartfelt petition on my behalf, her words echoed from my inner soul. In her prayer, she requested that if I must join with Prince Otto, he might break the demon's hold on Muniche's essence. Since he had leveled the curse upon the city, he must have the authority to reverse it.

When Joel and I retired to the spare bedroom that evening after dinner, his brow furrowed at the sight of our bags lying beside the single bed. "I'll take the floor," he said as I lit the candlestick upon the bedside table.

After a long day of bearing the weight of an unwanted destiny, his comment rubbed me the wrong way. Spinning toward him, I placed my hands on my hips and snapped, "If I repulse you *that* much, maybe you should slide into Lorraine's bed tonight. She's been giving you googly eyes at every meal."

"What?" Joel scratched at his chin and stared at me.

"Clueless as always." Dragging my bag to the head of the bed, I pawed through it in search of the camp blanket.

"Swanie, I just spent the afternoon hearing how only reprobates like Judas Iscariot commit suicide," Joel responded in a weary tone. "I don't need you telling me I should mess around with a girl twenty years younger than me."

Heinrich must have given him a hard time. "Lorraine's twenty-seven and you're forty," I reminded Joel, tossing the rolled blanket his direction. "Time travel screwed up our ages compared to everyone else around here. Hasn't it occurred to you yet that Wuotan wouldn't have bothered to try to kill us on our way here if we weren't fated to do something meaningful?"

"Hasn't it occurred to *you* yet that all I want is to see my wife again?"

The tragedy in Joel's voice cooled a portion of my irritation. I heaved a sigh and set my neck pillow atop the bed, then dropped my bag to the floor. "You can do whatever you want. It's not like you've got an unbreakable bond crying out for a mad Prince."

I sat upon the bed and looked up at Joel, who stood before the wardrobe with my rolled blanket in his hands. "Has Muniche started drawing you toward the Prince?" he asked in a low voice.

"She's been calling to him all day. And . . . I'm pretty sure he's noticed. I'm worried he might show up in my dreams even though our bond isn't complete."

"Isn't complete?" Joel cocked his head at me and began unravelling the blanket.

I shoved my hands beneath my thighs as embarrassment heated my cheeks. "The bonds of a Teuton city are finalized by a traditional wedding. Once the Lady and Keyholder have shared blood, he assumes responsibility for her heart and their spirits can meet in their dreams." *And the sexual union of their elements reaches ecstasies no words can describe.*

Joel was in the process of spreading the camp blanket upon the floorboards. "You think the Prince is going to propose to you once he shows up?"

The mere idea made my stomach churn. "He can't do that even if he wants to. I'm already married."

My ex-husband froze in a crouch, and I saw him look at his left wrist. "Not to you," I rushed to explain. "Augustin and I got married in the cathedral two nights before I played the Song of Time. He even has a written record of it somewhere." I smiled at the memory of the greatest victory in our relationship.

"Then . . . why did Muniche choose you as her Lady?" Joel looked confused.

"Because it was holy matrimony, not blood marriage. The spirit of a Teuton city considers a woman free unless she sports the scar." My hands were in my lap now, and I traced a finger across my clean wrist.

Joel removed his shoes and stretched out on the floor, his features twisted into an unhappy expression. "You know, this whole thing is really unfair," he said, placing his hands beneath his head and gazing toward the ceiling. "You don't love the Prince, but Muniche's forcing you to bond with him. You've barely had any time with the man you actually love."

"We don't always get what we want in this life," I muttered, a cliché I did not particularly like, though it often proved true. "But Augustin and I have a couple weeks to figure this out. I'm going to find him after you've done your thing."

"My 'thing.'" Joel snickered, then turned his face toward me. "How come you don't call any Black Priests by their chosen names?"

His question took me by surprise. "What do you mean? I call Günter by his chosen name."

"Who's Günter?" I gave a brief description of the Cursed One who had long inhabited the Black Castle in our era, relaxing my body upon the mattress as I did so. "Okay, so you call him Günter because you don't know his birth name. But you won't call your son 'Gust' or your husband 'Wolfgang.' Seems a bit disrespectful of their chosen identities, you know?"

I pursed my lips at Joel, unsure why he would equate the filial curse with a person's identity. "My son named himself after Augustin. That's where the name 'Gust' comes from. He gave me permission to call him 'Max,' but even if he hadn't, I wouldn't have referred to him with my husband's name. That would be awkward. And Augustin never demanded that I call him 'Wolfgang.' He said I should, but he left it up to me. His mother chose his birth name, anyway, not the Prince."

"That's fair, I guess," Joel said.

In the glow of the candlestick, I attempted to situate my head against my neck pillow, ultimately deciding to pass it to Joel instead. If he had to deal with the uncomfortable floorboards, I should at least offer his neck some support. "If I wake up screaming because Prince Otto or Wuotan invaded my nightmares, I apologize," I murmured to him. Joel breathed a vague response, and within moments he was snoring. Lucky.

Once my exhaustion pulled me into slumber, my awareness drifted from one scenario to the next, from a roiling sea to a misty forest, always seeking, never finding. Wuotan stalked me throughout the night, shrouded in shadow, his grating laughter clawing at my serenity. *Your feeble heart belongs to me, Muniche,* I heard him growl more than once. *Not to your faithless Keyholder, not to the Black Priest who spurned love long ago. You are mine. Your Deity has no power to save you.*

At one point I found myself in a fiery realm that must have been hell, black glass scorching my bare feet as I fled from a monster with gnashing teeth. Prince Otto appeared in the distance surrounded by smoke, reaching a red-fired palm out toward me. "I can protect you, Muniche. Come to your master," he called.

Then I heard Augustin roaring in anguish, brandishing a cerulean sword as he leaped from the flames to attack the monster that pursued me. There was a clash of teeth, but I could not force my body to move toward Augustin, to help him. Red fire began to eat at my ankles, and the Prince grabbed hold of me, his voice twisted into something demonic: "The nameless one can't assuage your needs, Muniche."

I'm more than Muniche! I'm Swanhilde von Thaden, I wanted to scream, but I could not find my voice. The fire licked through me, melting my ice, driving me to madness, and I wept as I reached in vain for the priest I could not have.

Each time the nightmares roused me from sleep, I saw Joel passed out with his mouth open, unconscious without a care, despite the calamities he had faced in his own life. I longed to freeze my body and send my spirit into the atmosphere, like I used to do when I had no priest to guide me into pleasant dreams. But I feared that Wuotan might confront me in the spiritual realm and drag me into an underworld where I must give myself to Prince Otto, my traitorous Keyholder.

So I passed much of the night watching the candle-light's flickering shades.

I drifted off again before the bells for sunrise but arose shortly thereafter. Making my way around Joel's somno-lent form, I sat before the washing table and cleaned my face and hands with fresh water and herbal soap. I would have liked to bathe my entire upper body, especially since my deodorant was wearing off. But with my ex-husband on the floor behind me, I had no wish to strip, even though he had shown no sexual interest in me. So I took up some fragrant sage from a small dish before the mirror, sprin-kling it along the folds of my dress. Good enough.

My braid had survived the night fairly well. I pinned back a few strays, then turned for the chamber pot. The single rag lying upon the floor beside it prompted me to cringe. Joel would doubtless take a shit in there as soon as he awoke. This was my last chance to wipe with a fairly clean rag.

I should have stuffed a couple rolls of toilet paper into his bag.

Joel stirred as I finished at the pot. Grumbling a few curses in English, he admitted that his head ached. "No coffee here," I reminded him, "but I'll go look around the kitchen for some feverfew."

I found Freia at work beside one of the young servant girls, baking wheat bread for the day's meals. She greeted me with a fond smile, and I told her about Joel's plight, catching sight of a teapot simmering at the edge of the cooking fire. "That's just mint and chamomile," she said when she saw me looking at the teapot. "But I can get some linden and feverfew from the pantry."

We went to the storeroom together, and Freia murmured that her family was running low on feverfew thanks to the pestilence. "Lorraine's going to harvest some willow bark this morning to use instead."

"Linden's good enough. I don't want you running out thanks to Joel. If you have any mallow seeds, that should fix him up just fine."

While we prepared the tea, Freia informed me quietly that Jarvis had passed away during the night, along with baby Swanie. "Lorraine and Heinrich confirmed that their souls have departed, so there's no need to hold a wake. We'll bury Jarvis this afternoon beside his wife, and I just sent Johann to give the news to Katchen and Max." My good friend sighed, sorrow straining her visage.

"Joel and I are planning on spending the day checking in on our children, but I think I'd like to be there for Jarvis' burial," I said, inhaling the woodsy scent of steaming linden.

Freia's expression grew ambiguous. "Swanie, are you sure that's a good idea? Even though you look different from the mother she remembers, I'm certain Cammie would recognize you. She mourned your death for years.

How would she feel if she finds out you lied to her all her life?"

I crossed my arms and considered for a moment. There was one way around that problem, but I did not know if Joel could manage such a thing. Dropping my arms to my sides, I reached out to pour two cups of tea, one for me and one for my ex-husband, the American Teuton. As I turned for the spare bedroom, I told Freia, "I have a few ideas about that, but it'll depend on what Joel has to say. We'll likely be away for most of the morning, but we'll come back here for lunch."

Chapter Five

The Next Generation

Joel gawked at me as though I had grown a set of horns when I described the concept of the *Gæstelort* to him. In his nearly sixteen years of living as a Teuton with other Teutons, he had never learned that he could magically separate his spirit from his body through the power of his element. I had to explain several times that traversing the atmosphere in spirit form was not inherently evil, just because the blood-transfer involved a similar separation.

"During the blood-transfer, Wuotan tears your spirit away from your body. Once you claim an element, you call it forth to shield your body in your spirit's absence, so no human or demon can possess you in the meantime. And so your body doesn't die without your spirit's life," I told him. "Your heart continues to beat, and your blood continues to flow, uniting with your element to shield you from harm, from death."

"But what if someone tries to cut your head off while your spirit's floating around miles away?" Joel asked. He stood with one shoulder propped against the wardrobe, his arms crossed as he eyed me doubtfully.

"Your element won't allow your body to die. If someone tries to harm it, your wind would summon you back to defend yourself. It's easy to attack someone as a spirit. I've done that a few times before."

Joel frowned. "Why didn't the Prince think to do that against the Saxons? If he'd left a battalion or two in reserve to fight in spirit form, we might have made some real progress."

Frustrated, I threw my hands in the air. "Don't ask *me* that question. Maybe he did do that in the final battles. The point is, if we visit Cammie, Max, and Helmut in spirit form, they won't notice our presence unless they're using their elements to enhance their vision. Most people don't do that constantly since it takes effort."

"Your irises have been blue with ice since we got here."

"Because my vision is 20/160 without glasses or contacts. Dork." I sneered at Joel and stretched out upon the mattress. "Now if you'll excuse me, I'm going to pay a visit to our kids." I shut my eyes and invoked the full power of my ice.

Within seconds, its frosty essence coated my body from head to toe, dress included. For a protracted instant, I held my breath as my lungs froze inside of me, and then my spirit broke free, rising above my inert body to hover in midair. The urge to breeze through the log wall into the firmament seized me, my ice elated by the Rhine's proximity. But I forced myself to remain in the bedchamber as I waited to see how Joel would react.

He still stood before the wardrobe, his crossed arms loosening, his clenched jaw shifting a bit before he whispered, "Swanie?" He leaned forward to gape at my frozen body.

I chuckled, and he jerked upright, his eyes growing as round as a full moon. "Did you just . . . *laugh* in my *brain?*"

Maybe you should call your wind into your irises and check out the ceiling, I suggested, amusement peppering my spiritual robes with artistic flakes. As soon as his eyes met mine, I zoomed into the sky, letting my laughter ring in his mind. *Come on, windy novice. The atmosphere's waiting for you.*

I caught a wisp of stratus cloud about two hundred meters from the ground and set myself upon it, marveling at the low mountain range below with the azure Rhine snaking its way northward. Some early morning fog draped the peaks, and a strange unease crept along my spirit, convincing me that Wuotan prowled in the mists, waiting to drag me away.

You're just imagining things, I told myself, turning my gaze to the dense woodland south of Eisenwald, where Augustin's cottage lay. I tried to focus on my memories of the dances we shared in our dream world, blue fire and ice bound as one, forever joined. It had to be possible to restore what we once had. Freia would not want me to lose hope, and I clung to it with my last threads of faith.

When my ice finally sensed Joel rising to meet me, I grinned and turned my attention to him, prepared to congratulate him on achieving one of the greatest wonders of Teutonic magic. His light gray robe billowed grandly around his spirit, making it difficult to delineate his shape; and his irises were a hypnotic ash gray, round and vigilant as they observed the clouds dappling the ether. His blond hair complemented the glory of his countenance, the flawlessness attainable only in the *Gæstelort.* I felt his wind permeating the atmosphere, mingling with the clouds in a curious dalliance of air and water.

Reaching a hand toward him, I smiled in encouragement as he poked his whirling robes with a finger, then shot a glance at the ground below. *Well, what do you think?* I asked, my hand passing through his sleeve. I felt nothing but a steady breeze that whisked my spirit.

Joel looked me up and down, then shook his head in astonishment. *Swanie, you're as stunning as a goddess.* He reached out to touch my hair, which draped my ethereal robe in the style of youth, black wreathed with a frosty cerulean.

I would have blushed, had I not been a spirit. As it was, Joel certainly must have detected my embarrassment.

Everybody always looks perfect in spirit form, I told him, shrugging off his amazement. *Come on, let's go back to the house and see how Erika is fairing with the fever.*

Moments later, we entered the chamber she usually shared with little Anna, who had apparently moved into Lorraine's room to avoid contamination. Erika tossed and turned on her mattress, her black hair tangled and soaked with sweat, her eyes screwed shut. She moaned sporadically, her shapely figure hardly hidden by her nightdress as she called for her betrothed, Edwin Denlinger.

I noticed her wedding dress hanging on the door of her wardrobe, the fabric light and flowing, patterns of sky blue and white. A smaller mattress lay upon the floor not far from Erika's bed, alongside an empty cradle. A dark-haired boy who looked to be around three years old lay curled in the fetal position beneath a linen blanket, his chapped lips sucking a thumb.

That must be Max's son Otto. And the cradle probably belonged to baby Swanie, I noted, directing my thoughts toward Joel alone.

The baby passed away? Joel inquired, his concern agitating the room's air.

Last night, along with Jarvis. Heinrich said Otto and Erika are improving. Joel gave what seemed like the mental equivalent of a snort, his swirling gray eyes riveted upon our daughter. Fear darkened the gray of his robes.

I really hope the rest of our kids are okay, he admitted at length. *I don't like seeing Erika suffer, even if she's going to live.*

Lorraine came into the room with a tray of tonics and broth, so I beckoned Joel to follow me outside before she perceived our presence. She certainly knew how to detect Teuton spirits, since she had confirmed both Jarvis' and Swanie's deaths. Behind the Denlinger house, we found a pair of servant men at work digging Jarvis' grave. Several older tombstones already dotted the landscape.

Let's go somewhere with less death, Joel urged. *How about Cammie's farm?*

We drifted toward the north side of Eisenwald, quickly finding the abode of Cammie and Alger, situated on a hill surrounded by grain fields and berry bushes. I would have recognized my daughter's ice anywhere, and when we glided through the fields, I saw her drawing water out of a well just behind the house. She wore a dress of bright blue linen, her blond hair braided and pinned beneath a matching covering. The skin of her hands showed signs of farm labor: threshing grain and cooking meals, sweeping floors and washing clothes.

Her eyes glimmered with contentment and maternal pride when her two small boys came tumbling out of the back door to greet their mother. I heard them exclaiming that the day was far too perfect for lessons, that they would much rather help their father with the planting. Cammie would hear none of their pleas. She shooed them inside kindly but firmly, passing the pail of water to her eldest son and glancing toward the fields and the sky before disappearing into her home.

Now that was an uplifting sight, I commented to Joel, who lounged atop the well, swishing his legs from side to side.

Yeah, but both her sons have dark hair like Otto's. I guess my foreign genes were subdued by her Teuton husband. He snickered and looked at Cammie's farmhouse. *I'm going to take a peek inside.*

I let him go alone, for I had seen enough to satisfy me regarding my oldest daughter's happiness. She was the mistress of a productive farm, and she had two healthy little boys who adored her. Freia's earlier remark returned to me while I watched Heino come outside and strike out for the fields. *How would Cammie feel if she finds out you lied to her all her life?*

It was better for me to hide away with Augustin after Joel departed. Better to forsake the village and avoid the stress of coming clean to my children. *I never loved your Daddy. My heart belongs to a Cursed One.*

Next, Joel and I headed for the riverbank and followed its course upstream toward the hut where Max lived with

Katchen and their children. On the way there, Joel insisted that I should have gone inside Cammie's farmhouse, for her husband had lost part of one ear in battle and kept his hair short enough for it to be obvious. I shrugged it off, stating that as long as our daughter loved Alger and he treated her well, it did not matter how he looked.

We found Max and Katchen speaking softly to each other at their front door, misery enveloping them in a dark shroud. Our oldest son was preparing to visit the Denlinger house and retrieve his deceased daughter, his wife's pale cheeks shining with tears. Max had grown tall and lanky, sporting a carefully-trimmed beard and hair as sleek as an obsidian rock. He kissed Katchen gently on her brow and turned to go, revealing their oldest daughter clinging to her mother's skirt, her childish face bleak.

I'm starting to wish I'd just jumped off the cliffs outside the Black Castle, Joel muttered as we drifted back toward the town. *Sickness and death everywhere we go. Can't catch a break.*

Our timing could have been better, I responded, thinking of the many tomes that recorded Prince Otto's death in June of 1074. Muniche's spirit pined for him deep within my heart, and it occurred to me that the Prince might have died any other way had Augustin's volume not summoned me here. I could sense my fated master's inquisitiveness through our tenuous connection. He would come here to find me, and then he would die.

Because of me.

We reached the tanner's shop before I could thoroughly contemplate that issue. A few people ambled here and there on the streets, though all of them had their faces covered with cloths. Some of the stores had opened, a welcome sight, yet I doubted any shopkeepers planned to conduct business all day with the pestilence raging.

The tannery had not yet opened its doors, but we passed through the wall and found Helmut's in-laws hard at work on a pair of hides. They looked like a pleasant couple, the man stooped with a short gray beard, his wife plump with a heap of curls piled atop her head. Joel and I left them behind without comment, gliding up the rickety staircase to the second floor, and from there to the garret where our son resided with his Rhenisch wife.

We encountered Holda first, a beautiful blond who was obviously pregnant. Bending over a boiling tub of laundry, she removed articles of clothing one by one and wrung them out at the window. She hummed a song while she worked, her voice occasionally breaking free in a few lines of Latin, likely a tune she had learned in a convent.

She does sing well, like Freia said, I observed as we hovered in the corner of Holda's parlor, observing her work. *I wonder if Helmut—*

My thought would remain forever incomplete. The Rhenisch maiden had finished her sacred tune and now she struck up a new one, one that made me gasp in surprise. After humming the opening chords, she began to sing a melody I knew well, *in English.* I just stood and stared at her with my mouth hanging open for the duration of the first verse and chorus. When she began the second verse, Joel sent an incredulous thought to my brain. *That's a Nightwish song, isn't it?*

"Wanderlust," I affirmed, shaking off my shock to join Holda on the chorus when it came around again. Though I bridled my mental singing voice so she would not hear it, our sopranos seemed to meld together from the mortal realm to the invisible place where Joel and I skulked. When the song ended, Holda moved on to a Rhenisch air, and I beamed at Joel. *Helmut must have taught her every song he knows, and he probably strums along on his lute while her voice rises to the stars. I wonder if he taught her what the English words mean.*

Before Joel could give his opinion on that subject, Helmut entered the room bearing a small basket of bread; apparently he had been trading at the bakery that morning. He greeted his wife with a kiss and invited her to enjoy some of his spoils. Holda giggled as he tweaked her blond braid. Then she dried her hands on a towel and followed her husband into the kitchen, where they sat down to spread butter over one of the loaves. And Helmut told his wife with a tender smile, "I could hear you singing all the way out on the street."

"That's because I was squeaking," Holda replied, pinching his hand, and we left them to their merriment.

You know, all of our kids look like they're happy with their lives, aside from the pestilence. Joel's muses drifted into my brain while we headed down the street toward the Denlinger house. *I guess we didn't do everything wrong after all.*

The colors of my icy robes shifted toward translucence. *I was the one who made the worst mistake. You deserved a wife who loved you.*

And you deserved a priest who viewed you as a peer, Joel supplied, humor weaving through his thoughts. *I hope you can figure out some way to give Prince Otto the slip, once he gets here. I don't mind keeping Jarvis occupied for a couple extra years.*

A caustic laugh escaped my mind. *His wife is already there, so I doubt he's bored. I hope heaven's timeline works differently than earth's, so you don't have to wait a thousand years for Melody and your sons.*

Me too, Joel echoed after a pause. I wondered if he had not considered that aspect before.

We might as well return to our bodies and get ready for lunch. Pretty sure it's been a couple hours since the bells rang for Terce.

Are we going to Jarvis' funeral like this or in our bodies? Joel asked as I prepared to condense my ice back into my blood.

If Cammie decides to show up, we'd better stick to the ethereal realm. Freia hinted that she'd be hurt if she finds out how much we lied to her. She took your death pretty hard, and apparently she mourned me even longer, I related.

Just before we returned to our physical bodies, Joel thought something I had never considered. *Maybe we should have told our kids the truth from the start.*

Chapter Six:
Joel's Choice

At lunch the mood was subdued, as the Denlinger household prepared for Jarvis' burial. The baby's death had saddened everyone, too, and Freia intended to spend the afternoon and evening supporting Katchen and Max. Their little son, Otto, had swallowed several spoonfuls of broth that morning, a sign of improvement. Before eating her salad, Freia murmured a fervent prayer that God would spare Katchen's family from further loss.

Joel did not speak much this time, concentrating on his food and avoiding Heinrich's gaze. I needed to talk to him in private and urge him to make peace with his good friend; I did not wish to see them part ways on a sour note. Lorraine shot intermittent glances at Joel beside her, inquisitiveness seeming to radiate from her aura. But my ex-husband either did not notice or keenly ignored her.

Lorraine remarked at one point that Erika spoke to her that morning and said she had sensed a wintry wind in her chamber. "She looked directly at me when she said it, as though the delirium had slipped away. But I advised her to rest, that what she sensed was only a dream. Not sure why she's envisioning her brother's element instead of yours." Lorraine quirked a smile at Edwin.

Edwin plied her with questions about his fiancée's condition, and I tuned him out and caught Joel's eye. His mouth was scrunched into a tiny knot, as if he worked incredibly hard to stifle a laugh. Immediately, I looked down at my food and stuffed a bite into my mouth, amusement quivering in my chest. I could just imagine Joel's thoughts. *So, ice plus wind equals a wintry wind. Really.*

Freia pulled me aside after the meal, requesting that I accompany her into the herb garden, for she had several concerns to disclose. The clouds had vanished by that time, the spring sunlight drenching the plants in a healthy radiance. The fresh aroma of mint trailed us as we walked, and I snagged a couple leaves to chew. The salad today had included rose petals, which awakened fond reminisces of my days in medieval Muniche.

"Cammie will be here for Jarvis' funeral," Freia told me, pausing to study the new growth on a patch of sage. "He helped her and Alger set up their farm and encouraged my son and Emilie to move their family there. If you and Joel plan to attend the burial, you'll want to conceal yourselves thoroughly. I'm pretty sure she knows how to use her element to enhance her vision, like you do. So if you go in spirit form, you'll need to hide amongst the trees."

I nodded, accepting her advice. "We'll keep our distance. I wish I could have actually talked to Jarvis, told him how grateful I am for his help running the estate all those years. He's the one who kept our finances in check, the reason my family had the means to flee here." I sighed and gazed toward the fresh mound of earth near the trees that bordered the Denlinger property.

"He set us all up for success, for sure," Freia agreed.

We rounded the corner of the garden farthest from the house, a bit of ivy crawling along its edges. "How did everyone . . . react . . . when you arrived here after telling your children you planned to stay in Muniche?" I asked, nervousness scratching at my gut. "Did you tell them

Augustin rescued you?" I had brought her to Eisenwald myself, actually, after a brief detour to the year 2000. But Augustin had held the Saxon warriors at bay while we made our escape.

Freia met my gaze for an instant before concentrating on the lavender sprigs not yet in bloom, grazing her fingertips through them. "I gave God the credit for my survival, but kept the details to myself. I said you were unable to get out of the city before the battle started, and Heinrich didn't find you among the survivors. Cammie struggled for a very long time, while Max declared that neither you nor Joel would want your heirs to wallow in sorrow. His fortitude gave the younger ones a boost, and Cammie projects happiness on the surface for the sake of her sons. Alger has told Heinrich that she's not at peace, not really."

Moisture welled in my eyes at the realization that my oldest daughter lived a life of hypocrisy, similar to my years in the eleventh century. "Joel said maybe we should have been open with our kids about everything. The time travel and our reasons for visiting this era. But now that we've come here to die, I doubt the truth would make any of them feel better."

"Heinrich doesn't think either of you should commit ritual suicide," Freia noted in an undertone. "He's afraid for your eternal souls if you do such a thing. He refuses to believe Prince Otto would do something so wicked. And I'll admit . . . I'm worried for you too, Swanie."

"If God's grace doesn't cover suicide along with all the other sins, then it's worthless," I said, prompting Freia to recoil. I looked up from a clump of verbena to meet her gaze.

"If God can forgive a man who murdered over a hundred people, then He'll forgive suicide, too. None of us deserve heaven. It's open to us only because of what Prince Otto and Paulus witnessed on their first journey through time. And it's completely ludicrous to compare Joel's death with Judas Iscariot's. Joel didn't betray God for money."

Freia looked stricken. "Well . . . I . . . that's—"

"Joel's wife and children were butchered by a group of Saxons, and he loved them dearly. He doesn't need his best friend telling him he's going to hell just because he wants to reunite with them. Heinrich needs to get his head on straight."

Freia wrung her hands in her apron and glanced toward the house. "I'll talk to him," she murmured, sounding chastened. "We all have to make our own choices, of course."

"Of course." I brushed a beetle from my sleeve, somewhat surprised at my frankness. *Never thought I'd defend my ex-husband so staunchly.*

"There's something else I need to tell you," Freia said, reaching out to link her right arm with my left. We turned our steps toward the house as I waited for her to speak. Her footsteps faltered, and the lines in her face deepened, crimson darkening her cheeks. "Your husband knows you're here," she confessed at length, her teeth scoring her bottom lip.

My heartbeat escalated, my ice casting itself in a wide net of its own accord, seeking those immortal blue flames I so deeply missed. "Has he been in the village today, or did you tell him?" I asked. If Augustin had passed through along the river, he would doubtless have noticed the presence of two unusual Teutonic elements in town.

"I went to his cabin last night in spirit form," Freia replied. I halted in place, staring at my best friend in shock. During our years together in Muniche, she had never separated her spirit from her body, to my knowledge.

"Heinrich taught me how to set my spirit free shortly after he came home to me," she explained, seeming to sense my confusion. "He thought I ought to know how to do that for defense, in case the Saxons ever send their armies to the Rhine. I don't do it often, but—"

"Did you tell Augustin why I'm here?" I interrupted, fear gripping me in its vise. *To die with your treacherous brother after ten days in the forest.*

Freia lowered her eyes. "I didn't. All I said was that you had come to check on your children, that you planned to stay for at least a month."

"What did he say to that?" I cringed, preparing for a blow.

"He thanked me for telling him and asked how my family and yours were faring with the pestilence. I told him which plants Lorraine had found helpful."

My body relaxed a tad. "So he wasn't angry."

"No. He didn't show any emotion at all, not even surprise. But I think he'll make his way here within a few days. He was chronicling recent events with the pestilence when I found him."

My lips twitched at that. I had read that section in his 1074 encyclopedia not long ago, and I knew what saga came next. *Muniche's Prince and Lady: Their Unlikely Reunion in Death.*

"I'm going to his cabin tomorrow morning, if he hasn't come here by then," I decided. "Once Joel has gone, there's no reason for me to hang around here and keep avoiding Cammie and Max. Augustin and I have some work to do before the Prince gets here." Freia favored me with a determined nod as we reentered her house through the pantry.

That evening after dinner, I bathed myself with a sponge and herbed water. I combed my hair and redid my braid, resolved to offer Augustin my best when I sought him in the morning. Why he had shown Freia an impassive façade, I could hardly guess, but tiny needles of doubt poked away at my heart's desperate hope. What if Wuotan had tortured him mercilessly during our years apart, to the point where he no longer had the capacity to love? Or what if he had decided to cast his lot on the altar of sensual lust rather than devoted loyalty? What if he chose one of the demon's immortal sirens to be his consort?

"Augustin would never do that," I told myself in Bayerisch dialect, studying my face in the mirror as I cleaned my skin. "If he gave up on you, he wouldn't have shown up in the Black Castle that time Günter tried to kill you. He's the only reason Günter stayed his hand. He wouldn't have jumped forward in time if he didn't still love you."

Now all I could give him was a forty-year-old body and a wearied soul who had faced too much hardship. Would that be enough to meet the needs of an undead priest?

Joel entered the bedroom while I tugged the bodice of my light green dress into place. "Pretty sure I'm going out the window when it's time to end this," he griped in English as he closed the door behind him. He stalked across the floor to run his fingers along the windowpane, seeking a method to open the glass.

"Is Heinrich still giving you grief?" I rose from the stool and tightened the sash that supported my breasts.

Joel pushed the glass outward, and a cool breeze swept into the chamber, causing the candle atop the bedside table to sputter. "He apologized for being so harsh about it, but he's certain I'm going to hell. He says there's no way to be sure I won't, and once I've slit my throat it'll be too late to change my mind."

The bells for Compline pealed into the twilight, and Joel sighed. His hands gripped the sill, and to my surprise I saw that his forearms trembled. Cautiously, I stepped around the blanket that took up most of the floor and reached out to touch his shoulder.

"I don't think you have anything to worry about. I killed myself once before, when I took a quick trip to see my Mutti." Joel stiffened and eyed me with a frown.

"That was after I married my Keyholder. And that was when I learned that having two females sharing the city bond at once really messes with a Keyholder's brain. He hunted me down and I had to kill myself quick to jump back to the future. When I did it, all I saw were the gates of time, not the gates of hell. I never felt like God rejected me after I did that, either."

Joel blinked at me, appearing bewildered. "How did you . . . do it?"

I dropped my gaze to the hem of my dress, heat rising in my cheeks. "I did the act of the filial curse. Ripped my radial artery wide open. I think I bled out in less than half a minute."

Muttering a curse, Joel ran a hand down his face. "I don't know what to think about you. You couldn't just slit your throat. You had to make it weird."

I chuckled. "Leave it to me to pretend I'm a Cursed One, right?" I nudged the camp blanket with my foot and noted, "Maybe we ought to organize our stuff so Felda doesn't have to. I'm heading for Augustin's cottage in the morning, and I don't think I'm coming back here."

Joel shut the window, then stooped to reroll the blanket and pass it to me along with my neck pillow. I tucked both into my bag while he sorted through his own, extracting each snack I had packed. "Think we should eat all this stuff now in case my bag vanishes after I'm dead?" he asked.

"Stay away from the nuts," I reminded him.

He spread all of the food out on the bed, and we picked through it slowly, sharing the water from the tumbler. I sat at the head of the bed while Joel sat at its foot, his countenance troubled, his gaze fixated on the half-open window. The night was dark and crisp, countless stars pinpoints of energy against heaven's tapestry. It seemed repugnant to taint such an idyllic landscape with blood.

"I have to do this at midnight, right? Vigils?" Joel glanced at the candle.

"Right. I added a nail to the candle to mark the hour, but we'll need to leave before it falls." Eisenwald's church bell rang for Vigils only on Sundays, so I had defaulted to ancient methods of timekeeping.

Joel fell silent, his hazel eyes staring vacantly at the candle's lambent flame. I chewed on a couple raisins and steeled myself to mention something that lurked in the far reaches of my mind. "You know, Augustin's record didn't mention your suicide at all. That means history doesn't bind you. You can do whatever you want here in the Middle Ages. Live, die, explore, settle down. You could even tell our kids the truth and become a wise old grandpa."

"Thanks a lot, Heinrich II." Joel wrinkled his nose and cracked his knuckles. "As nice as that sounds, Melody won't be here, will she? Not Andrew, Tyler, Dan, or Will. Not Gloria. Not my parents."

I turned a strip of jerky over in my hands, knowing he had a point. "You've got a stone knife in your bag, right? I totally forgot to bring one for myself."

Joel reached into his bag and produced a blade about as long as my hand. "Got this from Gust's armory. There were quite a few stone knives in there. Should have picked up one for you."

"Don't worry about it. I'll get one from Augustin, if . . . if I have to die with the Prince." I chewed on the strip of jerky, one final flavor of home.

"You have reasons to live," Joel said in a quiet voice, his eyes searching my face.

I shrugged and rose to my feet. "So do you. Cammie, Max, Helmut, Erika, and Johann. Pretty sure Johann would love to join you on a few adventures. And you've got four grandchildren who'd love to learn a bunch of English words from you while they're growing up. You could tell them stories about the future, about the twists and turns of time travel." I brushed my hands off on the skirt of my dress, restless.

"Put a lid on it, Swanie." Joel thrust his stone knife into the waistband of his trousers and turned for the window, pushing its glass away from the house. Before I could think of anything to say, he swung out onto the dandelions growing in the earth below.

Hurriedly, I snagged the shawl Freia had leant me from the washing table, wrapping it around my shoulders before slipping through the window myself. Joel had already struck out for the road, so I scurried to catch up, invoking my ice into my blood to protect me from the spring's chill.

"If you're not coming to witness my demise, you can turn around right now," Joel said in an irritated tone, quickening his stride.

"It's your choice to make, even if I don't agree with it. And yes, I'm coming to watch. I might need that knife of yours."

Once on the road into town, Joel glanced back at the Denlinger house, dark aside from the glow of candlelight at three of the front-facing windows. "Doesn't look like anyone's following us. But we'd better not waste time."

I stretched my icy spirit in a sphere around us, so I would know if Heinrich or any other Teuton tried to impede Joel's exit strategy. But we passed through the silent town undisturbed, naught but the starlight guiding our steps. I felt almost as though I walked to the gallows—ridiculous, since I was not slated to die tonight. But I would leave this world using the same method in a month's time, unless Augustin and I tossed destiny into the abyss.

When we reached the docks, we found them nearly empty of watercraft, the pestilence having slowed trade to a halt. The primary dock stretched at least forty meters from the shoreline, the Rhine's waters a glittering midnight blue on either side of us as we approached its far end. My ice-heightened vision picked out two figures standing at the edge, awaiting us.

"Tell me that's not Heinrich and Freia," Joel muttered, slowing his pace.

My element had already identified them both. "I can't."

Joel expelled an angry sigh. "This must be what it feels like when cops show up if you're trying to jump off a bridge. Leave me in peace to get this over with!" I felt his wind reach out, inciting a gale that created wakes upon the river.

I sprinted to the end of the pier myself to confront them, leaving Joel's fury behind. Freia's light enveloped both her and her husband in an angelic radiance, and Heinrich looked disgusted. "Please don't try to stop him," I begged them. "He's been longing to do this for months. It's not a rash decision."

Freia clasped her hands before her in what might have been pity, and her husband answered my plea. "I'm here to bid an eternal farewell to one of my closest friends. Nothing more."

I looked from one of them to the other, trying to judge Heinrich's intentions. Would he try to use his metal to stop Joel, knock some sense into him? My best friend took a half step toward me and whispered, "We know he has to do this. We're here to support you." She held her left hand out to me, an invitation.

Keeping a tight hold on my ice, I took her hand lightly, positioning myself so I could watch Joel's approach and shield him if necessary. The Rhine's waters roiled against the pier, Joel's fierce wind whipping Freia's skirt and mine around our legs as we awaited his end. His steps steady, he passed Freia and me before turning at the brink to regard Heinrich. Freia's light made his skin look ghostly pale.

"I want to thank you for everything you've done for me and my family," Joel said to Heinrich, his Teutonica hesitant. "If my heart could find a reason to stay, I would. I'll look for your children . . . on the other side."

Heinrich regarded him for a long moment, his right hand clenched behind his back, pain glinting in his metallic eyes. "I hope we'll meet again . . . my brother."

My lips parted at the term Heinrich used—an antiquated label referring to Teuton men who had shared blood during the blood-transfer. I put my left hand to my mouth, sickened. Joel should not spurn his blood this way, not with an infinite future on the horizon.

I hardly heard him exchange a few words with Freia, for my thoughts were in a panic, rushing to fabricate some way to convince Joel not to commit suicide. Now he stood before me with the stone knife held casually in his hand, the hysteria of his wind calmed. "Give the Prince the finger for me, okay?"

I shook my head, Joel's attempt at humor missing the mark. "I don't think you should do this," I said in English. "Why did Wuotan try to kill you in time's currents if you're meant to die this soon? What about the Teuton blood you took up at Heinrich's expense? Our people are scattered, decimated, and you could help preserve our heritage. You could have a child who challenges Wuotan's schemes!"

"It's not enough, Swanie." He cut me off, his expression set into a mask. And he pivoted back to the pier's edge, touching the stone blade to his left wrist.

A feminine gasp pierced the stillness, Freia's hand abruptly seizing mine in an iron grip. Beyond where Joel stood, my eyes caught sight of a dark form rowing steadily toward us from the shadows downstream.

My ice froze me into a statue as it identified the cerulean fire that embodied the robed figure's spirit.

Chapter Seven

That Dreaded Conversation

Augustin manned the stern of the same dinghy I remembered from times past, his baggage piled in the center, his paddle long and sturdy, stroking rhythmic currents in the waters of the Rhine. His black-hooded cloak cast his face in shadow, but I sensed the heat emanating from his body and saw those eyes glittering with cobalt fire. They locked with mine as he drew near to the dock, enslaving me with their hypnotic quality, inducing my heart to hammer, my hands to sweat in spite of my ice.

Joel reacted in similar fashion. He stood without moving on the edge of the pier, the point of his knife digging into his wrist, which leaked blood. It was as though time had stopped, the four of us ogling the immortal specter approaching from the water. Augustin halted his boat centimeters from the pilings, his face on the same plane as mine due to the disparity between the water level and the pier. His eyes shifted from my face to Joel's, then to Freia and Heinrich and back again. No one spoke, but I could hear Joel's erratic breathing.

My heart pounded so hard I could feel it behind my ears, but I could not force my feet to move forward. When

Augustin finally spoke, his familiar voice sent a rush of yearning through every part of me. "How dare you permit your mystical blood to spill upon the dock, Lord Joel Richard Hudson von Thaden?"

He spoke perfect English, his fiery blue eyes riveted upon Joel's visage.

Freia gasped softly beside me, but Joel did not reply, nor did he lift the blade from his wrist. Blood stained his deep blue sleeve and fell one drip at a time to land beside his shoe. I wished I could see his face from where I stood with Freia.

"It seems an improvident venture to visit this era for the express purpose of departing the mortal realm for good," Augustin went on, his eyes narrowing at Joel. "Forsaking five living children who look toward the future . . . abandoning them as though they mean nothing . . . as a certain disgraced Keyholder did when he cursed his city"—his eyes shifted to mine for an instant—"and discarded his Lady like a soiled diaper."

Joel stirred at last, the stone blade cutting deeper into the corner of his wrist. "*What?*" he whispered in an accusatory manner.

My chest felt tight, and I had to consciously force my lungs to breathe. Freia and Heinrich had no clue what Augustin said to Joel, but they stood silently watching, the atmosphere heavy with foreboding. None of us had managed to convince Joel not to offer his body to the Rhine, but my instincts told me Augustin was about to do exactly that. And in the worst way possible.

"Did you know that I am well acquainted with your son Helmut?" Augustin raised his eyebrows at Joel, his fingers tapping the edge of his paddle. "He imagines you as something of a hero, an honorable Teuton warrior who died in battle, defending his people from the Saxons. But today I shall tell him he has believed a lie all this time . . . that his gallant idol took his own life without reason in a blatant act of cowardice." Augustin bared his teeth in a horrific smirk as he finished, "Certainly your daughter Cammie shall appreciate the truth."

A strange sound tore at my emotions, and Joel fell to his knees on the pier, the stone knife clattering to the wood. "I can't do it." Joel choked out the words in ragged tone. "I can't do it. I'll have to tell Helmut . . . ." His voice petered out into a sob, and he buried his face in his hands.

Freia relinquished her grip on my hand and sailed forward to fold Joel into an embrace, her light stretching forth to soothe him. Though she understood none of his exchange with Augustin, she grasped the import of the situation and rushed to comfort. I saw Heinrich's wrinkled brow in my peripheral vision, and a moment later Augustin greeted each of us in turn.

"Master Denlinger. Lady Freia." He nodded once at each of my friends, then leveled his blazing eyes upon me as he finished, "Lady Swanhilde."

I stared back at him, attempting to appraise his fiery spirit as unobtrusively as possible, searching for some trace of the Augustin I had married in that ill-fated cathedral, the Augustin who had wept bitterly on the night he severed our heart-bond forever. I sensed his inquisitiveness, but aside from that he seemed detached and cool inside, belying the fire that smoldered perpetually in his soul.

Joel, meanwhile, was blubbering something about Helmut and Cammie. Heinrich had moved to his side, and Augustin regarded him again. "Your children are not as fragile as you believe. They can handle the truth, for they have faced far worse."

Then he looked back at me and asked in Teutonica, "For what purpose have you come here, Swanhilde? Merely to reunite with your children, as the Lady Freia suggested—or perhaps for some other, deeper motive?"

I shut my eyes, my ice ebbing enough for my body to quake. *How could I ever answer that question without provoking his anger? And how can I manage it in front of Freia and Heinrich . . . and Joel?*

"Perhaps a bit of rest would restore your intuitive abilities, for the hour is quite late." I opened my eyes a crack to see Augustin observing the stars. Then he held his left hand out to me. "Come, Swanhilde. Lady Freia and her husband have Joel's situation well in hand. Come home with me."

My eyelids sprang open at this summons. He offered me a *home*—something I had longed for since I left the Thaden house behind in the modern day, joining my cursed son in a place where nothing made sense. While I dreaded telling Augustin the real reason I had come to Eisenwald, we would have to have this conversation eventually. Better sooner than later, for Prince Otto should not arrive on the scene for nearly three weeks yet.

So I stepped forward to touch Freia's shoulder. She rose to her feet, leaving the shuddering Joel in Heinrich's charge, her green eyes holding my gaze. "Please be gentle with Joel," I asked her quietly. "I'll try to send you word ... once we figure things out." I jerked my head to my left, where Augustin waited.

Freia threw her arms around me, and we clung to each other for a lingering moment. "I'll be praying fervently," she whispered in my ear, "that God will show you the best way forward."

When we parted, we exchanged meaningful nods. Heinrich had helped Joel to his feet, and Freia moved to offer them her support. Then I turned to enter Augustin's dinghy, preparing myself to embark on a desperate quest to evade my recorded destiny.

I took my husband's hand, feeling its warmth as he wrapped his fingers securely around my wrist, guiding me into his dinghy. He gestured for me to take a seat at the bow, so I could lean against his baggage. While I situated myself, I heard him call out a farewell to the others. Then there was no sound but the swish of his oar in the water, accompanied by the gentle rocking of the boat as it began its course upstream to the untamed portion of the forest.

After a peaceful interlude of silent rowing, Augustin addressed me as I lay lazily watching the sky. "You did not heed my counsel." I frowned, twisting my neck around to look at him. His countenance was stern as he continued, speaking our private dialect of Teutonica and English. "In that final letter I wrote to you, I advised you to remain in the twenty-first century, to represent your city there and consign me to the past."

I winced but said nothing. If Augustin thought about it long enough, he might realize why I had come, saving me from the burden of explaining myself. But he continued with the same subject, his tone growing darker.

"I recall that I also pledged to meet you in the future, if I discovered a way to free you from Muniche's bonds. However, since I did *not* come to the twenty-first century to liberate you from your aged Keyholder, you should have deduced that I have *not* yet found a way to break your chains."

I sat up, turning my upper body around to face this fiery Black Priest who seemed intent upon criticizing me with every sentence he spoke. Before I could voice my own opinions on his last letter—which I had torn to pieces and flushed down one of the Black Castle's toilets—Augustin added with a caustic leer, "Or perhaps you are here to set some tide of history in motion, to ensure that I shall indeed discover a way to claim you once more, far in the ether."

"You never found a way to free me," I said, suddenly certain.

"And how can you be so sure? Have you lost your faith in me—*you*, the woman who once insisted upon the necessity of such lofty beliefs?"

"If you *had* found a way, you wouldn't have waited so long to come get me," I declared. "You're a Black Priest imprisoned on earth and unable to age, with a vigor even young Teutons can hardly withstand. I'm *forty*, Augustin, and not only that . . . not only that . . . ."

I feared his reaction to what I was about to assert, but Muniche's influence overtook my discernment. "You've waited too long. Muniche's ties have bound me so securely, deepening as the years go by. I don't know if I still have the will to leave her behind. She's vanquished me, just like you said would happen." I stopped my rant there. An unusual fatigue had come over me, exhaustion brought on by a stressful day laden with illness and death.

Augustin's face had grown livid. He looked away, plunging his oar into the waters with a vengeance. "You ought to sleep now, Swanhilde," he advised in a gruff voice. "We should not speak of sensitive subjects here for fear of capsizing the boat. I do not wish to ruin the goods I gathered today, since trade has diminished thanks to this recent epidemic."

Frowning, I positioned myself more comfortably at the bow. It figured that he would fret about material things when there were far more noteworthy matters to discuss. But I took his advice and leaned my head back against the roll of fabric, relaxing my muscles with effort. When I closed my eyes, focusing my senses on the serenity of the night—the gentle lapping of the waters against the dinghy and Augustin's paddle—he addressed me in a kinder tone. "Sleep peacefully, my swan, and lay your cares aside until daybreak."

The sky had transformed from midnight blue to the muted gold of sunrise when I awoke. Above me, a cluster of trees formed their canopy, bearing new leaves of late spring, oaks and birches. I stretched a bit, propping myself up on my elbows, and saw that I lay upon a thick blue blanket spread over the ground, a black pillow marking the place where my head had rested.

I pushed myself into a sitting position and found that Augustin had placed me beneath the trees at the edge of the clearing where his cottage stood. I saw the cabin now, surrounded by wild berry bushes. Not five meters away, my husband crouched before a pit of blue flames, frying eggs. He caught my eye and grinned, beckoning me to join him.

I did so, bringing the blanket along for a more comfortable seat. "What did you do, put me under an enchantment so I'd sleep until dawn?" I had no memory of leaving the boat or of Augustin carrying me to the tree-ringed dell.

"It is not my fault you find me so charming, my dear Swanie." He favored me with an authentic smile, display-ing his formidable teeth, which shone like pearls in the sunlight. "You have awakened just in time for breakfast. It is all for you."

He cocked an eyebrow at me and flipped the now-cooked eggs onto a plate, offering it to me with a spoon and a roll. Though I did not feel especially hungry, I accepted the victuals, remembering the fork tucked away in my packed bag. At some point I would have to retrieve my things from the Denlinger house.

My husband excused himself to bring a bottle of wine. In his absence, I stretched my limbs again, trying to shake off my fatigue. I had no reason to be tired after sleeping for five or six hours in the open air, but weariness clung to me like a stubborn child. I cast away Freia's shawl, for the balmy morning likely foretold a warm day.

Crossing my legs under my light green skirt, I tackled the eggs, which were scrambled and delicious, despite my lack of appetite. Augustin returned with a wine bottle and two glasses, which he filled without a word, handing one to me and keeping one himself. He said nothing for a while, sitting back against a bulky stump as he watched me eat, sipping from his glass every now and then. I could not guess what he was thinking. Although I could detect his curiosity, I also saw no passion in his eyes, sensed no desire in his blue-fired spirit.

Maybe he had given up on love after all.

Eventually he stirred, several locks of his black hair sliding forward when he used a stick to poke at the embers of his fire. He was still the most attractive man I had ever met, even when he kept his hunger on a short leash. It was a privilege to sit upon the soft blanket and observe him candidly, the educated priest who viewed me as more than just a warm body for his bed. Muniche's sturdy bonds pulsed around my heart, crying piteously for her traitorous Prince; but if anyone could help me pinpoint a solution to my dilemma, that man sat before me now.

"So you did not come here to ask me to free you, nor did you come merely to reunite with your children," Augustin discerned, situating himself back against the stump. Dread tainted my spirit's quietude as I recognized that I could no longer postpone this discussion. I nodded at him and chewed on a bite of egg.

"Would you mind telling me what inspired Joel Hudson von Thaden to end his own life in such a ceremonious fashion?" My husband took a long sip from his glass, his expression inquisitive. "You and the Denlingers seemed fully resigned to his fatal plan."

"Unfortunately, Joel had a difficult life in the twenty-first century," I said, hoping the simple account would satisfy my host. "He lost his wife and sons and was at the point of suicide already. He decided to come here with me to see our children, since they're living happy lives."

A long silence ensued, during which Augustin stared so piercingly at me that I was forced to drop my gaze. "You also came here to die." He said it without a trace of uncertainty, but I sensed his disapproval.

I sighed, realizing that I had no more appetite for eggs. "The future didn't treat me all that well, either," I admitted, setting my plate beside me on the blanket. I shivered, tracing one finger around the rim of my wineglass, gazing blankly at the deep red liquor within.

"Was Hans cruel to you?" Augustin's voice sounded abruptly dangerous.

I laughed once, then reassured him. "No, no. He was never cruel. He was a decent man, a faithful Keyholder, one who took his responsibility seriously. We got married right after . . . you told me about him. He welcomed me into his dreams so my heart could heal. He was a very devoted Keyholder, and I loved him." I fell silent and took another sip of wine. My mouth seemed intent upon going dry during this conversation.

"Was he good in bed?" Augustin questioned, his tone evocative.

That query brought my head up, and I frowned when I saw his smirk. What business did he have, asking me such personal questions? I felt the blush staining my cheeks, and my frown slowly dissipated as I thought of my *other* marriage—the one where Augustin came to me on my wedding night to learn whether or not Joel gratified my lust.

"Well . . . *spiritually* . . . nothing compares. It really is an indescribable glory, the union of a Lady and her Keyholder . . . and Hans was hardly inexperienced." I grimaced at the memory of his sexual exploits, the images so vivid thanks to the lasting impression of blood truths.

But I shoved those memories aside, although I knew Augustin had caught my grimace and would ask me about it later. I staved off his questions by adding, "Hans was good, far better than Joel. He made sure to please me every time. But he wasn't . . . particularly . . . violent."

Augustin chuckled and poured himself another glass. "Ah, Swanhilde the masochist. It is a relief to know that Muniche did not erase *that* part of you." His eyes burned into my spirit, sending shivers down my spine.

"We had two children, a son and a daughter," I went on, trying to lead our dialogue back toward benign topics. "And I started a business to offer support to survivors of domestic violence. I taught classes for the young on Teuton lore, so the children would never forget their magical heritage." Augustin made a sound in his throat, his blue eyes glittering with approval. "It seemed like a decent way to use the wisdom I gained from the past. If Teutons are taught to respect their gifts and each other, a defeat like that of 1066 would never happen again."

"You were always one to be admired," Augustin praised me when I paused to take a drink. "I can hardly predict how this laudatory life of yours could end in tragedy sufficient enough to lure you here to die."

I almost choked on the wine, belated tears welling in my eyes at the thought of how satisfying my life had been before everything crumbled in 2018. I had never fully appreciated it until it had been taken away. "But perhaps you could begin by explaining that look of distress that crossed your face when you spoke of your Keyholder's talents in the bedroom," Augustin said.

I nibbled a few bites of the roll to allow myself one last moment to sort those painful memories. Then I met my husband's gaze and related the first chapter of torment. "Hans passed away less than a month before I came here." Sympathy appeared upon Augustin's face, but I waved a dismissive hand. "It's no matter now. When he was on his deathbed, I found out he had an affair with my Mutti."

Augustin's eyes bugged, and I recounted the highlights of the tale. "Hans didn't meet my Mutti until after he took the keys, so there was really no chance for them romantically. He even introduced her to my Pappi in an attempt to put some distance between them. But eventually they couldn't fight it any longer. It turns out my brother Dane was Hans' child. And every time he got in bed with me, he was thinking of my Mutti." I smiled grimly, raising my glass to my lips as I awaited my husband's reaction.

He gawked at me in apparent stupefaction for a time, then shook his head and said, "What a miserable bastard. For pity's sake, that is worse than wishing for a siren whenever I am with you." The fire in Augustin's pit flared more brightly in response to his antipathy.

"Well, it took me a while to forgive him," I confessed. When I saw the silent question in Augustin's eyes, I clarified, "At least twenty minutes."

"Swanhilde, you forgive too readily." My companion eyed me distrustfully.

"Maybe that's because I know I make just as many mistakes as everyone else," I said with a shrug, remembering how many times Augustin had chided me for absolving his horrible iniquities. Before I could call the words back, I heard myself saying, "If I'd stayed in my time too much longer, I might have gotten in bed with my son."

Augustin choked once on his wine. He set his glass down upon the grass as his hands balled into tense fists. "*Excuse* me?"

"Hans made him the next Keyholder." That was the only defense I was willing to divulge at the moment. No need to complicate things by mentioning the curse or the name Max had chosen for himself. "That's why I had to get out. Muniche's influence can be really confusing at times."

Augustin's face had grown stricken, his jaw muscles tightening, his hands sinking into the grass to grasp the verdant blades in a devil's grip. Ice trickled into my veins as an instinctive defense, but I felt more vulnerable than ever. My undead husband rose to his feet, his hands flexing as he leveled me with a critical glare.

"The *Keyholder* has enclosed your heart in an unbreakable prison, and Muniche has distorted the last vestiges of your individuality." I gaped up at him, the heat of his element cutting through my dress, melting the ice in my blood. He took a step closer to me and intoned, "If you cannot deny these hypotheses, then refute this one: you came here to die with the *Keyholder*."

I withdrew from him, but he strode after me, kicking my wineglass to the dirt. "*Please*, Augustin!" I exclaimed, all of my fears descending upon me in a cloud heavy with rain. "I have no choice! Muniche punishes my heart if I don't—"

"*Swanhilde!*" he roared in a voice so terrible it caused the birds to halt their singing. "How could you dare to come here to *my* house and eat *my* food, when you have planned an ignoble death for yourself? How could you cast your heart to the fiend who cursed me, to jump into the Rhine in union with *him*, while I must stand back and watch? It is *shame*, Swanhilde! The greatest treachery!"

My back pressed up against one of the oak trees, its bark digging into my spine. I clung to it, terrified yet knowing I could go no further. Augustin planted his feet directly in front of me, keeping his hands at his sides while his inner fire threatened to burn away my dress. I tried to speak, but all that escaped my lips was a feeble squeak. On the second attempt, I cried out, "Augustin, I—"

"Do you think I *lied* at our marriage altar?!" he cut me off, his hands descending upon me, taking hold of the bodice of my dress. "Do you think I intend to renege now, and throw myself at the feet of a siren, or of some whore? I promised my faithfulness to *you*, and *this* is how you thank me?! Would you ask my permission to run off with your precious Prince Otto, so you can experience your 'indescribable glories' with him without a troublesome conscience?"

"Augustin, it's already written in history!" I interjected, crying out as he pulled me to my feet, pressing me ruthlessly into the tree trunk. "I read about it in *your* records. I'm supposed to die with the Prince!"

"Lies!" he snarled, his hands closing tightly on my shoulders. "If I did write such sacrilege, it was a blatant lie! I shall kill him myself before he can throw any claim upon you."

"Don't suggest things like that!" I cried. "You'll lose control of your death if you kill him. I know it now. I found out from—"

"I have spent six torturous years without you," he stated through clenched teeth, ignoring my pleas about the Prince's fate. His hands slid from my shoulders to my neck, singeing my skin, though his touch had turned disturbingly gentle, his sapphire eyes seething with the passion I had sought in him earlier.

"If you must die here, I would not dissuade you. But if you believe I would abandon you to that once-brother of mine, wasting those sweet hours that could belong to us." His eyes smoldered, not with anger, but with desire.

In the heat of the moment, I had forgotten that I ought to tell him I wanted to reject my recorded destiny because of him. But his husky reference to our years apart rubbed me the wrong way. Lifting my hands to shove his fingers away from my neck, I snapped, "Six years, what a pity! *I* spent eighteen years without you! And don't you dare think it was easy for me just because I had Hans.

"You have no idea how it feels when your own heart stabs you every time you think about the man you love, gaslighting you until you doubt your own reality. And six years is plenty of time for sorcery. You promised you'd devote all of your resources and intellect toward breaking the bonds that hold us apart. If you really did that and still have nothing to show—"

"I have been avenging your blood, *Muniche!*" Augustin retorted, grasping my wrists in a vise-like grip. "Your enemies are not the simplest people to kill. If it were not for you, I would have left those heathens in peace. And I *have* sought the key to that unbreakable bond. Time remains yet, but you asserted that you may be too far enslaved to accept freedom. Where is that willpower I once admired, if you would die with the man who cursed you?"

"He deserves a chance to repent," I said, "and I'm here with you now to learn how to avoid this destiny you laid out for me!" I glared at him, struggling to free my wrists from his grasp.

"Is your pitiful heart willing to say farewell to your beloved city?" Augustin asked in a disparaging tone. He released one of my wrists and took hold of my chin, tilting my head upward to look directly into my eyes.

"Would you be willing to undergo agony you have never known, more horrid than anything you experienced during the blood-transfer? Would you be prepared to face a division akin to the finality of death, to rip Muniche's spirit away forever? Breaking a heart-bond causes torment, but to sever a tie wrought by forces beyond this world?"

I began to quiver at his pronouncements, rethinking all of my wishes for freedom as Muniche's spirit jabbed me afresh. But Augustin had not yet finished.

"It would be nigh comparable to the flames of hell, I imagine. Unlike those flames that liberated me at Wuotan's command, your torture would last weeks, months, even years, likely accompanied by insanity and an unquenchable longing for death. This is what I have seen in my mind, every time I have sought a way to free you. Thus far I have hesitated, unsure whether you would agree to madness of an eternal caliber. I ask you now: *would* you do it . . . for me?"

His hold on my chin and right wrist had not slackened. I trembled now with a helpless panic coupled with the fatigue that had become my permanent partner. Augustin awaited my reply. He breathed heavily upon me, but I no longer felt the heat from his fire.

I tried desperately to organize my frazzled thoughts for his sake, but I hardly managed to choke out, "I don't...I'm not sure."

He blinked at me, moisture welling in his eyes, his expectation dimming into stoicism. "Then the Swanhilde I loved no longer exists."

His hand moved from my chin to the left side of my face. Before I could process his intensions, he bit down onto my artery, his strength smashing me against the tree. Augustin depleted my vitality within seconds, and my awareness sank into a dark oblivion.

<h3>Chapter Eight:</h3>

Morass of Delirium

It could have been a week, a year, a lifetime that I remained incarcerated in that obscurity brought on by my husband's thirst for understanding. My mind refused to form a coherent thought for the majority of my captivity, but the sensations that wracked my body made up for my lack of lucidity. If I had hoped for the persistence of that initial calm unconsciousness, I was to be disappointed.

My body writhed in a burning haze, my mouth desiccated, my limbs useless to free me from this prison. I heard my own voice moaning from time to time, felt strong hands restraining my convulsions, a relentless jailor blinding my eyes to the truth, no water cooling my parched lips. There was no point in struggling against an adversary I could not see, an antagonist who had depleted my vigor to the very precipice of death, eliminated any relief my ice could have granted to my seething veins. If my mind had been well enough to form a rational wish, I would have begged for death with both my voice and my heart.

Sometimes spirits would visit me, memories both good and bad, floating in a torrent of boiling water, its waves drenching me in an ever-deepening confusion. Joel passed before my eyes in many forms: an eleventh century land-owner with a full beard and longer hair . . . a college student wearing a bathing suit and carrying a boogie board . . . a broken father, body lean and short hair sprinkled with gray, his mind shackled in depression. In every form, his voice droned about his wife Melody, how she embodied all of his dreams.

Hans appeared often, calling me to dance with him at the stream on Thaden property . . . defending me before München's council . . . sealing our bond through marriage . . . seducing me so tenderly with his words, his touch, his devotion to our city . . . insisting that I must be strong for the sake of our children, for the sake of our city, our people, never give up the Torstein. But then I would see a face so similar to mine, her eyes an entrancing icy blue, her arms locked around Hans' neck in an erotic embrace, his eyes black with passion, with lust, with rebellion against the destiny he chose for himself. He wanted Camilla more than me, more even than Muniche. She was his chosen love.

Prince Otto arose occasionally in a blistering smog of red fire, nimble hands grasping the keys of Muniche, the responsibility he had rejected. I heard his voice speaking to Wuotan, pleading for the demon to accept his offerings, payment for his dark sorcery that had doomed the Teuton people. Was it not enough that his heart remained chained to an accursed city? Could he find relief in the heavenly sphere, where his one true love had awaited him for a thousand years? He wept tears of blood as he pined for Kezia, the mother of his children, the woman who showed him the glory of untainted love.

And *he* would come always, cropping up in the midst of other reminisces, nearly able to inspire a poignant yearning in my soul. I saw our first dance, when he introduced himself: "I am Lord Augustin von Bayern, and you are the Lady Swanhilde von Thaden." I viewed him in all of his royal splendor, in the robe of the Teuton priest, organizing the archives, teaching me Ælte Teutonica, drawing my heart from my chest when he cast his spell on me forever. I felt his knife cut me open when I granted my Teuton blood to Freia, felt his claws tearing my skin when Wuotan possessed him that night in the forest, felt his lips brushing mine as he murmured, "You are *still* a goddess . . . the pinnacle of Teutonic splendor." I watched him sever our bond again, that moment of abject horror flashing across his face when he realized what he had done, what it meant, what we had lost. And I heard him say it, with no trace of indecision or pretense: "*I love you.*"

Of all of the specters that visited me in the sultry sea of delirium, Augustin was the only one who managed to break into a blurred reality from time to time. Sometimes I believed that I saw his face above me, lit by an aura of blue fire, desperation sizzling in his eyes as he laid a cloth on my forehead, tried to pour a bitter tonic into my mouth, quietly urged me to be still, to rest. While I could make no sense of these vague moments, my body automatically relaxed in his care, trusting him to protect me as I had so long ago.

Once I almost believed I saw him hunched on a chair in a room where all of the candles had nearly burned out, all ten of his fingers wound around a hand that must have been mine, though I could not feel it. Tears streamed down his cheeks, dampening his robe, his lips forming the very words that returned to me too often in those feverish memories: "I love you." Then another phrase, one that brought me back almost to the surface: "Please . . . stay with me."

When the sickness began to loosen its grip at last, my tormented brain had doggedly pieced together the truth. *Augustin is the man who loves me for who I am. Muniche or not, young or old, beautiful or wasted, intuitive or thoughtless. He may have anger problems, he may like to argue, he may have awful obsessions with blood and gore, he may even be dead. But he loves me. Why did I tell him I wasn't sure?*

There was no point in these games, in these imagined impediments. Though my heart belonged to Muniche and therefore to the Keyholder, the man I *should* be with was Augustin, even if Muniche's spirit stabbed me every minute of every day, even if she killed me, even if I had to turn my back on heaven. I had not come back to the eleventh century to give myself over to Prince Otto, the madman who had cursed my city. I had come for Augustin, for the man I chose to love. Now I had to find my way out of this feverish morass to tell him I wanted to be with him no matter the cost, to spend every possible second with him alone.

Finally I awoke, sensing a fiery touch upon my wrist—the first perception of a temperature hotter than the prison that had boiled my blood since I passed out beneath the tree. I blinked my eyes at the ceiling, at the dark tapestry covering it in a rectangle, its background a deep navy blue decorated with coiled flowers of black. The warm hand moved to my forehead, repositioning a moist cloth. With effort, I rolled my eyes to the left, where the owner of that hand sat upon a chair, clad in black from chin to the floor, his light blue eyes appraising me.

For some reason my gaze fixed on his hair, those locks of gorgeous obsidian, the bangs pulled back as always, likely held by the traditional clip, while the rest cascaded around his shoulders in silken perfection. My eyes locked with his as I struggled to find my strength, and I sought my voice inside, tried to pull it from my chest. I coughed, and his arms caught me, steadying me as he urged me to rest. But I had to tell him, whether my tongue felt like sandpaper or not. "Au . . . gus . . . tin." This would never do; my voice sounded like a frog at the bottom of a well.

A wry smile crossed his lips, and he propped my head upon one of his arms while his other hand brought a glass of potent wine to my lips. "Drink, Swanhilde, and sleep. You are still very sick."

I obeyed his first request, swallowing a few mouthfuls of wine, grateful that it soothed my parched throat. But when he pulled the glass away and laid my head gently upon its pillow, I moved my right hand toward him, trying and failing to snatch his robe. He rose to hover over me, snaring my wayward hand and placing it back upon the sable blanket, his severe expression telling me that I had better relax before he forced me to submit. But I managed to lace my fingers with his just for a moment, and I whispered in a ragged voice, "Augustin . . . I . . . would . . . do it . . . for you."

He smiled and let go of my right hand, sitting down again and taking my left in both of his. "I know you would," he said simply.

I blinked at him, uncomprehending, and he explained, "I saw it in your blood." My lips curled, and Augustin went on, "I have seen many things in your blood while you fought against this fever. It seemed a logical method of lowering it, as well as keeping you sedated so your system could recover."

I raised my eyebrows at him, and he leaned close to whisper, "To bleed you often and replace your feverish blood with mine. Now sleep, my swan, before I must drain your vitality again." He kissed my forehead and reached forward with one hand to slide my eyelids shut.

The next time I woke, I felt sweaty and stiff. I stretched my limbs as I blinked at the rectangular tapestry, absently wondering why it hung upon the ceiling. I ran my eyes around the room from right to left, passing over Augustin's washing table and mirror, pausing at the window. Its pane stood open with black curtains pulled back, sunshine brightening the chamber. One blue-flamed candle burned on the windowsill. I studied it for a while, then ran my gaze across the wardrobe, the high-backed leather chair at Augustin's desk, and the iron cauldron in the corner, out of which rose an odd-looking curl of whitish smoke.

I frowned a little, allowing my eyes to pass by the closed door and the empty wooden chair where my husband had sat while I writhed with illness. Then I lifted my gaze to the ledges on the wall to the left of the bed, noting the sheaves of paper, the sculpture that may have represented Azrael, the candlestick with four burning flames. My gaze fell upon a single candle at the center of the uppermost shelf, a lonely little thing, its flame casting a muted azure glow on the portrait that adorned the wall above it: *Leitalra* Marelda von Bayern.

A sound must have escaped my lips while I stared at that painting, recalling how Augustin had rescued it from her chapel before Muniche crumbled. The next thing I knew, I was staring at her son, his clawed hand reaching out to touch my neck, checking my pulse.

"You seem to be improving, slowly but surely," he said, pulling the wooden chair nearer to my head and sitting upon it. His hand brushed damp bangs aside. "Your fever has certainly broken, for you are drenched in sweat. I may have to lead you to the river for a bath, once you regain your strength." He took my left hand in his and kissed each of my fingertips, his eyes never leaving mine.

I smiled at him, relishing the touch of his lips upon my skin. "How long have I been sick?" I queried, then winced, putting my right hand to my throat. It still felt drier than a bone.

Augustin noticed my distress, for he helped me sit up in bed and offered me a mug of warm milk. I drank it thirstily, suspecting he had gotten it from his goats. It had a creamy flavor that soothed my throat and my empty stomach. While I drank, my husband answered my question.

"You have been ill for four days now with the same pestilence that struck Eisenwald. Your immune system was not prepared for the maladies of the past, it seems. The first three days, you refused all nourishment, remaining unresponsive to my ministrations. Although your lack of excess weight has greatly enhanced your loveliness at age forty"—he smirked at me rather suggestively—"it has done little to preserve you during this fever. I fear you are naught but skin and bones after such a protracted fast."

I looked down at the fingers of my right hand wrapped around the mug, noticing that they did seem bonier than usual. Dropping my gaze to my chest, I found it coated in a layer of sweat, my ribs visible above sagging breasts. "Well, maybe you should cook a meal for me now, before this milk puts me back to sleep. I might be able to force something into my stomach."

He handed me a small bowl of broth, commenting that he had killed one of his chickens that morning to prepare food for me. I sipped slowly at the soup, its warmth seeping into my weakened blood. My stomach seemed to have shrunk to the size of a walnut, my vague hunger ebbing quickly away.

Augustin remained silent while I ate, but he held my left hand in both of his, feeling my pulse from time to time, then running his fingers slowly up my artery and back. "Darling Swanhilde," he murmured when I gave up on the broth and set the half-empty bowl aside, "you could never understand how it pained me to watch you struggle with the fever, your body rejecting all sustenance, your mind lost in oblivion, unresponsive to my voice." Tears gathered in his eyes as he clutched my hand more tightly, kissing my wrist with a fierceness that drew a gasp from my lips. "I felt so helpless. I was afraid I would lose you."

"Oh, Augustin." My right hand plucked at the blanket, for I longed to reach over to stroke his hair, to reassure him. But my muscles were utterly spent; I had used what little strength I had to lift the bowl of broth to my lips. "If I had died of the pestilence, you know I'd have gone back to the future, not to eternity. I couldn't leave you that way."

"That does not make it any easier for me," Augustin said, holding my hand against his chest. "If I must watch you drown in the waters of the Rhine, I would rather not experience your death twice." He pursed his lips and moved the bowl to the bedside table, then gave me a look of despair.

Lying back upon the pillow, I breathed out a sigh, shifting my gaze from his face to the ceiling. "If you sifted through all my memories when you bled me, you should know I can't obey your record's prophecy. I love *you*, not Prince Otto. There must be some way to escape his sway."

"It may not be as simple as you believe, to tear you away from Muniche."

I closed my eyes and tried to force my wearied brain to think rationally. "The bonds of a Teuton city are broken at death for sure. That's been true throughout all of history.

That means if we can't find any other solution, maybe you can trail me to the brink of paradise and summon me back to earth. Like you pulled me away from time's gateway three times before."

Reopening my eyes, I favored Augustin with a resolute look, prepared to defy fate's claws until the very end. My husband reached out to stroke my hair, his pointed fingernails lightly grazing my scalp. "You would turn away from heaven for me?" he asked, his expression appearing both grateful and restless.

"For you," I promised, smiling weakly at my lover.

His eyes glittered with devotion, and he rose from his chair to take hold of my right hand, bringing it into my line of vision. "I have a gift for you, Swanhilde," he said, pulling something from a pocket of his robe. I felt him slide it onto my ring finger, and a tiny squeak pealed from my lips when I saw the candlelight reflecting off of the sapphire. Marelda's ring—the symbol of our wedding vows.

"It has been waiting for you to come back to me . . . my wife." Augustin laid my hand gently upon the blanket, and I closed my eyes as his lips caressed mine.

Chapter Nine:
Gradual Recovery

My physician insisted that I remain in bed during most of my recuperation, for he feared that if I pushed myself too soon, the fever may throw its net upon me once more. Initially, I was all too ready to agree with this prescription, since I had eaten so little for four days and barely had the strength to sit up. Augustin cared for me like I was the most important thing in his world, bringing me water whenever I asked for it and ensuring that I ate every drop of the soups he prepared for me, which grew meatier and more appealing as days passed.

He sat beside me when I was awake, holding my hand more often than not, quietly talking on any subject I wished to discuss. I discovered that while I knew my husband very well from the twenty-three years we had shared the heart-bond, there remained some aspects of him that surprised me still. Perhaps that was due to the fact that we had been apart for eighteen years—for me at least—but some of our conversations deserve to be recounted here.

After I woke from a long and restful sleep with my wedding ring adorning my finger, I brought up the subject of Joel as I relished a flavorful soup. "You did what neither

Heinrich, Freia, nor I managed to do. You convinced him not to kill himself when he was certain he had nothing left to live for."

"Life is too precious a gift to discard out of despair," Augustin said, crossing his arms and leaning against the back of the chair where he sat beside the bed. "The error you and the Denlingers made in your attempts to dissuade him was that you failed to personalize the act. You did not threaten to tell his children the truth."

He was right. Heinrich and Freia would have kept the story of Joel's ritual suicide to themselves, not burdening our children. I swallowed a bit of soup, the tang of fresh oregano enhancing its savor. "Have you had a chance to check on Joel while I've been sick? Make sure he didn't try again after we left?"

A slight smirk graced Augustin's face. "I visited the Denlingers briefly before you woke on the fourth day of your illness, primarily to retrieve the pack I saw in your blood memories. Your former husband also fell prey to the pestilence. He is currently in isolation, but Lady Freia mentioned that he plans to speak to your children one-on-one, to reveal the reality of time travel."

"I hope he doesn't tell them I'm here to commit suicide with the Prince," I mumbled with a grimace. Glancing at my lover's expression, I appended, "Or that I'm plotting an insurrection against my destiny with the Black Priest south of town."

Augustin chuckled and said, "You must return to a full measure of health before we attempt any insurrections."

A spoonful that included a bite of egg slid down my throat, and I counted backwards in my mind. "Eighteen days with you, and five have already passed. We have thirteen left?"

"Thirteen days," Augustin confirmed, blue fire flaring in his irises.

The subsequent day, we discussed at length the things Augustin had seen in my blood. He had drunk enough of it during my fever to give him a rundown of my experiences in the future and the motivations that drove me. "Being

Leitalra has influenced you down to the core of your soul," he told me that afternoon as we sat together on his couch in the parlor. My legs had wobbled when he led me there, my wiry fingers clinging to his sturdy arm; but it was a relief to use my legs for more than a quick trip to the chamber pot.

"You have grown into someone far more complex than the eleventh century Swanhilde," Augustin went on, his right arm holding me against his side. "Now you make decisions based on the good of the Teuton people, teaching both the young and old to respect their mystic heritage. You take an active role in Muniche's future rather than standing by to watch her burn as a woeful spectator."

I laughed hollowly at his commendations. "Maybe that's why she took me back in 1066. Maybe she got mad at me for standing by, for not fighting with the army or something. She wanted to ensure I wouldn't fail her again."

Augustin made a thoughtful noise, his warm fingers massaging my own. "You are certainly not the flighty invalid who pledged her eternal fidelity to me in a Catholic cathedral, knowing it would all come to naught soon enough. I doubt you would approve today if I planned to slip outside and slay a group of beggars. Your city's survival is your main purpose now, superseding even family love."

"Not necessarily," I disagreed, though I could see how he had reached that conclusion. Most of my twenty-first century family had died while I tried to protect the secret of time travel. "It was because of the Torstein, not Muniche, that I taught those classes and lost my family."

"And the Torstein is the brainchild of Muniche's most famous Keyholder," Augustin pointed out with a nod. "See, your whole life boils down to *her*. I saw the pain in your soul, the anguish that torments you at her destruction. But it is good to have such a significant purpose in life, for without a goal, humans tend to waste away into hopeless shadows longing for death."

I cocked my head at him, suspecting that he referenced himself with that assertion. For the past eight years, Augustin's goals had involved avenging Muniche and seeking a solution to the gulf between us. What he would do after my death became a gnawing burden on my heart. For so long, I had been his everything, and I knew that his regard for me had not diminished in the slightest.

I saw his love in his impassioned eyes, felt it in his gentle touch, tasted it in his kisses, in the nourishment he provided for me. My heart broke all over again at the notion that Muniche would win this fight if I died with the Prince. Why should I abandon this Black Priest again, when my Keyholders had given me nothing but a compulsory devotion?

"Though I spurn his infidelity with your mother, I can give Hans credit for one thing," Augustin said, noticing that I was at a loss. "It was a laudable move on his part to grant Muniche's keys to his cursed son. That guarantees that the poor lad shall always have a reason for existence, namely, to protect his city and provide for his Lady. He is one Black Priest who may never face the loneliness that so often accompanies this fate."

"Pretty sure that's how Hans saw it, too," I noted, my gaze drifting toward the blue-fired embers smoldering in the fireplace. Remembering his aversion to Joel's attempted suicide, I leaned closer to his chest and asked, "Do you think Max shouldn't have given up his life in order to stop the NVH and protect the Torstein?"

Augustin sighed, his lips gently brushing my temple. "I cannot judge him; his reasons were sound. But he likely mourns his loss as other Cursed Ones do. No one truly comprehends life's wonder until it is gone."

Clouds thick with rain descended in the night, and Augustin decreed that we remain indoors while the heavens pelted the earth with moisture. He admitted that he would have to leave me alone for a few hours once the rain tapered off, for his stores of food were running low. He usually traded the cheeses and butter he made from his goats' milk, along with the produce from his garden. Like my cursed son from the future, Augustin argued that it was pointless to eat dead plants or animals when his immortal body required no sustenance, adding with a wistful sigh that the death within him consumed anything he swallowed.

"But doesn't food still taste good to you?" I inquired as I enjoyed one of the last rolls he had bought from a settlement across the river. His homemade butter was smooth and delicious.

"It would be better if it carried the life I lack," he answered with a smile.

That afternoon I lay in his arms on the couch while the rain pattered heavily upon the parlor's window, a sense of tranquility relaxing my body against his in the cerulean glow of firelight. We talked about recent goings-on in Bavaria, with the Teutons scattered and the Holy Roman Empire controlling the trade routes. Augustin predicted that the fallen Teuton cities would be reestablished soon enough, since most of them had been prominent centers for commerce.

"Traveling merchants do not like to alter their habits with the whims of government," he said, "for many of them pause in their journeys near the sites of the ancient strongholds. The Saxons have urged others to repopulate the land, and settlers have come already from the north and east. Augsburg and Regensburg are in the process of rebirth now, and undoubtedly the Teuton refugees shall return to their homes once the Empire directs its attention elsewhere."

"Muniche will be restored in the twelfth century," I remembered, "and you'll have a castle to build in the mountains."

"A castle," Augustin repeated in a mocking voice. "The *Toteheri* should keep me occupied for at least another year. There are only five left, and they have grown skittish as a result of my retaliation. I spent much of the year 1073 tracking them across the Sahara, killing six before the rest bolted northward. They likely believe the cold shall deter me." Augustin scoffed.

The fact that my husband had gone to such lengths to eliminate the half-demonic force that destroyed my city warmed my heart, though Muniche's spirit continued to rebuke my devotion to a man who was not her Keyholder. *Prince Otto didn't figure out how to kill the specters that raped you,* I reminded her silently. I slid upward to give Augustin a heartfelt kiss, drinking the depths of that familiar aura of fire mingled with death—a flavor I had greatly missed.

"In case you didn't see it in my blood, I wanted to thank you for your fierce vengeance and for saving Freia's life last year," I told him, gazing into his eyes. "No matter how much Wuotan tries to drag you into the abyss, you continue to resist, to defend our people. You even managed a cross-gender blood-transfer, something none of the priests in my era dare to attempt."

Augustin's lips curved wryly, and he leaned his head forward to give my nose a quick smooch. "Just because I am a Black Priest does not make me omnipotent when it comes to deadly Teuton rituals. I agreed to it only to preserve your family's magic. I granted Wuotan something he coveted, so he refrained from tempting either of them in the bloody river."

I shivered all over at the mental image of my son Helmut facing that infernal pain. Augustin traced my spine in a tender fashion, prompting my desires to turn in a direction we had not yet traveled since my return. He had kissed and caressed me after I awoke from the fever, but we had not yet made love—something I longed to correct as soon as the opportunity presented itself.

"I officiated their Teutonic wedding after completing the ritual," Augustin said, his eyes reflecting the glow of his fires. My eyes bulged at that, and he gave me a chiding look. "There are no other Teuton priests near Eisenwald, and Holda wanted to claim the scar of Teutonic marriage. They held a ceremony at the church when they returned to their families."

"I kind of wish I had a chance to get to know Holda," I murmured, recalling how expertly she had sung Nightwish's "Wanderlust" just a week ago.

"You may have time for that," my husband responded, and I saw the angles of his face harden with determination. "Though I have yet to uncover a method certain to release you from Muniche's bonds, there are two scriptoria with Teutonic records that I have not yet visited. One in Wels, the other on a solitary mountain. Within a few days, I expect you shall be strong enough to accompany me when I go in spirit form to conduct a thorough search."

Excitement raced through me, and I pushed myself into a sitting position on Augustin's lap. "We'll figure this out. I know we will."

That evening, Augustin gave me a sponge bath with soap and herbed water, cleansing away the grime that clung to me with my sickness. I rested upon a towel on the couch while his gentle hands cleaned my body, the fireplace and a multitude of lighted candles granting the parlor a cozy atmosphere. By the time he toweled me dry, his touches had grown incredibly seductive, lingering around my breasts in a manner that lured a moan from my throat.

"Ah, darling . . . it is a crime that we have been together now for a week without unifying our bodies and elements," he purred, his hands sliding from my breasts to my navel, then to my thighs. I lay upon the couch with my hair wrapped in a towel, watching the candlelight grappling with the shadows upon the ceiling. I breathed out as Augustin drew my thighs apart, his heat arousing my yearning.

"Please . . . take me now," I whispered, my ice stretching forth to entwine with his fire. I closed my eyes as his fingers expertly worked my clit, my entire body shuddering beneath his command.

But before his strokes brought me to the edge, Augustin killed my paradise by groaning, "I cannot, Swanhilde, I cannot. Your life summons me with a siren's lure . . . if I take you now, I might drain you dry . . . and crush these flimsy bones of yours." The fingers of his free hand tugged at one of my nipples as heat built in my core, my hips leaning into his touch.

While my rational brain understood his point—he no longer held my heart, so if he bled me in the throes of passion he may very well kill me—my desire cried out for total union with the man who loved me without reservations. "I don't care," I managed to gasp. "I don't—"

His kiss smothered the rest of my protests, and an instant later my body shattered, my moans stifled by the consuming grip of death. When he released my mouth, Augustin turned his attention to the liquid adorning his clawed fingertips, sucking them dry one by one as his flaming eyes stared into mine. I watched him in a haze, silently wishing he would cast off his priestly robe so I could admire his immaculate body. Thus far, he had changed clothes only while I slept.

"Your life," he uttered in an ardent tone, "is sweeter than honey. Do you have any more to give?" His eyes traveled back to my crotch.

"You can have all of it. It's yours," I breathed.

Without pause, he lowered his head and took me in a way that Hans never had, his fiery spirit joining with my icy one as his tongue siphoned the life from between my legs. By the time he deemed himself finished, bliss had carried me into a reverie, safe beneath my immortal husband's care. I did not notice when he carried me to bed, but when I woke the next morning I felt more rested than I had in months.

Augustin went hunting that morning and returned around noon bearing two full bags of victuals. He confessed that his gift of death gave him an unfair advantage whenever he hunted game, since his weapon never missed. "Then you can sense the hearts of every living thing all the time?" I asked him as he laid out his kills in the pantry—a deer, two hares, and four trout from the river.

"If I focus on that, yes. I usually ignore it."

I told him that idea reminded me of "Halt," a song by Rammstein. Augustin grinned as I explained the variety of interpretations for that song, and I updated him on the Gothic and metal music he had missed between 2002 and 2020. While he cured his kills, he asked me to sing some of the newer Nightwish songs, but my voice cracked on the higher notes. "The darn pestilence has taken more out of me than I like to think," I grumbled.

We enjoyed a real feast that evening—herbed venison garnished with radishes and field garlic, topped off with a few hard boiled eggs, fresh raspberries, and wine. Augustin ate some of it at my insistence, and I offered to help him make more goat cheese and butter during the week to come. Vigor returned to my blood at last, the lingering shackles of the pestilence falling away.

After dinner, Augustin brought a trunk down from his attic and invited me to sift through its contents. Stepping to his side, I gasped at the sight of a wide array of fabrics. "I always hoped you would return to me someday," he said, "and when that day arrived, I had no intention of letting you parade around in rags."

"But it's okay if I parade around naked?" I raised my eyebrows at him. Until then, I had not laid eyes upon any dresses since I woke from the fever.

He wrapped his left arm around my bare waist and kissed my neck. "You are most attractive without clothing, my swan."

I swatted him and took a closer look at the contents of the trunk, my eyes growing wider at the sight of gowns made of everything from the standard linens and wools to silk. All were dark in color—varying hues of blue, violet, forest green, and maroon interspersed with the ever-present black. "Where exactly did you find all of this? Did you steal it from the Saxons?"

Augustin chuckled. "I acquired these during my journeys through Bavaria and the adjacent territories. With all of the noblewomen evacuated and a ravaging army drawing ever nearer, who else could make use of such spoils?"

I ran my fingers through some of the fabrics, surprised when I came across the three dresses I had brought from the future. Each appeared clean and pressed. I retrieved the modern-style one of flowing blue, deciding that it was about time I appeared somewhat presentable. My husband vacated the parlor while I pulled the dress into place, and when he returned I saw that he carried his dark blue blanket rolled beneath one arm.

"Would you like to watch the twilight descend with me?" His expression carried a hint of shyness as he eyed my outfit.

Dropping a curtsey, I responded, "It would be my pleasure." I offered him my hand, and he led me out the front door.

Augustin spread the blanket before his fire pit, and we stretched out upon it to watch the stars appear. He decreed that I must spend as much time outdoors as possible, in order to build up my strength. This new plan filled me with joy, for I longed to explore the woodland and tend Augustin's animals and garden. He had two gray goats that he allowed to forage in the forest during the summer months. They returned to his pen most nights to rest with his stallion and enjoy cultivated feed. Five chickens completed his tiny menagerie, each producing an egg nearly every day.

While we lay side by side watching hues of crimson paint the darkening sky, I opened the subject that had festered in my mind since the night I sought Günter's assistance. "In my era, we were apart for eighteen years. Until you showed up out of nowhere in the Black Castle looking as radiant as an angel." I rolled my eyes to the right to look at his face.

His jaw clenched, and his black eyebrows slanted downward, though he kept his gaze on the heavens with his hands folded behind his head. "Do you imply that you wish I had not come?" His tone sounded cautious.

"No, no. You were the only reason Günter didn't kill me. I felt his death prickling around my heart before you came." I shivered at the memory, invoking my element into my blood to console me and welcome the evening's coolness.

Augustin's features grew even more chiseled. "That arrogant fool had no right to offer your blood to hell's minions."

I knew he spoke of the ghoulish Cursed Ones that Günter resurrected to celebrate the sacrifice. Augustin had met the four eldest ones in 1045, after Prince Otto had cursed him. I tried to suppress a smile at the memory of Kasimir and Konrad, the two dead priests who met me at the castle's main entrance and gushed about their busts in the memorial passage.

"How did you know Günter was going to kill me?" I asked my husband, still observing his face. "I didn't think it was possible to see the future."

Augustin met my gaze at last, his eyes seeming to harbor arcane knowledge. "The powers of darkness can reveal some things, but divination is clothed in shadow, ever shifting, like the smoke. I used the fires within my cauldron to watch over you after our heart-bond dissolved, but it was difficult to see specific events. Until the day I saw you die at the hands of one of my successors."

His face broke, and flames churned in his irises, the fires in his pit flaring higher toward the sky. I reached my right hand out to his cheek, wanting to soothe his anguish. "Augustin . . . ."

"Ah, Swanie." He extracted his hands from beneath his head and took hold of mine, his fire seeking to bond with my ice. "I realize that you went to him to ask for help. But I love you, and the other Cursed Ones do not. They bow to their master willingly, glorying in the macabre, and Hans *owed* that wretch something already! It was madness to go to him. Madness!" He leaned forward to kiss my forehead twice, his lips burning into my flesh.

"But how did you come?" I whispered, marveling at the depth of this Cursed One's commitment. To watch my life through a cauldron was one thing, but to actually step through time to interfere? *No one could ever love me the way Augustin does.*

His lips quivered, and he sighed, dropping his gaze from mine as his fingers continued to warm my right hand.

"I am still unsure how I managed it," he said after a pause, his forehead creased in contemplation.

"I knew I could force that wretch to yield if I appeared in his dungeon. Such a vision would give any man pause, especially with the others scrambling around like skeletons. But just *how* it happened . . . desolation splintered my heart, and my fire exploded with a virulence that may have been enough to ruin me. And I leapt bodily into my cauldron, pleading with any entity that might listen to open a portal for me, to spare us both from infinite loss."

I gaped at Augustin, seeing tears trembling on his eyelashes as he blinked at the gloaming. "Somehow I found myself standing there so close to you, sensing all of your fear, your shock, the chill of your ice . . . all of this nearly diverting me from my purpose—to threaten Günter Setzer." He grimaced, then met my gaze at last as he finished, "So it worked, but I would appreciate it if you would avoid other Cursed Ones in the future."

Looking back toward the sky, my eyes traced the deepening shades of navy blue that gradually eclipsed the remnants of sunlight. He had not mentioned Wuotan at all in his explanation; he had saved me in some miraculous way he could not identify. *God hasn't given up on him yet,* I thought.

But I gave a soft sigh, my brainlessness from that night drenching me in a wave of remorse. "I was such an idiot. I should have said I loved you."

When I turned apologetic eyes to look into his, my husband's gentle smile calmed my fears. "You did say it," he murmured as his lips brushed mine. "Your love is evident every time you say my name. You are the only living soul who calls me Augustin."

Chapter Ten:
At the Riverbank

The forest around Augustin's cottage was truly sublime, bursting with life and growth of all sorts. Each morning when I awoke in his bed, my husband would open the window to invite in the sunlight, along with the sounds of birdsong and chickens scratching in their pen just outside. I watched Augustin feed them as I prepared for the day, saw him groom his black stallion and milk his goats before allowing them to roam free. He caught my eye when he turned for the pantry with pail of milk in hand, his smile appearing peaceful even though our time together grew ever shorter.

He tended a small vegetable garden against the northern wall of his cabin, which sported cabbages, cucumbers, radishes, onions, and carrots. Although he consumed its yield only rarely, Augustin stated that he preferred his home to be surrounded with life rather than death and decay. He experienced enough of that in his travels and in Wuotan's realm, as well as inside his own body. Therefore he cultivated a multitude of plants—from the raspberries, bilberries, and elderberries gathered along the front of his cottage to the herbs and wildflowers that sprang up in the clearing and along the pen. A lengthy trellis hung with grapevines stood not three steps from the front door, and a cherry tree marked the path to the Rhine.

On my ninth day at his cottage, my husband invited me to join him at the riverbank after I savored a tasty breakfast of scrambled eggs and buttered bread. He said that he had something to accomplish there and that it was high time for my ice to revel in the camaraderie of its primary—water. I already wore one of the dresses from the trunk in the parlor since my period started that day, for I had no wish to soil Augustin's floors and blankets with blood, even if he believed I looked best naked. But I asked him to grant me a few minutes to prepare myself for such a venture, and he waved me to his bedroom, an eager glow lightening his face.

It took me a while to deem myself presentable. I spent close to a half-hour in front of Augustin's washing table, straightening the dress—which fit me decently enough, the skirt brushing the ground, the short-sleeved bodice hanging somewhat loosely off my shoulders—perfecting the bow I tied in its wide violet ribbon, combing and parting my frizzy hair, washing my wan face and hands. My cheeks still appeared devoid of color, so I longed to spend the day drinking in the sun's life-giving heat.

When I made it to the shores of the Rhine, I had to consciously refrain from breaking into a jubilant dance. It was such a beautiful day, the sky a perfect azure with a few cumulus clouds brushed along by the warm breeze. The waters of the Rhine called to my blood, urging me to transform my eyes to match their deep blue, to usher a welcome chill to the heat of summer. Summoning just a trace of my magic into my eyes to hue my vision in a pristine blue, I halted a few steps from the water, watching a pair of ducks floating along. Nature's glory relaxed me, and I breathed a contented sigh, then swept my gaze up and down the bank, seeking my husband.

He sat with his back against a mulberry tree near a clump of reeds not far from the water's edge, his outer robe lying in the grass beside him, his black tunic and pants hardly blending him with the virescent foliage. Sunlight shone on his countenance, which was tilted downward, his concentration on whatever sat in his lap. As I approached him, I saw the pen in his right hand and the inkwell resting atop his cloak, one sheet of paper spread across a slab of wood that served as a buttress.

A smile broke across my face, and I was about to make some snide comment about my husband being a fanatical chronicler who refused to abandon his writing even in the sphere of nature. But then I caught sight of the artistic strokes adorning the parchment, a sketch in black ink that depicted me asleep on Augustin's bed, the outline of his body taking shape beside me, his face trained upon mine, his hand curved around my wrist.

Fascinated, I crept onto my husband's cloak and sat down, folding my legs beneath my skirt, taking care not to tip the inkwell. Neither of us spoke while his pen filled in the contours of his clothing, the details of the headboard, the shadows of devotion upon his face. "I intend to call this one *The Slumbering Angel*," he said at length, his hand guiding the pen so expertly, forming a faultless drawing.

"I didn't know you could draw." A stupid statement, but it was true. I knew Augustin was a skilled chronicler, a capable physician, a ruthless avenger, an able priest ... but an artist? And one who worked so proficiently with such a demanding medium—medieval pens and ink?

"It is something that caught my interest about six years ago," he explained, raising his eyes from his picture to look into mine. "It seemed a useful method for expressing my inner feelings, less destructive than indiscriminate killing sprees." He chuckled once, a mordant sound, putting the finishing touches on his drawing and laying it down upon a flat rock to his left. "The ink shall dry soon enough, and after titling and signing it, I shall add it to my collection."

"You have a *collection* of these drawings?" I gaped at my husband, who nodded. "Well, you should have figured out earlier that you have a creative talent with pens. If you can shape sentences so artfully, why not pictures? After all, your mother was a painter." I thought of that rendering of my city that I had seen in the Bayern castle—the work of Marelda, Muniche's *Leitalra*.

Augustin said nothing to my musings, giving me a thoughtful look as he put his pen back in its inkwell and set it near the base of the rock. I turned my head back toward the river, another disquieting question rising in my mind. I swallowed, gathering my courage, and asked in a whisper, "How many people . . . did you kill . . . because of . . . because—" I could not form the words. *Because you lost me.*

"None," he responded, his gaze also upon the Rhine. "But it was not a good year to be in this forest." He pressed his lips into a thin line, then reached over to touch my left hand. "How do you feel, Swanhilde?" he inquired, checking my pulse, then scrutinizing my color with an expression of dissatisfaction.

"A little tired, but happy to be outdoors."

He released my wrist and felt my forehead, then suggested that I keep my ice on a short leash, since my spirit still appeared weakened to his eyes. He reached to retrieve something from behind the rock and said, "I may cook the evening meal at my fire pit, assuming my artwork does not appall you enough to cause a relapse." He smirked and handed me a leather folder containing a thick stack of parchments.

"You're actually going to let me look at them?" I traced my fingers slowly down the howling wolf imprinted upon the cover.

"Yes, now that you have sufficiently recovered. Many of the earlier ones are not particularly pleasant to the eye, but you have known for years what evil lurks within my heart." Augustin's expression suggested that he was not looking forward to this artistic disclosure. But he drew me against his side and wrapped his right arm around my waist as I hesitantly opened the folder.

The sketch that greeted me almost prompted my heart to skip a beat; it was undoubtedly the first he had drawn. A distorted rendering of Augustin himself, a gaping hole torn in his chest where his heart should have been, his face contorted in a scream of anguish, his left hand clawing at the wound in his chest, his right clenched before him, hemorrhaging blood. A jagged darkness surrounded his body, and I felt a lump form in my throat as I turned the paper over. The initials *W.W.* were scrawled across the back, and one single word in English: *Why?*

I shuddered, abruptly regretting that my husband wanted me to look at his drawings. The second was worse. Me, naked and shackled in irons, a chain tight around my throat, my eyes blindfolded, my lips parted in one final breath, a key with serrated teeth slicing into my heart, dark blood running down, pooling between my fettered feet. This one was labeled: *Beauty Destroyed.*

My hands had begun to shake by the time my eyes locked upon the third sketch. A portrait of Augustin on his knees in darkness, his clawed hands digging into the flames around him, his eyes wild and desperate, his teeth bared like those of a beast. I could practically feel his pain by looking at that drawing, seeing how hopelessly he had sought an escape, a reason to exist. *Empty.* A suitable title.

I closed my eyes before I could see the fourth picture. "I can't keep looking at these. I'll ruin them with my tears."

Augustin's hands gently slid mine aside, and I heard paper rustling. "Here, Swanhilde. There are happier moments."

Cautiously opening my eyes, I saw a picture that radiated beauty in style and subject. Augustin and I floated in spirit form, depicted with godlike perfection, my robes enveloping me like the clouds, my hair's tresses rustling around my face. I gazed at Augustin in obvious adoration, and he smiled back at me affectionately, his right hand curved protectively around my heart. I recognized the scene as the moment I basked in the wonder of our newly formed heart-bond, my spirit overwhelmed by the sense of trust that swelled in my heart, an abiding devotion to the priest who guarded it. When I turned the paper over, I found that it was titled simply: *Love.*

I looked through quite a few of Augustin's drawings that afternoon, scenes of glory from our past mixed with sketches depicting portions of the cottage, the yard, the river, Eisenwald in the tranquility of sunrise. It became evident that he preferred to draw either me or himself or both of us in any pictures that involved people. I found only one portraying another subject—Helmut and Holda kissing at the Teutonic altar, their hands stabbed together on the post.

Many of his sketches brought back a rush of fond memories. Augustin and I sitting on a couch in the Meldorf parlor, poring over our dictionaries; resting in his lap upon the bench amid the roses; dancing in the Bayern gardens in winter; walking beside him toward the cherry tree at the Meldorf stream; whirling together as spirits through the Rhenisch forest, upon the waters of the Rhine; pledging eternal love and faithfulness in a darkened cathedral.

And of course, I found many explicit depictions of our sexual encounters, from that first sinful fling to the copulations upon the Catholic altar. I suspected Augustin had drawn out every single position we had ever assumed, including the brutal ones, for I found at least four sketches of my beaten body chained to the ground or sprawled on a stone altar, ravaged by a vicious demon.

After sifting through a stack of nude portraits of myself in every shape and age—all of them bearing suggestive titles like *Teutonic Perfection, My Luscious Siren,* and *The Erotic Swan*—I shot Augustin a reproachful look. "I think you must have a one-track mind."

He answered with a grin, "You know that sex has always been one of my greatest pleasures, even before I was cursed." His grip tightened on my waist, and he nibbled at my ear, effectively distracting me from his artwork for the time being. I ended up laying the folder aside before wrapping my arms around him and pulling his mouth to mine, drinking his love with what vigor my frail body had. His natural scent of smoldering campfire infused my soul with a sense of belonging, of acceptance, of safety. Sentiments I would have to forgo if fate had its way.

We bathed together in the river that evening, the glow of the waxing moon providing enough light for me to ogle my husband's immortal body at long last. The sculpted muscles of his chest looked heartbreakingly attractive in the moon's silvery glow, his blue-fired eyes glimmering with love. His aura simmered with heat as we passed the soap back and forth, the waters around us as temperate as a modern day bath.

"Ah, how I long to claim you as I once did," Augustin crooned while he pressed my back against his chest, his hands lathering my breasts. He bent down to inhale the scent of my hair. "Your heart should beat in *my* hands . . . not in the callous grip of a city."

I moaned and brushed my lower back against his firm length; our difference in height rendered a comfortable copulation impossible while we stood on equal ground. "Swanhilde von Thaden's heart belongs to you alone," I murmured, biting my lip as I felt Muniche's collective soul stab me in response. Must I resign myself to a life of constant torture just to stay with the man I loved most?

It would be worth it.

Easing myself around to face him as he rinsed away the suds, I raised my eyes to his and offered a sultry warning. "If you don't give me your body tonight, I'll tear your dead heart from your chest and freeze it solid. I'm as healthy as I'm going to get, and I want to indulge in some cerulean fire."

Augustin chuckled, and he ground himself for an instant against my stomach. "Black fire did not satisfy your needs?"

"Not when it imagined my Mutti the entire time. And you know blue is my favorite color." I snagged one of his nipples in my lips and suckled it, wrapping my arms around his lithe back.

Augustin groaned and swept me into his arms, his sharp teeth gnawing at my throat. "I shall try my hardest not to bleed you to death, Swanhilde," he growled as he carried me back to his cabin. "But I fear I can make no promises."

He did not kill me that night; in fact, he made love to me so sweetly that my shackled heart melted into a limp puddle, weeping for a miracle we could not see. Prince Otto would arrive on the scene in just nine days, but I longed to stay with Augustin, to abandon my responsibility to Muniche just as the Prince had done. Why should I cast my life into the Rhine's maw when a Cursed One's heart beat for me alone? If I forsook him, would he hand himself over to God or descend into the abyss with the others of his ilk?

Augustin and I spent most of the tenth day beside the river, dabbling our bare feet in the shallows and speaking on whatever subjects came to mind. He told me that he intended to probe the archives of Wels the following day, for he judged my strength sufficient enough to permit me to join him. We would likely spend the entire day as Teuton spirits, sifting through tomes and scrolls in a desperate search for a way to defy Muniche's cords. He promised to cook a big breakfast and dinner for me that day, to ensure my vitality would not fade.

I brought up several questions while I lay folded in his arms that afternoon, clad in the light green frock I had brought from the Black Castle's collection. My husband wore his priestly robe overtop a simple tunic and trousers —his standard outfit whenever I was around. He knew that I found him most attractive in the garb of the Teuton priest, its blackness suggesting mystery and authority.

He told me the stories of the half-demons he had slaughtered on my behalf during the past eight years, relating the gruesome ways they attempted to fight him when he cornered each of them. He had subdued each one for the purpose of bleeding before invoking his fire to scorch their blood, sometimes calling down the sun's rays to assist. He left their cindered bodies behind as a testament to his power and as a warning to anyone who wished to challenge him.

"And you're one hundred percent certain they're really and truly dead," I said, my toes creating flakes of ice amid the Rhine's waters.

"Without question. I watched their souls—if what drives them can be labeled as such—disintegrate in a torrent of screams. I know not what sort of eternity awaits them, for demons were never meant to procreate with humans. Offspring of such perversions may find themselves beyond grace."

"But if there's still some humanity in them, they should have a chance at heaven," I noted, wondering whether I should have asked Augustin to offer them the gift of repentance before ending their lives.

"I am the harbinger of death. Their fate is in God's hands, not mine."

We went back and forth on that topic without reaching a certain conclusion. So I eventually agreed that God would have to handle their sentence, that as mere humans we could not fully comprehend the results of demonic lineage. Augustin mentioned in passing that despite the death that roiled inside of him, his spirit pulsed with life in the ethereal realm. "I have spent weeks apart from my body when the decay grows too onerous," he confessed in a wistful tone.

My muses drifted toward the Augustin I had known in Muniche, the noble lord who cultivated a steady relationship with the local working women—and who took sexual pleasure from each of his female sacrifices. I thought of the comfortable bed I had occupied throughout my stay in my husband's home . . . and I felt something twitch in my gut.

"You don't need sleep, but you have a really luxurious bed," I said during a lull in the conversation. I gazed at the tree line across the river while his fingers toyed with my hair, and his body tensed beneath me. After considering the potential repercussions for a half-second, I blurted, "Do you screw a bunch of sirens in that bed or what?"

Augustin held his peace for eighteen seconds; I counted them off in my head. Then his chest expanded in a sigh. "I fear you would not believe the truth if I told it to you."

My forehead wrinkled. I pressed my thighs together in an instinctive attempt to stave off the truth. "Got some local squeeze like Gisela who stops by every few weeks?" Jealousy sliced at the edges of my heart, but I knew that my husband was a sex addict. He had to have gotten his release somewhere during our years apart.

"Swanhilde, I promised you my fidelity at our marriage altar. That was not a lie." His arms tightened around my body in a possessive fashion.

"You . . . you mean . . . you've been *abstinent* . . . all this time?" I twisted my neck to the left in an attempt to meet his eyes, but they stared off across the Rhine as mine had done, his lips pressed into a stern line.

"It has not been easy to abstain," he said in a ragged voice. "But sex without love is incredibly unfulfilling. I learned that shortly after I fell under the curse, when the sirens kept throwing themselves at me. The elemental rush they offer is nice, but it pales to insignificance in light of your ardent passion."

A single tear slid down my face as Augustin's love rebuked my destiny anew. But I leaned back against his chest and twined my fingers through his, wanting to focus on the positives. We were together now, and tomorrow we would search the tomes for a way to remain together.

"So you built that bed just because you believed one day I would return to you," I gathered, working to surmount my gloom. Augustin affirmed it, and I traced my index finger down one of his claws. "Then it basically sits there all empty and lonely unless you sleep in it yourself."

"A dead man does not need sleep, Swanhilde," he reminded me, his fingers twitching beneath my grip "I do not prefer to indulge in pastimes which bring no sense of satisfaction. I rarely slept more than five hours per night when rest was a requirement for my system."

I turned my neck to look at him again, perplexed by this fresh snippet of information. "How did you survive on such little sleep?"

He scowled and narrowed his eyes at me as he said, "It was a necessity, to circumvent the nightmares. The people I sacrificed haunt me when I sleep. The rush of power such massacres offers is sweet but fleeting, replaced by the ponderous weight of offense inherent to a destroyer."

I gasped, stunned at this revelation from a hardened murderer. I always assumed Augustin drank the high of power and then forgot his crimes. But now he admitted that their souls haunted him, that the guilt he bore was punishment in and of itself.

"I am still human, my dear swan, as much as I would wish otherwise," he related, his tone pained. "Though I have not slept in six years, I still see their faces in my memory, sometimes."

Giving his chin a gentle kiss, I whispered, "I love you so much, Augustin. You aren't the villain those in Muniche imagined you to be."

Chapter Eleven:
A Complex Puzzle

Wels' scriptorium proved a disappointment. After two full days of sorting through scrolls, papers, volumes, and etched tablets from as far back as the early Roman Empire, Augustin deemed our efforts a waste of time. The city archivist—an elderly Teuton shadowed by a young apprentice—proved unwilling to direct our search, muttering often to his young lackey that only an evil witch would seek the knowledge we pursued. His distrustful eyes, glimmering the orange of fire, trailed my spirit as I moved from one collection to another, and he grimaced at the sight of Augustin assisting my efforts.

My husband told me, when we returned home on the second evening, that the aged chronicler did not believe women should be permitted to enter the spiritual realm without a master's help. "He believed us to be mages who wished to invoke evil magic on the battered strongholds," Augustin said as he cooked a stew of venison, vegetables, herbs, and eggs over the fire in his kitchen. "It upset him to see us working together so seamlessly when I do not hold your heart."

"Typical of this backward era," I commented while I laid out the last of his rolls and a slab of butter. "We're lucky he didn't call the city authorities on us. I thought he might when we slipped past the energy barrier on the first day." One section of that city's archives was under lock and key of a supernatural sort.

"He would have, had I not insinuated that he had best not interfere. Quite intriguing to learn that Wels' Keyholder concluded a deal with Wuotan to spare his city from the *Toteheri*."

"Right? Meanwhile the Prince figured it was better to just curse his city after it was too late for any favors." I scrunched my nose while Muniche's spirit lamented her destruction within me, my focus on the roll in my hands, my fingers buttering it meticulously.

"Wels' Keyholder paid an atrocious price. It will be enlightening to see what comes of it as the years pass. I shall update my private chronicles tonight while you sleep, and tomorrow morning we move on to holy ground." Augustin dished a heap of stew onto my plate, a sly smirk adorning his lips.

As I burrowed beneath Augustin's sable blanket upon his bed that night, I reflected on the odd bits of information I had learned at Wels. We found little about the mystical bond between a Lady and Keyholder, but I had spent at least an hour analyzing a scroll that told the story of a woman who wanted to purge herself from all emotion after her husband cheated on her. Written in elegant Ælte Teutonica, the record claimed she had begged Wuotan to punish her spouse and turn her heart to stone. She became an undead siren . . . and her unfaithful husband perished in a torrential storm alongside two mistresses.

Before she vanished from the mortal world, the woman had wielded the element of whirlwind. The scroll inferred that she created the tempest herself, and that for years afterward, young men could hear her voice wailing in every gale.

There were a lot of tales about sirens in the restricted section of the archives, most portraying them as soulless vampires who rendered virgin males infertile. A latched Latin tome detailed methods of summoning every known demon, from the standard Germanic deities like Wuotan, Saxnot, and Thunar to ancient entities like Moloch, Baal, Lamashtu, Nergal, and Lilith. Truth to be told, I was relieved when Augustin decided it was time to move on. The longer we spent in that scriptorium, the more I felt as though Wuotan lurked just behind my spirit, his sinister hands grasping at my heart through the veils of Prince Otto's curse.

A windy siren visited my dreams that night, as my husband composed his private records at the desk in his bedroom. I looked on while she cast herself at a cruel demon's feet, pleading for release from her tormented feelings. I saw Wuotan's phantomlike hand reach into her chest and turn her heart to stone, ending her individuality, confining her in an empty shell. And I realized, when I awoke, that I would never wish to do the same, despite the anguish love had brought me.

The second stop on our hunt for unknown Teutonic sorcery was a place my husband had never visited before, so he could not simply carry our spirits there on the power of vision. At breakfast, he identified our goal as an abbey perched upon a mountain peak not far from one of the primary Italian trade routes. A common waypoint for those making religious pilgrimages to Rome, Augustin knew that it was run by monks and friars from the Italian and the Germanic side of the Empire. He had heard that some of the chroniclers fleeing the Saxon onslaught had deposited records there, and that was the collection we intended to browse.

To my surprise, when Augustin changed reality around our spirits, I found my icy eyes looking down at a city with new stone walls under construction, nestled in a valley along a pristine Alpine river. The landscape looked vaguely familiar to me, and as I glanced over each summit below, my husband's mental voice illuminated my recognition. *Innsbruck*. He gestured downward, his robes flaming sapphire.

Chuckles escaped my brain as I remembered sweeping these environs in a far different place alongside my girlfriend Vreni. *Went hunting for an elusive Black Priest east of here before I left the future,* I told Augustin.

Disapproval radiated toward me from where he hovered just a handbreadth away. *Yes, I saw that in your blood. You had best take my warning to stay away from others of my kind seriously, Swanhilde.*

Hans said the same thing. Pretty sure that Cursed One was insane, even though he didn't agree with the council members using females as magic practice. Catching hold of a warm zephyr, I allowed it to carry my spirit along the river below as I asked, *So where do we need to go to find this abbey?*

Southwest, I believe. Augustin pointed toward what appeared to be a well-traveled road winding around the mountains below the city. *We should come upon it before reaching Bozn.*

He took my hand, and we breezed along with the winds, keeping our eyes peeled for the sight of manmade formations upon the peaks. I told Augustin about the priestly conference Hans had attended in 2011, when Innsbruck's *Leitaeri* inadvertently revealed one of the most repulsive practices perpetuated by Teuton priests. Augustin's disgust was palpable, stretching forth to alter the hues of my icy robes. His tutors had him practice his sorcery with his peers and demonstrated the mysticism of the heart-bond upon their own wives, not on young slaves.

Did any of them show you how to hurt a woman's heart using the bond? I asked him, wondering whether he would admit to it if they had.

If a man claims a destructive element, such things do not need to be shown, Augustin responded, his ethereal fingers tightening around mine as he nodded at a splash of gray in the distance. *Our goal is in sight.*

Since his immortal eyesight was far sharper than even my elemental vision, I did not question him. But as we neared the abbey—a small edifice of gray stone perched atop a forested mountain—I gave words to the notions that churned deep inside my heart. *Hans promised never to use his fire against my heart, and he kept that promise. But you burned my heart more than once.*

Augustin gave a mental sigh. *Swanhilde, I know full well that I have not been guiltless in my treatment of you. I wish I could purge those sensations from your mind forever.*

I'd rather our relationship be honest, even when we make mistakes, I rejoined. *One of my girlfriends was bound to an awful priest who blurred her memories until she questioned her own reality. He met a horrid end, but Ina struggled for a good many years.*

I said I wish I could do it. Not that I would *treat your mind with such scorn.* Augustin's broad smile warmed my heart, and he gestured for me to remain amid the clouds while he descended to the abbey to scout it out first. I knew he did so to protect me, so I let him go and set my spirit upon a wisp of cumulus drifting a meter above the structure's primary turret.

In his absence, I observed the landscape below in its entirety. The primary building contained a large chapel with several wings surrounding it, one of which I could tell belonged to the kitchen, due to the scent of baking bread rising from a chimney. There appeared to be at least one smaller chapel, dormitories, a library, and a separate bath house, stable, and barn. Vegetable gardens ringed the edifice, and I saw small crops of grains some distance below the peak, before the tree line. Several gravestones dotted a meadow around the well.

I noticed several people at work amongst the grain, and plainsong rose from the chapel below. Perhaps this was a brief glimpse into the religious culture Freia had experienced in the convent during her childhood. Tangible peace seeped into my spirit while I waited for Augustin to give the all-clear, and I smiled as I allowed my element to brush each soul upon the mountain. Aside from my husband, three others harbored Teutonic magic. Earth, smoke, and water.

Suddenly, Augustin emerged beside me, a worn tome with golden letters stamped upon its cover tucked beneath his left arm, his ghostly face paler than I had ever seen it. Holding his right hand out to me, he projected restless thoughts into my mind. *Come. We must go.*

I frowned, hesitant, for I wanted to explore the abbey in its entirety. *Did you have a run-in with one of the Teutons or something?*

Swanhilde, we must go. Now. Augustin's tone demanded no objections. He snagged my hand in the next instant and sent our spirits back to his cottage.

When I opened my mortal eyes, my element contracting itself back into my blood, I blinked at Augustin. Hints of smoke rose from his robe as his fire confined itself to his irises, his expression severe, his gaze traveling from my face to the couch, where he had laid the tome. Following his example, I looked at the volume myself. It was not particularly large, two golden embossed leather straps sealing it shut. Its title read *Teutonic Cities* in Latin, which hinted that we might have finally hit the jackpot.

Returning my gaze to Augustin's, I detected what could have been a muted terror clinging to his countenance. "Why did we have to get out of there so fast?" I whispered, fearing he had stolen the volume.

Augustin stared into my eyes in without speaking for a long moment, as though trying to decide just how much to reveal. At length he exhaled heavily through his nostrils and said, "One of the chroniclers in the library recognized me."

I did a double-take. "That doesn't happen all that often, right?" My husband had been cursed—and dead—for nearly three decades now. The Teuton community at large had long since forgotten him.

"Not often. We may need to return there at another time, once we have reached a viable solution to our dilemma." Augustin placed his hands on his hips and looked toward the window. It was a cloudy day here at the Rhine, weak rays of sunlight casting insufficient light into the parlor.

"Another time, then," I said, gears turning in my brain at such a prospect. *Maybe the person who recognized him offered some sage advice on my destiny. Maybe my hopes haven't been for naught after all.* A smile curled upon my lips, and I pulled a few stray hairs back from my face, ready to tackle this day's challenges.

Augustin retrieved the book from the couch and carried it to his bedroom, suggesting that we browse it together upon his bed. I agreed to this plan and asked to borrow one of his clips to secure my hair out of the way. Not long afterward, I lay beside him on my stomach as he opened the book to its first chapter, a myriad of blue-fired candles providing light for us to read, alongside the clouded daylight arching in from the open window.

Chapter Twelve:
Loitering Ghosts

Foolishly, I had hoped for a miraculous breakthrough, as if my life experiences had not proved that such marvels rarely materialized. The tome taught me secrets far contrary to my dreams.

The first chapter, a lengthy one, offered descriptions of the spells and rituals required to found a Teuton city. Augustin had a notion to skip ahead, for he had witnessed the founding of Amberg during his teen years. But I insisted that we read the entire account, to refresh my knowledge of Latin if nothing else. I soon found myself imagining the scenes in my head—the moment when a city birthed its soul through the combined power of the elements, human spirits, and magical blood. Gate keys forged and enchanted by Teuton metalsmiths and priests, dipped in the Lady's blood to seal the bond until death.

"It's a good thing you're reading through how to do this," I commented to Augustin as he proceeded to the second chapter. "For all we know, you might play a role in Muniche's rebirth next century, since who knows how many records are left to describe the process."

My husband's body stiffened beside me. Turning his head to the right, he favored me with a pensive frown. "You are certain, from history, that the Muniche of the future shall harbor an entirely different essence than the soul that inhabits your heart?"

I felt my forehead wrinkling in thought. "Possibly?"

"That would mean you became *Leitalra* twice," Augustin said, traces of blue fire sparkling deep within his eyes. "Once when your current Keyholder cursed his city, killing his enfeebled Lady. And again when you stepped out of time's gateway upon your return to the year 2000. You mentioned that you sensed Muniche's soul rejoicing inside of you and attributed it to the fact that she lived. But perhaps she simply filled you with joy to make the transition easier for you, her human host."

I cringed at his choice of words; they made Muniche's bonds seem like a parasite. I shook my head slowly, trying to rationalize what he implied. "But is it possible for a woman to represent two different Teuton cities? Or are you saying the Muniche from this era released me in time's currents? That might actually be feasible . . . since I think the Prince meant to destroy the keys and the city's entity when he cursed her to Wuotan."

"That is likely what he meant to do," Augustin agreed, scowling as he looked back down at the open book before us. "But doubtless abject treachery cannot be performed with such abandon. This volume may educate us further."

As we read on past the introductory chapter, anxiety rooted itself within my heart, convincing me that the only way to eliminate my connection to Muniche was to die, to commit ritual suicide like history implied. Maybe that was the reason I had to join myself with a traitorous Keyholder for ten days before the new moon. Maybe it was Prince Otto, not Augustin, who would help me unravel the tangled chaos of my fate.

We had gotten about halfway through the volume— learning the steps required to choose a new Keyholder if one died before passing the keys on, as well as an odd spell that inhibited the romantic aspects of the city bond when a Lady claimed one of her sons as Keyholder—before another disquieting concept arose in my brain. I focused my concentration on Muniche's essence within me for a moment, trying to sense whether Prince Otto still searched for me . . . and whether my presence here had duplicated the bonds.

"When you drank my blood, did you see that fiasco where Hans persuaded me to visit my Mutti and get her advice on my destiny?" I asked Augustin.

"I did."

"And you saw how the younger version of him hunted me down since I'd 'perverted' Muniche's bonds? Existing in the same time frame as Bertha Lohr?"

Augustin gave a quiet snort. "I saw your frustration at his actions."

"That jerk saw me kill myself and thought it'd be awesome to keep it a secret from me," I grumbled, rolling my eyes on Hans' behalf. "At least you wrote about me dying with Prince Otto so I'd know before I came here. I appreciate that, by the way."

I glanced briefly at Augustin's face, and he nodded once, his eyes on the page before him. "But I was just thinking, did Muniche *not* choose a new *Leitalra* after I returned to the future? I've felt the Keyholder's inquisitiveness about me, but he hasn't freaked out like Hans did."

"Perhaps when the Prince cursed the city, it affected her spirit in ways we do not yet perceive," Augustin proposed, raising one eyebrow at me.

"Probably means the city's going mad inside my heart. Lovely." I flopped onto the blanket and asked my husband to read the book to me for a while, for the scratching in my heart had grown vexing. Shutting my eyes as his educated voice related the Latin in a scholar's tone, I tried to send a silent message to the Prince, to wherever he lurked, disconsolate and alone.

I don't appreciate what you did in the heat of the moment. But I'm waiting for you here by the Rhine. Waiting to see your face when you repent of burning your blood upon me as an offering to your demon lord.

Toward the end of the tome, we came upon a brief section that outlined the tales of two Teuton Ladies who had attempted—unsuccessfully—to break the city's hold on their hearts. The first, a *Leitalra* of Freising named Waltraud, from the 900s, had consulted a forest witch to weave a spell that would release her heart from her master, an elderly brute who raped her every morning and night. She had tried to reason with him first, to no avail, and the strength of the city bond would not allow her to slay him herself. The forest witch did some sort of ritual involving Waltraud's blood, the earth, the water, and herbs. Her sorcery drained the vitality from Waltraud and her Keyholder, both of whom died within a week. The witch was tried before the council and executed for murder.

The second story happened during Augustin's childhood and was far worse. In the 1020s, a young maiden named Millicent became *Leitalra* of Ingolstadt, but she already cherished an abiding love for a local carpenter. Surprisingly, her Keyholder sympathized with her and worked with the priests on the city council to wear away the chains that bound her heart. The process lasted for weeks, and the young *Leitalra* eventually lost consciousness, her spirit weeping wordlessly for the carpenter. On the night of the full blood moon, the priests and Keyholder believed they had succeeded, for Millicent awoke and the Keyholder sensed the city bonds drawing him toward a new woman.

What the priests did not realize was that Millicent did not actually awake. She had died, and in the instant her soul departed, a demon took possession of her body. The false Millicent married the carpenter and proceeded to drain his blood; she drained a handful of others before a Catholic bishop managed to exorcise the demon. Then her body crumpled to the ground, degeneration wiping away the last of her beauty.

Nothing else in the volume gave any suggestions on how to free a Teuton Lady from her city and Keyholder. My hopes were unfounded, our efforts in vain. I would remain bound to Muniche until I entered eternity.

Augustin closed the book and sat in silence on the edge of his bed, his back turned to me. I pushed myself into a sitting position, too, realizing that my stomach felt famished; noon had long passed. But my icy spirit sensed despair sizzling deep inside my husband's aura, his own hopes disintegrating. My love was the sole thing holding him back from evil . . . and he was about to lose it permanently.

Wringing trembling hands in my lap, I cleared my throat and tried to find a way to reassure him. "Maybe . . . maybe . . . if I die with the Prince . . . and go to the very threshold of heaven . . . maybe Muniche will release me then . . . and you can pull me back to earth." An impossible fortune, one that might be our only hope.

Augustin's shoulders sagged, his clawed fingers gripping the edge of the bed. "If I did such a thing . . . you would return?" he asked in a low voice.

"For you," I vowed, sidling to his side and laying my head upon his shoulder.

Augustin sighed and wound his right arm around me. "We still have the rest of today, and five days after that," he noted. "It may be best to enjoy each other's company while we can. I shall pursue darker research after your Keyholder claims you."

His disgust was palpable, but I recognized what he planned to do. He would commune with Wuotan and other demons in a final bid to free me at the brink of eternity. "Please don't make a deal you'll regret," I begged, reaching up to trail soft kisses along his jawline. "Don't damn your soul to hell on my behalf."

Augustin's jaw shifted beneath my lips. "No price is too high to obtain further time with you," he murmured. Then he captured me in his arms and pinned my body to the bed, effectively distracting me from my discontent.

That night, my daughter Freya visited my dreams for the first time in a while. Together, we revisited a memory from when she discovered her element. She had come home from a friend's birthday party, her black hair in matching pigtails, her cheeks flushed with what I identified as consternation. "Mutti . . . something bad happened . . . at the party," she confessed in a high voice so similar to my own at that age, her dark blue eyes glistening with apprehension.

I guided her into the sunroom, away from her older brother's prying eyes, and sat down with her upon the settee. "Did you do something bad, Freya?" I asked her gently, reaching out to stroke her head.

Tears welled in her eyes, and her body started shaking. "I didn't mean to. I didn't mean to!" Her voice rose into a shriek before hitching in a sob.

I gathered her into my arms, grateful that her sweet heart compelled her to confess to me rather than conceal her troubles. For a long interval I consoled her, rocking her tenderly and assuring her that everyone—even people like Mutti and Pappi—made mistakes. In time, she managed to admit what she believed to be a sin. She had accidentally hurt one of her good friends.

"Selina . . . showed me her fire . . . she has fire . . . like her Mutti," Freya said, her voice breaking over the words. "So I tried . . . I tried . . . ."

"You tried to invoke your own element?" I prompted, pride building within me at the fact that my daughter had harnessed her magic. My ice sensed what simmered in her spirit, but I waited for her to tell me what it was.

"I don't know what happened!" Freya cried out, shrinking back from me. "I touched her hand, and something snapped. She fell down and started crying. I don't want my element to hurt people!"

"Your element can't hurt me, darling girl," I soothed her, folding her into another hug. "I think you ought to tell your Opa about it. He can teach you how to control how it reacts to other people."

"You mean—" Freya sniffed and wiped at her tears, which appeared just a shade darker than standard liquid. "You mean . . . it's energy? But I saw darkness when it came out . . . I thought it was darkness like Max!"

Looking into her innocent eyes, I offered her a knowing smile. "Looks more like *dark* energy to me. And that's way cooler than what your Opa's got. You're the perfect combination of him and your brother."

"Wow!" Freya exclaimed. Seconds later she zoomed into the house, her shrill voice calling out for her beloved Opa.

The dream left me feeling empty when I woke, the night's obscurity cloaking Augustin's bedroom. Two blue-flamed candles brightened opposite sides of the chamber—the one upon the windowsill and the one that illuminated Marelda's portrait. I stretched beneath the blanket as latent grief seized me, tears of simple salt water dampening my cheeks.

Augustin lay awake at my side, and he tucked me against him when he heard me crying. One of his hands stroked the artery in my neck for a while, and then a claw pierced me momentarily, extracting a single drop of blood. The pain did not upset me, for my inner anguish penetrated far deeper. Through a veil of tears, I watched my husband suck the blood from his fingernail, his light blue eyes shining with understanding.

"Your daughter's ghost has visited you," he said softly, gentle fingers massaging my tense shoulders.

"She suffered so much from the NVH," I whispered, struggling to speak around the lump in my throat. "I don't know if she'll ever forgive me. I should have cut the Torstein out of my hip and chucked it into the ocean. Where only the fish could find it." I sighed and cuddled myself beneath Augustin's arm.

"You did what you believed was right for the sake of the Teuton people," he murmured, his warmth gradually quieting me. "I doubt those fiends would have left you alone had you destroyed the stone. They would have oppressed our people until they obtained what they sought."

"Freya was such a sweet child. She really had a gift with electronics. Sango started showing her programming techniques right before they kidnapped her. She deserved to live . . . but she suffered and died because of me." My tears had begun to run dry, leaving me emptier than before. "So many people died because of me. When all I've wanted is to help others, to shine a light in the darkness."

"It is difficult to achieve any lasting changes for good in this world," my lover sighed after a pause, his fingers continuing to knead my shoulders and neck. "That is why Wuotan's enticements are so tempting . . . to propagate hatred and tumult, two ruins that humanity embraces. Short term pleasures with long term decline. Those who imagine their lives to have no meaning often fall prey to such deception. Spread anger and offense, cast the blame anywhere but where it belongs."

"But we have to keep trying," I mumbled automatically, Augustin's eternal fate replacing Freya's at the forefront of my mind. "We have to keep fighting against evil, doing our best with what we've got."

"And you have done that very thing, Swanhilde." Augustin's eyes smoldered down at me in the darkness. "You continue to stand for goodness even while you shoulder demonic persecution. Your faith is a breath of fresh air in a realm of death, a vibrant candle in oppressive darkness. There is something I do not think you have realized about your influence."

I caught sight of his sharp teeth smiling at me in the candlelight. "What?"

"I observed and recorded the destruction of multiple Teuton strongholds during the Saxon onslaught. Bamberg, Regensburg, Muniche, Augsburg, Salzburg, Ingolstadt. In nearly all of those settlements, the majority of the population remained until it was too late to flee, and those who fled ran to the nearest Teuton city set to fall within a year. But five of the eight landed families around Muniche escaped to the south and west, along with many merchants and producers.

"Though your peers may have treated you like a madwoman—crying out for everyone to fly to the Alps in the wake of the apocalypse—*you* are the reason so many Teutons still live today, preserving their magic for generations to come. If you had not journeyed to eleventh century

Muniche, the Holy Roman Empire may have wiped Teuton blood and its sorcery from the earth."

I stared at my husband, aghast. "Are you serious?" I managed to say.

Augustin bent forward to give my forehead a light kiss. "*Never* discount the smallest actions, my darling wife."

Much needed relief flooded over me, perking my spirit once more. "We need to check on Joel sometime today," I declared, sliding my body atop my husband's and leaning my ear against his chest to listen to his slow but powerful heartbeat. "Make sure he's gotten over the pestilence. And find out whether he's told any of our kids the truth yet. I'm hoping none of them incite a march on your cottage to rescue me from the Cursed One."

A chuckle rumbled in Augustin's chest. "You had best sleep again if you wish to embark on such a venture," he advised, softly rubbing my naked back. So I tried to relax again, closing my eyes to concentrate on the reassuring thuds of Augustin's immortal heartbeat. Slow and steady, perhaps once every two seconds. No life to offer . . . but a fidelity that soothed my spirit, edging me back towards a restful sleep.

I talked to Joel briefly just after lunchtime that day. Augustin and I visited Eisenwald in spirit form, and he remained beyond others' reach while I sent my thoughts to Joel as he finished a meal of roast hare, bread, and greens along with the rest of the Denlinger household. I noticed that Erika was back to a full measure of health, and that Lorraine continued to observe Joel from beneath her eyelashes from time to time. My ex seriously needed to take the hint. I invited him to meet me in the chamber we had shared upon our arrival.

Positioning my spirit before the window, I waited while Joel entered and shut the door behind him. He wore a different set of clothing—a green tunic and brown leather trousers—and his cheeks appeared hollow. "Guess that pestilence wasn't the flu after all," he said in greeting, invoking his wind into his irises as he regarded my spirit.

I could not smother a smile. *Yeah, I had it too. Still some weakness hanging on even after fourteen days.*

"Has it been that long already?" Joel stretched his back with a grunt before leaning against the door and stuffing his hands in the pockets of his trousers. His windswept eyes drifted toward the window.

It has.

"Have you and your husband found a way to avoid your suicide yet?" he asked, looking back at me.

The pity upon his visage surprised me, as well as his reference to Augustin as my 'husband.' *We're working on it,* I answered evasively, folding my ethereal hands beneath my icy robe. *What about you? You're not having second thoughts about ritual suicide, are you?*

Joel gave a quiet scoff. "Not when your Cursed One will shatter our kids' perceptions of me if I do. I'm going to do some work with Heinrich at the foundry starting next week, see if I can get back in the groove."

Augustin had been correct. Joel had decided to continue on only to spare our children from heartache. *Good. I really think you ought to give Lorraine the time of day, once you get settled. You seem to have enchanted her.*

Joel shrugged, his cheeks flushing just a shade. *Have you talked to any of our kids yet?* I asked, nervousness peppering my robes with wintry sprinkles.

"I'm going to do that tonight, actually. Freia and I are having dinner with Cammie's family, and afterward I'm going to tell her the truth." Joel extracted his hands from his pockets and rubbed them together, looking as nervous as I felt. His windy gray eyes refused to meet mine.

Sorrow merged with my anxiety, prompting my spiritual lungs to pull at the air uneasily. *You're not going to tell any of them I came back . . . are you?*

Joel met my gaze, his sandy eyebrows arched in concern. "Not unless you want me to."

I shivered and closed my eyes, casting a thicker sheen of ice over my vision. *Tell Cammie I love her so much. And I'm so sorry.*

From behind my translucent eyelids, I saw Joel shaking his head, and he implored, "Could you at least . . . ask your husband to come by and tell us . . . whether you actually commit suicide with the Prince?"

I nodded and opened my eyes. *I'll ask, but it might be a while before he can do that. Freia said he mourned me for an entire year when he first lost me.*

Joel raised his eyebrows at me meaningfully and said, "Sounds like you need to make sure he doesn't lose you again."

<h2 style="text-align:center">Chapter Thirteen:</h2>

Grasping at the Wind

Sensuality and long discussions filled most of our hours throughout the next few days. After confirming that Joel was safe, I tended to agree with Augustin's earlier suggestion: to relish each other's company in the limited time we had. We danced together through the forest and amid the Rhine's waters in our bodies and in spirit form, gathering nature's glory around the two lovers fate held apart. We tended his animals and his gardens, and I helped him prepare several meals, long forgotten medieval traditions coming back to me in the process. I even practiced my handwriting with his fountain pens while he sketched more portraits, my muse entranced by how creatively he directed the ink.

Augustin made love to me so sweetly as my body continued to recover from the pestilence, his claws and teeth leaving no mark on my skin. He told me one morning without a trace of deception in his eyes that he could grow used to such placid lovemaking with me as his partner. It truly amazed me that he could control himself so strictly after six years of abstinence. I certainly could not do the same, for my blunt fingernails dug into his muscles as I drank death and fire from his lips.

"I think you're as bewitched as I am," I scolded him afterward, as I clad myself in an amethyst-tinted summer dress. "What will the Prince say when I tell him how kind you've been these past weeks? I doubt he'll believe me." I chuckled, wiping a damp cloth across my face while Augustin brushed my hair and pinned my tresses back in one of his clips.

He managed a smile that appeared strained for some reason. As I finished primping myself at his washing table, Augustin threw on a black tunic and pants, securing his garments with a thick leather belt. Then he took up the brush himself and combed his satin locks with deft strokes, tying all of it into a knot between his ears. "Your Keyholder shall arrive tonight," he commented suddenly, checking his hairstyle in the mirror.

I froze where I stood before the window with my eyes following his chickens. "You mean . . . it's *already* . . . how do you—" I could not finish my thought.

"Twelve nights until the new moon." His eyes drifted from his mirror to the window and the blue sky above the trees. "I can sense his red fire in the distance, drawing ever closer. I would recognize him anywhere, after trailing his army for nearly seventeen years."

I slumped against the sill, forcing my lungs to draw breath. I had a strong desire to beg Augustin to run away with me now. My heart hammered in my chest, and my ice turned my vision blue, my mind struggling to prepare itself for this rendezvous with a man I did not want. "But why . . . why is he coming so *early?*" I wondered. "Your record said we spent ten days together, not eleven."

Augustin came to my side, his hands lightly rubbing my arms, coaxing my ice to thaw. "Who can say?" he muttered, bending down to nuzzle my ear. "But he is coming, and thus you must ready yourself for your destiny. For now, we shall not bother to speak of him, and eat breakfast as if we had centuries before us." He eyed me gravely, then kissed my lips before leading me to the kitchen.

After breakfast, I attempted to bury myself in menial work, but every weed I removed from Augustin's garden reminded me of some part of Prince Otto—his beard, his hands, his serious eyes that matched Hans' exactly. What was worse, a Keyholder who cheated on his aged Lady with an icy vixen, or a royal Prince who preferred a woman from centuries ago, who abandoned his duties under pressure? I felt like fate had dragged me into a twisted fairytale. But I gathered the produce and eggs anyway, ordering myself to maintain my poise.

Augustin set his death loose upon a duck dabbling at the riverside, and when he brought it back to his cabin, I helped him butcher it outside the pantry. Neither of us spoke while we worked. I suspected that my husband struggled as much as I did with cruel reality bearing down upon us. Once I disappeared with the Prince, Augustin would probably not bother to hunt or eat.

In the afternoon, we took a stroll along one of the woodland trails, pausing at a raspberry bush to pluck from its fruit. We speculated on the past and future, on our fates once time separated us. We joked about the Black Castle—Augustin's project to keep him occupied for the next hundred years. I insisted that he build four corner towers and one in the center that reached high enough to see the spires of Muniche in clear weather. I reminded him to install an organ and prepare a grand library and set aside a hallway for the busts of Cursed Ones throughout the ages. He pledged to do all of it, but admitted that it might be a while before he felt comfortable undertaking such a complex task.

During our return trip I sang a few newer Gothic tunes Augustin had not heard before, along with his favorite, Nightwish's "Two For Tragedy." Trying to allow musical loveliness to purge my mind of its anxieties, I cast all of my emotions into my voice as I covered Sirenia's "My Destiny Coming To Pass," Tarja's "Our Great Divide," and Within Temptation's "The Last Dance." Augustin seemed to appreciate each song, remarking that they were all appropriate to our situation in one way or other.

We held hands during our entire walk.

Later, we lay in the grass near his cottage on the shores of the Rhine, watching the waterfowl floating with the current, the birds fluttering from tree to tree. My eyes closed of their own accord, my body resting tranquilly despite what lay ahead; for my husband's arms were around me, his warm chest beneath me, his ubiquitous eyes shielding me from harm. I imagined that we relaxed alone in an idyllic paradise, safe from the cold dictates of fate.

Presently, Augustin stirred, his hands undoing the stays of my bodice, his fingers reaching beneath the fabric to touch my skin. "Tell me," he began in a strange tone, his right hand working its way to my left breast, "have you changed your mind about removing Muniche's chains?"

I gasped and stiffened, my ice churning through my veins at the idea of such blasphemy. I had seriously thought Augustin had given up on that after the awful stories we had read in that Latin tome. And earlier, he had said that my Keyholder would come for me tonight.

Then it hit me. *This may be our last chance to try . . . just to* try *to bridge the gulf that separates us. Though it may be painful . . . though it may not succeed . . . we certainly have to try.* "No, I haven't changed my mind." The words came out dry and shaky. I trembled at the way his right hand seemed to dig into my chest, to physically mold that organ that pulsed deep inside.

Augustin exhaled, a breath that rang of finality. The next thing I knew, he had wrapped a strip of black cloth around my face, blinding my eyesight, his left hand knotting it at the back of my head. My heartbeat sped, whether in response to my lack of vision or Augustin's right hand pressing against it so firmly, I am not sure. My whole body tensed, and a whirl of horrific images raced through my mind—memories of the other time he had tried this, when my city was dying inside of me. His left hand crept forward to cup my throat, pushing my head back against his chest while his legs wound around mine, pinning me to the earth.

"This is not going to be simple, or pleasant," Augustin warned me as I struggled to stave off the hysteria churning in my blood. "You must trust me with every part of you, every portion of that soul shackled within, that woman who belongs to *me*, the woman Muniche stole away."

My body shivered at these words—a terrible depiction of my destiny, yet so true, so *true*. My husband's breath touched my ear, his hands tightening upon me as he murmured in a voice that was almost a growl, "*Trust* me, Swanhilde, and do not resist. Open your heart to me, to the priest who loves you more than he loves his own soul."

Heat pounded into my blood, spreading outward to the edges of my limbs, displacing my ice entirely with a power I could not counter. Augustin continued to whisper commands in my ear, and they were commands—orders not to fight, to open my soul, to let him inside where he belonged. The air around me seemed to thin, and I gasped, feeling the fire creeping through my veins, centering around my heart, that rebellious organ that throbbed thickly now, sensing those deadly fingers that sank so deep, endeavoring to touch my very soul.

I cried out involuntarily, and my body jerked, though I had lost the ability to control my limbs. My eyesight returned in a flash, and it was as though I looked down at myself from above, seeing my prone form in the grasp of a black-clad devil, his right hand a flame that penetrated my heart. His eyes aglow with determination, his lips fabricated syllables of endearment, of adultery, of *treason*.

He was all I could see—a blue-fired demon reaching into my chest, touching the cords that bound my heart, attempting to burn them away. Intense pain shot through my soul, igniting an animal inside of me, a beast that had fully awoken on one other occasion, in 1066, in a crumbling tower.

My soul screamed in rage, and my body followed suit, convulsing in the grip of this priest whose voice tried to calm me while his hand ripped my heart in pieces. The hands of my soul clawed at his grip, Muniche's vigor reinforcing my frailty, her voice pealing from within, roaring,

Let GO of me! My lips spewed a hiss, for Muniche recognized this tyrant, this priest who refused her once before, this man cast out from her forever, exiled unto death.

His left hand slapped my face hard. I felt it in the mortal world and in this realm above, this place where Muniche's soul reigned supreme, eliminating all truth from my mind except that I belonged to *her*, to her Keyholder, not this fiery enemy who attempted to break that connection through force. I growled at him, thrashing against his iron grip.

Swanhilde, cease your struggle, he commanded, slapping me again. *Stop fighting me. Fight her. You are stronger than her, if you would cast off this insanity.* His left hand grabbed the nape of my neck, his eyes burning me to the depths, his teeth bared as he tugged harshly at a heart so unwilling to relinquish its chains.

I AM Muniche, my lips snapped at him, my mind still enslaved. *And there is nothing you can do to change that, wretch of damnation.* I wailed in the next instant, a cry of agony directed to my Keyholder, pleading for his aid in a struggle against an opponent who wielded the scepter of death. His grip on my heart was so fixed now, chipping away at my defenses, throwing waves upon waves of pain through every fiber of my being. But Muniche continued to struggle, her spiritual legions bolstering her bonds on my heart, rendering it impregnable.

Augustin abruptly switched tactics, his lips consuming mine, engulfing my soul with fire. He kissed me viciously, the fingers of his right hand stroking my heart seductively but with an unyielding force behind it.

Swanhilde, he pleaded, the eyes of his spirit holding mine with a flaming desperation, *do not let her do this to us. I must hurt you to set you free, and you must embrace the torture to discard your chains. Please, I know you love me more. Please.* He kissed me again, and I shivered, the torment in my heart warring with the elation in my lips. I *did* love this man, this deadly wraith. I would renounce everything—my life, my soul, these last twenty years representing my city—for *him*.

So I tried to do as he asked, though she speared me vengefully, rebuking my treason. I tried to relax, to welcome that flaming hand still thrust into my soul, scalding my heart. I closed my eyes, trying to block all memories of my responsibility, of this destiny that had shackled me for so long. Trying to focus on my faithful husband, my priest, my deliverer, though it felt as though he slew me now, raking claws of liquid fire through the chambers of my heart, infusing it with his influence, his authority, his control. I should not belong to a stupid Keyholder. Augustin should be my master, my only love. I wanted to say it, to open my lips and name him my master, to promise my eternal fidelity.

But she was stronger than me, in spite of what he had said.

She retaliated with a suddenness that shocked me, quashing my hopes. My ice erupted within me, bursting from my spirit at her command. My eyes flew open, and I saw Augustin's look of horror, his right arm suddenly translucent, still embedded in my chest. *NO!* he shouted. And then oblivion took me.

When I opened my eyes again, I saw the leaves and branches of an elm tree spreading their canopy above me, beneath an orange sky. The light hurt my eyes. My right arm lifted of its own accord to shield me from another form of fire.

Sensing the ice chilling my body, I rolled to my side and discovered that I lay in a pile of feathery frost, the black cloth that had blindfolded me earlier lying at the base of the tree. I thought of that last moment before I blacked out, realizing that my element must have really gone haywire, coating the summer ground with this slowly-melting ice. I hardly knew what had happened to me, here at the riverbank or there in that misty firmament I could not see with my mortal eyes.

Then it finally occurred to me that Augustin was not here, not holding me in his arms as he had been before my ordeal began. I pushed myself upright, then climbed to my feet while holding onto the tree for balance. I blinked my eyes at the Rhine, so resplendent in the reddening rays of sunset; then I turned my neck this way and that, seeing no trace of my husband. He must be somewhere nearby, and I must find him, to beg forgiveness for my weakness, for being unable to conquer the stronger will of Muniche.

I stumbled to the trail, following it with the steps of a drunkard, brushing my hands against tree and bush as I walked, trying to stop my head from spinning. That was the first time I had ever gone to the realm of the spirit without elemental help since the day of the blood-transfer, and my system did not appreciate the exertion.

I found Augustin crumpled on the ground before his fire pit, his face bowed in the dust, his shoulders shaking with silent sobs. The pit sent forth a soft curl of smoke, an indication that a few flames smoldered within, their presence doing little to comfort my grieving husband. I fell to my knees at his side and threw my arms around him, my own tears spilling from my eyes in droplets of ice. I could think of nothing to say, no words to properly express my anguish. Muniche would claim my heart until the day I stepped through heaven's gates, and tonight I must leave with my master, my Keyholder. Our final hopes had been destroyed.

Augustin lifted his head after a time, wrapping his left arm around my back, his expression so broken that I could hardly bear to look at his face. "I tried," he whispered when I leaned my head against him. "But your city is stronger even than a dead man. Her warriors of the past would not allow me to spurn her."

"I'm sorry . . . Augustin." I sniffed, my tears dampening the rumpled bodice of my violet dress. "I tried to stop her . . . but it was no use."

He grimaced, his face taking on a strange grayish hue. "She is very powerful, to extinguish the fire of a Cursed One so absolutely. My blood feels like sludge, a final reminder that I must not attempt such a feat again."

I frowned, perceiving that the fingers of his left hand held no trace of their familiar warmth. I opened my mouth to ask him to explain, but then he raised his right hand from the earth, holding it up for me to see. It was frozen solid, covered from the elbow to the tip of the middle finger with a layer of ice.

"Augustin," I gasped, stretching one finger out to touch it. I recoiled at its chill, a cold far more profound than the ice that coated my skin whenever I released my element. "Is it . . . is it ever going to go away?" I shivered in horror at the prospect of my husband's strong hand cursed forever by a wintry spell.

"In time," he replied, cringing as he laid it back upon the ground. "I feel the fire pumping outward from my heart even now, driving the chill from my blood. But I fear that Muniche wished to warn me not to meddle with her human frame again. She shall not willingly release you until death, Swanhilde, and perhaps our only hope now would be what you suggested after we read through that tome. To die, to go to the very threshold of heaven, and then turn around and fly back to your corpse."

Dread crept over me at the notion that I might have to truly renounce my faith in order to stay with my chosen love. "Would that really *work?*"

"I do not know." Augustin squeezed me once, then sat back to look seriously into my eyes. "But I do promise that I would not call you away from your reward unless I was certain."

His pledge would have to be enough to sustain me through the next eleven days, though I felt more reluctant than ever to disappear with Prince Otto. Augustin prepared the duck for dinner, setting it on his kitchen table along with a salad, but I could hardly force myself to eat more than a few bites. My gaze kept drifting to his right hand, thawed now but resting on the table like a squeezed lemon, scrunched and inert.

He had stuck it in the cooking fire to accelerate its recovery, and I could not evict the memory of his resultant scream from my mind. How Muniche could do such a thing to an immortal man, I could not comprehend. As I watched him flex his defrosted fingers, I knew that we would never be able to break down the barrier she had erected between us. It had been a fading hope from the very beginning, a futile grasping at the wind.

Augustin had no appetite either. He cast the remainder of the food outside after we had consumed a few forkfuls, grumbling that his goats could root through the vegetables. Not long afterward, as I sat fidgeting on the couch in the front room, my gaze shifting from the flames in the fireplace to the medical cabinet to Augustin writing at his desk by candlelight, my heart began to throb with a familiar longing, answering the call of a Teuton approaching the cottage. I could hear the soft clopping of horseshoes on the leafy soil, and my ice sensed the presence of a scarlet fire creeping cautiously through the forest, seeking the Lady who had called him.

My husband rose from the desk and strode to the door. Before I could order my feet to follow him he stated in an emotionless voice, "Wait here until I signal you. The Prince of Muniche must be greeted by the owner of this cabin, not by a visiting woman." He smiled dangerously and swung the door open.

I flew to his side and choked out, "Please . . . don't kill him."

"That is not my intention," he assured me. Then he stepped into the yard, and I waited in the shadows, hearing the Prince's horse halt at the edge of the trail, neighing rather uneasily.

"I had not expected to find you here, Wolfgang." The Prince sounded weary and surprised, maybe annoyed. I heard him climb down from his horse.

"Your senses are undoubtedly preoccupied." There was blatant mockery in Augustin's tone, but then he said, "The Lady you seek is here."

Chapter Fourteen

The Defeated Prince

My element froze me just inside the doorway, darkness still concealing me from the gaunt man standing beside a chestnut-colored horse. If Augustin had beckoned me to emerge at that moment, I would have been unable to comply. This Teuton adventurer eyeing my husband guardedly looked so unlike the haughty Prince I recalled from the prosperous days of medieval Muniche. He even looked far different than the battle-weary warrior who guided his knights into the city walls for a last stand.

His hair and beard had gone completely gray, bushy and unkempt. His clothing was soiled, the tunic torn in several places, the leather trousers tattered, the boots dusty. His hands twitched as though they longed to grab the sword that hung from the saddle and slash it wildly at the trees, the night, the blue flames in the pit before him, the cursed sentry who stood near the grapevines. He wore one chain around his neck, its gold and medallion tarnished, hardly giving off any glow in the firelight. But his eyes were the most unsettling aspect of his being. Though I could not discern their dark blue color in the dim light, I could see their roundness, a tension that boded insanity.

The Prince's gaze roved from the fire pit to the cottage door and finally to Augustin, the Cursed One who stood beside his trellis, clad in a black tunic and trousers that looked far more striking than the other's rags, despite their simplicity. "I should not be surprised," Prince Otto said, running a hand restively through his hair. "For years, you have trailed my armies to gloat over my defeats without lifting a finger, and now you have incarcerated my Lady here at this hovel in an attempt to undermine me yet again." His hands balled into fists, but he did not reach for a weapon or step forward.

"On the contrary, I held my powers in check out of knowledge," Augustin said neutrally, not stirring from his place at the trellis. "It is not permitted for man to direct the hand of God. If it were possible to alter His record, you or your brother would likely have pulled His Son from the cross." He paused, and I saw the Prince's eyes glitter red, though his hands relaxed a bit.

"For the same reason—out of knowledge—I have kept Muniche's Lady here for the past month, readying her for one final reunion with her Keyholder. She returned to this dark era for you . . . Prince Otto." Augustin ducked his head, his expression betraying no trace of scorn now. Before the Prince could formulate a reply, he lifted his right hand in my direction, summoning me forward.

I stepped into the grass on quivering legs, clasping my sweaty hands before me, my chest rising and falling with swift, shallow breaths. At first I could not find the courage to meet the Prince's eyes, for I felt so unworthy all of a sudden, a flighty *Leitalra* from an era of plenty. So I stared blankly at the fire pit, watching its light blue flames flickering upward, framing the Prince's boots in an igneous outline. I heard him gasp, sensed the recognition in his fiery spirit when it reached out to me, carefully touching my ice. But I could not speak, nor could I approach him. I had frozen just four paces from the doorway, incapacitated.

Warm arms enfolded me in black, lending me a portion of enduring strength. "Pull yourself together, Swanie,"

Augustin murmured in my ear, his hands rubbing heat into my frigid arms. "He is not going to murder you, after all." He offered me the briefest of smirks, then shoved me gently in the Prince's direction.

I wanted desperately to cling to Augustin like I had done the night he had blown Hans' cover, but I knew that would not be prudent. This man beside the horse was not a mere comrade I had known since childhood; he represented a lost epoch, the time of Teutonic success. My feet led me timidly forward while my eyes remained riveted on the grass, and I wiped my damp hands on the violet dress.

Then I heard the Prince make a strangled sound, distressing enough to bring my head up at last. Just a short distance separated us, and he stared at me with a look of madness, sweat beading on his brow. His lips, which looked parched by the summer sun, quavered, then issued an indictment that pricked my heart. "My Lady . . . you . . . you *deserted* me."

My breath went out of me, his heartrending words answering the question that had grated on me for the last few days. He had been alone all this time, without a *Leitalra* to twine the city bond. I pressed one hand to my forehead as the forest seemed to spin. The Prince's eyes glowed with crimson fire as he stared at me, his teeth clenched, his hand fiddling nervously with his tunic.

There were a thousand things I could have said, but when I managed to stammer a reply, it was this: "You cursed me . . . and gave me the means to escape . . . *Leitaeri*."

The Prince sighed, his shoulders drooping. He must have seen the truth in my words, though I should have held my tongue, considering the poor man's wretched state. What a wonderful reunion this had become, with both of us throwing pointless denunciations in each other's faces. I was such an idiot. Why had I rushed to defend myself against the charge of a madman?

Augustin likely snickered somewhere in the background, though I could not hear or see him now. My heart was shackled by a Keyholder, by a dead city, fate pulling me inexorably toward Prince Otto. "I have failed you," he said in a ragged whisper. He could not meet my gaze.

Muniche's soul groaned within me at her master's meekness. I took three steps forward, wanting to speak some sort of ancient phrase of devotion in Ælte Teutonica, a pledge of lasting fidelity and forgiveness. But he raised his eyes and whispered in a tormented voice, "Why did you come?" Tears warred with the red flames in his irises as he reached his right hand out to stroke my cheek. His fingers felt coarse and weathered, but my heart raced at the touch of its guardian.

"I came to die with you . . . master," I breathed, trembling from head to toe.

A wry smile broke across his lips. "Appropriate." He let go of my face, his hand pausing for an instant on its way back to his side, as though it wished to take hold of mine but feared it had not earned the privilege. The Prince glanced over my shoulder, then looked into my eyes and queried, "You read of my . . . of *our* death?" Despite his mental instability, he was quick. Why else would Augustin claim that he kept me here out of knowledge?

I nodded at the Prince, not trusting my voice; thus far it had sounded airy and tremulous, qualities I did not appreciate. He turned to his horse and adjusted the saddle and baggage, mumbling under his breath that we ought to go, to ride further into the forest and seek a private place to converse. His words cut me like a knife and I shook myself, extricating myself from Muniche's influence just long enough to turn back, to catch my husband's eye.

He stood at the threshold of his cottage, the blue flames in his fire pit gradually dying, his right hand resting upon a nearby bilberry bush, his glowing eyes fixed upon me. He knew that I must go, that I must leave him behind and prepare myself for the death his records described. But defiance flared up in my soul, shoving aside Muniche's rebukes. I stretched my hands toward him, though my feet remained rooted to the grass. "Augustin," I mouthed, not wanting to speak his cursed name where the Prince could hear.

He was with me in a flash, his hands reaching out to take hold of my waist, swinging me onto the Prince's horse. My Keyholder situated himself in front of me, but I clung to Augustin's hands when he let me go, breathing hard as I stared into his fathomless eyes, all of my screams tethered within. "You must go with him," he reminded me firmly, holding my hands in a strong grip. "You must fulfill your duty, your destiny."

I saw the agony in his fiery eyes, how desperately he clung to his control, crushing his anger to the dust, not allowing it to explode and kill the man who cursed him, the man who now would ride away with his wife. Wuotan likely urged him to stretch his deadly anger forth and slay the Prince while he had the chance. Tears dampened my eyelashes, and I knew that we had no time for proper farewells. All I could do was hope one last time.

"Eleven days," I whispered to him fiercely in English, blinking back my tears. "Eleven days, and twelve nights." I squeezed Augustin's hands, letting my eyes speak all of the words I could not say. Now he must seek dark magic to rescue us both from this obligation. At length, I added in an undertone, "I haven't changed my mind."

He lowered his gaze briefly in acknowledgement, then admitted in English, "Neither have I." A ghost of a smirk appeared on his face, and he kissed the sapphire on my hand and remarked, "After all, you read only the *official* record."

Augustin winked at me, then let go of my hands. I started having a heart attack right then, for neither of us had brought up the concept of false information in his records. Could all of his official encyclopedias be second-guessed? *Historians should not lie, though sometimes they misinform,* he had once told me.

"Take care of her, *Leitaeri*," Augustin said, maintaining his dignity. The Prince spoke a brief reply, and I secured my arms around his waist. Then Augustin slapped the chestnut horse on the rump, spurring it into the forest, away from him, away from the answer to all of my questions.

I buried my face against the Prince's back as he guided his horse deeper into the trees, closing my eyes, trying and failing to keep my new uncertainties at bay. *Why did he have to wait until the last second to bring that up? If Augustin admits to actively misleading his readers, these next eleven days may hold more trials and complexities than I ever expected.*

What if this is really not *the end? What if Prince Otto actually dies alone in the Rhine, while I spend the rest of my days with Augustin? What if something else happens . . . some way of breaking my bonds . . . some way of freeing Augustin from his exile on earth, of sending him to heaven with me?* Before I worked it all out, the Prince had reined in the horse on the banks of a small tributary sporting a trickling waterfall, a place to rest for the night.

It was a serene dell he had chosen, a clearing of smooth rocks and leaves, the former of which jutted into the brook to form the tiny fall that poured like water from a faucet. I bent over the stream to study its current in the moonlight while the Prince fastened his horse to a low-hanging linden branch, afterward removing his packs and spreading their contents on the ground. I sat upon a rock beside the stream, shooting covert glances at my Keyholder, watching his movements.

He unrolled a pair of frayed blankets, arranging them on the leaves with a space between them about a meter wide. He laid most of his belongings on the thinner blanket: his sword and scabbard, two ragged tunics, a tent tarp, a small kettle, a skillet, a spoon, several lengths of rope, a comb, a sheaf of parchments, several pens, and a knife.

I noticed that he laid the blanket meant for me closest to the stream, likely in deference to my element. An instant later I saw that the blade of his knife was made of stone, not metal. Quickly averting my gaze to the brook, I tried not to pay close attention as he laid two parcels upon my blanket—a voluminous oilskin and a leather pouch with what appeared to be dandelion greens poking through its flap. How often had Prince Otto tasted meat during his wanderings? His sword would not be particularly useful for hunting.

The fact that he put the food on *my* blanket prompted Muniche's soul to croon inside of me. A blatant offering of sustenance, something a Teuton man was expected to prepare for his bride on their first morning together. But we were just a pair of doomed representatives from an ill-fated city, not a romantic couple.

"I have traded most of my possessions already," the Prince said. It was the first time either of us had spoken since he suggested that we camp for the night. I continued to watch the moonlit brook as he went on. "You caught me on the last leg of my journey, *Leitalra*, for I intended to make this forest my grave."

"The waters of the Rhine could serve you well," I heard myself saying, my fingers sliding through the shallow rivulet.

He did not reply, but I heard him rustling in the brush, then digging amid the leaves that coated the ground. When I turned to face him, I saw that he had cleared a small pit in the soil between the blankets. Now he grouped sticks into a pile, casting three miniature red flames upon them. Within minutes, his campfire crackled lustily, casting the dell in a cerise glow that seemed to vanquish the silver moonlight.

The Prince sat cross-legged upon his blanket, his eyes trained on the fire, the keys of Muniche hanging from his belt at his right hip. I wondered why I had not noticed them before; maybe they had been stuffed in his pocket. He raised his eyes to mine and gestured toward the other blanket, his hand glowing scarlet in the firelight. "Sit, Muniche, eat and warm yourself. You ought not to squat upon the rocks all night, or you might turn into stone." His smile was shaky, uncertain.

"I'm more likely to turn to ice than stone," I answered, vacating my rock and settling myself onto the thicker blanket, colored a faded hunter green.

"Then warm yourself," he repeated, holding his hands out to the fire. "If the plants do not satisfy you, I could do some hunting in the morning."

"With your sword?" My eyes fell upon it for an instant; then I tugged the leather pouch into my lap. Digging through it, I uncovered a pile of roots, dandelion greens, field garlic, mushrooms, crab apples, and raspberries.

"My element can take out the hearts of larger prey," the Prince responded. He had a point, but I cringed at the thought of a fawn crying out as red fire singed its heart into ash. Honestly, Augustin's death gift seemed more merciful.

"Or I could set some snares for squirrels and hare," my companion added, doubtless noticing my uncertainty. "I must admit that your presence nearly drove the last strands of lucidity from my mind. If nothing else, you have successfully delayed my end." He raised an eyebrow at me, the fingers of his right hand sliding down the keys at his hip.

I felt his touch through our incomplete connection but tried to disregard it, chewing on a crab apple while I studied him. I was not quite sure yet what to make of this gray-haired, unstable adventurer who also happened to be my fated master and Muniche's most famous Prince. "Well, you could always take your life at any time if I don't please you." I dropped my gaze to the bag in my lap, thinking that I might prepare a stew from its contents in the morning.

"You please me, Muniche," he murmured, scooting a few centimeters forward on his blanket. "I cannot fathom how you could forgive me enough to come here."

I smiled shyly, setting the pouch aside and tossing the apple's core into the brush. "We all make mistakes," I said, feeling an uncanny shiver running up my spine. Something in the Prince's demeanor reminded me of Augustin— a lonely and misunderstood Teuton priest searching for acceptance, for understanding.

He smiled back at me, his dark blue eyes glittering and tragic. "Please tell me what brought you back to this dismal era," he requested, warming his hands over the fire again. "You must have used my song to escape to the future. I felt it resounding in my soul just before you vanished. Only then did I recognize who had taken Lady Maria's place."

I shivered a little, edging closer to the fire. "Truthfully, I never thought of what it would mean for you, when I leaped through the gates of time," I confessed, seeing a replay of that day in the ruby flames: the Saxon onslaught, Augustin urging Freia and me to go, his sword raised to avenge and conquer.

"Maybe if I had died to return to my time, another Lady would have taken my place. I was too busy thinking of myself, wondering about the future, the Keyholder I didn't know, everything I was leaving behind forever." *Namely, Augustin,* I added silently.

"Was your Keyholder a good man?" the Prince inquired, retrieving one of his ropes and fiddling with it, forming and loosening an array of knots.

It figured that everybody had to ask me *that* question. I glanced up at the Prince, then down at my hands. There was no point in lying, since I would be spending eleven days with this man, a Teuton priest who would certainly bleed me somewhere along the line. *If he's hoping to prove himself better than Hans, he might get his wish.*

"He was decent, a good Keyholder, very loyal to our city and a talented leader. The Teutons in modern Muniche respected him, for he held the keys for almost fifty years," I said. Prince Otto gasped at this, and I saw the fire reflected in his eyes, his mien implying admiration. Time to trample that notion.

"As a husband, he could have been better. We represented Muniche for nearly seventeen years, but before he died he told me that he had loved my mother once, long ago. They never had the heart-bond, since he was already the Keyholder when they met. But they shared a strong and forbidden love, one he never forgot." I ended the tale there, awaiting the Prince's reaction.

He eyed me solemnly for a while, the firelight creating a myriad of shadows upon his aged face. He made a slip knot with the rope and tugged it free, his eyes on his hands as he asked softly, "Did you love him?"

I looked down again, wishing I had a rope to play with, although I did not know the first thing about tying knots. Instead, I fingered the sash of my dress, seeing that my bodice showed signs of wear from that afternoon, when Augustin had attempted the impossible. I looked upward at the starry sky framed with black branches, then admitted, "I did love him. He was the first Teuton priest I ever loved, even before I came here the first time. Apparently I was fated to be *Leitalra* all along, whether I agreed with my destiny or not."

The Prince's mouth twitched, and he began fashioning a square knot. "How long were you with the Cursed One before I came? I believe I first heard you call for me nearly three weeks ago, while I sojourned near Speyer."

"It's been about that long," I said, still fumbling with my sash, avoiding his gaze. "I was lucky I came across him, for he cured me of the fever that ravaged Eisenwald earlier this month. He's a skilled physician." A lame commentary on my motivations for residing at Augustin's cottage for such an extended period, but I felt hesitant to discuss him openly with the man who had cursed him.

"The last time I saw you," Prince Otto began in an inquisitive tone, the rope now motionless in his hands, "was on the night before Muniche fell, when I led my defeated forces back into her walls for one final respite. As I recall, you stood with him beside the bulwarks of the gate, your black clothing undulating around your bodies like the claws of death, in the power of the storm. He held you in his arms, quite possessively it appeared, and kissed your throat."

Chapter Fifteen:
Realizations

All the words that could have explained my decades-long relationship with Prince Otto's cursed brother evaporated from my mind as I sat with naught but the campfire between us, my body gradually surrendering to the chill of ice. Memories of that night—our last night together without Muniche's bonds driving a wedge in our devotion—played out in the flames. Death and smoke, weary warriors lifting parched faces to the sky, drinking the rain's temporary relief. Augustin's powerful arms around me while we stood above the devastation, never imagining that our commitment would take a blade to the heart the following afternoon.

"We were married." The words fell bluntly from my frozen lips, my eyes focused upon the ocher glow of the embers. "Holy matrimony. For all of eternity, we promised." My voice hitched, and I wrapped my arms around myself, trying to stifle the pain that saturated my spirit. "Then she took me. After you cursed the city. Why did you do it? Why would you hand Muniche over to a *demon?*"

I raised my eyes to my Keyholder, the city's essence filling me with an anger redolent of that afternoon in the turret, when I denounced Augustin for standing by while the *Toteheri* and their Saxon overlords ravaged his birthplace. That was the only reason Muniche's soul seized upon my heart in her throes of destruction. Because Prince Otto cursed her to Wuotan . . . and that demon wanted to separate Augustin from my love.

The haggard man before me dropped his head into his hands, his rope cast aside onto the gray blanket where he sat. "It should have ended her," he mumbled in a defeated voice. "Her spirit should not have continued on after I cursed her by Teuton law. That spell meant our people relinquished our claim on that settlement, consigned it to—"

"But it didn't," I cut him off, my element retreating into my spirit as wrath churned in my blood. "It drove Muniche mad and tore me away from the priest who held my heart, the man who saved my life during the blood-transfer and saved Joel when *you* didn't. The man who never judged me as some flighty maiden who leaped into the past for a careless fling. The man who chose to love me for who I am, not because of some ridiculous bond I can't control. You renounced the duty you chose the moment you took those keys from your father's hands, and ensured that Muniche's spirit would mourn her loss forever." I glared at the iron keys that he clutched in gnarled fingers, wishing for a way to eliminate them for good.

But the city's soul stabbed me viciously for my dark desires, her reproach sealing my lips shut for now. *Are you just as cowardly and selfish as Prince Otto? He forsook his calling and now you seek to follow in his steps.*

Eyes brimming with remorse, the Prince met my gaze through his crimson fire and began to speak. "Muniche . . . my precious *Leitalra* . . . Lady . . . Swanhilde. If I had the power to free you from this burden, I would. These keys should have disintegrated in my hands when I burnt my blood upon Muniche's stones. No one . . . no Teuton woman . . . should suffer due to my failure."

My frosty spirit sensed the sincerity permeating his warmth, but sentiments could not wholly still my disgust at him. "Teutons in my era like to say that a city's spirit never chooses the wrong Lady. But the position of Keyholder is in the hands of man, and men make wrong choices. A lot." I narrowed my eyes.

Prince Otto sighed, his hands taking up the rope to fidget once more. "The spell I laid upon Muniche's stones . . . the curse of cindered blood . . . I invoked it because she came to my dreams the night before."

I blinked at him in confusion as his eyes met mine. "My *Leitalra*, the Lady Maria. The siege had sickened her body and her spirit, weakening her and encumbering her with unbroken torment. She begged me on her knees to release her, to guide her into heaven."

My lips parted and I gawked at him, his actions abruptly making much more sense. "In the twenty-three years that we led Muniche, she had never once bowed before me. Our enemies had broken her, and I could not bear to watch her fade on account of my mistakes."

"So you cursed Muniche to help her die," I translated, my indignation having cooled to something more like loathsome comprehension.

"Yes. Her spirit whispered to me when she departed, relating her earnest gratitude. I did not recognize that another woman had taken her place until much later, after my knights and I retreated south of the city. The cries of Muniche's soul infiltrated my heart, but I imagined them to be naught but phantom agonies."

"But you had the keys." I nodded at them, where they hung at his belt.

Deeper regret appeared on the Prince's face. "I abandoned them upon the wall where we burnt our blood," he divulged, his bearded jaw quivering in shame. He stared at the knotted rope in his hands. "When I realized you had taken her essence with you . . . upon your journey to the future . . . I returned that night in spirit form and retrieved them, determining that this was the penance I deserved. To embody one half of a severed bond evermore."

Sympathy began to ease my body's tension, gradually releasing its grip on resentment. "You've been alone, with no *Leitalra* to complete the bond, for eight years," I whispered. The pity that stirred me stemmed from my own soul, not from the city's essence.

"It is what I deserve," my Keyholder repeated, still staring at his hands holding the rope in his lap.

Fate wished to smile upon the shamed Prince one final time, sending his Lady back to him as a comfort in his final days, a companion in death. The words from Augustin's encyclopedia came back to me, the history he set down about my reunion with my Keyholder. Eight years of loss and loneliness, eight years hearing a mystical entity weeping for an incomplete bond. At least Hans and I had shared over a decade of peace together despite his preference for my mother. The Teuton community of modern München had flourished under our guidance, but Prince Otto had wandered alone, defeated and ashamed.

I recognized that comfort might be the greatest gift I could offer the fallen soldier before me, comfort and companionship for the brief time he had left. But he needed to know that Augustin would work dark magic in the shadows, one last hope to restore what the city stole from us. Perhaps Prince Otto would understand.

"Have you eaten anything lately?" I asked, my eyes sliding toward his pack of vegetables.

"Just a few crab apples this morning," he answered, still looking morose.

I crawled around the campfire to retrieve his skillet, which I loaded with the roots, greens, garlic, and mushrooms before dashing it beneath the tiny waterfall. My Keyholder held our stew over the flames while I stirred it using his stone knife, its blade prompting me to envision extremely morbid things. He pledged to set a few snares in the morning and noted that we could endeavor to trade for victuals at Eisenwald.

"I might be able to get some currency from the blacksmith for my medallion," he said as he pulled the skillet away from the campfire, deeming its contents sufficiently boiled. I glanced at the medallion's tarnished gold, where it lay against his chest, wondering if he had already traded his more valuable jewelry.

"Heinrich Denlinger runs the ironworks in town," I mentioned, gesturing for the Prince to eat from the skillet first. The only utensil we had between us aside from the stone knife was his spoon. I should have brought my bag from Augustin's cottage before riding away with my Keyholder. So much for my fork.

"I thought I detected a fair number of Teutonic spirits in the village when I passed through earlier today. But I confess that I did not take the time to identify any of them, in light of Muniche's soul calling to me through you." He talked with food in his mouth, his royal manners tainted, his round eyes riveted upon my face.

"All of the histories from my era state that you died a ritual death in the Rhine River on the night of the new moon, June 27th, 1074," I said, deciding now was the best time to reveal the whole of it, while the food distracted him. "But the only record that mentioned your Lady dying with you was written by the Cursed One. The only witness to your . . . to our suicide."

"You can call him by his name if you wish, Lady Swanhilde," my companion said through a mouthful of vegetables. That caught me off guard, and my eyebrows came together as I recalled what happened the last time I spoke Augustin's name before the Prince. He had slapped me twice, and hard.

"I know that you never stopped speaking his name." Prince Otto's charge brought a sense of dread into my heart, along with a feeling of devilish anguish. He watched me now from somewhere beyond the veil—the villainous demon who insisted that Augustin belonged to him, not to me. A strange tightness descended into the darkness around us; and when the Prince passed me the skillet, its handle slipped through my fingers. The simmered plants splayed across the dirt between our blankets, ruined.

"When you cursed the city to Wuotan . . . I think you gave him access to my heart," I managed to say as I quailed into a tight ball. "He's been haunting me ever since I got here . . . and he tried to kill Joel and me in time's currents. He knows I came here to lead Augustin back to the light . . . and he won't . . . he . . . ."

I could say no more. Spectral hands reached into my spirit to scratch at the heart of my soul, drawing a choked scream from my lips. Obscurity impeded my vision, but I clearly heard Wuotan's deep laughter, his sinister voice growling in my ear. *Your heart belongs to me, my child. I have the power over your fate. This man you commiserate with now handed you over to me as payment for his access to time's portal, not because his aged witch begged for death.*

Wuotan's clawed hands gouged my spiritual heart as he mocked me, and I found that I could not escape his grasp. My voice had failed me, but I desperately pleaded for God's help in the confines of my mind. Only the Almighty Creator had the power to save me from this curse.

After what seemed an infinite interval of brutal torment, my consciousness found its way back to my mortal body. Just where it had traveled in the interim, I could not say, but Prince Otto's arms held me in a sturdy embrace, Latin prayers falling softly from his lips. Had the combined strength of our faith guided my spirit away from the dark? How could we break this demon's hold upon my heart?

The Prince's body odor was not particularly pleasant, his sweaty beard brushing my neck as he murmured rote prayers. I endeavored to extract myself from his grip; he held me on his lap with my face tucked against his left shoulder. "I think . . . I think he's left us alone . . . for now," I whispered.

My Keyholder's arms dropped to his sides, his round eyes staring at my face as though I had turned into a ghost. "He tried to take you from me."

I sidled my way off of his lap and onto the gray blanket, suspecting that I had better stay close to my fated master even if he smelled like he had not bathed in weeks. "When you cursed Muniche with your blood, you handed her soul over to Wuotan. I think . . . if I didn't belong to God, he would have possessed me."

Prince Otto's right arm wrapped around my waist, keeping me from moving further away. "I had not expected . . . he . . . he has stalked you since your return? Has he hurt you like that before?"

"It hasn't been that bad until now," I responded, gazing into the crackling flames in a daze. "He keeps saying he's in control of my fate. I know that's a lie, but . . . I'm starting to think being Muniche's *Leitalra* is a worse curse than Augustin's."

"The curse of cindered blood lingers upon a settlement for a hundred years," the Prince said in a repentant tone. "I have failed you. I am so, so sorry."

I shuddered into the Prince's shoulder, shutting my eyes as I tried to bring my reason to the fore. There had to be some way to break Wuotan's hold upon my city's soul. He came from a realm of fire and sin, a place where hatred reigned over all. But love could conquer hatred, and love could conquer death.

The mystical bonds connecting my heart with my Keyholder's mirrored the tie I had cherished for so long . . . a more potent form of the intricate sorcery that united a Teuton priest with his chosen one. The heart-bond of *love*.

Truth stared me right in the face; we had no other recourse. I touched Prince Otto's cheek, its scraggly fuzz stained with tears. Looking into his eyes, I breathed, "We have to complete the bond. We have to get married."

Chapter Sixteen:
Unsettling Dreams

"Love is the only magic that's strong enough to defeat hate, to defeat death. It's what triumphed over sin when you and Father Paulus traveled to the time of Christ. It's what's necessary to create the Teutonic heart-bond. It's what's held Augustin back from demonic slavery all this time. I believe . . . I believe love can free Muniche's soul from Wuotan's clutches."

Prince Otto's eyes took on a quality I could not identify. He wrapped his left hand around mine, drawing it away from his face. "You love me?" he asked in a tone laden with disbelief.

I chewed on the inside of my cheek for a second as I considered how to reply. "Well, I don't hate you. And I don't despise you like I did before we had this talk. I'm starting to see what drove your choices . . . and Muniche pines for you already." I paused to rub my left palm agitatedly upon my bodice, failing to appease our city's silent yearning. "If we complete the bond, that may be enough to save her."

The Prince's forehead wrinkled as he considered my suggestion, his right hand tightening upon my waist. "Is there love to be found at the end?" he said in a voice that implied he talked to himself. He turned my right palm over in his lap, revealing Marelda's sapphire. "You are already married, Lady Swanhilde."

"In holy matrimony, which wasn't enough to keep Wuotan away from my heart. Blood marriage should return Muniche's soul to her Keyholder, to where she belongs. If your death . . . and my death . . . doesn't finish the cursed city for good, some innocent woman could find her heart chained by a demon, the way it stands now. We have to fix this for our people's sake."

I stared into the Prince's eyes with determination, hoping that his damaged mind could grasp the truth. We needed to summon love and forgiveness between us, not for our sakes alone, but for our people's future. Teutons would restore the city of Muniche in the next century, and we could not allow Wuotan to wield the power over her heritage then.

My Keyholder exhaled heavily, his eyes fixated upon the sapphire ring. "If we are expected to die just eleven days from now, we must thoroughly open our hearts to one another, to properly restore this relationship beyond mere blood ties. Are there any Teuton priests in Eisenwald aside from the Cursed One?"

Prince Otto lifted his chin, his eyes burning into mine as I faced the flaw in my plan. To completely repair the mystical bond between *Leitaeri* and *Leitalra*, we would need to absolve each other's mistakes and pledge fidelity in a Teutonic wedding. The only local man capable of performing such a rite was Augustin. My husband. The Black Priest who loathed his ex-brother.

The man whose death could erupt with his anger and kill.

The Prince could not ask such a thing of Augustin. But I could. And he might agree to it if I explained our purpose. When I related this to my companion, his dark gray eyebrows came together. "You did not tell him that his demon master has unsettled your heart?"

"I've been able to push it aside until we got together tonight," I explained, deciding an instant later to be a bit more upfront. "After he helped me heal from the pestilence, we spent most of our time seeking a way to free me from Muniche's bonds. He's going to keep researching while we're apart. But I can't separate myself from our city now, not until we break Wuotan's hold through love. I don't want any more of Muniche's daughters to suffer his wrath."

I thought I caught a glimpse of pride in my Keyholder's eyes as he nodded. "Then we shall seek to regain the beauty inherent in our fated union."

We ended up settling in on his blanket to rest until dawn. My companion insisted that I use the hunter green blanket myself, since his fire provided sufficient warmth for him. My mind continued to muse long after Prince Otto began lightly snoring, fantasizing visions of Augustin's anger reaching out to stop my heart once I asked him to wed me to his ex-brother. Hopefully if he did not allow me to explain, he would bleed me like he did on the morning the fever had struck me, so he could see that we needed to do this to give Muniche's sons and daughters freedom in the years to come.

As I began to drift off, other images danced behind my eyelids. Pictures of myself frolicking with a red-fired spirit, seizing the glory of the atmosphere and the river . . . sitting side by side with him before a scarlet campfire, talking through the countless trials and mistakes we had made over the years . . . and an aged warrior enfolding my naked body with his, my ice yoking with crimson flames in infinite rapture and release . . . the Keyholder and Lady as one.

Would our attempt at reconciliation be enough to liberate Muniche from a devil's authority?

Would Augustin succeed in luring me away from this path at the very brink of paradise?

I could only hope.

My dreams took a disturbing turn that night. My body and spirit swept away into oblivion with Augustin brandishing a cerulean fiery sword at my side, while my hands held a dagger of stone. Invisible entities attacked us, blocking us from reaching our goal. Somehow I knew that if we made our way out of the darkness, we would stay together at long last with no supernatural ties holding us apart. As we slashed at the creatures gnawing upon our limbs and spirits, I caught a glimpse of dawn breaking over a row of trees in the distance, signifying the hope I had long cherished.

But as I turned to point it out to Augustin, a shrouded monstrosity arose in an aureole of black flames, singeing my husband's sword into ash and winding a thick cord around his neck to drag him away from the light. Screaming, I tried to grab hold of him, to save him, to fashion my fervent love into something tangible, something that could spare him from hell. Wuotan's dark laughter reverberated in the blackness, mocking my feeble attempts to redeem an accursed priest. Icy claws extended from my fingers, cutting uselessly at the cord around Augustin's neck.

Hell's lava seethed around me, raising indestructible barriers between me and the man who had given his life for mine, long ago when his royal brother had cursed his blood. The anguish was too much to bear, coupled with the knowledge that my beloved husband refused to turn from evil, even for my sake. Parted for eternity, no matter how ardently I prayed otherwise. And the demon continued to laugh, his malicious triumph swallowing my heart in depression.

I woke shaking all over, the sky above still dark, the embers of the Prince's campfire casting an eerie glow upon my ankles that reminded me of the abyss I had wandered in my nightmares. Shivering, I forced myself to roll over, turning my back to the fire's uncanny glimmer and focusing on the reedy man who slept at my side.

Prince Otto Eduard Hildebrand von Bayern. The fifty-two-year-old Keyholder of Muniche. He lay upon his back with his hands clutching the length of rope that had stilled his anxiety while we conversed, his face twisted away from me, trails of saliva moistening his beard.

You're actually going to marry this man? The jealous sibling who damned his brother to hell, refused to complete the city bond with Lady Maria, brought the Empire's forces down upon his people thanks to his foray into time travel. The man who ended an era . . . whose influence led you into hell's bowels.

But forgiveness may be the only way to fix his mistakes, I told myself as I mentally took a step back from the repugnance that dogged me when I looked at him. For all I knew, he might suffer from nightmares, too, maybe the variety that refused to permit the victim to awaken. So I pushed myself upright and shuffled closer to him, laying a gentle hand upon his left shoulder. His muscles felt as tight as a drum.

"*Leitaeri?*" I murmured, giving his shoulder a careful shake. His jaw shifted a bit, and another title trembled in my heart—one my individual self would never wish to grant to this man when Augustin waited in the wings. But it intruded upon the night's stillness anyway, cracking from my lips like destiny's knell: "*Truhtein?*"

The Teutonic word for *master*.

His eyes opened, blinking the sleep away as they locked upon my face. "My . . . Lady?" he gasped out in Ælte Teutonica, the ancient phrase prompting my heart to hum with adoration. *Muniche's avowed protector . . . her master guardian.*

"The demon's been haunting my dreams, and I feared he might do the same to you," I said, giving him space as he sat up, his eyes narrowing at the embers. Red flames lit up our campsite in an instant.

"I should have expected this," the Prince said, taking a few short breaths and sitting back on his hands. His round eyes slid to mine as he added, "Quite likely, he listened in on our conversation earlier and knows that we plan to complete the bond. If he troubles our dreams now, he doubtless assays to prevent our ritual marriage. And that means—"

"Love will break the demon's power over Muniche," I finished, thinking back to the images Wuotan sent to my dreams. Prince Otto had not appeared at all; the demon wanted me focused on Augustin, the man he sought to enslave. Could my free will manage to echo Muniche's love for her fated master? Maybe it would be enough for us to reconcile, to forgive the past.

"I . . . I might love you already . . . Lady Swanhilde," the man beside me said unexpectedly, the fingers of his left hand twitching as though they longed to take hold of mine. He looked over my body, with the green blanket swathing my dress, then studied my graying black hair, still pinned back with one of Augustin's clips. He breathed out a shuddering sigh. "You came here just to provide me with solace in my final days, a gift I do not deserve."

"Call me Swanie. Please," I requested, wanting to dispense with formalities. Gathering my nerve, I reached my right hand out tentatively toward him, and he gasped when I wound my fingers through his, cool ice against simmering heat. His gratitude rushed over my spirit in a flood, and I shut my eyes for a moment, trying to keep my reason in control of the emotions Muniche stirred within me. Issues I needed to lay to rest roiled in my blood, so I brought the Prince's hand into my lap and broached the first one.

"Could you tell me . . . why you never completed the bond with Lady Maria?"

I watched a multitude of sentiments play across his face in the firelight, his fingers resting tamely in my hand. His response took me completely off guard. "We intended to marry as Teutons on January 1st of 1044, to celebrate the New Year and a new epoch for our city. But my brother and I took our first journey into the past just three weeks before, and you know what came of that."

He paused, and I nodded, remembering his tale of the time of Christ. He and Paulus traveled back to witness the crucifixion and resurrection, and afterward they had assimilated with other Christians in Judea. There, the Prince had met the only woman he chose to love—Kezia— and raised her children. When he continued his explanation, I felt as though a gruesome hand clasped my throat.

"Of course, I could not keep the story of our journey from my *Leitalra*. That very night, I related the good news of God—that He had truly come to this world for the sole purpose of redeeming humanity. But somehow . . . she sensed the truth that I endeavored to conceal . . . and she bled me. In my blood, she saw my abiding love for my wife Kezia."

His next words made me sick. "I remember the hatred in her wintry eyes when she pulled back from my neck and wiped my blood from her lips. The disgust in her tone when she said, 'I never dreamed you'd taint your body with a *Jew*.' She never forgave me."

If there had been anything in my stomach, I would have vomited. As it was, I arched away from the Prince to retch in the direction of the campfire. I had not known Lady Maria was anti-Semitic. Although Hans had not approved of my deep relationship with a Cursed One, at least he had agreed to seal our bond, to raise our children, to support our community in partnership.

"It really . . . grosses me out . . . how prejudiced our people can be," I groaned, rubbing my queasy stomach with my left hand. My right held my companion's in a death grip, his warmth hardly touching my spirit.

"It's completely ridiculous. *Anyone* can have Teuton blood, no matter what race they come from. One of my friends from my era was a Teuton of stone born to parents from . . . Constantinople." I had to think about the proper name for a second, since I did not know any other medieval cities in Asia Minor. "And the Teuton of energy who controlled security for my family's house had African descent. There's no reason whatsoever for a Teuton to look down on any outsider. We're all human, and that means we all make mistakes. We're all the same."

Prince Otto gazed back at me with an expression of respect. "You are a truly remarkable woman, Swanie," he declared, his fingers squeezing my own. "I am so thankful you chose to be here with me."

Offering him a wavering smile, I glanced at the blanket beneath us and said, "Maybe we ought to try to get a little more sleep so our brains work properly today. I have to convince a Cursed One to perform our wedding, and you have trading to do."

The Prince chuckled and invited me to curl up beside him, so perhaps his nearness might stave off the worst of the nighttime terrors. I did so, lying on my left side facing the firelight while my Keyholder wound his right arm around me, drawing me back against his chest. It felt bony and hollow, but it was a relief to sense his fiery presence close behind me, even if I longed for a different man.

"I must find two witnesses for the ceremony while I pass through Eisenwald later today," Prince Otto mentioned after an interval of silence. "I shall likely ask Master Denlinger, but do you have preferences for our second?"

Freia's sunny face arose in my memory, but I knew that Teuton law required male witnesses, at least in this backward era. Truthfully, there was only one option. "Joel," I answered. "Joel Hudson."

"He returned here with you?" The Prince sounded surprised.

"To live the rest of his life with our children."

"Ah. I wonder if he will approve of our marriage." My companion yawned.

"Pretty sure he will," I murmured back, closing my eyes in an attempt to gain a few final moments of slumber. Joel was not the love interest we needed to worry about. The one whose devotion spanned the heavens—and whose ire tapped the finality of death—resided in a cabin not far from where we rested.

In the morning, the Prince dropped me off outside Augustin's cottage and struck out for the town, promising to return by nightfall for our wedding. The fact that he chose to grant me a full day with my immortal husband was not lost on me. I would have to repay his generosity after we left civilization behind for good.

My ice sensed Augustin's blue fire scorching rather potently within his cabin, so at least I would not have to waste time hunting for him. When I pulled open the front door, I found his body in the fireplace, encased in cobalt flames. I frowned, realizing that I would have to attempt to summon his spirit back to his body. Was he already skulking demonic territory in a final bid for my freedom?

Calling my element from my blood, I fashioned a tiny dagger of ice, its chill refreshing my spirit as I approached my dead husband's blazing body. He crouched on his heels with his hands flat upon the hearth, so I thrust my dagger straight into his temple, hoping that was violent enough to provoke an immortal's attention.

A half-second later, a sweltering hand gripped my wrist, pressing the nerves to the point where my ice retreated into my spirit. Augustin's scorching eyes met mine as he hissed, "Swanhilde . . . what *have* you done?"

Chapter Seventeen:
The Spell

Fear turned my brain into mush, for Augustin's suspicion bore down upon me like a swarm of greenheads. My knees buckled as he tightened his grip on my wrist, all hints of my magic wiped from my reach. I was supposed to explain why the Prince and I needed to complete our bond—to protect Muniche's future representatives from Wuotan's deceit. But when I opened my mouth, I heard myself asking, "What happened to my dagger?"

I had driven it into his flaming temple, and the void had swallowed it.

Augustin growled, baring his teeth. "Maybe you should check my brain. Did your master send you here to kill me?" He stepped away from the fireplace without releasing my wrist. In an instant, he had me pinned against the wall.

"I'm here of my own volition," I spat at him, his assumptions irritating me. "Last I checked, no human has the power to kill you, anyway. The only way I know to call someone's spirit back to their body is by attacking their elemental shield."

"You certainly succeeded," Augustin said with a sneer, letting go of my wrist and taking a step back. He wore a maroon tunic and leather trousers, an outfit that implied he intended to travel soon. "And what, may I ask, has brought you back to my home? Did you tire of your Keyholder so soon?" He looked toward the window, his jaw tense.

Silently praying for divine courage, I set myself upon the couch beneath his window and related what the Prince and I had concluded last night. That his penchant for leveling Wuotan's curses brought demonic retribution upon our city and upon my heart, as Muniche's Lady. That our people's former demon lord well-nigh envisioned himself to be my Keyholder in Prince Otto's stead, haunting me in the darkness, inducing me away from the light. That the only power great enough to sever his hold on Muniche's spirit was love—true love between Keyholder and Lady, its magic sealed through blood marriage.

Augustin remained standing while I explained, his arms folded, his fathomless eyes staring at me . . . through me. I sensed no black knives of anger probing my heart; in fact, his fiery spirit felt empty of feeling, closed off with lock and key. When I found that I had no more to say, he looked at me for a moment longer before saying in a flat tone, "So you would practice polyandry in your final days and greet your Almighty God as the wife of two husbands."

It was a statement, not a question, and I detected a hint of reproach exuding from his aura. Heat rose in my cheeks at the implications of his charge. "It's not something I *want* to do," I emphasized, bowing my head to gaze at my hands. The blue of the sapphire screamed a rebuke at me, and I covered it with my left hand. "It's the only way to triumph over hatred and torment. Wuotan could torment my successors indefinitely if I don't—"

"It never occurred to you to mention this during our weeks together?" Augustin interrupted, creases appearing between his eyebrows. "You would rather bind yourself in matrimony with the man who cursed you to a demon, instead of asking Wuotan's servant for a way to liberate you from his influence?"

Pain stabbed my heart as my allegiances battled within me. Augustin would not forgive me if I married the Prince. That was infinitely clear. He might even give up his search for a way to restore our relationship. If love and forgiveness were the sole way to conquer Wuotan's sway over Muniche's soul, we *must* complete the city bond and allow its mysticism to heal our hearts.

At the cost of Augustin's eternal destiny.

Icy teardrops began to fall upon my lap as I tried to put my harried thoughts into words. "Augustin . . . I can't . . . I can't keep following the dark for a solution to all my problems. See what that's done to our people, to my son from the future, to *you*. The Prince cast the filial curse upon you to ban you from Muniche, but it turned you into a dead man enslaved to a demon. I believe . . . I believe love and goodness are powerful enough to fix this. I have to stop messing around with evil for a fleeting glimpse of the light."

I blinked at my husband through my tears, my spirit pleading for his understanding, if not for his acceptance. But to my consternation, I watched his perfect face shatter into agony as he muttered, "Then your devotion to Muniche supersedes your love for me. I suppose I have earned it."

He vanished from the parlor before I could begin to think of a reply, a single sob trailing in his wake. Augustin's distress broke me, and I curled into a ball on his couch, weeping tears that sliced at my corneas. I did not have the ability to make this decision. Augustin or Muniche. Choose Muniche, lose the man whose strength had buoyed me for decades, whose skills rooted an inhuman army from the earth. Choose Augustin, and hand the fates of Muniche's children to Wuotan for as long as the Teuton people existed.

Then the horrific verity broke me further.

Wuotan had never once touched my heart in all the years that I represented modern München. That meant his sway over Muniche's soul was nullified.

That meant I chose the Prince.

Unless I wanted to destroy history itself, I must choose the Prince.

This was the end of my sanity, the end of Swanhilde's individual self. I could not forsake Augustin unless I allowed Muniche's influence to supplant my will.

Why?!

I know not how long I lamented upon my husband's couch, my defiance giving way to destiny at last. Eventually, I opened my eyes to see Augustin standing before me, all kindness absent from his countenance as he said, "You seek a Teuton priest to conduct your wedding. I shall perform the rite for you in exchange for a fair trade."

I took a shuddering breath, while part of my soul died within me. He had stepped back from our relationship himself, and viewed this as a transaction between one supplicant and a Black Priest. Gripping one arm of the couch, I dragged myself into a sitting position and nodded once. "Name your price."

Cobalt fire smoldered in Augustin's eyes. "I require a measure of authority over your fate by means of an irreversible spell."

My body recoiled at that concept. I could not envision the devious methods a priest of Wuotan may use against me to upend my fortune. "I can't agree to it if it would mess up my brain," I warned him, preparing to haggle with the dead.

A crass smirk crept across Augustin's face. "Your mind is yours to use as you wish. I would never disgrace your character in such a manner."

Maybe this is his way of not giving up on us, even if I have to marry Prince Otto for our people's sake, I thought. *Maybe he's trying to work things in his favor . . . in our favor . . . so we can be together in the end.* Clearing my throat, I lifted my chin and accepted his terms. "If your spell won't alter who I am, you may cast your sorcery upon me."

"It certainly shall not, but I cannot perform it until twilight." My husband jerked his head toward the kitchen and noted, "A stew of squirrel simmers in the kettle, if your stomach requires nourishment."

Glancing out the window, I noticed that the sun had nearly reached the peak of the sky. I had spent more time wallowing in misery than I thought. Getting to my feet, I followed Augustin into the kitchen and tossed a few sprigs of herbs into the pot. He mentioned a few bland comments while I checked his pantry for more ingredients—I needed to repack my bag with items appropriate to a short, woodsy holiday; he could grant me an extra blanket and some wine. I hardly noticed what he said, for a pile of skinned carcasses lay beside the garden's entrance.

I counted at least a dozen squirrels.

My husband had fled from me and unleashed his anger upon wildlife.

If I do nothing else in the eleven days before the new moon, I have to make sure Prince Otto commits suicide in the river, I recognized. *I can't let Augustin lose control over his death by using his anger against the man who cursed him.*

That resolution might be enough to sustain me.

After lunch, Augustin went outside to prepare the grounds for the wedding. I retrieved my bag and sorted through its contents. Since my husband offered to grant the Prince and me small comforts like a blanket and wine, I figured I had best pack my clothing separately. Choosing two plain dresses of sturdy linen from the collection Augustin gathered during his travels, I rolled them into a bundle along with my underwear and socks, securing them with a thin length of twine.

As for the bag itself, I left the neck pillow in there, figuring my Keyholder might be fascinated by its "futuristic" style, along with my fork. I tucked my Latin-German Bible into the center of the pillow beside my knife and wooden hairbrush. Then I snagged the metal tumbler and headed for the Rhine, intending to fill it whether we needed more drinking water or not. The river was clean enough some distance away from the shore.

I found Augustin at the riverbank, positioning the wooden table from his pantry about six paces away from the Rhine's waters. I paused at the edge of the trail to watch him for a moment, admiring how his sable hair shone in the sunlight, its locks contrasting starkly against the maroon of his tunic. A black clip held his bangs back from his forehead in the style I loved most, his sturdy fingers setting a variety of items onto the table.

You're abandoning this man today for the fucking Prince, I thought to myself, *and here he is casually preparing for your marriage because he loves you more than he loves himself. You don't deserve Augustin. At all.*

He acknowledged me with a brief glance when I bared my feet before the river, wading into its waters to fill my thermos. "I would advise you to bathe once I have finished here," he remarked as I endeavored to hold my violet skirt above the surface. "The day's traders have passed by with their boats. You should be able to cleanse yourself without spectators."

The fact that Augustin did not suggest that we bathe together brought a touch of disappointment to my heart, but I shoved it aside. "Hopefully the Prince will do the same while he's in Eisenwald today," I said as I made my way back to the bank. I shot Augustin a meaningful look while shutting my tumbler's cap. "He smelled as grubby as a hog last night."

"The twenty-first century has spoiled you," Augustin observed with a hint of irony. I stuck my tongue out at him and reentered the path, carrying my shoes and socks along with my tumbler.

When I returned to his cottage after my bath some time later, dripping and wrapped in a towel, Augustin declared that I might as well remain naked until I completed my half of our bargain. That prompted me to raise my eyebrows, for I could fabricate a thousand reasons why he might want me nude for his schemes, none of which were particularly pleasant. He gestured for me to look through the extra items he had added to my pack while he checked on the stew from that morning, which had spent the day heating above a bed of coals.

In his absence, I lugged the leather bag to the hearth to examine its contents. Augustin had stuffed it with a decent array of food: the produce of his garden, eggs, several goat cheeses, raspberries and cherries. He had included a plush blanket, three bottles of wine, two cups, and at the very bottom of the bag, a sealed envelope bearing the instruction, *Open on the final day*.

I eyed the packet warily, recalling another last letter that had given me fine threads of hope for some eighteen years. Was there any hope left now, hours before I must bind myself in wedlock with the Prince of a ruined city? Despite the spell he intended to cast upon me, Augustin must not have given up on us yet. So I left the envelope where it lay and finished drying my body, spreading the towel upon the hearth before pointing my feet toward the kitchen.

The heavens had begun to darken with sunset when Augustin led me into his bedroom, stating that he would attempt his sorcery there with the cauldron burning blue. I stood meekly in the bedroom doorway as he tossed a batch of azure flames into his iron cauldron, their heat drawing sweat upon my brow right away. He ordered me to lie upon his bed, and while I did so, he opened the doors of his wardrobe and disappeared behind them.

Nervousness sent chills along my spine despite the heat of his fires. I had no idea what to expect from a spell that would grant Augustin 'a measure of authority' over my fate. My eyes drifted from the cauldron to the wardrobe doors, then to my breasts, which still appeared feeble and unimpressive although I had long shed the shackles of illness. The candlesticks positioned on the desk, window-sill, and ledges around the room all burst into flame, their sapphire glow evicting the gloom from the chamber. Then Augustin stepped away from his wardrobe, closing its doors behind him. He was darkness itself, attired in an imposing robe of blackest black, his hood shielding his face from my sight.

He returned to his cauldron first to hold a wicked-looking knife over the flames, its blade razor-sharp and serrated toward the handle. My heart skipped a beat at the sight of that blade—deadly enough without the excess heat of fire—and my mind raced here and there, trying and failing to figure out just what Augustin planned to do to me with that knife. I had seen him use a burning blade only twice before; once for the sacrifice, once for the blood-transfer.

Before I could reason out his intentions, he stood at the bedside, his fiery eyes sweeping over my naked body from head to toe. Now he held a small bowl in his left hand and the burning knife in his right—and I realized, to my dismay, that its blade was made of stone. Its gray did not hold the standard shine of metal. "Are you going to kill me before my time?" I asked in a tremulous voice.

"Your fate is in your hands in the place where you go," Augustin responded. He no longer looked at my body; he moved the point of his stone knife artfully in his bowl, its contents emanating a curl of soft white smoke.

I stared at the tools in his hands, my age-old fear of doctors prodding my nerves. "Are you going to cut me with that?"

"There will be pain, Swanhilde," he said solemnly, his focus still upon the contents of his bowl. "But if you choose to return from where you go . . . ."

My breathing had quickened, and I could sense my heart thudding against my rib cage. "You're sending me somewhere alone?" I croaked.

"I cannot go to the place that summons you." Augustin's eyes locked with mine, and he bent close to my face as he murmured in English, "Be wary of the one who shall speak to you."

"Wh . . . *what?*" But my innumerable questions would never be answered, for Augustin's lips began to weave the spell in a language I could not fully translate. Some of it sounded close to Ælte Teutonica, and other words may have had Latin roots. But I sensed his magic suffusing the atmosphere, rendering my body inert. And he reached over my pelvis to take hold of my right wrist, the point of his stone knife glittering with an entrancing liquid as he inserted it into my flesh, carving the shape of a rune.

The pain from the cut knocked my rate of breathing up another notch, and a simmering sensation spread upward from my wrist. Augustin continued to utter unspeakable words as he carved a different rune into the flesh at the inside of my left ankle, between the bone and heel. I probably should have screamed at that point or at least attempted to struggle, but his influence held me motionless upon his bed, the flowered patterns on the tapestry above me seeming to swirl.

I caught sight of a diminutive flame in his hands, situated atop what might have been beeswax, judging by its yellow hue. His sorcery traveled throughout my body in blistering waves from the two runes he had sliced, and to my chagrin, he proceeded to set his beeswax candle into my navel, its heat piercing me deep inside. My lungs panted shallowly, refusing to take in sufficient oxygen, and the ceiling blurred high above, transforming into a looming portal. What was Augustin doing to me? Why had I agreed to let him work dark magic over my wearied body?

The next thing I knew, the shrouded priest had placed the rim of his bowl between my lips, pouring the rest of its smoking contents down my throat. His free hand pinched my nostrils shut as he crooned in a lover's voice, "Swallow . . . and surrender the reality you hold dear."

The potion burned me from the inside out, and the portal overhead seemed to yank me into its jaws, scratching at every part of me while my cries remained shackled within. Then a brilliant light cast me in sharp relief against a towering collection of mirrors above, below, and around, effectively caging me. Blinking, I stared back at my own face before me, then a few centimeters to my left, then a few centimeters more, my nude body glowing like a candle. I thought I detected other images in the distance of the reflections, indistinct like negative film.

I folded my arms over my breasts, which did nothing for the pubic hair and ass cheeks standing out like sore thumbs all around me. A crackling sound seemed to draw ever closer to me, and I turned in a circle, seeing no escape from my mirror prison. Belatedly, I thought to try out my voice. "Where . . . what is this place?"

Vibrant giggles rang out around me, compelling me to start. "This is naught but echoes of your past, your beloved ones come to judge your life's path. Do you dare to stand before them as you are?" The mirrors bent toward me and shattered, their shards tearing at my flesh. A single set of eyes captured mine from the vague reflections just before they fragmented—Hans staring up at me from a hospital bed, his familiar face wasted by cancer and chemo.

The mirrors reformed as an older set of memories marched my way. I felt my heart pounding while my eyes checked the body mirrored before me, finding no blemish, cut, or rune. Only the ancient scars from my blood-transfer with Freia and the thinner line from my C-section that birthed her namesake marred the woman whose dazed eyes blinked at mine. Reaching both palms out to touch one of the mirrors, I shoved against its solidity as my daughter's eyes appeared behind my right shoulder, her lips parted in censure.

"Freya?" I managed to gasp just as my prison shattered over me afresh, the pain pulling a cry from my lips. Dust coated my hair and skin and then vanished. My cage reformed to reveal a terrified woman, breasts heaving, hands knotted on the glass before her. My cousin Beth's brown eyes seized my attention, displeasure crimping her forehead as snowflakes swirled around her body. Was I doomed to look into the eyes of each person who lost their life due to my mistakes?

"No," I moaned, covering my eyes with my hands. "Please don't—"

The glass smashed over me again before I could go on, and the female voice that spoke earlier filled my ears with unwelcome delight. "What lovely people have shared your life's path! Just a drop in the bucket, inchworms on an infinite quest."

Inchworms? The mirrors gouged me again, and other faces belonging to my twenty-first century family arose in my memory, even though I covered my eyes. And this time I heard their voices, their contempt.

She should have destroyed the Torstein the second she learned of its devilish roots. Why didn't she keep its curse to herself? What sort of Leitalra *craves one of Wuotan's minions instead of her fated Keyholder? She brought the Saxon horde down upon us.*

Crumpling into a ball upon the mirror beneath me, my eyes stared in horror at the reflections as my cruel cage contracted around my chosen posture. Trapped in a replay of ghosts that already haunted my waking hours, I feared that Augustin had cast me into a hallucination from which I could never escape. Glass crumbled upon me, and I saw Ina declaring her liberty from Walfrid, Marga sobbing because her prejudiced boyfriend had dumped her, Joel's young wife Melody beaming as she tried on a graduation cap.

"Augustin, where have you brought me? I can't do this," I moaned, putting my hands to my temples. The indistinct reflections had subjugated me, rendering me unable to look away from their judgment.

"To free yourself from this influx of memories, let them go," the feminine voice advised me, its tone sounding too enthralled to be proper. "Leave your past behind you . . . embrace the mantle of destiny."

It was too much, my brain too besieged to seek my magic inside, to liberate myself from this cage. So instead I shut my eyes and climbed to my feet, breaking through the glass that enclosed my body as I seized the power of faith—of an entity far beyond mere mortal downfalls. "God spare them all," I whispered, willing it to come to pass. "May He triumph where I cannot."

Suddenly I felt the gentle touch of fabric cradling my spine, air that tasted of candle smoke passing in and out of my nostrils. My eyes were still closed, but I sensed that I had returned to my cursed husband's bedroom, the silence broken only by the quiet sounds of flames flickering in the cauldron. I smelled no trace of blood in the atmosphere and felt no pain anywhere in my body, not even where Augustin's knife had burnt runes into my flesh. Had it all been an illusion—and if so, what had it accomplished?

A strange vigor seemed to pulse through my veins, erasing my weakness, even the stiffness that often troubled my neck. I opened my eyes to squint at the patterned tapestry above me, surprised at the extent of its details visible in the blue candlelight. Augustin appeared above me, the hood of his cloak pushed back to reveal his face, its muscles taut in what looked like incredulity. His fiery eyes roved over my body, and he held my left hand loosely, checking my pulse.

"How do you feel, Swanhilde?" he questioned in an odd tone, laying my arm back upon the bed and reaching forward to touch the artery in my neck.

I closed my eyes for a moment, relishing the sensation of his warm fingers upon my skin. Then I thought about his question, uncertain how to answer. I felt quite decent, even healthier than I had been before my illness.

"Well . . . I guess I feel pretty good," I replied at length, "considering that you just trapped me in some sort of mirror realm and scraped incidents from my life over my body." I snickered, opening my eyes again; and Augustin let go of my neck, his expression quizzical.

"What exactly . . . was the point of that spell?" I lifted my right arm, turning my wrist to see the rune his knife had traced upon my flesh. It had healed into a whitish scar, the skin around it tight and youthful, absent of creases. My lips parted in bemusement, and I averted my attention to Augustin.

My husband smirked down at me, his teeth immaculate and sharp. Then he climbed atop the chair he kept at his bedside and raised his hands to take hold of the tapestry adorning the ceiling.

Chapter Eighteen:
Destiny's End

"Look here, Swanhilde, and see for yourself."

Augustin swept the fabric away in a swift motion, catching the whole of it in his arms. There above me I saw a mirror image of myself, naked and young, cheeks ruddy, muscles firm, abdomen absent of the C-section's scar. The four lines stretching outward from my heart remained the sole flaw—along with a collection of odd grooves surrounding my navel. I counted ten of them.

My reflection's forehead wrinkled in confusion as I tried to comprehend Augustin's motives. His spell had transformed my body into virginity's perfection, the hints of gray gone from my tresses. *He wouldn't offer this sort of glamor to his ex-brother without cost,* I recognized. My eyes slid toward where Augustin stood at my left side, his expression satisfied. *But what's the price?*

"Somehow I just . . . don't believe you had me drink from the Holy Grail," I said, pushing myself effortlessly into a sitting position. No soreness in my joints whatsoever.

Augustin chuckled and sat upon his chair, raising one eyebrow at me in an incongruous fashion. "Christian mythology means little to one who has walked where demons tread. The beauty you now claim is Ashima's gift, that of a persona who imagines herself a goddess of time and fate. Her dominion is a sham, but she offers ephemeral gifts when petitioned respectfully."

He reached the index finger of his left hand out to trace the grooves around my navel. His touch inspired a tingling sensation centered at my womb, the source of life. "These ten marks represent the ten days that remain to you. Once you and your Keyholder complete your bond in blood matrimony, the stone knife that caged you to Ashima's whims shall cage your master as well. If you choose not to end your lives on the night of the new moon per history's record, the two of you shall die at dawn as your transient youth decays into ruin."

Augustin massaged the skin around my navel as he invoked my doom, and my revitalized hormones urged me to do things that were hardly appropriate under the circumstances. I seized his left hand and tugged it away from my abdomen, longing to guide it to where desire mingled with my frosty element at my core. But first I had to clarify a few things. "You've sentenced me to death," I said, holding Augustin's gaze.

"I hedge my bets," he corrected softly, leaning forward to press a gentle kiss to my forehead. His fiery scent enveloped me as the sable locks of his hair tickled my cheeks, and I shut my eyes, my heartbeat escalating. "If your cherished belief in love proves ineffective at freeing you from Wuotan's grasp, death shall certainly succeed." I opened my eyes to see his gazing back at me solemnly.

"Then you'll come for me at heaven's gates?" I wanted to be sure.

"For all of eternity," he quoted, his lips ensnaring mine in a sensual kiss.

When he pulled back, I deemed his revelations sufficient enough. I must die on the night of the new moon with Prince Otto, and afterward I would return for the man who loved me at my worst. The Prince did not need a virgin bride. Shifting my eyes briefly toward the window, I inquired in a silky voice, "How much longer until my wedding party arrives?"

I sensed Augustin's immortal spirit expanding far beyond what my finite ice could manage. "Soon . . . but there is time enough for this."

No further invitation needed. I released my grip on his left hand to undo his trousers, his tunic already cast to the floor as his flaming hands drew my lips to his. Within seconds, our bodies and spirits had thoroughly entwined, the living and the dead defying fate to claim a glorious Elysium.

Some time later, I lay still upon Augustin's chest, my right ear mesmerized by the steady thumps of his heart, my arms buried beneath the black pillow upon which his head rested. I was acutely aware of every sensation upon my skin, from the heat of inner fire that engulfed me to the stickiness of my own blood seeping from where his claws had gouged my flesh. One of his hands busied itself with my hair—weaving it, tugging it, scraping at its roots—while his other hand stroked my back, occasionally prodding tender points until I groaned.

My eyes were closed, my mind drifting in a confusing haze, fantasies of the next ten days running together with the painful knowledge that, in fulfilling the destiny of Muniche, I must leave my true mate behind again, possibly forever, or at best for four centuries. Though I clung to a desperate hope that Augustin would uncover a way to free me, my reason told me this moment was all we would ever get. This moment, with his body sheathed securely in mine, our elements drinking life in a realm we could never reach.

I lifted my head slowly to look into my lover's eyes, reading all of their anguish, their devotion, their silent determination to fight my fate until death took me. His lips formed a broken smile as his left hand crept upward to grasp my right, to drag it out from beneath the pillow and finger the sapphire ring. I pulled myself forward just a bit, disengaging our joined bodies. Augustin growled and bound me tightly in his arms, an unspoken rebuke.

"Wait," I whispered, as I saw his eyes flash with fire and focus on my neck. They flicked back up to meet mine, questioning, and I brought my left arm out from beneath the pillow, gently turning his face a little to the side, combing his silken hair back to bare his neck. "Just relax . . . for a moment," I murmured, holding his gaze. Then I sank my teeth into his neck to taste a few drops of his blood, seeking only one thing: reassurance.

I vaguely heard him murmur "Ah," when I bit him, but he slackened his hold on me, allowing me to drink freely. I released his neck after just two swallows, grimacing as I wiped the blood from my mouth. It still tasted horrible, no matter what Teuton priests thought. My stomach gurgled a few times, but I took several deep breaths, determined not to be sick.

Augustin pressed my face into his chest as I fought to regain my composure, my mind more in danger of sickness now than my stomach. He rubbed my back with one hand and stroked my throat with the other, probably an attempt to calm me, but the tears came anyway. I should never have drunk his blood, especially not with the intentions I had. Behind my eyelids all I could see was myself, always out of reach, while a maddened Black Priest bared his heart before me, pleading that I stay with him, his love for me more intense than anything I had ever known.

"Did you find what you sought?" Augustin asked as I raised my head from his tear-stained chest, his fingers kneading tender circles on my back.

Cold air escaped my lips as I blinked harshly against my tears. "You really . . . didn't have sex with anyone . . . all this time." My voice hitched.

Augustin grunted, his gaze turning slightly reproachful. "Of all the truths you could have sought." He rolled his eyes at me.

I choked out a weak laugh. "Your love for me . . . it's just . . . no words can express how powerful it feels."

Augustin took my face in his hands, wiping away the salt water before resting his forehead against mine. "Did you honestly hope that my regard for you had diminished over the years?"

Sighing, I stared into his gorgeous eyes, just centimeters from my own. "But I have to marry my Keyholder tonight . . . and die with him in the Rhine's waters."

"Death may be the only way to free you," Augustin said, his gaze assuring me that he understood what compelled me—Muniche's deathless spirit, pleading for release from Wuotan's clutches. Our lips met in a long, lingering kiss.

When he let me get up, I did not feel tired or shaky, despite the vast amount of blood it seemed like he had drained from me. Augustin led me to his washing table and helped me clean the blood and sweat from my body, then arranged my long hair himself, braiding it intricately and weaving it into a gauzy black veil. I studied my appearance in the mirror while he worked, noticing that although my body still looked young and healthy, slight bruises discolored my ribs and arms, marks that no amount of blood control or elemental first aid could erase. Augustin had paid careful attention to my throat, for several deep scabs marked where his teeth had found my arteries and veins.

For a moment I thought about summoning my ice to cool the wounds, but I decided to leave them alone for the Prince to deal with later. He was Muniche's lover, not Swanhilde's, and the maiden in the mirror was Swanhilde. I did ask my husband the meaning of the runes he had carved into my right wrist and left ankle. Augustin told me that they symbolized life and destiny, two constructs that surged onward beyond my control.

"I have a gown here that would be appropriate for your wedding, lovely Muniche," Augustin informed me as he turned for his wardrobe, beckoning me to accompany him. Raising my eyebrows, I walked to his side, then gasped at the sight of an exquisite satin gown—the bodice maroon dotted with gray flowers, the sleeves and skirts black as midnight, patterned with intricate grayish circles. Augustin helped me into the gown, securing its black ribbons while I slipped my feet into my sensible leather shoes.

Returning to the mirror, I gazed at myself in awe while Augustin tied a black-flowered choker around my neck. Then he stood behind me, studying my reflection with a look of approval. He squeezed my shoulders and murmured, "Our fallen city must wed her Prince in splendor, not simplicity."

I managed a smile, though it seemed so surreal to see myself looking and dressed like a virgin princess rather than a weary, forty-year-old matron. Augustin let go of me and turned to retrieve his priestly robes from the floor on the opposite side of the bed, but I caught his right hand, clinging to him. He halted at the edge of the bed and I kissed the palm of his hand, trying to think of something profound to say now, while we still had a few moments of privacy. He said nothing, but his eyes glistened, the fire in them swallowing his pupils along with his irises, spilling over in burning streaks down his face.

I broke away from his tormented gaze before I started crying myself. I had to control my anguish before I went out to face my final matrimony. Still holding his right hand in both of mine, my eyes locked on the black scar running from his wrist midway to his elbow—the sign of his damnation. Stroking the cursed mark with my fingers, I perceived the toughness of it in contrast with the smooth skin of Augustin's forearm.

"Four hundred nineteen years." I stared at that black scar, unable to think of anything else to say.

The hand moved, taking hold of my left, lifting it to its owner's lips. "I shall have the memory of your love with me always, to carry me through those years," Augustin reminded me, but his voice was ragged.

"Will that be enough?" I queried, meeting his desolate eyes.

"If I cannot find a solution to our predicament by dawn of the eleventh day, it will have to be enough." Augustin wiped at his fiery tears with his free hand. I heard the sound of sizzling flesh.

"You have to try," I whispered with renewed vigor, grasping his right hand tightly. "You can't give up on us, not ever."

He nodded, his visage grim. "I shall seek a way for us to be together from the moment you ride into the forest with your Prince until the moment your heart fails in the waters of the Rhine. I shall search, with everything that I am. I shall not interfere with your appointed destiny unless you can truly be mine."

He took hold of my right hand, removing the sapphire —our wedding ring—and clasping it in his fist. "I take this as a token of my pledge, a memento of you. If I do not succeed, I shall cherish it forever, with your candle." He gestured toward the small one upon the windowsill, the one I had never seen absent of flame.

When we exited his cottage, Augustin instructed me to wait in the yard for a time, so he could ensure the stage was set for Muniche's binding. A blue glow filtered through the trees in the direction of the river, so I knew Augustin must have lit a fire in the pit with a spare thought during our intimate activities, to guide my Keyholder and guests to the appropriate venue.

"I shall see you soon," he said as his fingers left mine bereft, his course set for the riverbank.

In his absence, a chill swept through my body that did not quite match the warmth of a summer's night. Focusing on my element out of habit, I allowed my spirit to sweep over the place where I must unite my blood with that of a man I respected but did not love. I sensed Augustin's potent blue fire at the edge of the river, the Rhine's spirit inviting my ice forward. Three other Teuton spirits were grouped together a short distance away from Augustin— metal, wind, and light. Freia had chosen to attend despite this era's chauvinism, doubtless an effort to support me. Her light wound its way through my spirit with gentleness, granting me the courage I needed to proceed.

Prince Otto's red fire awaited me at the far end of the short trail between Augustin's cottage and the clearing at the riverbank. It was time to finish this. So I headed for the pathway, brushing my right hand against the bark of the cherry tree as I passed by.

What will the Prince think when he sees me like this— in a satin dress with the beauty of youth? Will he be angry when he learns I've condemned us both to death?

The air tightened around me when I drew near to where the Prince waited in the darkness. I sensed a threatening presence encroaching upon me, Wuotan's abysmal voice ringing inside my head. *Do you truly believe feigned love can tear your heart away from me, naïve Leitalra? Death calls to you from behind the table . . . no precious sentiments can shield your heart from my servant's wrath.*

My feet faltered, and I put a hand to my mouth at the implications of the demon's portent. Wuotan would spend the entire ritual stoking the flames of my undead husband's aversion for the Prince—the man who had cursed him. What if Augustin was not strong enough to fight his master's influence? What if the demon possessed him and set his anger loose, slaying everyone gathered at the riverbank?

The Prince stepped onto the trail from behind a cluster of oaks, his right hand proffered to take hold of my left so we could walk to the table together. But I stood frozen in terror, panting shallowly as all sorts of morbid possibilities flashed before my eyes. Maybe my Keyholder and I should flee now, leave the city bond incomplete and pray that reconciliation would be enough to sever Wuotan's hold on Muniche's soul.

My partner detected my distress, his irises flashing with crimson fire as he reached out to stroke my cheek. His elemental vision must have shown him my altered appearance, for he whispered, "What has he done to you?" in an accusatory tone.

I sensed Wuotan's hands scratching at my heart again, echoing his insidious laughter. This was exactly what he wanted—for Prince Otto to be frustrated enough to incite the Black Priest's anger.

But we needed to finalize this marriage so my Keyholder, too, would bear the curse that had shortened my lifespan. That way if he did not grant the Rhine his slain body, Ashima could claim it instead—and Augustin would forever retain control over the death inside of him.

So I invoked my ice into my eyes to perfect my vision and looked directly at his face, confining his right hand in my left. "No matter what . . . don't make him angry. Don't say anything except the vows. Please."

Chapter Nineteen:
Not Enough

When we reached the opening of the trail, I ran my eyes over the group waiting at the riverbank—three living Teutons unaware of the mortal danger before them. Heinrich, Freia, and Joel stood to our right, all of them decently attired. Behind them I saw the Prince's chestnut horse and the three my friends had ridden, all tethered to the branches of a cluster of lindens. Between Freia and the water, I discerned the dark wood of the post, where the stone knife would join my blood irrevocably to the unstable Prince whose fingers twitched beneath my grasp.

Directly in front of me stood the table bearing the necessary instruments of the Teutonic wedding—the knife, bowl, cup, book of vows, silver oak leaves, iron stirrer, vinegar, bitter herbs, a small pile of dirt. I wondered briefly if Augustin had gotten the silver oak leaves from his own tree, which had not yet reached the age at which its fairy would appear. But as the Prince and I approached the table, I kept my focus on my cursed lover. He waited with the Rhine at his back, his pale hands standing out against his midnight robes, his hood cloaking his face.

Cautiously, I reached my icy spirit out toward him, endeavoring to catch a hint of his mood. Had Wuotan begun to aggravate him already, while he watched his traitorous ex-brother step forward beside his one true love? We halted before the table, and I stared at Augustin as he reached down to take up the book.

Though I was expected to keep silent until it was time to exchange vows, I breathed a plea in Bayerisch, knowing my Black Priest would hear and understand. "Don't kill him. Don't submit to temptation."

Augustin gave no sign that he had heard, instead speaking the opening lines of the ritual wedding in a tone absent of feeling. "Tonight, we come together to bind two Teutons by blood, oath, and love, representing the incomparable union of the Keyholder of Muniche and his Lady." Those were the same words Rudi had used to initiate the marriage of Hans and me—an event so far from this place —but when Augustin spoke the phrases, they sounded caustic.

The Prince and I stood solemnly, our hands joined, as Augustin performed the rite with the fire and oak leaves, closing the door of my escape. I followed my Cursed One out of the corner of my eye when he stepped to the right to speak with Heinrich and Joel regarding the duties of witnesses, his voice revealing no hint of emotion whatsoever. *He can do this. He can keep control of his anger long enough to finish this ritual,* I told myself, my left hand reflexively squeezing the Prince's.

My Keyholder's red-fired spirit reached out carefully toward me, wariness evident in his aura although he kept his gaze on the waters and trees beyond. His insecurity was understandable, since my physical appearance had altered so drastically after we parted ways that morning. I tried to offer a sense of comfort through my ice, despite the fear that chugged within my veins as Augustin retook his place behind the table. With a touch of shock, I realized that Prince Otto had never married anyone in a Teutonic wedding before. He might be nervous about the custom itself, not just about my mysterious youth.

I continued to watch Augustin minutely as the ceremony progressed, trying to maintain an essence of peace and tranquility around the three of us. I hardly felt the sting when his stone knife sliced my left wrist to form the marriage scar, but I sensed an unusual stiffness to his fingers when they turned my wrist downward to capture the trickle of blood in the cup. Somehow the blue firelight did not touch Augustin's face at all. I wished I could see his expression. *Don't kill him or you'll kill us all,* my spirit pleaded silently.

After we sipped from the cup of sorrows and the Prince tossed it over his left shoulder, we faced each other at last, and I took a moment to observe my Keyholder in the firelight. Heinrich must have given him his outfit, or perhaps he had traded something for it. He wore fresh black trousers, a clean tunic of brocade, shiny boots, and a black leather belt with a polished brass buckle. He still sported that tarnished medallion on a chain around his neck, and the keys of Muniche hung conspicuously from the right side of his belt. He had cut his hair and beard, his red-fired eyes gazing deeply into mine as I repeated the vows to him.

"Until we are parted by death." The last phrase of my latest oath fell from my lips, a mad relief spreading over me in its wake. The final recourse for the living bound in Teutonic matrimony—the event that ended my marriage to Joel in 1061. It cleansed my wrist from the scar that bound me to Hans, in the moment he breathed his last. *But Augustin and I vowed for all of eternity, since he's already dead. He's yet to agree that he can't keep that vow unless he turns from evil.*

It took effort to keep my focus on the Prince when he repeated Augustin's words, for my Black Priest's tone leaned more toward a snarl, as though he fought tooth and nail to avoid lashing out at the man who would soon ride away with his wife. Anxiety brought forth a light sheen of ice over my skin when Augustin paused before reading the last sentence, and I felt certain I heard him grind his teeth.

"Do this. Please," I whispered out of the corner of my mouth, my tongue stumbling over the Bayerisch words.

"I pledge to stay with you and you alone, as your husband, until we are parted by death." Augustin pushed the words between his teeth, and I shot a glance at his face. This time I saw his eyes aglow with blue flames, sweltering fury.

We needed to get this over with before he could no longer contain his death. As soon as the Prince finished speaking, I tugged him toward the post, my impatience drawing a quiet chuckle from one of our witnesses. I could not tell if it was Heinrich or Joel; neither of them knew that their lives hung by a thread. I laid my right palm atop the post as soon as we reached it, giving the Prince a pointed look while he took his place across from me. *Hurry up.*

My Keyholder's warm fingers closed over mine, and his left arm wrapped around my waist, drawing me near. I saw Augustin looming before us, stone knife in hand. I shut my eyes, praying hard that he had the capacity to finish this. The pause dragged long—too long—before Augustin spoke the final phrase in a tone of detachment, as if he remarked on the weather: "May the couple seal their marriage with a kiss, and may their union be complete."

This was the first Teutonic marriage I had experienced in which I actually *felt* the knife stabbing through my hand, just before the Prince's lips consumed mine. Tears of pain welled in my eyes, but I fought to ignore it, to concentrate on the sensation of his lips moving upon mine, his tongue exploring my mouth as my blood erupted with crimson fire. His spirit's ecstasy spilled over into mine, and I felt our magic binding us together, consummating Muniche's mystic ties, granting me a dedicated partner for life.

I had forgotten how glorious it was to sense the perfected city bonds pulsing between my heart and that of my Keyholder. I had missed this stability, this sense of absolute belonging.

If I did not take care, I might forget that Swanhilde desired a different bond entirely.

When Prince Otto backed away from me, I brought my right hand before me to look at it, to make sure the stab had healed properly. The fact that I had noticed the pain made me wary. Was that an aftereffect of Ashima's curse, Wuotan's meddling, or my individuality wailing for a different fortune? To my relief, I found no mark upon my palm or the back of my hand—but I saw the cryptic rune on my wrist and shook out my sleeve. Now was not the time to explain that to the Prince.

Suddenly, his right arm pulled me to his side, and he bent down to murmur in my ear, "Let us sign the certificate and leave this place."

Whether he had detected Augustin's tenuous control or my own anxiety, I could only guess. But I allowed him to guide me back to the table, recognizing as he did so that Ashima's curse had indeed fallen upon him, too. His hair and beard had turned quite black, his muscles regained their solidity, his face absent of time's creases. I caught Freia's gaze for an instant on our way to the table. Her graying blond hair was tucked beneath a lavender head covering that matched her dress. She looked worried.

Augustin stared down at us like the Grim Reaper as we took turns signing our full names onto our marriage certificate, our commingled blood serving as our ink. I had a strong feeling that he had placed his hands behind his back solely to keep them from wrapping around the Prince's throat. My Keyholder's spirit was radiant with elation when he signed after me, his respect and adoration throbbing along our mystical connection. Prince Otto loved the woman he had once despised as a foolish vixen who traveled time lightly.

But I sensed spectral claws delicately slicing the edges of my heart, quashing my hopes for an easy reprieve. *Your blood belongs to* me, *Muniche, not to your adulterous Keyholder,* Wuotan growled in my ear. *He granted me dominion over your spirit as payment for his jealous schemes.* I tried to block the demon from my thoughts, mouthing a silent prayer to God for protection.

The Prince finished signing and raised his head to meet Augustin's gaze, but I shoved him toward where our friends stood. "Go talk to Heinrich," I urged him under my breath, though I knew Augustin could hear. "I'll be there in a second."

To his credit, my Keyholder moved away, leaving me standing alone before the table—before Wuotan's priest who held the authority to kill us all. I peered at the darkness that obscured his face, his blue eyes invisible now, no longer glinting with fire. "Thank you so much for doing this," I said in Bayerisch. "I'll keep him away from you until we—"

Augustin thrust our marriage certificate at me before I could speak further; he had signed it in ink after he caught our blood in the bowl. I saw that Heinrich and Joel had already inscribed their names, so I took the parchment from him, my eyes lingering upon my own bloody signature: *Swanhilde Rolande von Thaden und von Bayern.*

"Until parted by death," I whispered, taking a deep breath as I tried to push aside the demonic presence marring my peace. There must be some way to make this work out for us, after the Prince and I shattered Wuotan's hold upon our city. Bound by death . . . parted by death.

Augustin handed me the stone knife and said, "You may have need of this. I shall return in a moment with your bags."

He vanished in a whirl of cerulean fire, prompting the heads of the four who stood near the post to turn in obvious surprise. I heard the Prince say something crass to Heinrich, but I marched straight for Joel, wanting an update on his status with our children.

Joel's face still appeared wan from the pestilence as he cracked a smile at me. The beard he had begun to grow sported more gray than blond. "You want me to kidnap you real quick?" he asked me in English, jerking his head toward the horse he had ridden here. It was Erika's favorite tan-and-white mare.

I did a double-take, my eyebrows coming together. "What?"

He raised one brow and glanced at my newest husband. "I know you're doing this for Muniche's sake, not your own. Pretty sure Heinrich's over there trying to convince your Keyholder not to commit suicide. You shouldn't waste this on him." He gestured at my youthful body.

Sighing, I folded my marriage certificate around the stone knife. "There's a lot more going on than you realize. But the Prince and I need to get out of here, or Wuotan might incite Augustin to kill us all."

Joel's hazel eyes bugged. "Okay then." He edged closer to the mare.

I reached out with my free hand. "Did you tell our kids . . . about you?"

"Yeah." Joel slid his hands into the pockets of his trousers, his body language implying discomfort. He did not meet my eyes as he said, "Cammie's not taking it well. She thinks I'm lying about you, that you're here somewhere too. You might want to steer clear of Eisenwald while you're hanging out with the Prince."

Shame enclosed me in its shroud, and I dropped my hand to my side, my teeth scoring my bottom lip. "If only I had more time."

"Max didn't believe me until I started speaking perfect English to him," Joel went on, his eyes darting from the blue flames flickering in the pit to where Freia stood two paces from her husband and the Prince. She clearly wanted to speak with me, too.

"Helmut said he thought that was why you played the organ. Because you were a time traveler like the Prince." Joel snickered, his solemnity broken at last. "Erika and Johann are just happy to get to know their Daddy. And before you ask, I *did* tell Lorraine, too. She's still reeling from the news." He looked amused.

"Technically, you should be the same age as her Mutti, but here you are looking like a handsome adventurer awaiting a fair maiden," I joked, giving Joel's arm a firm pat. "I wish you a long and happy life here, whatever path you choose."

"Thanks, Swanie." He glanced at the stone blade peeking out from the paper I held and added, "Good thing your Black Priest thought to give you one of those. I'm saving mine for old age." He winked.

Shaking my head slowly, I turned my attention to my best friend, who pulled me into a hug, her light reinforcing my element's verve. We embraced each other in silence for a moment, but when she stepped back to hold me at arm's length, the fear upon her countenance prompted my angst to multiply. "Wolfgang did this to you," Freia said in a hushed tone.

Whether she referred to my youth or the marriage itself, I could only guess. "It was the only way he'd agree to wed me to the Prince," I explained. "This renewed youth will kill us both on the morning after the new moon, setting a limit to our . . . whatever this is we have." I shot a glance at my Keyholder, who was in the process of securing my bag and bundle of dresses to his horse. The Cursed One stood in the shadows, his arms folded beneath his robe.

Freia looked at me for a long while, her green eyes sad. Then she squeezed my arms and reminded me, "Swanie, you mustn't lose hope."

I nodded and headed for the Prince's horse, suspecting that any further goodbyes must remain unsaid. Augustin's silence made me nervous. I had no clue how strongly Wuotan tormented him right now, urging him to end his murderer's life. Heinrich offered me a smile as I passed him, and the Prince helped me mount his horse before situating himself in front of me. I twisted my torso around so I could stuff our marriage certificate and the knife into my pack, and my eyes met Augustin's. They smoldered with anguish and hurt.

I froze with my hands atop my pack, unable to force my fingers to undo the flap and place the items inside. Augustin's essence seethed with pain and loss, no trace of anger remaining. *Why can't I think of something to say when I'm about to run off with the man who cursed us both?* My lips quivered as I tried to remember how to say something, anything, to reassure my most faithful partner that nothing had changed, no matter how Muniche's spirit altered my yearnings.

The Prince murmured at me over his shoulder, asking me to wrap my arms around his waist so we could be off.

Crumpling the parchment in my hand, the most meaning-ful phrase found its way out of my lips in Ælte Teutonica. "I love you, Augustin."

He did not reply, his burning eyes communicating everything words could not. But I managed to open the bag's flap and cast the knife and certificate inside before securing my arms around my fated mate's waist, the firm-ness of his muscles evident beneath his brocade tunic. He nudged his mare onward, and I squeezed my eyes shut as I leaned my forehead against his back.

"We're not having sex tonight," I stated bluntly once we left those at the riverside behind. "There's a lot we need to talk about, and the only safe place to do it is in the realm of dreams."

Chapter Twenty:

Our First Night

Prince Otto used his influence over my heart to lull me into slumber shortly after we lay together on his gray blanket from the previous night. His expertise at such things reminded me that, although he and Lady Maria had not finalized their bond, he had shared the heart-bond with a woman from ages past, the one he chose to love. The similarities between his situation and mine with Augustin agitated me as I fell asleep. Just how much of this man's soul would he reveal to me during our ten days together? Could we reconcile and compromise, forgive the mistakes that led us to our doom?

Would that be enough to break the blood curse my Keyholder had laid upon his city? Or would each woman who embodied the fallen Muniche shoulder a demon's hex for the next ninety-two years?

When my dreaming spirit rose from my body at the Prince's call, I turned for the trickling waterfall and drifted upstream, preferring to indulge in nature's serenity while I bared my heart before him. Though my curiosity needled me about his own dark secrets, tonight I must lay it all on the line so he could understand the fate that loomed before us. Our days were numbered by my own doing.

The Prince's spiritual robes glistened around him in tongues of crimson fire, providing light to guide our path beneath the trees. I kept my ethereal feet in the water, its cool dampness soothing me, while he floated along the bank at my side. After about five minutes of silent wandering, he spoke first, the tone of his voice charming the collective soul that held sway over my heart.

"Something tells me this beauty we've obtained is not a gift from God."

Maybe that was the best place to start. I slowed my pace and looked toward my Keyholder, who had pushed back the right sleeve of his robe to bare his wrist. The rune carved beneath his thumb glimmered in an eerie fashion. Anxiousness sprinkled my robes with icy flakes as I looked at my own wrist. I had not realized Augustin's spell had marred our spirits alongside our bodies—like the filial curse. I wondered if that was something that happened anytime a mortal dabbled with demonic sorcery.

"It's not Wuotan's gift, either," I responded, shaking my sleeve out around the rune so I could concentrate on the spiritual realm's peace. "Augustin demanded recompense for conducting our wedding. He didn't consider my request valid, since I'm already married to him."

"Not as Teutons," the Prince noted.

"Yeah. But I'll still have to answer to God for marrying two men. In a way, it's almost like those romance books from my time where the woman has her own harem of powerful males." I gave a bleak laugh and muttered, "My two priests, one of red fire, one of blue. Both trying to tame the icy witch."

"It seems that no fiery priest has managed that yet," my companion said, his tone amused. "So the Cursed One put you under a beauty spell that involves neither God nor Wuotan," he prompted.

"The runes that mark our wrists and ankles signify life and destiny," I said, "and a giddy female entity has decreed that we must die at dawn on the eleventh day. This youth we claim will fall away and drag us into death."

The Prince had halted in the midst of a tangled batch of nettles, their stems sizzling beneath the flames that comprised his spirit. "A giddy female entity?" he repeated, giving me a look of bewilderment.

I shrugged, digging my toes into the sandy creek bed. "Ashima."

"I have never heard of her. A demon?"

"Probably. Aren't all false deities demons?"

The Prince stared through me, the forehead of his spirit wrinkling. "So the Cursed One gave us this fleeting youth to ensure that we would commit suicide on the night of the new moon, like his histories imply."

"All of Teuton history implies it," I corrected. "But . . . I think Augustin was the only actual witness to your . . . to our demise."

"It would make perfect sense if this youth was to kill me. But you? He has fought to preserve you all this time." The Prince rubbed his forehead, confusion evident in his expression and in the frantic licking of his flames.

"He believes death would break Wuotan's power over Muniche's soul, if our attempt at absolution does not," I explained.

Comprehension dawned on the Prince's face. He slipped his right hand into his robes to clutch my heart, his ruby eyes boring into mine. "Merely completing our bonds through marriage was not enough to liberate you."

"No. And that's why I wanted to talk to you here, since no one can intrude upon dreaming spirits. Wuotan spoke to me before and after our wedding, warning me that love isn't enough to break his hold on Muniche. The curse you and your knights laid was really strong. I think Wuotan's going to creep on us until we end this . . . and he wants Augustin to kill you."

"That is why you urged me not to speak to him," the Prince discerned, his eyes watching me closely.

My spirit shuddered, and I sat down in the creek bed, welcoming its waters to flow through me. "Did you even know . . . what the filial curse means . . . when you laid it upon him?" I asked my Keyholder, raising my head to look at him, where his fiery spirit towered over me upon the bank.

Prince Otto's shoulders sagged, and he eased himself down beside me, his buttocks upon the earth while his fiery feet created strange ripples in the stream. "According to what I read, the filial curse presented his soul to the demon he served, giving Wuotan authority over his eternal destiny. It was a fitting penalty for a man who sacrificed human blood in his hunger for power, to grasp sorceries beyond the ones I wield as Keyholder."

"He died," I said when the Prince fell silent, his words proving he still imagined that his wayward ex-brother deserved his terrible fate. My companion turned his face toward me, and I looked him square in the eyes as I revealed the lurid details of my beloved's fortune.

"After you exiled him from the city, he traveled to the Alps, where he met his predecessor, the Black Priest who had walked the earth alone for a thousand years. One of the four cursed when our people accepted Christianity, he carried Augustin into Wuotan's realm against his will and sacrificed his body while the demon looked on. Then Wuotan took him to hell's gates and offered him a delay of judgment. So he returned as a dead man, and he'll be trapped here until another Cursed One accepts the same offer."

Prince Otto stared at me, his horror and dismay reaching out to touch my spirit. "He is dead then. That is why he has not aged, why a darkness suffuses his aura."

I narrowed my eyes and asked, "What exactly happened to that superhuman army the Saxons commanded, after you surrendered the city to them and cursed her stones with your blood? Did they continue to spread their disease throughout Teuton lands, or were your forces able to cut them down?"

"He found a way to slay them." The Prince's ruby eyes glinted with abrupt understanding, and I sensed his horror transforming into something like pity.

Muniche's collective spirit powered my voice as I said, "At *my* behest. You failed me, betrayed me, left me to rot in my enemies' hands. When I demanded vengeance, an exiled priest came to my aid."

"Your Keyholders have failed you too many times," the Prince whispered in a chastened tone, his gaze focused on his fiery toes fashioning swirls in the water. "I intend to do all that is in my power to regain your trust and confidence in the short time we have together, *Leitalra*."

Hesitantly, he lifted his eyes to meet mine, and I felt his fingers touch my heart anew, reverence pouring from his spirit. "Muniche would like to forgive you," I admitted in a low voice, sensing her fidelity awakened by his touch. "But you'll have to prove yourself worthy of redemption if you expect Swanie to pardon your mistakes."

"I shall do all that you ask of me. Truly," my companion promised. "And you may call me Otto, if it pleases you. You stand far above me as our people's royal mother, and I shall find a way to free your heart from Wuotan's tortures. I should bear his punishments, not you. Never you."

My Keyholder's crooning voice shattered what resistance I may have wished to offer, as he drew my heart from beneath his robe and massaged it tenderly, each touch entrancing me with devoted magic. My lips parted unconsciously, and my eyelids slid shut, casting the world in a translucent sheen of ice while Muniche's essence concentrated on her master's ardor. Maybe Otto believed he could evict Wuotan's hold through love and fidelity alone. His touches guided me into a blissful trance, his fire gently warming my spirit.

But I extracted my individuality from its reverie before he drew me in too deep. Opening my eyes, I reached out to trace his cheek. He averted his gaze from my throbbing heart to my face, though my fingers passed through his spirit, and I forced myself to remind him of the truth. "No matter what happens between us these ten days, Augustin will be seeking a way to reclaim my heart. He promised to never give up on us until my soul departs for good."

Otto looked into my eyes, sensing all of my conflicting emotions through his grip on my heart. Realization seemed to cross his features as he replied, "Swanie, I hope for your sake that he succeeds. But in the meantime, we ought to do what we must to sever Wuotan's hold upon our city."

For the rest of that night, we lounged together with our feet in the stream, our spirits close enough that I could sense the change in his heat with every shift in emotion. I told him about the trials I faced in the twenty-first century, pausing in my discourse here and there to concentrate on his magic pouring into my heart. He asserted, after I bemoaned the friends and family who lost their lives at our enemies' hands, that I had done well as *Leitalra*, protecting the Teuton people from extinction. Wicked criminals must not be granted access to time's gateway.

"Leadership is a difficult burden to carry, whether it comes through heritage or circumstance," Otto told me. "If you had given the Saxons what they wanted, it may have spared your loved ones temporarily only to slaughter them later. To this day, I still second guess my actions regarding Paulus, whether I should have let the Saxons have him without repercussions. Would they have spared our kingdom if I had not led my armies against their settlements?"

"It's best not to agonize over past decisions. We made them, and now we must live with them and move forward." I caught another deferential gaze from my companion and added quickly, "Not that I've always done that myself."

Otto hummed in agreement. When the sky began to lighten with the coming dawn, we returned to the Rhine to watch the sunrise over its expanse of dark blue. "The one choice your *Leitaeri* made that I cannot condone is his failure to pull your children from school when your enemies focused their efforts on your family," he observed as we situated ourselves upon an outcropping of rock within a copse of birches, fifty meters from where our sleeping bodies rested. "His shortsightedness there astounds me, though I trust that your daughter has offered him grace in their shared infinity."

I sighed, my icy eyes focused on the rippling hues of the water below us. "Freya's ghost haunts me more than any of the others," I confessed. "She blamed me for her pain. They convinced her to blame me, not her Pappi. Her censure has weighed heavily upon me since—" I could not go on. Images of the box bearing her preserved body parts tainted the tranquil scene before me.

A thick blanket of peace folded over my spirit as Otto's fingers instilled my heart with his reassurance. "Those hauntings are Wuotan's schemes, his efforts to draw you away from the light."

Part of me knew he was right, while the deprecating corner of my mind told me Freya would have been better off with another mother, any other mother. My husband's comfort bathed me in quietude, so I endeavored to concentrate on that and enjoy the artistic glory of the sunrise. Freya and I would meet again soon, and in the interim I needed to spurn demonic deceit.

When we awoke, Otto went off to check his snares. He wanted to prepare a hearty stew that we could leave simmering in his kettle throughout the day. In his absence, I changed out of my wedding dress into a simpler frock more appropriate for a forest holiday. The bruises upon my arms and ribs had begun to fade, and I noticed that one of the ten grooves encircling my navel had vanished. We had nine days left after today.

It occurred to me, while I sorted through the victuals Augustin had packed into my bag, that it might be wise to relocate to somewhere with better shelter, in case the weather turned sour. The dew dampened our blankets and clothes each morning, so we ought to scout out a place amid the boulders further upstream from our faucet waterfall. As I sliced a carrot and radish with the knife I had brought from the Black Castle, my thoughts drifted in a carnal direction.

Thus far, Otto had not changed out of his wedding attire, and I knew he had at least one extra pair of pants and three tunics. He had traded his parchments and pen along with his saddle the day prior. His chestnut horse now occupied herself with a fresh bale of hay, which Otto had brought back to our campsite while I spent the afternoon lamenting how terribly I must break Augustin's heart. But now I claimed a master of red fire with a body time had not ravaged . . . and we were married.

Last night I had declared that I did not want to have sex with my husband. He needed to grasp the seriousness of our situation before we took that step. This morning, after having spent multiple hours of the night basking in the sensations of his spiritual hands preening my heart, my youthful hormones urged me to finish our union once and for all. *Leitaeri* and *Leitalra* must mate and seize the rapture Otto had not yet experienced.

He returned with four squirrels, approval glinting in his dark blue eyes when he saw the batch of chopped vegetables waiting in his skillet—my cutting board. I had added some water to the kettle, which sat beside the embers of his campfire, awaiting the meat. "I have dishonored you, allowing you to wake before I prepared a meal," he remarked, dropping the squirrels next to the kettle and taking up the stone knife to butcher the first.

I gave a careless shrug and leaned back on my elbows, watching his hands as they skinned his prey. He crouched upon the ground, leaving the gray blanket to me. I noticed, when he caught my eye, that his irises nearly mirrored Hans'.

"Our ten days don't have to follow every tradition. I don't mind preparing the vegetables," I said, lowering my eyelids to gaze at Otto through my lashes. "I've been wondering, actually, what we're going to do after we eat."

My Keyholder caught the hint in my tone, and his lips curled into a naughty smile as he diced the meat of the squirrel and tossed it bit by bit into the kettle. "I gather you have no intention of holding me at arms' length for much longer."

"Muniche's cravings are rubbing off on me. And I'll admit that I'm curious to see what Ashima's curse has done to your body."

"I share that curiosity about your body," he said, the sunlight seeming to reflect off his teeth as he smiled. A blush appeared on his cheeks.

"You know, some of my girlfriends in the twenty-first century used to muse about how marvelous it would be to dance, kiss, and dream with Prince Otto von Bayern, the talented musician who travels time."

He laughed outright, the heat of his fiery spirit toying with my ice in a realm our mortal eyes could not pierce. "A thousand years from now, I am remembered as a paramour. What a magnificent legacy."

"I'd have shared my girlfriends' opinions had you not given me the cold shoulder at our first meeting," I mentioned, remembering how his handsomeness had struck me when he stood among other members of the Teuton Council of Muniche so long ago.

Otto exhaled heavily. "Another choice I have regretted."

"Destiny wanted to smack us together whether we liked it or not." He smiled again and shook his head, seemingly entertained by my humor. "We're to be honest with each other in these final days, right?"

"I see no reason not to." He had finished with the first two squirrels, his knife at work on the third. But he glanced at me for a second, his focus on the curve of my neck. He would bleed me at some point; there was no escaping it.

Just how often had Lady Maria bled him?

"Then in an attempt at full disclosure, I advise you not to be deceived by my maiden-like body. I've lived for sixty-two years, and I've slept with three men. And if you're too brainless to take the effort to get me off like a certain windy ex of mine, I want a refund."

My companion threw back his head and laughed, the half-gutted squirrel forgotten in his hands. "Swanie . . . you mean to tell me . . . that Joel Hudson . . . used you like . . . a common harlot?" He wheezed, dashing moisture from his eyes.

"He wanted me pregnant or nursing constantly so I wouldn't run away with Augustin. So there was a lot of sex in the Thaden manor, and a lot of fake moaning on my part." I rolled my eyes at the memory, hoping that Joel had matured enough to communicate with Lorraine, if the two of them ended up together.

"He feared he could not measure up to a fiery priest."

"He wasn't wrong."

The Prince gave one final chuckle before turning back to his kill. "Do you intend to run away from me?" he queried, looking at me from beneath sable brows. His voice wove around me like a sultry breath of jasmine, inspiring my ice to surge within my core.

"Not until after I've slit my throat," I answered in the same tone.

Otto made a guttural noise as he finished with the third squirrel. "We had best speak of something else, or I am likely to stain your dress with animal's blood."

We continued our banter while enjoying the stew some time later, his hands stroking the heart of my soul in a way that transformed Muniche's yearning into an abject need. This Keyholder had the power to make me forget Augustin entirely, though I trusted he would not use the city bonds in such a way. My heart throbbed at his command, and the crimson flames enhancing his irises entrapped me in a hold that Muniche's essence had no desire to break.

Wuotan's authority crumbled when a Keyholder and Lady worshipped one another. To my delight, Otto proved himself to be a capable lover, his fiery fingers pulling me to the brink of bliss, his warm lips swallowing my cries. If he noticed the fading marks of my erotic triumph with Augustin, he gave no sign of it, his lips memorizing every portion of my face, neck, and breasts before he thrust his body into mine. Already nearing my second release, I sank my fingernails into his back as he rode me, pleas for more spilling from my lips.

When Otto's teeth sank into my neck as our bodies moved in tandem, ecstasy enveloped me from deep within, moans of wonder bursting into nature's idyll while I gave my heart to my fated master.

Afterward, as our mortal bodies gradually relaxed from our triumph, Otto released my neck from his hold, his magic sealing my wound before I found the wherewithal to heal it myself. Blood control? What was that? My icy spirit drifted in an elated trance I had not achieved in many years.

My hazy eyes recognized pain contorting Otto's face as he hovered over me, and he gasped, "Swanie . . . your heart . . . it is torn . . . because of me."

Chapter Twenty-one

Otto's Confessions

Crimson fires simmered in Otto's irises as tears welled in his eyes. He pushed himself away from me before I could formulate a lucid response, and in his absence, my ice's chill washed over my body. Muniche's cries pealed from my lips in quiet whimpers, for she had not finished drinking her Keyholder's devotion. She wanted more, and the hormones charging through my veins agreed.

But I could not lift my body from the blanket bunched beneath my back, so I stretched my left hand out in the direction my husband had gone. "Otto?"

"Ah, Swanie, perhaps I should not have drunk so freely of your heart's truths," he mumbled from some distance away. I managed to twist my head toward his voice, and I saw that he had curled into a ball beside the embers of our campfire, his kettle resting atop the coals. He had found the rope from the previous night, his hands twisting it frantically, forming no knots. Sweat slaked his naked torso, and steaming tears poured onto his hands and ankles.

I groaned quietly, my instincts telling me I could not expect further intimacy from this man until he had relinquished his latest torment. With effort, I propped my head up onto my left fist, my pulse still slightly elevated from our mortal and spiritual mating. "And how exactly are you responsible for my heart's ruin, may I ask? Pretty sure the heartbreak I feel is a result of my choices."

Otto shook his head, the locks of his hair dangling to his jawline, hiding his face from me. I saw smoke rising from their tips. "Everything your heart has suffered is a direct result of my meddling. Everything. You bared your soul to me in our dreams and I know I must do the same, for I am not worthy of your grace. Not at all."

Sighing, I stifled my urge to contradict him, for sentimentality would get us nowhere. He had listened patiently last night, and now I ought to grant him the same deference. "Go on. I'm listening." Otto's broad shoulders rose and fell in a heavy sigh, and he straightened his back just enough to meet my eyes through his tousled hair as he related the darkness of his past.

"There seems to be no better place to start than with the final portrait my mother finished in the weeks before her death. I believe you saw some of Marelda's artwork in the Bayern library, many years ago." He paused as his eyes darkened, and I nodded.

"The last painting she ever created was an image of your Cursed One, exactly how he looks today. The long hair, the shrewd eyes, the sturdy body with powerful yet noticeably agile hands clasped before him. She drew him as a Teuton priest with a halo of blue fire adorning his head."

Otto paused again, his eyes watching me astutely. I gawked at him, wholly confounded. "How . . . is that possible?" I asked in a squeak.

"Perhaps God sent Marelda a vision of how her most beloved son would look in adulthood. I know not. But she titled the portrait *Prince Augustin von Bayern*. I remember seeing it as a young child before Lady Maria hid it away, before the subject of that painting descended into darkness. The image stayed with me as I grew, as I watched him work spells I could not. He was a sorcerer who fol-lowed Wuotan, while I was a child of God. It seemed unfair that he could bend fate to his will without cost to himself.

"'It must be possible for me to do the same,' I convinced myself, even after I learned the price he had paid to wield the powers he claimed. But that plays no part in this story. After my father sent him away for foreign education, Lady Maria crowned me officially as Prince, demanded that her Keyholder recognize me as his successor. But my father held to the ancient traditions—his oldest must be offered the keys first, no matter what a wraith he had become. Lady Maria and I expected him to take the keys and ruin the city.

"But he proved himself unworthy of the honor. Instead, he strode down Muniche's streets like a personage, slaying the criminals, gambling the Bayern funds, ravaging the harlots. Sacrificing the outsiders. I knew what he did, and in a moment of weakness in November of 1043, I sum-moned Wuotan into the fireplace of my private chamber, begging for magical knowledge his servant—my rival—had not yet uncovered. He had begun to lead young women astray with his healings, and I did not want him to craft Muniche's destiny in my stead."

Otto broke off for a moment, his palms raw from wringing his length of rope. His eyes darted from the twine in his hands to the kettle to the stream, unable to meet my gaze. I waited, inquisitiveness coursing through my blood along with traces of ice. Despite the twenty-three years Augustin and I had shared the heart-bond, we had rarely spoken of his youth. He preferred to focus on the present, if not on language studies, during our dreams. I knew that was because he was ashamed of the depravities he had savored before we met.

"Wuotan told me," Otto went on at length, his voice hesitant, "that at the cost of human blood, he could teach me a sorcery my rival could never know, for he had avoided music since Marelda's death. My talents at the organ could open a gateway to the past, the demon said, to histories unknown to man. He had already guided my muses during composition in recent months . . . I had the Song of Time nearly finished, though I did not comprehend its significance. Wuotan would teach me those final lines if I did the perverse ritual his servant performed on the regular. But at a cost too dear even for him to pay."

The fire gone from his eyes, Otto stared at me, his face cast in shadow from the branches spread above us. My breath had quickened, and a sense of dread came over me as my brain endeavored to translate his words. What price was too high for Augustin to pay? He had sacrificed adult women, children, animals on the stone altar.

All at once, his statement from thirty years ago struck me between the eyes. *You are a Teuton. When I kill you, it will not be so wretched.*

"You had to sacrifice one of our own people," I whispered, horrified.

Otto bowed his head in shame. "The cost of those final lines was the heart of a Teuton woman. That was my initiation onto the dark path. Though I sinned far worse in later years, her eyes have never left me. They were the same color as yours. I was her Prince, her Keyholder. She trusted me, even as I bled her upon the altar, set her blood aflame, dedicated her heart to our demon lord."

As my husband outlined one of his most atrocious sins, I sensed Wuotan's presence descending upon our campsite, the sunlight dimming. Sharp blades jabbed at my heart, the pain prompting me to cry out, my lungs unable to inhale sufficient oxygen.

I know you can feel her suffering. The demon's threats scratched at my mind, mingling with his spiritual tortures. *I know it pains you to watch your dear one writhe on account of your misdeeds. Would you grant me the price necessary to undo the curse you leveled upon your ruined city?*

"Leave us in peace, damned creature!" Otto declared in Ælte Teutonica. He rose to his feet as scarlet fires ignited around his naked body. "Neither my *Leitalra* nor I have invited you to disturb our sanctity here."

Wuotan's chuckle rang out between my ears; apparently he spoke to both of us this time. His claws continued to probe my heart, seeking a place to find true purchase. I whimpered aloud, pressing my hands against my chest in an attempt to smother the discomfort. *God, I need You,* my spirit cried involuntarily. *Your presence lives within my heart . . . even if Wuotan holds sway over Muniche . . . does my faith count for nothing at all?*

A surge of peace and security bolstered my heart, repelling Wuotan's claws and granting me the stamina to climb to my feet. Ice enhancing my vision, I blinked at my Keyholder, whose muscles rippled amid his flames as he demanded that the demon depart, invoking the name of the Almighty Creator. The air around us noticeably shifted and Wuotan's waning voice advised, *Remember my words, conquered* Leitaeri.

Silence followed, and my husband stepped forward to take hold of my arms, his fires vanishing into nothingness. "Swanie, are you all right? I am so sorry, *so* sorry my recklessness brought this upon you!"

Belated shock drove my body to sag in his arms. His warmth reinforced my vigor as I took several slow breaths, my father's fears from long ago arising in my memory. *He wants you, Swanie . . . and he didn't say whether he wants you dead . . . or something worse.*

"My Pappi warned me . . . after I came back from my lifetime here . . . that Wuotan wanted payment . . . for all the times I've used his magic," I managed to say, my breath hitching in strange places. I buried my cheek against my husband's smooth chest hair and gasped, "This is what he wanted . . . worse than death . . . he wanted a way to torment the heart . . . of God's child."

"And I gave it to him," my Keyholder groaned. "I am a failure."

"What price did he offer . . . to break his hold on Muniche's soul?" I asked, unsure whether I really wanted to know. Doubtless it was too terrible to pay.

Otto's chest rose and fell beneath my cheek in a lengthy sigh. "If I give my life to your Cursed One and allow his death to slay me, he would take that man's heart instead of Muniche's."

I jerked away from Otto, slipping out of his arms to stare up at him. "No."

His lips formed a tragic smile. "I could not agree to such a crime. Not after seeing the depths of your regard for him." He glanced at the place where he had drunk from my neck during our binding.

"We'll just have to find another way to free Muniche's essence. Our marriage wasn't enough, our sex wasn't enough, our mystical union wasn't enough. We still have nine and a half days to figure this out."

Otto's smile turned a trifle shy as he said, "An idea did occur to me, but we had best discuss it in our dreams, since it appears our adversary wishes to hound us in the mortal world."

I raised my eyebrows at him. "If you think we should spend most of our time sleeping, we'd better move our campsite to somewhere with shelter. I noticed a few alcoves in the rocks last night that might work well if we add some branches and your tent tarp."

We spent most of the day constructing a shelter in the rocky niche nearest to our tiny waterfall. Thick clouds made their way across the sky as the day wore on, and my ice detected the water gathering among them. Otto guided his horse to a glade of thick pines that would protect her from storms, and we carried the hay bale there together. It was a fascinating experience to work beside my Keyholder, for while he took on the harder tasks himself, he accepted my help without offense.

He confessed more of his iniquities while we worked on our shelter, shame evident upon his countenance more often than not. Augustin had committed his devilish sins openly, while Otto shielded his dark deeds behind a holy façade. He performed only one human sacrifice, insisting that the demon require other payment from that point forward. So Wuotan had claimed the lives of the Prince's citizens in ways apart from Otto's interference—childbirth, sickness, accidents.

Otto had convinced himself that the occasional fatality was necessary to augment the respect he had garnered as Muniche's Keyholder and Prince. He used Wuotan's sorcery to help other Teuton Princes maintain their autonomy over the kingdom. He held the authority to bend time over the heads of anyone who dared to challenge him, even though he had learned during his first journey that history could not be changed. He had not expected the Saxons to use his song the way they did—to destroy the present with the help of semi-demonic entities long banished from the earth.

"I went to confession every week, pouring out my heart to my brother and to God, pleading for His understanding. Did I not do these things for our people's good, to preserve the only known race God has blessed with mystical gifts? But it was not repentance, for true repentance requires change. I did not change."

Using one of Otto's spare tunics, I brushed the last bit of brambles from our stone nook as he reinforced the branches we had arranged to form our roof. The shelter was about eight paces from front to back and four from side to side, enough room to sleep comfortably and store our goods. I had to duck my head beneath the section where the rocks joined at the back, but that gave it a cozy ambiance. Now we just needed some firelight to chase the shades away.

"Then Muniche, and the Teuton kingdom as a whole, succumbed to the Empire as recompense for your dark sorcery." I stepped onto the sand before our shelter and shook out the tunic. The stream trickled along just six steps from the opening.

"I was not the sole Keyholder who dabbled with Wuotan's devices. Our combined hypocrisy was enough to bring divine wrath upon us all," Otto said from the collection of boulders above. Sweat glistened on his bare chest as he wove his tarp between the branches, his eyes catching hold of mine. "Our kingdom would have fallen eventually, but my machinations with time certainly brought it sooner."

A disquieting thought came to me as I draped his tunic over a branch beside the stream. "Maybe it would be better if Teutons breed with outsiders until our blood gets diluted enough to make us equal with normal humans. If our powers come from a demon . . . ." I let it hang.

"Many have argued toward that very thing since our people learned of God's gift to humankind. All of our written records attribute our magic to Wuotan. Thus, many Teutons have stifled their gifts and hidden away in monasteries and convents in an attempt at achieving deeper holiness."

"I take it you don't agree with that," I charged as I carried our bundles into our shelter. Otto was the same as every Teuton priest I had questioned. *We don't know the terms of our people's deal with Wuotan. If we use our magic for good, then we walk the path of light, where demons fear to tread.*

"I would, if our magic did indeed stem from Wuotan's dominion."

That brought me up short. Pausing with one foot inside our shelter, I tilted my head upward to meet my husband's gaze. "You think it doesn't?"

"I have reason to believe that our blood and the powers it contains courses from somewhere far purer than hell," Otto responded in a low voice. "But that is a discussion for our dream world, not here."

Once Otto finished with the roof for our shelter, he declared that we ought to dedicate the inside through a vivacious round of sex. Muniche's collective soul purred within my heart at such a prospect, and before I knew what I was doing, I started yanking his trousers to the ground. Thank goodness he had discarded his tunic while he worked. He ended up taking me from beneath my skirt, seductive growls rumbling in his chest as he clutched me against him, his fingers tangling themselves tightly in my hair.

By the time we finished, our blankets were a wreck, and some of the seams in my dress had loosened. But I could get used to such passion, for my icy spirit welcomed the seething heat of Otto's red fire. Whether we figured out how to break Wuotan's hold on our city or not, at least my youthful hormones were appeased.

That's not enough, I rebuked myself as we went back outside to prepare our dinner. *We have to undo Otto's blood curse for the sake of our people's future.*

That evening, as we sat outside our shelter beneath the lowering sky, eating the stew that simmered upon a new batch of coals, my Keyholder told me that he felt responsible for the path I had taken that led to my heartbreak. "If I had never colluded with Wuotan to reveal a portal through time, your heart would have beat for Hans Meissner alone, never falling prey to lesser men."

I stared at Otto, where he sat cross-legged before the embers, eating straight from the kettle. Did he really mean to imply that my heart would have been better off yearning for an old man who wanted my mother? "Think that if you must, but I'm grateful for the years I spent with Augustin, the one man who loves me without reservations. He loved me before and after I became *Leitalra*. In my experience, chosen love is more intense than anything fate can cough up."

Smoldering flames reflected off of my companion's eyes as he gazed into the embers. "If that is the only sort of love that would free Muniche . . . ." He chewed on a bite of stew, looking contemplative.

"Whether our death destroys Wuotan's hold on our city or not, the one thing that bothers me the most is that Augustin still hasn't turned from evil," I admitted. I recognized that the eternal fate of one man seemed insignificant in light of our city's imprisoned spirit, but I pushed aside Muniche's agitation within my heart.

"I tried to tell him more than once, during our weeks together. It's still possible for a Cursed One to accept God's grace. My son did it, and so did his predecessor. But Augustin changed the subject whenever I brought it up. He's convinced himself that Wuotan will torture him if he walks the path of light, but I *know* otherwise. I've prayed so hard for him, and it's like I'm shouting into a void."

I grumbled and took a giant bite of squirrel and carrot, trying to cling to that fading hope that had carried me throughout a lonely life without him. Otto's next statement was not encouraging; in fact, it grated on my patience. "Sometimes God answers prayers with a no rather than a yes."

Incensed, I swallowed a bite and narrowed my eyes at my Keyholder. "I'm well aware that sometimes God says no. I prayed for my brother to be healed, and He said no. I prayed for Freya to come home. He said no."

Otto's shoulders drooped, and he ran his hands through his hair, his eyelids squeezed shut. "It is difficult . . . so difficult . . . to find peace when divine plans do not match our own."

His sorrow struck me through our bond, a gloom that far outweighed what guilt I had sensed in him due to his own sins or Muniche's destruction. My intuition told me that he mourned his chosen love now. Had Otto begged God to spare Kezia and their children from the Romans? "When did God tell you no?" I asked.

My husband reopened his eyes to stare into the embers again. "Long ago, I told you that I had traveled time thrice, and that the third time was for personal reasons." I nodded when he glanced at me, for I remembered that well. During his first journey to the past, he had spread the news of Christ's resurrection alongside his brother Paulus and his wife Kezia. Then the Romans crucified his wife and three children while he and Paulus were away in another town.

I always assumed Otto took a brief trip back to share a quickie with his cherished wife. But the tale he related that evening mortified me.

"When I led my army home the winter after Paulus was taken, I fell into a deep despair that prompted me to question my entire life's path. Maybe I did not deserve to hold Muniche's keys. Maybe our city should be in the hands of a righteous man, not one who colluded with dark forces. My wife here did not love me; I had no children, no legacy. So I played the Song of Time during a heavy blizzard and fled alone to my family.

"The evening when Paulus and I returned to our home to find my wife and children hung outside upon crosses is a blur in my memory, for I could not control the grief and rage that rent me asunder. But I recall seeing an empty cross right beside the one where Kezia's body hung. Ropes wound around its beams, discharge sullying the ground beneath. But the cross itself was empty.

"So I chose, in my infinite despair, to mount that cross myself. I returned to my first century home for the sole purpose of holding my loved ones close before dying at their sides. And I died, the last of us, gasping, gasping out for God's mercy, to permit me to enter heaven with Kezia and our sons and daughter. To spare me from having to return to this place where I would never feel the glories of devoted love pulsing through my spirit . . . where my soul must walk alone."

Bitter anguish creased his face as he raised his eyes to mine with a glare that seemed to come from the abyss. "And God said *no*."

I breathed shallowly, my fated master's resentment enshrouding me in a ponderous cloud. The first words that left my lips exposed the wretched truth. "You haven't forgiven God for that."

Chapter Twenty-two:
The Gatekeeper

Dreams became our escape throughout our days together, the serenity inherent in that realm releasing us from Wuotan's oppression. Even though Otto and I made a habit of praying for divine protection and wisdom each morning, the demon continued to invade our solitude, threatening to drag every future *Leitalra* of Muniche to the depths unless my husband offered his life to the Cursed One. I suspected this was Wuotan's climactic attempt to bind Augustin into slavery. If Otto took his own life, Augustin would never lose control over the death inside of him, so he would never be forced to hide away from humanity.

Therefore, I insisted that Otto and I pass our time south of our shelter, not straying toward where the Black Priest's cottage lay. Hopefully Augustin had gone to seek a feasible way to restore our relationship—perhaps from that chronicler he met at the abbey west of Innsbruck. But we gave his territory a wide berth, though his demon lord sought to lead us straight toward him.

Otto believed that he had no authority to judge God's providence, as a mere human being; therefore he could not "forgive" God's failure to allow him to die with his first century family. I argued that he ought to make peace with that inside his heart before he ended his life, since it was unhealthy to harbor bitterness at the brink of eternity. Wrong or not, my elderly mentor Bertha Lohr had urged me to forgive even the worst harms, so I enjoined Otto to do the same.

That issue was a sensitive topic for him. He agreed to compromise on many things, but preferred to hold that burden close to his heart. When I implored Otto to forgive, he asked harshly whether I would pardon God if He gave up on Augustin. I could not answer that question, although I knew deep down that if my chosen love descended to hell, I would beg God to damn me with him. It appeared that each of us would carry our personal afflictions to the grave and beyond.

Otto's story of why he believed that Teutonic magic stemmed from a source more celestial than devilish prompted me to rethink many of my opinions. Our spirits floated over the Rhine's waters as a rainstorm passed through them, inspiring my ice to celebrate while my husband noted that his fire felt uncomfortable. I pointed out that we could always rise above the clouds beyond the rain, but he said that our current venue was apt for the story he had to tell.

That night, I learned that the Bayern family had fallen under an affliction after Lady Maria took Marelda's place. Although Otto's father, Prince Ulrich, already had three healthy sons, he longed for more. He had experienced the city bond with an older matron in his younger years—similar to Hans' situation with Bertha Lohr—and intended to have as many children as possible with the fertile maidens our city chose after his first *Leitalra's* death.

Lady Maria's body remained barren for the first four years of their marriage. When Otto was five, she gave birth to a daughter who passed away after only two months of life. She bore two stillborn sons and miscarried a third, her misfortunes prompting her to evince a cynical character. She was certain the Bayern line was cursed, for her two sisters had seven children between them. Shortly before he sent Augustin away for schooling, Prince Ulrich took Otto along on a furtive journey to a lakeside hut south of Muniche—the abode of a forest witch.

Our people tended to distrust true witches, the type who lived in union with nature and cast spells unknown to Teuton priests. Whether those sorts of women existed in the modern era, I knew not; as Lady Muniche, my experience had been confined to what could be found in the records and whatever the priests agreed to share. Long ago, I had read that witches could summon arcane spirits to protect Teuton women in childbirth. That was as far as my knowledge went.

Otto's father asked the witch for guidance regarding his Lady's failures to achieve motherhood, whether anything could be done to help her. The witch had taken his father into an attached chamber, where she invoked wisdom from beings beyond mortal reach. Otto did not witness the summoning himself, for his father relegated him to a nook in the witch's parlor, where he befriended a brown tabby cat. Upon their departure, Prince Ulrich's mien appeared stricken, and he sent Augustin away shortly after their return home.

"My father told me that my *brother*"—Otto spoke the word as though it were a curse itself—"had connived with the demon lord to ensure Lady Maria would not bear viable heirs for our family. He never accepted the mystical bond of the keys, how they pulled Prince Ulrich to his new *Leitalra* so soon after Marelda died. The forest witch knew not how to undo the curse my brother had wrought, so my father sent him away in hopes distance would do what magic could not. His hope proved unfounded, for her womb returned to its barrenness."

"Wait," I interrupted my husband as the rain froze into intricate sparkles upon my icy robe. "Augustin was four when Marelda died. He told me he turned away from goodness at age five. How could he have wrought such a curse when he was only *five?*" I held up five fingers for emphasis.

"He has always been gifted, intellectual, and shrewd," Otto responded, his glistening visage reflecting pain. "Lady

Maria told me much later that she had a lighter miscarriage the day before my brother emerged from Marelda's chapel. She did not tell my father of that one, but she knew who to blame for her trouble."

I ran my fingers through my ethereal hair, unhappy with the direction of our conversation. "So this forest witch couldn't help your father because the curse was something demonic. How does that factor into your belief that Teuton blood doesn't come from Wuotan?" I inquired.

"I returned to her later, alone, not long after Paulus and I took our first trip to the past," Otto explained. "I brought several gifts for her, for I desired to learn at least a portion of her ways, that I might not fall utterly into Wuotan's deceits. My father said she drew her power from heaven and spirits with no connection to hell's legions, and I had no other recourse. I had prostrated myself before the demon to earn the robe of the Teuton priest, so I knew my peers could not help.

"She had grown quite old by then, and while she accepted my gifts, she told me that she could not share her methods with one who walked the dark path. If I had come to her in my youth, she could have instructed me to the point where I would never have thought to bow to a demon. 'You have followed social pressure to walk the path of the thief,' she said.

"'The thief?' I asked, and she told me that our magic comes from a source beyond Wuotan's lair, that the demon stole it millennia ago and granted it to our people to make us a scourge against divine intentions. She said that one needed only to commune with the spirits of nature to understand that all mystic gifts come from God, but how we choose to use them determines our own destinies. Before I left her in peace, she deigned to teach me a single invocation that has served me well over the years, one that may help us free Muniche's soul."

I ogled him when he fell silent, his statements churning in my brain like the Rhine's currents. A weight I did not realize I had carried rose from my heart at the notion that Teutonic magic may *not* be demonic after all. But could we trust a long dead forest witch to tell the truth? "How can you be sure she wasn't just repeating a legend?" I asked him.

A satisfied smile curled across Otto's face as he replied, "Because the spirit of the Isar confirmed it, as did the spirit of the Danube."

My jaw dropped, though no sound escaped in our dream world. "You've . . . *talked* . . . to the river spirits? They *exist?*"

My gaze shifted from his face to the choppy waters of the Rhine beneath where we hovered. Recollections of my dance upon the Leutascher Ache before I discovered the Torstein flooded my brain, the certainty I had felt that other spirits danced along with me. I had imagined them to be the *Eihalbae*—silver oak fairies whose trees liberally populated that forest. Maybe the Leutascher Ache *itself* had gamboled with the ice maiden.

"If any entity can give us guidance in our final days, I believe the Rhine would be a fair place to start," my husband said.

But of course, our desires for a simple solution proved unfounded. The next morning, Otto taught me the spell required to call a river spirit, patiently coaching me until I had the incantation and elemental symbols memorized. Although Otto assured me that we had cast our spells correctly, the Rhine did not respond at all, not even with an unusual ripple of water.

"Maybe the Rhine's spirit doesn't feel obliged to answer Teutons," I mused as my husband sat back on his heels upon the bank, his countenance discouraged. "This isn't our people's territory, after all."

"Or maybe God wishes to tell us no, that nothing we do can revoke Wuotan's authority over our city." Otto's jaw clenched, and he beat upon the earth with his right fist. "If only that devil had not wiped those final lines from my memory . . . then we could fly to the nearest abbey, and I could repair the damage my rashness inflicted upon your heart."

Raising my eyebrows at my Keyholder, I kept my distance for fear that his frustration might drive him to injure me along with the earth. "How exactly would that fix anything? The past can't be changed, only observed. You know that."

"There must be something . . . *something*." Otto rubbed dirt into his hair.

But a method to release Muniche from Wuotan's hold— or to free my heart from Muniche's grasp—eluded us as the days passed. We continued to share our hearts with each other in our dreams and bind our bodies and spirits daily in the throes of passion, but Wuotan continued to graze his claws through my heart, a pointed reminder of Muniche's place. Shackled beneath his influence.

No matter how much respect and gentleness I offered him, Otto seemed to withdraw further into himself as the lines of Ashima's curse vanished from around my navel one by one. He cried out to the Rhine's spirit every morning with no response, and my thoughts returned to that letter Augustin had written with the instruction, *Open on the final day.*

How was I to do that when I had to keep a close eye on Otto's ravings? What could my Black Priest possibly offer me now? If love was the magic that could break Muniche's essence away from her demon overlord, she would remain bound after Otto and I passed on; for though I tried, I could not force myself to love him. Offer him deference and comfort, sex and forgiveness . . . but love? My free will had no capacity to fabricate that sort of fidelity where it did not exist.

Maybe Augustin was correct. Maybe death was the only way to free the city and free my own soul. *Thus, Muniche's Keyholder and Lady were both dead, reflecting the unfortunate fate of that grand Teuton stronghold that lies as rubble along the Isar, awaiting life again.* That was what Augustin wrote in his official encyclopedia, and my reason gradually accepted that there was no alternative. Otto and I must die and pass Muniche's legacy on to others. Her soul was to be reborn in the next century, and Wuotan would claim no power over her fortune then.

On the morning of our eighth day together, a peculiar strain escalated in our spiritual dream world. Otto and I had discussed Augustin extensively that night, how my influence had reawakened honor and goodness in him over time. My love had challenged him to rethink his bleak view on the world, and Otto admitted that the man he saw in my blood memories must share some similarities with the young Prince that Marelda adored, the child to whom she spoke her last words.

By the time dawn's earliest rays lightened the summer sky, my Keyholder's spirit radiated obvious despair. He refused to share his grief with me, but instead left me alone as a dreaming spirit, promising to awaken me after the sun rose. For a while, I drifted in private along our stream, reminiscing on the hours I had shared with Augustin, the priest who had offered me a love beyond anything my fated masters had granted.

Otto's love burned bright for Kezia and their children, not for me, not even for Muniche. He knew he could never match what the Cursed One had provided for me . . . and for Muniche. Only five *Toteheri* remained, and they had fled to the tundra. Augustin extended his skills to preserve my family and Freia's—Muniche's children. His commitment to me superseded the constructs of fate.

I sent my spirit into the atmosphere after I returned to our shelter and found Otto's body gone, my own curved comfortably on my left side with Augustin's deep blue blanket cast over my nakedness. Our kettle stood empty upon cold ashes, so my husband was not in the process of preparing a meal. His chestnut mare snoozed peacefully beside what remained of her hay, so he must not have gone far. I thought I detected something akin to mad desperation pulsing through our bond, so it was time to seek him out. The sun had already cleared the horizon.

Once above the tree line, I turned my gaze toward the Rhine, startled at the sight of a watery plume rising from its eastern bank. Had Otto finally succeeded in his attempts to invoke the mighty river's spirit? Curiosity welled within me, and I allowed my spirit to drift forward with the breeze, situating myself amid the upper branches of a linden as I watched the unfolding tête-à-tête with wide eyes.

Otto crouched with his limbs in the shallows, his hair damp but steaming, his body completely nude. Wild red flames flared in his irises as he stared at the entity before him—a humanoid form comprised of silvery water, its crowned head poised at least five meters into the sky. Its eyes caught the glittering light of dawn, its fingers sporting what seemed to be amphibious webs. The currents that swirled upon its chest revealed brawny pectorals that set my heartbeat racing. The Rhine was male. Of course I knew that.

And his watery spirit crooned wordlessly to my ice, which began to create artistic flakes all over my robes.

"There is no way my *Leitalra* and I can manage that," Otto choked out in a voice that sounded far from his own, his chest heaving as he gazed at the towering spirit. "My heart would not allow it . . . and neither would hers!"

Then you know what must be done, Leitaeri. The Rhine's voice eased into my brain like a sultry tonic, and my ice started to shed traces that fell to the ground. Had I missed *this* all this time, not learning how to speak with the rivers? But the Isar—the dearest one to me—was female. Had she made love to Otto in spiritual fashion whenever he invoked her presence?

"It is not enough," Otto groaned, running muddied hands through his hair. "My *Leitalra* and I are cursed by a demoness. We must die three days from now. Muniche's burden must soon pass to someone else, someone inno-cent of this spell that cages us in darkness!"

Your path lies ahead. I advise you to relinquish your fixation upon the past and allow another to guard the keys to time's abyss.

The river surged over Otto's body, drenching him and nearly snuffing his fire. But I saw crimson magic tighten-ing in a sphere upon the waters between his hands. I saw them shaping something out of the mud, his lips forming words I could not discern over his creation. The Rhine's spirit watched him work, droplets showering down from his crown.

My heart continued to seethe with craving, and I wished I was in true spirit form, so the river could see me, see how vibrantly my element preened for him. My icy attire looked more spectacular now than I had ever seen it. Otto needed to hurry with his sorcery and awaken me, so I could run here and invite this magnificent river to dance.

"Help me. Please!" Otto wheezed, gazing up at the river spirit with crazed eyes. "I want this gateway to have no connection to him!"

We have already made sure of that. You have blasted it with your heat. Now it needs your Leitalra's *cold.*

I thought I detected a hint of amusement in the river's tone, but before I could react, my physical body launched itself upright in our shelter, the deep blue blanket falling gently around my waist. My element already chilled my blood and sharpened my vision. Without further ado, I sprang to my feet and leapt for the stream, following its trickling path to the Rhine. Ice propelled my bare feet onward, and shining claws extended from my fingers and toes.

I did not think to put on a dress first.

My heart raced in exultation as I dashed into the river, summoning a frozen wave to thrust me toward where my Keyholder and his watery companion waited. The Rhine's eyes glistered with what appeared to be delight, as I nearly ran smack into his waterspout. But his large, webbed hand stretched forth to catch my waist, the water's freshness reinforcing my element's verve. *I believe we have danced before,* Leitalra, the river greeted.

He spun my body in a whirl, which I transformed into an elegant pirouette, my heart pounding visibly above my left breast. The spirit smiled at me, steadying my torso before the currents beneath my toes swept me toward Otto. He crouched in the shallows with the scarlet sphere ablaze between his hands, his head cocked in an absurd fashion. "Would you prefer to become a river yourself, I wonder?"

I chortled, all thoughts of our anxiety in the dream world forgotten. "I think I'm supposed to be a human, unfortunately." I halted by his side, digging my toes into the riverbed, and turned to regard our gigantic acquaintance. "Thank you kindly for answering my *Leitaeri's* call, my lord," I said in full propriety.

Only rarely do I heed the whims of humanity, for my experience is ever shifting, ever renewed, the Rhine told me, his crown sprinkling me with a fresh set of dewdrops, which my ice welcomed and promptly froze. *Your* Leitaeri *seeks my counsel on a wise gatekeeper to protect time's portal, and we both agree that the gatekeeper is you.*

Shivers cooled my body further from the inside out, and my eyes widened at the imposing being before me. "But . . . I . . . have to die."

The Rhine winked one enormous eye and said, *Time and tide wait for none but the dead.*

A strange sensation contracted my throat as my thoughts raced back to that mysterious Black Priest from the twenty-first century, the one I met only once. He had said the exact same thing before rescuing me from certain death. Had he talked to the Rhine River at some point during his death, or was that a truism all rivers liked to recite? I could not ask the towering spirit, for this river was hardly the same as the modern day Rhine. His waters were ever shifting, never constant.

So instead I focused on the magic simmering in my Keyholder's hands, my forehead wrinkling as I saw that the sphere had shrunk considerably. It appeared that Otto held a thumb-sized clot of blood and dirt in his right palm, misshapen and viscous, oozing into the creases of his skin. Otto looked down at it, then up at me, for he still crouched, while I stood. And the truth became clear in my mind as I stared at his creation, steaming and emanating magic. "Is that—"

"It awaits the mystic ice of Muniche's greatest *Leitalra*, to shape it into a perpetual gateway to the past, to serve as an instructor of those things which cannot be understood any other way." Teutonica flowed in a spell from his lips.

Why had I not realized Otto would create the Torstein during our ten-day holiday . . . and why had I not imagined that *I* would play a role in its design? I closed my eyes for a second and shook my head, trying to concentrate on my ice, to extend it from the index finger of my right hand as I reached out to touch that blood-red amulet. Opening my eyes, I watched the orb coalesce into stone, shining a dark ruby in the early morning sunlight.

The privilege of gatekeeper has fallen upon you, Lei-talra, the Rhine stated, his solemnity cautioning my spirit. *Use it wisely.*

Chapter Twenty-three

Eternity's Threshold

"Every time I think I've got things figured out, some Teuton priest has to totally upend reality," I complained to my husband when we returned to our shelter. We had bathed thoroughly in the Rhine's waters after the river's spirit left us in peace. Innumerable questions boggled my mind about the Rhine, the Isar, the tiny stream on Thaden property in the twenty-first century . . . the entirety of nature in general. Did every mountain, valley, lake, tree, blade of grass harbor a spirit—a distinctive manifestation of the life inherent in all of creation?

"Even priests cannot fathom the whole of heaven, earth, and all realms in between," Otto said with a chuckle, his right hand lightly gripping my left as we made our way through the brush. I had the Torstein clutched in my free hand, its potential prickling at my blood. "From my experience, humans have a very limited outlook."

"I'm just wondering if the Isar and the Danube seduced your element the way the Rhine did to mine," I mused, skirting a patch of briars. "Most German rivers are female. Did our ancestors figure that out because they invoked each spirit first to see how they exhibited themselves?"

"That is likely the case. I must admit the Rhine intimidated me. I had never conversed with a male river before." Otto stooped under a low-hanging birch branch before appending, "And no, neither the Isar nor the Danube enticed my fire the way the Rhine's waters did to your ice." He raised an eyebrow at me.

"The Rhine made me want to screw him," I confessed, blushing.

The Prince gave a hearty laugh and smacked my bare ass playfully. "Pardon me while I check the snares, lovely courtesan. I am famished after expending my magic in such a way." Otto snagged a set of trousers from just inside the entrance to our alcove, tugging them into place before setting off into the forest. He patted his horse's nose as he passed by where she stood in the pine grove. She neighed quietly and nudged his fingers.

I set the Torstein inside our shelter in the center of my neck pillow, its ruby glimmer standing out against the faded cover of my Bible. My eyes kept straying toward the stone as I clad myself in a plain linen frock. *It's honestly a little late for Otto to give me that, and to expect me to take the position of gatekeeper,* I thought, my brow furrowing.

I glanced briefly at the two indents remaining on the edges of my navel before pulling the dress over my head. *The two of us are to die three nights from today. Unless Augustin pulls off a miracle, he'll be time's gatekeeper for the next four centuries, not me.*

The Rhine's spirit had instructed me to use the Torstein wisely. Not much of a chance left to do that now, was there? Part of me wished I could sneak off to Augustin's cabin at some point before my suicide, so I could tell him that this rock had no connection to Wuotan whatsoever. Prince Otto had created it with help from the river spirits, who claimed some sway over time since it also progressed like a river. But Augustin had written that the Torstein stemmed from dark devices, and I spent the majority of my life fearing that I owed Wuotan recompense.

I owed that demon nothing. Whatever debts I may have incurred during the blood-transfer had been squared long ago.

So why did he insist upon afflicting the city that lived within my heart?

We had eaten most of our initial provisions already, so our lunch consisted of the last of Augustin's goat cheese melted atop hare spread with acorns. I offered to do some foraging that day, while Otto remarked that he needed to build a raft for us to use when we cast our bodies into the Rhine. He rattled on for a while about lashing branches together with vines from the forest.

"Do you think the Rhine will be offended when we . . . commit suicide in his waters?" I asked when my husband paused to concentrate on his food. He raised his dark blue eyes to mine as I said, "I read a fiction book in my time where a man who fought in a really awful war came home to find his wife had cheated on him, so he tried to drown himself in the Elbe. But the Elbe vomited him back out and said he wasn't finished yet."

"The Rhine knows our intentions, Swanie," Otto answered, but I detected a glint of uncertainty in his eyes.

"I'm really starting to question what Augustin's record claims I did," I went on, pushing what remained of my meat around the skillet with my fork. Otto had already finished, but my ruminations troubled me. "If the Rhine believes I'm meant to be the gatekeeper of time's portal . . . or did he mean I'm supposed to pass the Torstein on to Augustin, since he's a Black Priest?"

"If you refuse to let me fix your past and are unwilling to do it yourself, perhaps your Cursed One will pry the Torstein from your corpse and find his own subtle way of altering your destiny." Otto left me beside the campfire and ducked into our shelter, emerging a moment later with the Torstein in his left hand and the chain that held his golden medallion in the other.

Returning to my side, he presented the medallion to me and said, "This is the last of my royal jewelry, a remnant of a kingdom long past, similar to Marelda's sapphire." I had told him that Augustin had retaken the symbol of our marriage as a reminder of his vow to fight my fate. Had he made any progress?

"You can see that this pendant has an empty socket for a jewel, the ruby that matched my element," Otto said, as I studied the beaten gold in his palm. "I traded that long ago, but it seems that your stone of the gate could serve as an appropriate replacement." He set the Torstein into the medallion's center, and to my surprise, I heard it snap into place. A whiff of magic glistened around it as it settled into its new abode, and Otto hung the chain around my neck. "For Muniche's *Leitalra*."

My Keyholder shaped our raft that day and finished it the next, while I spent my time foraging and reading my Bible in hopes of keeping Wuotan's torments at bay. He seemed to have backed off since our dialogue with the Rhine's spirit, yet I knew not to let down my guard. Dark claws continued to graze Muniche's soul from time to time, a wordless reminder of my place. It was a joy to lose myself in nature, harvesting field garlic, dandelion and salsify roots, wild raspberries and cherries, acorns and pine nuts, edible mushrooms.

On the tenth morning—our final morning—Otto and I reveled in passion's embrace when we awoke, my ice entwining with crimson fire in the realm beyond. My body seemed desperate to claim his one last time, Muniche's influence bringing ardent cries to my lips. It felt as if she knew what we intended to do that night and wished to enchant us into forgetting. But eventually we slipped away from each other and dressed, a morbid silence falling between us.

Otto and I discussed those we longed to meet in heaven while we savored the final prey from his snares, a dabbling duck. My Keyholder could hardly wait to embrace Kezia and their three children, along with his father and a variety of friends from days of old. Since I had no clue how things worked in eternity—whether I could reunite with my friends from the twenty-first century or whether I would have to wait a thousand years for them—I mentioned saints from this present era. Augustin's mother Marelda, my daughters Gloria and Bethany, the baby I had miscarried, Jarvis and Ulka, Count von Meldorf and his wife. Most of all, I longed to meet Marelda Swanhilde, the child Augustin and I had created together.

Though I would have liked to spend the entire day imagining eternal glories, Otto laid a hand upon my shoulder while I cleaned our utensils and skillet at the stream. When I tilted my head upward to meet his gaze, he said that he had to leave me for a few hours to complete one final duty. Retrieving Muniche's keys from the pocket of his trousers, he favored me with an apologetic smile. "I have to choose a successor for our desolate city."

"Are you sure about that?" I asked, rising to my feet and shaking the water off of the skillet. "I think once we die, Muniche's spirit should vanish completely, rendering the keys meaningless. Augustin's record didn't mention a successor for either you or me."

Otto looked troubled, and he turned away from me. "We cannot be certain, Swanie. I tried to burn the keys more than once during my exile, always without success. I simply assumed that Muniche will live on in spite of my failures."

"But the München I represented in the future is a separate entity from our city here," I pointed out.

"That may be true, but it is my duty as Muniche's *Leitaeri* to pass on my responsibility before death. If the keys crumble to dust after our suicide, so be it; but since we cannot be certain, I must complete this task." Otto smiled wanly at me and brushed his fingers against my cheek.

I trailed behind him when he headed for his horse, watching his hands untying the rope that secured her in the glade of pines. "Are you planning to look for your successor in Eisenwald? Because if so, you need to find another way to the main road . . . and avoid Augustin's cottage. Today is Wuotan's last chance to force him to kill you, so you need to stay far out of his reach." I gave him a pleading look.

My husband sighed as he swung himself atop his horse. "That will take time and effort, for the forests in this area are dense."

"Better than dying before your time, right?" I took hold of Otto's tunic and clung to it until he looked down at me. "Please don't think you're doing me a favor by asking him to kill you in order to free Muniche from Wuotan's grasp. Please. No matter what you do this afternoon, I have to die at dawn tomorrow. All of the lines around my navel have disappeared." I nodded toward his right hand, which held the reins. The rune carved into his wrist emanated a muted glow.

"I seek an honorable Teuton man to take charge of Muniche's keys. Nothing more," my husband pledged, though his eyes wandered fretfully. Something odd passed over his countenance, and he frowned down at me. "Do you plan to escape with your Cursed One during my absence, Swanie?"

Recoiling, I let go of his tunic and crossed my arms over my bodice. That very idea had occurred to me, a smoldering fire deep inside my heart that nothing could put out. But I masked my dark cravings and said, "Even if I go to him . . . and trust me, I'd like to . . . I don't think he has the power to break Ashima's curse. This youth will kill me tomorrow if I don't die with you."

"That sort of death would send you to the future. There is only one sure way a time traveler can enter eternity. The magic has been set in motion to ensure that." Otto eyed me seriously.

"Do you think I *ought* to run off with Augustin while you're giving the keys to some poor soul in Eisenwald?" I gawked at my Keyholder uncertainly. "Muniche still chains me in slavery, binding my free will."

Otto sighed and nodded, as though accepting my stance. "Promise me then that I will find you here upon my return. Promise me on the honor of Muniche."

Bowing my head, I locked myself into the fate Augustin had recorded. "I'll be here to die with you. I promise. Now go and pass your authority on to a young man who would wield it honorably."

"I shall discuss this with Heinrich and seek the Lord's help. Perhaps your youngest son could take up the duty." He blew me a kiss and turned away. "I will return by sunset to join you for our final act, *Leitalra*." Knocking his heels against his mare's sides, he departed into the forest.

His last statements prompted me to envision Johann, my youngest son who preferred to spend his days outdoors, hunting and gathering from the wild. He had only just learned that his father lived, and why. How would he react if Prince Otto von Bayern offered a dead city's keys to him? Had Joel told any of our children that their hometown would ultimately rise from the ashes to become the largest city in modern Bavaria?

Shaking my head, I carried our utensils and skillet into the shelter, unsure how to distract myself for an entire summer afternoon. I probably ought to read my Bible again or forage for more edibles so Otto and I could consume a last meal upon his return. Once inside our alcove, I looked around at the few possessions we had left. Our clothing and blankets, our crockery and cups, the last third of a bottle of cherry wine, the Bible and medallion, the empty leather bags.

No. My bag was not empty. An envelope lay at the bottom, sealed with my chosen love's wax and bearing the enigmatic inscription: *Open on the final day.* I had the chance now to read Augustin's letter in private, learn if it contained some mad solution I had not anticipated, some way for me to break Wuotan's hold on my city and rend Muniche's ties from my heart. Tenuous seeds of hope sprang to life within me, and I carried the letter to the stream, settling myself onto a smooth boulder as I broke the envelope's seal.

Two mottled parchments lay within. When I unfolded the first one, I gasped, vicious grief striking my heart. I saw my name written repeatedly in jagged script, interspersed with long and meaningless scribbles that could be construed as the pen's cries of agony. On the second page,

Ælte Teutonica flowed like a raging river, revealing Augustin's despair after he had broken our heart-bond.

I cannot survive this . . . so bleak . . . nothingness. How many times have I torn out my heart and screamed for it to stop, to let me die?! No use . . . no amount of blood or life can erase the memories . . . the pain . . . hopeless. I walk through hell without a heart, without a head, without myself . . . she was . . . she IS . . . without her, I am worthless, begging for death. Swanhilde, so precious, so loving . . . all annihilated . . . Muniche's punishment for my infidelity, my stupidity. Why did I scorn her? Damned fool I am . . . . She eliminated my one chance at hope, at salvation, at heaven, reparation for my mockery. 'Give them to the son you love.' WHY?! Muniche laughs, but Swanhilde persists beyond my reach, smothered, her candle reflecting a compulsory fate. How I long to undo that moment when I let go of her heart! Why did I surrender the fight? Why did I hand her over to that city, to forget me? Another chance, yes . . . then I would hold her tightly, never loosen my grip on her heart, keep her, love her, be everything she needs, her master, her husband, her Keyholder. Anything. Swanhilde, my love, how I long to recreate what we have forever lost . . . and if I can, darling, I would never forsake you, for our souls belong together. I love you. For all of eternity.

It took all of my control to refrain from racing into the forest, from throwing my ice in a wide net until I found that blue-fired priest and begged him to ravage me while my Keyholder was away. I wanted to do it, to spend my last afternoon with the man who really mattered, but my pledge to Otto held me back. If I went to Augustin now, I would stay, use the Torstein to return to my own time, and then leap back to spend my last years with my real lover, the one who wanted me even if I was Muniche, even if I was sick and weak.

Instead, I plodded back to the shelter and threw myself onto the blanket to weep my final tears for the man I had lost, the fate that had been shoved out of my grasp. When I felt nothing left but emptiness in my soul, a void that could never be filled, I dried my cheeks on my bodice, then ripped the dress off, replacing it with the one I had worn for my wedding with Otto. I ran my brush through my tangled hair and braided it, making myself presentable for heaven's gates.

Then I retrieved the envelope to stuff the parchments back inside, and a small slip of paper fell onto the blanket, one I had not noticed before. On it I found six words in Bayerisch, the language of *my* soul: *Nothing has changed. I love you.*

Tonight, I would forsake the man whose soul matched mine, abandon him for a reward I did not deserve. A hollow sob pealed from my chest, and I yearned to curl into a ball upon his plush blanket and weep until my Keyholder returned. But we needed something to eat for tonight's meal; wine alone would not suffice at eternity's threshold. So I crawled into the sunlight of late afternoon and struck out for the riverbank, prepared to seek more roots and greens.

As the resplendent sunset darkened into nightfall, I coaxed a collection of flames from the embers we had used to cook the duck at lunch. Setting Otto's kettle upon the coals, I tossed my harvest from that afternoon into its water—dandelion, field garlic, acorns, mushrooms, and a patch of wild chamomile I found near the river. We would be vegetarians in our final hours, although now that I knew every plant had a spirit, I recognized that no one could eat without inflicting death. *We kill and kill again, and glory in its taste,* I thought grimly when I heard Otto's horse approaching our campsite.

My husband came to the fireside and took up the cup of wine I had poured for him, sitting down with the fire between us. As he drank, I passed him the spoon, which he accepted without a word, proceeding to eat straight from the kettle like I did. Neither of us said anything in greeting.

I studied him covertly while I chewed on some acorns, glad for the darkness of night to hide my scrutiny. The natural flames alighted his face in an ever-changing glow, mirrored in his eyes, highlighting his coal-colored beard.

Agitated, his gaze darted from me to the kettle to the fire, then scoured the woods beyond our camp and the moonless sky overhead. His left hand shifted restlessly, and I saw that it plucked often at the pockets of his trousers, seeking something that could no longer be found.

"I did not bother to tie the horse," he said at length through a mouthful of stew. "Hopefully she will make her way to the village."

I thought about that for a moment, then replied, "Someone will probably clean up whatever we leave here." Both of us knew to whom I referred. His cabin was just under a kilometer downstream. Thank goodness Otto had taken the long route through the forest at my insistence. Despite his tension, he looked no worse for wear.

Otto complimented the stew after another pause, but offered no information on his escapades. I could sense the bareness of his heart whenever I focused upon our bond; but if he felt uncomfortable bringing that up, I had best not broach the subject. So I mused about my son Johann while we finished eating, wondering if he might leave Eisenwald to return to Bavaria when he grew older. He would live the longest out of all of my children, but not quite long enough to see Muniche's rebirth. Prince Johann, Keyholder of a fallen Teuton city.

My husband washed our dishes at the river when we deemed ourselves done with the stew. I sorted our possessions inside our shelter, rolling the blankets and arranging the packs in an orderly fashion. My hands closed on the medallion after I stuffed Augustin's envelope into the bottom of my pack, and I pulled it out to study it for a moment. Beaten gold, about five centimeters in diameter with pine cones etched around the center where the Torstein lay. I hung the chain around my neck, then located the stone knife Augustin had given me and secured it to the black ribbon at my waist.

We walked to the Rhine's bank together, Otto's left arm wrapped around my waist as our bare feet trod along the stream's bed. Every sensation of the summer night left its mark upon me, farewell gestures of the mortal world—a wispy breeze caressing my cheeks, the pebbled sand beneath my feet scratching at my toes, the scents of pines and dying embers tantalizing my nose. At the river, my husband hesitated for a moment before guiding me toward the raft, his gaze fixed upon the tree line beyond the Rhine.

"It is good that I am to die tonight," Otto murmured, a hint of pain tainting his tone. His beard brushed against my cheek as he kissed my right ear, his breath prompting the bits of ice that had entered my veins to recede, welcoming his ruddy fire. He released my waist and admitted with a sigh, "I could not remain here long after resigning Muniche's keys to another. Even though I still have you, I feel like I have lost part of my soul, taken the first step toward death."

I knew not what to say to that, for my heart sensed Muniche's presence, her spirit humming in satisfaction at the nearness of Otto's fire. The emptiness he felt did not touch me, as I had wallowed in a much darker place earlier that afternoon. Collecting food from nature had distracted me to some degree, yet a knot of anxiety had settled in my gut, refusing to dissipate.

I was about to commit ritual suicide, and I was not at peace.

After we climbed onto the raft, Otto observed, as he shoved it away from the bank, that God had granted him certainty about his destiny. "I spent more than an hour in prayer this afternoon, rooting out the iniquities I had cherished throughout my life, repenting of them at long last. I managed to do as you suggested, to forgive God for decreeing that I remain here while my family passed on."

That figured. Shame inundated me, for I had been too overcome by anguish connected with Augustin to rid my heart of its infinite shortcomings. I sat in the middle of the raft without speaking while Otto paddled us toward the center of the Rhine, searching my own heart, trying to decide whether I had forsaken all of my besetting sins. I tried to do it then, shutting my eyes to the world around me, focusing on the pleasant sounds of the river, bullfrogs, and nightingales breaking into my meditation.

Just one concern troubled my heart after I finished, polluting the serenity that encompassed my spirit through my Keyholder's influence. *Augustin watches us now, from somewhere along that darkened shore, prepared to write the next page of Teuton history,* I knew, unhappy at the thought. *If only he could come with me somehow. Then I'd be glad to die.*

I glanced toward the eastern bank when Otto stopped the raft near the midpoint of the river, but the night was too dark to discern anything aside from the crowns of trees. *But he's there, and I'm leaving him. This is not a peaceful night, no matter what my fated master believes.*

My brain seemed unwilling to comprehend my body's actions as I got to my feet, steadied by Otto's strong hands. My fingers mechanically removed the stone knife from my sash, winding themselves around its handle. I stared at the blade, the serrations near its hilt appearing so wicked now, yearning to taste my blood. Ice sprinkled my skin with a translucent shimmer, and clouds of frosty breath puffed like smoke from my quaking lips. *Augustin, you're running out of time.* My eyes darted toward the eastern bank again.

Had it not been for Otto's hand rubbing my back and his spiritual fingers instilling my heart with a peacefulness it endeavored to fight, I would have dropped the knife and sprinted across the surface of the river on the power of my element, throwing myself before Augustin and crying, pleading for another way, any other way. The tolling of a distant bell jolted me into some sense of reality, reverberating along the water from the church at Eisenwald, beyond the starry horizon. Sunday. Today was Sunday.

Otto's voice reached my ears. "It is Vigils now, dear Swanie. We should delay no longer."

The knot twisted in my gut as I drew a shuddering breath, trying to prepare myself, to hope that maybe Augustin could trail me to heaven's gates and summon me away. Had he not done something similar three times before, when the portal of time arose from the mist in an attempt to launch me back to the twenty-first century?

What about the time Günter tried to kill me in the Black Castle? I had *felt* the knives of death gouging my heart before Augustin bothered to arrive in power and glory. Maybe he relished the thrill of saving someone at the final instant. Maybe he thought dragging things out proved his authority to those who wielded the keys of life and death.

He would come for me and I would return to him. Even if he waited until heaven's infinity arose before me.

But my husband was ready to die, so I met his gaze, displaying a courage I did not feel. "May the soul of our city bloom again for future generations," I heard myself saying. What a trite, bizarre thing to blather now; I nearly rolled my eyes at myself. But Otto favored me with a satisfied smile.

Then we positioned ourselves facing opposite ends of the raft, intending to leap together, but in different directions. I raised the knife, ordering my hand not to quiver, biting my lip as I sliced it across my left wrist. The blade stung me almost as acutely as that familiar pain in my heart.

Gritting my teeth, I shifted the knife to my other hand, cutting my right wrist before I had time to reconsider. As the blade tore my flesh asunder, I glimpsed the rune Augustin had carved below my thumb. It signified life, he had said.

Not anymore.

The coarse scent of blood polluted the tranquility of the night. I could feel it pouring into my palms, between my fingers, splattering the branches beneath my feet. My self-preservation instinct struggled with my reason as my Teutonic magic fought to seal my wounds, but I ordered my blood to flow uninterrupted. I closed the fingers of my right hand around the handle of the knife again, preparing for the finale. Focusing on the stars, I ordered myself to be happy, to be ready. I raised the stone blade to my throat, its blade damp against my skin.

My Keyholder murmured, "I love you, Swanie. I will meet you at the gates."

. . . But in spite of my attempts at quietude, my voice croaked out a sentence in my native dialect, a promise sputtered from my bleeding heart, one last gasp of weakened lips sinking into a watery grave: *"I'm still waiting."*

~*~

When it comes to storytelling, there are some tales that cannot be suitably related by one who was not present for the event . . . and with an event so significant, I can hardly attempt to do it justice myself. Therefore, I turn the next sheaf of pages over to that chronicler who shakes his finger at me now, insisting that he may find it challenging to recount the tale in English.

Excursus

**Composed in English by Wolfgang W. Wolfe,
once known as Augustin Abelard Ulrich von
Bayern**

As the sun ascended to the height of the heavens on that tenth day, the Black Priest scarcely gave a thought to nature's radiance, so consumed was he with his absolute failure. Frustration blurred his perfect vision; his eyes glowed a boiling cerulean as he stared unseeingly before him, at his fire pit. Numerous birds warbled in the trees surrounding his dwelling, nestled deep into the gnarled branches and vines on the edges of the Black Forest. Summer insects murmured their own songs as they flew about the few wildflowers that graced his thicket. Several chickens pecked at weeds along the forest's edge, relishing their holiday apart from the pen.

Had that day not been the tenth day—the final day, his last and only chance—the cursed priest may have laid aside his melancholy and allowed himself to admire the season's perfection. Unfortunately, yet not unexpectedly, he had not found the solution to his predicament, tried as he had. He knew that the end of this day would kill his soul, though not his body. Dejection had taken hold of him permanently now, his mind tense with the inevitability of his impending torment, his blinded eyes fixated on the blue fire flickering in his pit.

This was the end. He had known it would come.

Why then must he continue to exist, to wallow evermore in lamentation for his deserved retribution? He had died once before and could not die again until another cursed priest took his place. That would not occur for centuries, he knew, with the Teuton kingdom in shambles. What few Teutons remained after the Saxon conquest would be compelled to higher planes of loyalty than ever before, a fidelity that some in his time had never comprehended. None would dare to curse a child, a brother; the very method may have been lost in the invasion, burned to ashes, unrecognizable. He would be forgotten with no comfort attainable on earth. His pain would never cease, for he had not been able to solve the enigma of Swanhilde Rolande von Thaden, the Lady of Muniche.

Muniche had chosen her eight years prior, tying her with an unbreakable cord to that city—that fallen city, that cursed city. Never, the Black Priest knew now, would anyone discern a way to dissolve that connection. It would remain with Swanhilde *ad infinitum*, until the soul of that desolate city selected its next victim, another woman. Swanhilde could not have refused Muniche's bonds, and tonight she would die with them and her Keyholder, the man whom Muniche's bonds had forced her to love. She had never loved that man before Muniche sank her claws into her heart. The Black Priest knew that for a fact, for he had seen it in her blood. Swanhilde no longer had a free will. Muniche's grasp on her heart had ruined her, dragged her into delusions from which she could not escape.

Eight years earlier, the cursed priest had held her heart himself. Suddenly, on the day the city had succumbed, he had sensed a new opponent waging war with his protective grip. Muniche had seeped into her mind and soul, breaking her away from his influence, drawing her instead toward that very city which had cast him out. Ultimately he had released her, coming to the dismal realization that he could no longer satisfy her. Swanhilde would never belong to him again.

He had loved her. On this tenth day, as he sat wraith-like before his fire, he still loved her; and that love had begun to eat what ragged shards remained of his own heart out from the inside. He had loved one other woman long decades ago—Marelda, the woman who was once his mother. Her agonizing death had set him upon the dark path he had trodden ever since. Tonight, Swanhilde would die in the waters of the Rhine, just steps away from his dwelling. What would her death do to him? Inasmuch as he had loved Marelda, she could not hold even a faltering candle to Swanhilde. The icy swan princess had accomplished a feat that no other woman could ever achieve—she had taken him for her own, trapped him with her seductive goodness, caused him to forget his lot, forget his lust for death, forget his evil . . . even for a moment.

The Black Priest had run out of time.

For eight years, and especially during the past ten days, he had sought the knowledge no man had ever possessed. He had attempted desperately, frantically, to uncover the mystery behind the hold a Teuton city could achieve upon the heart of a woman. Before she had left him to embark on her ten-day honeymoon with her Keyholder, he had promised that he would seek the truth of that unmatched hold. He had vowed a solemn vow that if he could unearth a way to loose her chains, he would tell her so before she committed ritual suicide with the Keyholder.

He had clearly observed the hesitation in her eyes when she considered this possibility. Muniche had driven her mad, veiling her mind, making her believe that she would not want to break her chains. She had told him that according to the histories, she had come to die, nothing more. Nevertheless, she had promised to hope, even when she drew her final breath, wishing that he could yet determine a feasible method to mend their broken relationship.

Her insistence upon clinging to such an impossible hope soothed the Black Priest in some inexplicable way, for he had seen the conflict in her blood as though it had been his own. He felt confident that once Muniche's grasp on her heart had been broken, she would love him freely and completely, as she once had. He had made one final oath which he intended to keep if all others failed: *He would not interfere with her death unless he had found a way for them to be together.*

As the sun crawled across the sky, the Black Priest felt the lugubrious weight of despair descend upon his shoulders with its awful truth. He would not be able to help her this time. Instead, he would have to watch her die.

Everything good inside him would die with her. He had no more will to fight Wuotan, not without Swanhilde. Even if God Almighty offered to grant him superhuman strength to counter that traitorous demon, the Black Priest would have no interest in such futile victories once she had left this world. He would never sleep again. For every minute that he must remain on earth, he would seek his own death. He could not exist without her.

Sporadic tears trickled from his sightless eyes while he stared at the fire, all thoughts and reason having left him. Ten days, and she could not spend them with him, buoyantly whirling together in dalliance and joy one final time. Muniche had enslaved her, insisted that she spend her final hours married to that Keyholder—the one who had cursed him. He could never have her again. He had once laid eyes upon the gates of hell, but the awareness of his failure and its resultant torment punished him even more severely. *Damnatio aeterna.*

The sundial, situated amongst the bilberry bushes, reflected the approach of evening when the Black Priest heard twigs snapping in the forest not far from his dwelling. Someone had come to disturb his concentration, and the cobalt fire within him identified his unwanted companion almost as swiftly as his ears caught the sound of footsteps. His black heart hardened into iron, and he grudgingly forced himself to forgo his reverie, to return to the present circumstances until he could frighten away the intruder.

It was Prince Otto Eduard Hildebrand von Bayern; he could distinguish that wretched ruddy fire anywhere. That abominable Keyholder of Muniche, the one who had cursed him nearly thirty years earlier. Swanhilde did not accompany him; he discerned that immediately. Perturbation seized his soul as he rose to face his opponent, his blue fire flaring brightly in the pit. Wuotan's ominous voice crawled into the Black Priest's brain, the demon's presence also unwelcome. *He comes to you, just as I have foretold.*

The Black Priest endeavored to disregard the demon's warning as he looked toward the trees through which that bastard Prince emerged, alone, having left his chestnut horse somewhere in the woodland. The Prince looked far younger now than he had twelve days ago, when he had first encroached upon the Cursed One and Swanhilde in their transient bliss. He had come to die then, maddened and humiliated by the destruction of Muniche and the scattering of his army.

In her delusion induced by Muniche's chains, Swanhilde had convinced the Prince instead to marry her, the *Leitalra* of his city, for one last interval of glory before committing suicide together. The Prince had agreed, and the Black Priest, reinforcing his own condemnation, had officiated their wedding. He had not expected to see either of them again after they rode away on the Prince's horse ten nights prior. Now Prince Otto had reappeared, his face haggard, though his eyes shone with the release he had attained in the past ten days with the Lady of his city. The Black Priest hated him, for he had everything the priest could never have.

The Prince glanced briefly at the chicken wandering near the trellis that supported the Black Priest's grapevines. Then his eyes met the wraith's, and he nodded a greeting. "Wolfgang."

The priest stood still, attired wholly in black with a Gothic cross hanging on a chain from his neck, his arms folded beneath his outer cape. His eyes gleamed blue with more than just the fading daylight as he nodded curtly at the interloper. "Prince Otto." His voice was neutral, absent of feeling. "And why have you come to disturb me?"

The Prince studied the Black Priest for a long moment, then chose to waste time with trivialities. "You think I should be with her."

A touch of restrained emotion tainted the priest's reply. "Of course you should be with her. This is your last day." If it had been his last day with Swanhilde, he never would have left her side. On the day the Prince had come to extirpate their happiness, he had not parted from her except when he had to properly prepare for the wedding.

A hint of sheepishness crossed the Prince's face at his opponent's words, and he cast his gaze toward the Rhine, downstream in the direction of Eisenwald. "I had to visit Eisenwald today to pass the keys on to someone else." He appeared slightly bereft as he spoke, his expression downcast.

A derisive yet tragic smile emerged on the Black Priest's face. He knew that several families of Teuton children—five of them Swanhilde's children, in fact—lived at Eisenwald with the Rhine people. He knew each of the single young men, though none would associate with him, the Cursed One. Each of the youths boasted strong Teuton blood, but they were yet immature, innocent.

"So, into which of the poor babes' hands did you thrust those keys, with their abhorrent responsibilities?" In spite of the hardness of his heart, the Black Priest felt a brief pang of sympathy for whichever child the Prince had chosen.

The Prince looked his adversary straight in the eye and replied succinctly, "None of them."

At first, the Black Priest could not fathom the meaning of the Prince's statement. None of them. Why then had he gone to Eisenwald in the first place? Did he intend to keep the keys himself, in death? Then the realization struck him hard, and he took a step back, the flames in his pit blazing higher. *He would not have come here . . . .*

"*What* are you suggesting?" he roared, anger overtaking him.

The Prince's eyes flamed a deep scarlet, doubtless in response to the wraith's outburst. "Before I speak any of my 'suggestions,'" he began, vehemence creeping into his tone also, "I must ask you to do something for me."

An inimical smirk cracked the wraith's face in two, and he shook his head in wonder and no little irritation. "You would dare to come here and ask favors of *me?*"

"You are the only person who holds the information I must have." A challenge exuded from the Prince's rufescent gaze as he held the priest's eyes with his own. "I need to bleed you, Wolfgang."

The Black Priest recoiled again when his opponent revealed his intentions. Repulsive memories flooded his veins, nearly transforming him into blue fire on the spot. He had never taken kindly to being bled, as most Teuton priests did not. It seemed an intrusion on his privacy, for he knew his heart and the depths of his depravity. No one needed to dabble in his iniquity, especially this Keyholder of the cursed Muniche, the one who considered himself faultless.

You have the power to end this fiend's existence, my servant. Wuotan's foul thoughts intruded again upon the Black Priest's mind, prompting him to glance at his pit, to ensure that the demon had not manifested himself unannounced. His element sensed naught but his own fires burning there, but the demon spoke into his thoughts again. *You have long awaited this opportunity.*

But curiosity had encroached upon the Black Priest's revulsion, and he had no intention of eliminating the haughty Prince until he learned *what* exactly the man sought. What information could he possibly know that this arrogant ruler did not already have? For a transitory moment, the wraith considered subduing his antagonist with his element and ripping the questions from the arteries that pulsed so tauntingly along his neck, the life within them nigh screaming at him. He knew that he must resist such urges, especially when Wuotan himself skulked beyond the mortal plane, putting wicked thoughts into his rational mind.

So instead, the Black Priest asked, "What information could my blood hold that would have anything to do with those atrocious keys of yours?"

The Prince eyed him piercingly and said, "If I find it, I shall tell you."

The Black Priest frowned. "And if not?"

"I will leave you in peace."

This did not bode well, but even the worst of the Cursed Ones could not push aside that soul-eating inquisitiveness. So he nodded once, accepting, and drew back his collar. He did not sit down. "Let us be done with this," he said.

The Prince stepped forward to halt directly in front of the wraith, too close for comfort. He viewed the other's neck for a brief instant as the Black Priest stared at him distrustfully. Then he grabbed the priest's shoulder with one hand, placing the other firmly against the opposite side of his head, and bit down onto the carotid artery—the one that contains every thought, every memory, even the ones that have long been consciously forgotten.

The Cursed One stood stock still, his fists clenched at his sides, clinging to his control, ordering himself not to thrust his assailant away. His whole body had tensed the moment he felt the sharp pain of teeth, an instinctive reaction. He shut his eyes and endeavored to relax, ignoring the pounding pain in his neck. He wondered what Prince Otto was seeing, which terrible memories he now shared with the one who had cursed him. He wondered also how long the Prince would bleed him—until his blood ran dry, perhaps? He felt no fear, only impatience and discomfort.

He thought again of the keys, and the fact that the Prince had not yet found a proper home for them. How could he? No one in his right mind would willingly accept the keys of a ruined city. Muniche had been consigned to oblivion by Teuton law; it would not be rebuilt—by Teutons at least—until that memory evaporated. But the Black Priest knew Swanhilde. She was from the future, almost one thousand years in the future. She had been born in Muniche...she had been chained to the city by those bonds of hell. The city would not remain forever dead. What then?

This bleeding had lasted far too long. The Black Priest's irritation abounded. Would the Prince never find what he sought? He had doubtless already seen too much. Too much. *Stop.* The priest sent the order through his blood, but his adversary's grip on his shoulder and head did not waver, nor did he release his teeth. Damn him. *Stop!* He thought the word much more strongly this time, a command. Though the wraith's strength did not wane, he knew he had lost a vast amount of blood. If he were truly alive, he would be dead. The Prince knew better than this.

STOP!

His body finally flexed, and he pushed the Prince away from him, breaking his hold, ripping the teeth from his neck. The priest took several steps back, raising his left hand to his neck, knowing he had a rather ugly wound there now. His body abated the flow of blood within a few seconds, and he turned his fury on the Prince, who stood bent over several paces away, gripping his knees, obviously trying to recover.

"You bastard!" the Black Priest spat at him. "What do you think I am, a blood sacrifice?!"

The Prince looked up at him, still slightly bent over and breathing heavily; but his blue eyes, glowing just a shade red, held an accusation. "So it is true," he intoned, sounding resigned but not entirely surprised. He looked the Cursed One straight in the eyes and charged, "You love her, in spite of everything."

Initially, the priest could not fathom of whom his opponent spoke. His love, or lack thereof, had rarely come forth over the years. Now he thought of only one woman, but the Prince already knew that. "Swanhilde?" he asked, perplexed.

The Prince shook his head, triumph glistening in his eyes. "No. You love *her*. Muniche."

Blue fire shot from the Black Priest's eyes at such an illation. "You fool, how could I love that city, the city which cast me out?" He glowered.

That was when the Prince admitted something that took the priest's breath away, for he had never dreamed that such a concession could ever escape those proud lips. "It was not she who cast you out. I did it."

This admission disarmed the Black Priest more than anything ever could. His fire cooled considerably as he stared at his opponent in disbelief. He recovered himself enough to say, as an excuse perhaps, "You are her Keyholder. It is all the same to me."

But the Prince shook his head, something resembling regret veiling the fire in his eyes, and spoke another shocking statement. "You should not hold my sins against her."

Sins . . . sins . . . sins. The word revolved in the priest's mind, and he stared down at that dreaded black scar on his right forearm, the one that neither time nor blood control could erase, the one that had sealed his doom. "Then you admit . . . that what you did was wrong?" The priest's voice came out low; he had to be certain. He gawked at the Prince in astonishment.

"Whether it was wrong or not at the time, I cannot say," the Prince replied, looking down at the grass beneath his shoes. "The things that you did in those days, for pleasure or for edification, could not be allowed to continue in a Christian city. You do not know how many times the clergy confronted me, demanding that I do something to punish you and your propensities for murder and sorcery. That day when Swanhilde interrupted my blood-transfer—in *public*—to challenge Wuotan himself . . . and when you came to pull her back, under the eyes of everyone, from the townspeople to the clergy—" The Prince broke off, shaking his head, though his eyes still shone with regret. "I could not let it go on, Wolfgang. It had to stop somewhere or they would have killed you both."

The Black Priest's eyes blazed with fire. "So you had to curse me then, but you could not curse yourself—you, the one who bargained with Wuotan in secret, the one who wrote a song *at his bidding* that could open the gates of time, while you publicly retained the guise of a holy saint."

He pointed an incriminating finger at the Prince, who stared at him in consternation, and growled, "You *hypocrite*. At least everyone knew where my allegiances lay."

A long silence ensued as the wraith wondered how his opponent could possibly counter that accusation. It was laden with truth. How long had the Black Priest wished to have this conversation with the man who had cursed him! How satisfying it was to finally voice his own charges! He heard Wuotan chuckle softly in his brain, and the demon said, *Now you can show him what his curse has done to you. Show him your authority as the master of death.*

The Black Priest frowned and shook his head, wishing that the demon would stop interfering. This was hardly the time to cast a protection charm, with Muniche's Prince shamefaced before him.

At last, the Prince heaved a sigh and murmured, "Of course, you would know. Swanhilde would have told you everything. No, I was never a saint." He paused, raising his eyes again to the Cursed One's, and said, "Both of us should have been cursed. But Wuotan never appreciated me. He probably would have let me die. Paulus was the best of us, it would seem."

The blue fire in the pit flared at the Prince's words, and the Black Priest struggled to restrain himself from leaping forward and choking his opponent's life away, in spite of the repercussions. "You imbecile, Paulus was pathetic. If you had given *me* the song, Muniche would never have fallen. But no, you had to confide in the weak one, and look where it got us!"

Something more occurred to the wraith, and he added scornfully, "And who are you to suggest that I have any place with you or Paulus now? 'May it never be spoken again'!" He quoted the closing lines of the filial curse, his malice agitating the death within him.

The Prince sagged, stepping back and sitting down onto a rock in palpable weariness. "I cannot answer your charges," he said, gazing into the Black Priest's fire pit. "I have wished, in these final days, to discover another way into the past, to halt the terrible destruction of our people."

He paused with a sigh, then looked up at the priest again, who stood rigid, scowling. "But I have forgotten the end of my song. It will come to me no more, likely because of what I would do with it now. Swanhilde said that there is no point in bemoaning the past. We must look to the future. Everyone makes mistakes, but not everyone can choose his fate. All that matters is what we do *now*."

The Black Priest had heard Swanhilde speak this counsel before. She ought to have insight on that subject, since she had no choice when Muniche bound her. He nodded curtly and questioned, "What *do* we do now?"

"When I bled you," the Prince began, rising from the rock, "I wanted to see your true thoughts on our city. Though your former name has long been burnt out of the birth records, you were, in fact, born there. I wondered if you possibly had some loyalty to Muniche in spite of the past—in spite of *your* past."

He eyed the wraith thoughtfully, and a rather dreaded fear broke through his powerful veneer as realization dawned regarding *what* the Prince had sought. He started shaking his head slowly, negatively, but the Prince ignored it.

"What I found in your blood surprised me, nearly knocked me senseless, I admit. I discovered that your love for Muniche and your loyalty to our city is stronger than I can put into words. You have desired recurrently over the years to see her again, to walk her streets, though it was forbidden. You have drawn rough sketches of her walls and spires in the sand and in the fire. You felt physical pain when she fell to the Saxons. You wished more than anything that you could have unleashed Wuotan's gifts to kill them all, disregarding how that may have altered the course of history. You *love* her; you rue the day that she burnt to the ground. And some of this love—some of this loyalty—stems from your long relationship with Swanhilde."

The Prince paused again while the Black Priest gaped at him, rooted to the ground by his pronouncements. "I must admit, Wolfgang, that I had no inkling that your grip on Swanhilde's heart persisted for some twenty-three years after the council tried to break it apart. She told me herself that it was her doing. But that relationship, so powerful it was . . . and when Muniche took her, she left her mark on you both."

The Black Priest frantically struggled to find words to oppugn the Prince's report. He had never consciously considered his love for his birthplace to be so unshakeable; and these concepts the Prince had found in his blood could only lead to chains, yes, the very chains he had tried to avoid. At last, he voiced the only argument he had against the truth in his blood. "I love Swanhilde, *not* Muniche."

"They are one and the same," the Prince reminded him, and it was true. "I also saw that you have a candle burning in your bedroom for Muniche. You lit it with your fire the moment you returned from tracking the *Toteheri* across Bavaria. You look at it every time you lie in bed."

The wraith could not refute this, but he again shook his head, holding up both hands in a gesture of appeal. "No. Do not do this."

"Those children in Eisenwald need not know the burden of loving a cursed city," the Prince noted, reaching one hand into his trousers as the priest watched in horror. "Those few of us warriors who remained sprinkled our blood on her walls and set it ablaze, right before the Saxons burnt the city to the ground, cursing her by Teuton law. I expected these keys to crumble in my hands, to consign the city's bonds to oblivion, as they should. But they remained, and thus I knew: there is still some future for this city. And that future, I believe, is up to you, who knows what it is to bear a curse." He drew the ring of iron keys from his pocket, holding them out to the Black Priest.

The wraith arched away from the Prince, his blue eyes wheeling, his body trembling. He could not believe *this* was happening. No . . . no . . . no . . . not *again*. And he had no way of knowing whether the Prince had fabricated what he claimed to have seen in his blood, for he could not read his own memories. But that candle, with its bright blue flame, did indeed burn at his bedroom window.

Wuotan's gift of death churned fast in his blood as the Prince's words raced through his mind: *Who knows what it is to bear a curse . . . a curse . . . a curse.* Never before had he wished to kill Prince Otto so greatly as now, for it was apparent that the Prince had pondered his arguments fully. The wraith could not push this aside without damning himself further. He repressed his ire, for he remembered Swanhilde's warning and clung to it, ignoring Wuotan's dark temptations: *Kill him, my servant. You have always wanted this. Do it now and reach true supremacy.*

Instead, he focused with effort on his opponent and reminded him of the truth, his voice menacing. "I refused these once before." He glared at the keys, wishing that he could use his gift of death on *those*, if not on the Prince.

"You will not refuse them again." The Prince's riposte rang with confidence. He did not relax his stance, letting the key ring dangle from his fingers.

"Give them to one of the children, in spite of their inexperience!" the Black Priest expostulated, throwing his hands out. "They need to learn cruelty sometime; let it be now! Get those horrid things away from me!"

"If you would, for a single moment, let go of your selfishness and see the world apart from your lonely lot, you would understand that these belong to you, and you alone," the Prince informed him, his expression serious.

"You are asking for *death*," the priest threatened, the fire blazing hotter in his pit, leaping far past the treetops.

"Then you shall damn yourself further into the abyss," the Prince proclaimed, awful truth ringing in his words. "Pull the blindness from your eyes for once and think of Swanhilde. What would she want you to do?"

The Prince had him there, but the very mention of the name of his lover prompted the Black Priest to scream in ferocity, a devil's cry. "And SHE is why I want nothing to do with your keys!" he roared, ripping his clawed hands through ebony hair, shaking it out around his shoulders.

"I watched, helpless, as Muniche stole her heart. I saw that city gradually take over everything I loved in her, twist her desires to meld with the city and the *Keyholder*." He glared at the Prince, then finished, "She could *never* love me again, the way she once did, the way she did when she had a choice—*because of Muniche.* I do not want to lose myself as she was lost."

"Being the Keyholder of a Teuton city is not like that, in spite of what you have deluded yourself into believing," the Prince answered shortly, his expression critical. "You still retain a free will. If you wished to ruin the city, you could. If you wished to love another and abandon your Lady, you could. It is the woman who has the harsher fate, but the city never chooses wrong. Swanhilde told me that she is at peace with her destiny today, in spite of her pain and shortcomings. She did all that she could for Muniche; she represented her city well. How long it took her to reach that point, I cannot say. But it is true that the woman has no choice. The Keyholder has a choice." He looked at the Black Priest significantly, expectant.

The wraith grew thoughtful, the anger gradually seeping out of him while the fear returned again. He eyed his opponent apprehensively, where he stood by the rock, still holding the keys in his right hand. "And if I choose to say no?"

"Then I will leave you in peace and give them to one of the children." The Prince's gaze averted to the sky as he added, "If I must do that, you had better decide swiftly, for I am to die tonight. The sun is already setting."

The priest also regarded the firmament, seeing that it had indeed begun the transition from cobalt to a rich vermillion. The Prince's time ran short, as did Swanhilde's. Now the priest faced the choice before him in earnest, recalling his dismal thoughts from earlier in the day.

Once Swanhilde had gone on to eternal bliss, he would have nothing left in this world. He would seek death forever after, although he knew he would not find it. But these keys, this responsibility . . . .

If he agreed, accepting them as his own, his existence would have renewed purpose—to preserve the fallen city of Muniche, to pass her records along, perhaps even to fully punish the Saxons who had ravaged her. Acknowledging that his remaining time on earth was to be quite long, the feeling grew within him that *if* he accepted the keys, he would one day see Muniche reborn. He would walk her streets again. He would never be the outcast, not to her.

He was weakening. His reason always ruined him, always led him to the logical conclusions in spite of his impetuosity. He had one final argument, and he spoke it now, softly, meeting the Prince's gaze. "If I take them, she will compel me to love another, a woman I do not know. No woman would want to unite with a cursed Teuton priest. This mark speaks for itself." He lifted his right arm, baring it before the Prince's eyes. "I would have a city and a purpose, but I would never know human love again."

"Muniche will know you are cursed, and she will take that into consideration when she chooses her next *Leitalra*," the Prince replied. "She will not select a pious saint, for your sake. She will choose the woman you need."

The Black Priest stared at the Prince, then at the key ring. "You are certain?" he asked, his voice hardly above a whisper.

The Prince nodded solemnly, then made another observation. "Just think of what you could do for Muniche, with your gifts. You could be the one to make her rise from the ashes, to eradicate her curse." He stopped suddenly, looking down at the keys in his hand, then back at the priest, tears pooling in his eyes. "It is all I want," he whispered fiercely, his body quivering. "Please."

And there, the iron heart of the Black Priest broke, and he wondered idly what Swanhilde would think of him now. He had loved her most, but now he freely walked away. She would die tonight with the Prince, her husband. This very one had come to him at the eleventh hour, offering him a reprieve from everlasting melancholy at her death.

Swanhilde would want him to do this, in spite of what it meant. She would want him to have hope. She would want him to spit in Wuotan's face, to consider a brighter path again, to reunite with her one day in eternity. She had never believed in his curse. He must take hold of responsibility again, for her sake alone.

The Black Priest bowed his head, nodding in resignation. Then he stepped forward, meeting the Prince's eyes as he reached out his right hand, with its midnight scar. "I will take the keys." His voice shook a bit.

Relief brightened the Prince's face, but he masked it swiftly and recited the ritual words in Ælte Teutonica. "With these keys, do you accept eternal responsibility for Muniche, this city, and her Lady, swearing as long as you remain on this earth to love her and her people, to protect them, shield them, teach them, and always deal with them in fairness, pledging infinite loyalty to her children?"

The Black Priest closed his eyes as the enormity of this thing descended upon him. "I accept my duty, and I do swear it, on the eternal blood of Muniche."

The next instant, he felt the iron key ring placed into his right hand, with the four keys to Muniche's four gates and the key to her archives. He opened his eyes and stared down at them in amazement, recalling the other time he had held them himself—in the future, when he had revealed the Keyholder to Swanhilde just before they had broken their heart-bond forever. That time they had not belonged to him; he had almost stolen them, in fact. They had felt like ash in his fiery palm, contumacious at his touch.

This time . . . . Now they were his. He felt it in his blood instantly, a new and unfamiliar rush of loyalty, of fidelity, of *purpose*. He must bring Muniche back from the dead, he must help her regain her glory, and he could unleash his powers on those who attempted to stop him. His fingers closed around the keys protectively, solidly. He had not felt such resolution flowing through him in years, and he marveled at it.

"Before I go," the Prince uttered, shattering the dark priest's concentration, "there are two things." The Prince paused, drawing a shaky breath, averting his gaze to the heavens and the realm of nature surrounding the priest's dwelling. Then he shook himself and finished, "Two things for which I must . . . apologize."

The Black Priest frowned, his fingers closing more tightly around the keys. The pompous Prince would apologize for something at the end? Curiosity welled within him, and he urged, "Speak on."

The Prince took a few steps backward, putting a safer distance between himself and the Cursed One, it seemed. He inhaled again, looking frightened, then stared down at the ground as he began to speak. "In my lifetime, I have had three terrible regrets, and the greatest was that I never consummated the bond of Muniche until just ten days ago. When she vanished from my blood and from our time for those eight years, it practically drove me insane. I almost killed myself over it, knowing that I should have taken her while she lived, in spite of her misgivings. But now, I need not apologize for that."

The Prince paused again, and the Black Priest viewed him in mistrust. He did not give a damn, personally, about the Prince's sorrows over the late *Leitalra* of Muniche. He had refused her, himself. He waited, and at length the Prince continued, his gaze still riveted upon his boots.

"The thing I regretted secondly, and for which I wish to apologize now . . . was that I killed Marelda, at my birth." The priest grew rigid, shock and loathing coursing through his veins at the subject. The Prince glanced up at him rather uncertainly, then went on.

"If I had been able to die then myself and spare her, I would have chosen that. I never knew her, but I remember . . . I remember how dreadfully her death influenced you. I have wished for years upon end that she could have lived. If I could have altered history with my song, I would have saved her. I know that you have always blamed me for her death, but I do hope that someday you can find the ability to forgive me."

The Black Priest could not speak. He could respond neither positively nor negatively to the Prince's request for absolution. He stood still, amazed that the Prince had thought of this now and actually felt sorry. He knew he ought to say something, to accept or reject the Prince's offer, but he had lost his voice. The fire in his pit burned low, and he stared directly ahead of himself at nothing. He could not answer. He could not bear this now, not now.

The Prince saw that the Black Priest was at a loss, and his posture sagged, his expression resigned. He waited in vain for the wraith to speak, to say anything in response to his confession. At last he turned away, likely to return to his horse and ride like a sweeping forest fire back to where Swanhilde waited for him a short distance upstream. The Black Priest continued to stare vacantly, his reason having gone out of him, while the Prince withdrew toward the trees. *How could I bear to forgive him now, after fifty-two years?*

Suddenly, the Prince halted his retreat, and had he not begun the way he had, the priest likely would not have heard him at all. When he did hear him, at first he thought his ears had deceived him in spite of their acuity. The Prince had turned back to face him, his feet planted firmly at the periphery of the forest, and spoken one word—a name.

"Augustin."

Lightning flashed across the cloudless sky at the impossibility of his utterance. A strange rumbling sound pealed out in the distance, like the approach of a large mounted army, and the earth trembled beneath the Black Priest's feet as his mouth fell open in shock, shock, *shock!* His vision returned, and he gawked at the Prince in complete incredulity, seeing remorse and earnestness in his eyes.

"The last thing I have regretted, so horribly, for twenty-nine years, was that I had cursed you. Though I have excused it in my own heart a thousand times, the guilt has never left me. No one, not even the worst of sinners, deserves the fate I thrust upon you in my arrogance, handing your life over to the devil, to Wuotan. I should never have done such a terrible thing, and I realize you have no desire and no reason to forgive me. Just know now, at the end, that I would erase the cursed mark myself, if it were possible. I am sorry."

The Black Priest stared at the Prince, his thoughts spinning in confusion, in disbelief. *May the name of Augustin Abelard Ulrich von Bayern be burnt . . . . May it never be spoken again . . . may it never be spoken again . . . . He spoke it. The one who cursed me spoke it again. How could he do such a thing? How could he?*

Abruptly, his thoughts turned to Swanhilde and the many discussions they had over the years on the subject of forgiveness. In spite of the horrid wrongs that had been done to her throughout her life, she had concluded that she did not want to live like *him*—the wraith who could not forgive, who wallowed in bitterness, in self-pity, in hatred. She had to forgive everything, or she would never find peace. Nor would he.

Forgive even the unforgivable wrongs, she had said. That black scar on his forearm equated the most unforgivable wrong. Now, at the end, the Black Priest perceived that even he yet retained the capacity to forgive.

So at last he said truthfully, raising his eyes to the Prince's fearful ones, "I forgive you . . . *my brother.*"

The lightning sparked across the calm twilight with an accompanying roar of thunder, and the ground quaked again, throwing the priest to his knees, causing him to curl into himself, covering his head with his hands, crying out in anguish for what had been done. Wuotan was angry with him. Eventually he would have to face that demon and admit that he had forgiven the one he was meant to kill. What would he do to him then? What *could* he do? He had taken a firm step onto the path of light, and Wuotan wielded no authority there. *Thank you, Prince Otto von Bayern. I accept your apology, though it came far too late.*

When nature quieted herself, the Black Priest rose from the ground and looked around him. Otto was nowhere to be seen; he had gone to prepare for his ritual suicide. The blue fire in his pit had burnt out. His chickens had apparently fled from the sudden elemental storm; they had likely returned to their pen. The priest shook his head in amazement, the wry thought crossing his mind that he was not a devil after all. Devils could not forgive, but he had done it. He was still human, still a man. He felt his own heart pounding, his blood rushing through his veins. His gaze dropped again to his right forearm and that damning scar there. It would never fade, but what did that matter now? Forgiveness had lightened his heart, and he felt an elation he had never known before. He should have listened to Swanhilde long ago. This far outweighed bitterness.

When his thoughts turned to Swanhilde, dejection threatened to envelope him afresh. He opened his right hand and looked at the keys, thinking of his new duties as the Keyholder of a cursed Muniche. Soon—tomorrow even —his heart would begin to pound for another woman, and he would have to find her and make her his own. He would have to be gentle, not bleed her, not ravage her, handle her kindly in bed. His love for Swanhilde would one day pass into memory, while his love for Muniche would flourish. He was likely the first Black Priest in history to have hope, and that alone required much reflection. Presently, he trod down to the banks of the Rhine River, situating himself beneath a mulberry tree, resolved to thoroughly ponder what had transpired while the darkness of a moonless night descended upon the forest.

The Cursed One knew not how long he rested there, in tranquility at long last, a smile curling on his youthful face, gazing with lidded eyes at the dark water before him. He had not felt so free in many years. Otto had been right; the keys of Muniche were not chains. They held responsibility but also possibility. The priest would rebuild his city . . . he would seek his Lady . . . .

And that was when his perfect eyes caught sight of a raft in the distance, drifting slowly out upon the water far upstream of him, toward the middle of the Rhine. At first he frowned thoughtfully, his mind too occupied with the novelty of peaceful notions to identify the raft and its meaning. He could barely discern the two figures sitting upon it, together. Then suddenly, like a meteor shooting across the sky, the Black Priest remembered something abysmal.

Swanhilde had never stopped loving him, even though she was Muniche. If she had not . . . then he would never stop loving her.

His body boiled hot and he abruptly dropped the keys onto the grass as he recognized the truth of the matter, the truth he had endeavored not to see. Otto had said that the keys would induce him to love another Lady. There was nothing worse than loving two at once. Swanhilde had taught him that, when she vacillated between him and her Keyholders. Now he sat here, on the banks of the Rhine, the cursed keys of Muniche beside him, tying him to the city, to *her*. And he would have to watch her *die*.

No.

No.

No . . . .

It could not be.

He would have no hope without her. Those keys would not be his salvation. They would be his demise. They would drive him insane. His love for Swanhilde flared like the flames of hell, and he knew why. The keys were his.

It was not possible.

It was not possible.

No . . . no . . . no . . . *NO!*

All at once he remembered his vow, when she had left to be with Otto . . . *who was no longer her Keyholder*. He would not interfere with her destiny unless he had found a way for them to be together.

A way for them to be together.

She planned to cut her wrists and throat with a stone knife, then cast herself into the waters of the Rhine. History would label the act as ritual suicide, Prince Otto's fabrication, a respectable manner of escape from a tormented life. He could not stop her, not with human strength. Her blood would burst forth like the river itself; water would inundate her lungs. There would be no time. Already, the pair on the raft had risen, making gestures, positioning themselves back-to-back for their jump. He was too far away to stop her.

NO!!!!

In a flash, he leapt from beneath the tree and threw himself upon the Rhine, his blue fire licking up the waters of the river in his path as he streaked toward the now-empty raft with the speed of a comet. And he screamed an oath to the sky, to the river, to Wuotan himself:

IF YOU WILL NOT LET ME SAVE HER, I SHALL NEVER SERVE YOU AGAIN!

Chapter Twenty-four:
He Calls for Me

Had Augustin really imagined it was wise to wait this long?

That was my final thought when oblivion stole my soul away, ejecting it from a body that had cast itself into the Rhine. I remember subconsciously inhaling the water, a frailty and chill far more insidious than my ice plunging into my core. This was death.

For a fleeting moment, I may have believed I would open my eyes to see the labradorite gateway of time rising from the mist, its heavy doors creaking inward to return me to my son. To a future that had no place for me.

Instead, a radiant light caught my attention as my eyelids slid open of their own accord, granting me a view that I have no words to describe. Around me drifted clouds reflecting hues I had never seen before, even when my ice enhanced my vision, a gentle breeze shaping them into spectacular patterns, ever changing. In my peripheral vision, I noticed other souls converging in the same direction my feet carried me, some more distant than others. I sensed a unity with them, a grand relief of reaching the next plane in life's journey—the great expanse before us.

Heaven's landscape unfolded before my eyes, my vision perfect enough now to appreciate details that would normally have escaped me. The gates, which did not appear as if they could ever be shut, dazzled with a brilliance beyond anything I had experienced. There were no walls, the lush scenery summoning weary souls into everlasting peace. Winged beings clad in golden-flecked white reached out to each soul approaching from the clouds, guiding them into the realm beyond.

The earthly cares that once troubled me had fallen away into insignificance. When the soul who walked forward nearest to me paused to cast a knowing glance in my direction, warmth seemed to swell inside of me, assuring me that I belonged here. An eternity with God, with the angels, with the saints who had gone before.

Grace alone had brought me to this place.

I saw Otto smile at me before he turned again for the gates, his countenance shimmering and flawless. And then I saw a woman sprinting toward him with her arms outstretched, forsaking heaven's boundary to welcome her long lost love. Her eyes were a deep, earthy brown, her black hair flowing to her waist, her tawny skin glowing from within. She and Otto embraced, and they clung to each other without speaking a mere twenty steps from the open gateway. Husband and wife, together at last.

While I felt no jealousy at the sight of their reunion, something twisted in my heart in a manner hardly appropriate to the heavenly realm. Unhappiness had no place here . . . but my muses wandered back to earth . . . to where I had left my one true love behind.

I hesitated. My feet halted in place, the wispy clouds undulating around me.

I don't belong here without him.

The thought cropped up out of nowhere, assaulting the joy that had gripped me since I beheld heaven's grandeur. All of my intentions surged back into my brain—*die, break Muniche's hold, return to earth to be with . . . .*

Did Muniche still claim my heart? I tried to focus, tried to ascertain the truth.

Was my body too dead for me to return? Should I have pivoted my course long before I reached heaven's threshold?

I can't enter those gates without him.

Otto and Kezia had separated just a hair, their arms still clasped around each other's waists, their eyes noticing nothing but their most cherished partner. Twin souls.

Then I heard my name, called out softly from somewhere behind where I stood. Somewhere far distant within the clouds. Its tone permeated with desperate hope. A voice I would recognize anywhere.

I turned back just for a second, my perfected eyes narrowing at the clouds through which I had emerged. Other souls continued to journey forward, none of them evincing any care about what they left behind. Was I the only fool who would pause at the edge of paradise, asking myself whether I had *really* heard Augustin's voice? Could I go back? Had he found a way?

All at once, I remembered his promise, the one he had made right before he officiated my wedding with Otto. He would not interfere with my destiny unless he had found a way for us to be together.

"Swanhilde."

I looked toward Otto and Kezia, seeing that he, too, stared into the clouds with a bemused expression. His eyes drifted to mine, and a smile quirked upon his lips. He gave a single nod, as if granting permission. He knew my heart, and he knew that if Augustin called for me, heaven could wait.

I offered up an unspoken apology to God, hoping He would not take offense at my irreverence. I was not relinquishing my faith; I was simply taking a side trip.

Augustin . . . I hope you've managed to put my drained and drowned body back together.

Then I lunged back into the clouds, away from heaven, into the unknown, seeking the infernal arms of my one true love.

Chapter Twenty-five:
An Absurd Revival

My eyes opened to a moonless sky dotted with stars. Pinpoints of light blurred into one another, dark tree limbs obscuring them here and there, leaves shivering with the slight breeze of night.

It took me endless minutes to reconnect my reason with what my senses told me—I lay upon my back on grass, damp tendrils of hair chilling my neck, some sort of cloth enfolding me, shielding my soaked body from the cool air. A raw ache centered at my left breast spread throughout my torso, and every breath I drew seemed a trial, my lungs protesting at my system's need for oxygen. My entire body felt as heavy as a cement truck, my blood having gained an unwieldy weight as it pulsed like sludge through my veins. I tasted the nauseating combination of sullied water, disgorged stew, and death on my tongue. But that death . . . was it truly my own?

I shut my eyes and endeavored to roll onto my side, coughing in an attempt to rid my esophagus of whatever ailed it. I struggled to make sense of my situation. How had I managed to return to my body after those short seconds of heaven—this mangled body of mine, unquestionably broken beyond repair. Had it all actually happened, or had it been some sort of nightmare, one that shackled me still? Would I wake to find myself beside Prince Otto, my Keyholder, or had I really seen him embracing Kezia at those resplendent gates?

And if I had in fact been marveling at the entrance to God's paradise just moments ago—fashioned of something more brilliant than earthly jewels, to my foggy recollection—then *why* did I lie here upon the earth? Why had I hesitated when I saw countless saints converging to claim their reward?

That voice had arrested me, like it had done on several other occasions. In the past, I had left naught but the future behind when I followed those seductive commands. *Swanhilde, I cannot follow you there.* It could still be true, could it not? *Forgive me Swanhilde, but I love you too much to let you die this way.* He had demonstrated his love countless times. *Death cannot save you this time. You are mine.* Were these the phrases I should reconsider now, those uttered at a demon's behest, the ones that reinforced my slavery, physical and mental, to a dead man who had long degenerated into a wraith?

He had called me from behind, spoken nothing but my name, no sentence of entreaty, no explanation presented. What could he have proposed that would convince a sane person to turn away from heaven? Nothing. I knew that answer without having to form a coherent thought. My lips, so chapped and bloodied, stretched into a frail smile. Had breathing not still been a trial, I may have attempted to expel a cynical laugh.

Why did I listen to him? What unfeasible destiny could he possibly put before me? I have no option but to die tonight in the manner prescribed . . . so why did I allow this? A delay . . . just what Wuotan offers . . . what his servant suggests . . . and a delay of what? A fortuitous death . . . one carried out by Augustin himself . . . what he has always wanted.

Despite my silent reproof of myself, I knew why I had answered, why I had turned my back on Prince Otto, on paradise, on the welcoming hands of God. It was the same reason I had dawdled there in the clouds long after my soul departed my drowning body, my blood mingled with water, my heart ceased to labor. I had thought of him, recalled the times when I had greeted another gateway that merely opened to the future. He had come for me then, and I held doggedly to the hope that he may come again.

He had promised not to interfere with my death—my final death—unless he had discovered a way to free me, a way to salvage what we had lost over and over again. But wait . . . had he not also hinted that he might linger until the last moment, then entice me away from heaven in hopes that Muniche's bonds might release me in the face of eternity?

I opened my eyes again, the irregular puffs of air from my weakened lungs peppering the immediate atmosphere with frost. My ice was with me still; maybe that was what slowed my circulation so drastically. I focused on my element out of habit, calling it back, then quickly abandoned that plan when the ache in my chest increased. Death had drained my magic from me.

Gasping feebly at the cool night air, my hazy vision discerned the presence of the Rhine a few paces from where I lay, its waters sloshing against the bank. I wanted to crawl back to the grave that had been stolen from me. If the stone knife had been in my line of vision, I might have done just that. Instead, I simply lay still, choking out stray drops of blood, squeezing my eyes shut, trying to stave off the terror that threatened to devour me.

If he really came to save me, then why am I alone? How could he leave me half-drowned in the grass after apparently restarting my heart and breathing dead air into my lungs? Oh, and sealing the wounds in my throat and wrists. This is madness, Swanie . . . you have to find the strength to rise . . . to search for him . . . to demand his rationale . . . for at dawn, Ashima's curse will devour you.

So I tried to flex my arms and legs, to push myself off my side into a sitting position. Unfortunately, drowning— or more probable, bleeding—had erased the verve from my body. Wiggling just the fingers of my right hand seemed impossible, and I sank back into the grass with a groan, sensing the dust clinging to my wet hair. I should never have listened to him. I should have followed Otto, gone into heaven beside him and Kezia. She had seemed like a really lovely person.

Now that wondrous portal that had been close enough to touch had drifted beyond my reach, extinguished the instant I leapt into the clutches of a blue-fired demon. He had dragged me through the void, into nothingness, unconsciousness . . . and finally to this solitude at the shores of the Rhine. Maybe his efforts to rescue me had killed him at long last. Perhaps if I had the strength enough to send my ice out of me in a quest for cobalt fire, I would find no answer. Pulling me back from heaven into this revived corpse may have cost him his soul.

But I knew why I had responded to his call, for the same reason I had not felt peaceful about committing suicide on this moonless night. A heretical motive, but true nonetheless: *Without Augustin, heaven was not meant for me.*

I lay still, staring up at the sky for a long while, my body greedily drinking in the heat trapped beneath the black cloth that covered me, which I had finally identified as one of Augustin's priestly robes. It was a tedious process, waiting for the precious threads of life that remained after my suicide to run their course throughout my bloodstream, gradually restoring my strength bit by bit. I began to take note of the smallest improvements in my senses—the augmented clarity of my vision, the increase in my sluggish heartbeat, the warmth that spread to the very tips of my fingers as blood coursed through my capillaries. Conscious of the passing of time during my recuperation, my eyes kept straying to my right, checking for gray in the eastern portion of the sky. My hours were numbered, and since I had no clock, I could only guess just how long I had until sunrise.

With the return of my energy came the return of my full capacity to reason, and with it all of those nagging fears. It *had* really happened. I remembered slicing my wrists and throat after Otto pledged to meet me at heaven's gates. I remembered whispering that final plea to Augustin right before my lips sank beneath the water: *I'm still waiting.*

He must have heard me somehow, or he would not have come, a flaming spirit obscured by the mist, hands reached out to a saint bound for glory, silently entreating her to reconsider—not to forget her vow. But the stronger I grew, the more aware I became of those cords binding me still, the muted cry of a deserted city echoing in each beat of my heart. Muniche had not freed me yet, and therefore I had not died. What unthinkable scheme would Augustin set before me in these transitory hours?

Irritation crept through my blood at my body's intrinsic weakness. Although I sensed my magic returning, it did so much too sluggishly. Pity Teutonic magic did not include supernatural healing, like the shifters and dragons that starred in many of the fantasy romance novels I used to read. Blood control was not enough to fully restore my vitality. Apparently I would feel mostly dead for a good while. An absurd resurrection, not quite meeting divine standards.

Eventually I decided that I *had* to get up, whether my recovering corpse appreciated the effort or not. I needed to find that insane man who had trailed my soul to the threshold of heaven, who had gone to such lengths to bring me back to an imperfect earth. He must be somewhere nearby, probably weakened, comatose, or he would have spoken to me already. I had no concept of what it must have cost him—a dead servant of a devil—to accomplish my rescue.

I rolled to my side again and pushed myself onto my knees, gasping at the resultant pain in my chest, my limbs hardly able to sustain the weight of my body. Gritting my teeth, spitting another mouthful of blood onto the grass, I dragged myself a few centimeters away from the river-bank, toward the sturdy trunks that framed the woodland. There, sprawled facedown between two trees, I saw the unmistakable form of my most faithful husband.

I crawled gradually toward him, pausing every few seconds to catch my breath and clutch one hand to my throbbing chest. When I reached his side, I had completely expended my energy, and I collapsed on top of his back, my fingers plucking uselessly at the dark fabric that covered him. A rune glimmered eerily on my right wrist—the mark of Ashima's curse—revealing a faint scab remaining from where the stone knife had torn my flesh. *What can we do to fix this?*

I coughed again, pressing my forehead into his tunic, catching the familiar scent of inner fire mixed with blood, rancid blood. At first I thought it was just the odor of that red-tinted stream that continued to clog my throat. Once I could breathe again, I rolled onto my left side, planting my elbow upon Augustin's back, pushing aside the idea that I might be hurting him. Focusing my eyes on his head, I reached my right hand out to brush some of his drenched hair away from his face.

Suddenly my eyes fell upon his hand, stretched toward the river, coated with blood and grime. Dark liquid pooled on the ground beneath his palm, and I drew a sharp breath as I realized mine was not the only blood defiling the night air. He had given me some of his blood, yes . . . and before he could seal his own wounds he had . . . fainted? Died?

Anxiety threatened to engulf me as I lurched toward his hidden face, brushing both of my hands through his hair— which, to my relief, felt quite damp but warm. There must be fire inside of him still; and if that were true, his soul must also be within reach. The skin of his visage appeared as pallid as a specter, smeared with blood and something else. I could tell, considering how completely his face had sunk into the ground, that he was not breathing. A dead man did not need to breathe . . . right?

I bit my lip hard, drawing blood, and sought a pulse at the right side of his neck. The heat of his blood singed my fingertips, and I detected a strange, irregular throb—a dead heart pumping dead blood. I tried to say his name, but no sound came from my lips, so I coughed again, wishing for some water to cleanse my throat. Then, as I used both of my hands to pry his face out of the grass and dirt, I managed to whisper, "Augustin?"

Perhaps his soul had been waiting for my voice to call him back to earth, as my own had done earlier that night. When I spoke his name, his eyelids fluttered and his hands twitched. "Augustin?" I whispered again, pulling myself forward and easing his head into my lap.

His lips parted; both of his soiled hands balled into fists, then relaxed . . . and at last, his eyes opened, blinking fitfully as though part of him were still lost in the realm between life and death. I tried to wipe the blood and dust from his face, but my hands were too dirty to do much good. Then he must have sensed my touch, for his vacant eyes locked with mine, their irises suddenly flaming with fire and perhaps with triumph. He curled his lips back into a smile that looked gruesome on such a spectral face. I shook my head at him, massaging his temples.

"Oh Augustin . . . what *have* you done?"

Chapter Twenty-six:
Desperate Measures

$\mathbb{A}$ ghostly chuckle broke the stillness. In a strained voice, Augustin responded, "I keep my promises . . . my swan."

He began to raise himself from the earth, and I re-strained the instinct to constrain him. Since I scarcely had the strength to hold myself upright, I had no authority to insist that a reviving dead man take it easy. I let go of him as he sat up with a groan, extricating his filthy hands from the ground and wiping them on his tunic.

I abruptly noticed that he wore a Gothic-looking cross on a silvery chain around his neck. Ironic that a Black Priest would sport such an accessory, while I wore a magical amulet set into a medallion. My gaze dropped to that piece of jewelry for an instant, seeing the mud stains upon the gold from my stint in the river. The Torstein glimmered in the darkness, seeking its first victim to carry it through the gates of time.

"It was not simple to fulfill my promise," Augustin remarked in a stronger tone. After stretching his legs and arms, he propped his back against a nearby tree. Eyeing me with a singular expression, he went on, a smirk playing on his lips.

"To restore your life when I have none to offer without consulting heaven for a miracle. Ah, Swanhilde, I feared... I feared that I would not succeed . . . when I dragged your body from the water, so cold and still, your heart already silent. I wept while I purged the liquid from your lungs . . . while I shocked your heart with an energy that is not my own . . . while I breathed the air of death into your core . . . then fled from my body to chase your fleeting soul." He broke off and buried his face in his hands, soundless tears forging tiny streams in the dirt that sullied his cheeks.

I gawked at him, trying to decipher his motive. He had gone to great lengths to save my life, and it had apparently taken a lot out of him. All at once, I sensed a familiar scratching at my heart—a reminder that despite Augustin's attempt to save me, I was not free. Wuotan still stalked Muniche's soul, and she had not let me go. My lover had brought me back to an earthly prison.

Blotting his tears on the sleeves of his tunic, Augustin muttered that the events of this night had depleted his emotional stability along with his power. "I ought not to sit here blubbering at a time like this. Forgive me, Swanhilde. How do you feel? Are you in pain?"

My deliverer transformed into the concerned doctor, taking my face in his hands and tilting it upward to study my eyes, which likely looked quite glassy. I sat mute while he felt my pulse, while his fingers probed my throat, tracing the mended incision from his stone knife. "Your heartbeat is still incredibly weak," he observed with a frown, touching the artery in my neck a second time. "Are you having trouble breathing?"

I was, in fact, for not all of the blood and water had made it out of my lungs yet. However, my irritation erupted at his query, at his disapproving stare, as he cupped my throat in his hand when I swallowed. "Why does it matter . . . if I'm having trouble breathing?" I demanded in a hoarse whisper. "I have no clue why you decided . . . to call me away from heaven . . . when Muniche shackles my heart." My complaints ended in a cough that brought up nothing but phlegm.

His gaze grew gentle, and he crept closer to me, so close that his lips brushed mine as he crooned, "Darling Swanhilde, how do you think I restarted your heart?"

As I stared back at him, uncomprehending, I felt his fiery hand cover my heart, a familiar tinkling reaching my ears, his fingers permeating the very essence of who I was. An astounded gasp spilled from my lips as Muniche's cords sang inside of me, rejoicing, beckoning, yearning. My eyes widened at the realization that I stared into the gaze of *my Keyholder* . . . Augustin Abelard Ulrich von Bayern.

His left hand tenderly stroked the curve of my face, and he whispered words I had never expected to hear from his lips, laden with immeasurable devotion: "Muniche . . . my dear one . . . my precious *Leitalra*."

I could not speak. Had he not pulled me into his lap, his right hand firm upon my faltering heart, I might have passed out from sheer astonishment. It was too much to bear in one single night. A failed attempt at suicide, a voluntary departure from heaven's gates, an agonizing recovery at the edge of the grave, and now a new Keyholder—a dead Keyholder, a Keyholder Swanhilde had always loved, had wanted for over forty years.

My lungs began to gasp at the atmosphere, my mind struggling to smother the desperate hope that bloomed within me. Augustin's left arm held me against his chest while his right hand touched the keys to my throbbing heart, his voice murmuring comfort in my ear. I moaned, my eyes closing as this cursed Keyholder began to enchant me, to bind me more and more securely with his own soul, so fiery, so depraved . . . and yet . . . so ardent.

"I could not allow our city to chain me to another *Leitalra*," he said, his lips gently touching my eyelids. "A Lady whom Augustin could never love."

"But it is impossible," I croaked, hardly noticing that he had referred to himself by his cursed name so casually when there were more pressing matters at hand. I opened my eyes to gaze sorrowfully into those of my dearest love. "Unless there's a way to undo Ashima's spell, I'll die when the sun rises."

He winced, but responded in a consoling tone, "That would simply open the gateway to your future, though the death itself shall not be pleasant. You could conceivably return to the twenty-first century and then come back here to me, if you still wish . . . if you . . . ." His voice trailed off, and he averted his gaze.

That possibility had already occurred to me, but I shied away from the idea of experiencing death by accelerated decay. It reminded me too much of the Indiana Jones movie involving the Holy Grail. "What if . . . what if I just use the Torstein to go back instead?" I fingered it with my left hand as I spoke, trying to think the matter through. Exhaustion still fogged my reason.

"I would not advise that. Since Ashima considers time's currents to be part of her dominion—a lie, as I mentioned before—her spell would likely cling to you if you open the portal apart from death. But . . . would it release you with death, or would traces of it linger upon you as you return to the future, since such a death would slay only your body?"

Looking up at Augustin's face from where I lay curled in his lap, I saw that his forehead wrinkled in apparent stupefaction. Traces of blue fire flickered in his irises as he stared across the Rhine, his right hand sliding Muniche's keys away from my heart, returning them to a pocket of his trousers. "The runes. Did you notice if they appear on your spirit along with your body?" He touched a clawed finger to the glowing mark upon my wrist.

"They were on both of our spirits," I answered, dread creeping up my spine.

Augustin's mien cracked with pain. "Then her spell is the same as the spell that ended my life. Cursed for all of time. If you see morning's light and return to the future . . . you would likely die upon your arrival. Or you may become lost in time's currents until the Almighty declares their end."

My lips parted, and I stared at Augustin in horror. "You didn't think this through . . . did you?" It sounded like my best recourse now was to hunt the stone knife from the bottom of the Rhine and commit ritual suicide again. I had no wish to die in a grotesque manner twice.

"I did not realize . . . Ashima's gifts were so potent." Augustin's arms drew me securely against him, denial surging through the incomplete bond between us.

"I think I need another stone knife, so I don't have to crumble into dust on my way into eternity." I coughed, my throat still feeling incredibly ragged. "Maybe it all has to end for us tonight . . . no matter how much we hope otherwise. And you hold Muniche's keys now . . . so you won't be alone after I'm gone."

Augustin held me tightly, and when he spoke again his tone implied that he had not listened to my hollow attempt at comfort. "Since the youth that binds you is Ashima's creation, she must know how to undo it." His eyes blazed as he looked down at me, his lips descending upon mine for one sensual kiss.

When he released my lips, he stated, "I cannot lose you again, Swanhilde, not after working so hard to preserve you. You belong to me now, and you shall belong to me after the sun rises. Ashima does not readily respond to invocations, so we must go to the demonic demesne—both of us—to confront her and bargain for your life."

My ice—which had helped little in my recuperation, shielding my weakened blood from the warmth it needed— froze my body completely, encrusting my skin in defense against a demoness' deceits. Augustin's assertion, voiced in such a forceful tone, left no room for misunderstanding. We would descend to the abyssal realm whether I agreed or not.

My Keyholder's hands began to infuse my blood with numbing fire, and he reproached me for reacting so rashly when I teetered on the precipice of death. In spite of the influence of his element—which by then had regained its full potency—I shivered, burrowing my face into Augustin's chest. "I don't know . . . if that's the best idea," I told him in a shaky voice. "What if Wuotan challenges us while we're looking for Ashima? He still holds some sway over

Muniche's soul . . . and we know he hates me . . . because of how deeply I love you."

Augustin sighed, his hands releasing their hold upon me to concentrate on my sodden hair, winding it into a braid. "Since his lover's gift has drained your hourglass dry, I argue that we have no other choice. We cannot tread lightly if—"

"His lover?" I interrupted. "I thought the sirens were Wuotan's lovers."

"He uses them for erotic purposes, but most demons copulate with their own kind whenever the opportunity presents itself. I first met Ashima when she rode Wuotan's penis in a hammock of purple flames."

Heat returned to my cheeks at long last as my brain conjured up images hardly appropriate to the situation at hand. "Are we . . . are we going to have to . . . trade sex for my life?" I whispered, my voice breaking.

"If she requires that of me, I can grant it. As a mortal human, you cannot mate with a demon or siren and live."

"Wuotan might try to rape me." I began to shiver with cold, though my ice had retreated beneath my Keyholder's immortal blue fire.

I heard Augustin grind his teeth as his hands finished with my hair, sealing the bottom of the braid with one of his clips. "Wuotan had best tread sagaciously now that I wield the power over Muniche. If he harms you in any way, I can reject any of his plans for our city's future. We have dealt harshly with one another over the years, but Wuotan has no other Teuton servant on this earth. If he fails to please me and therefore loses me, his most prized possession shall slip from his grasp—authority over our people." Augustin met my gaze, a malicious smirk upon his lips; then he bent down to kiss my nose.

Though his words rang with truth, my fears refused to grant me reprieve. Observing my uncertainty, Augustin added, "Wuotan holds no sway over your eternal fate due to your faith in God. Ashima would not appreciate his interference while we bargain to free you from her hex. Demons prefer to close deals with humans individually. I can protect you from their wiles, but you must maintain a strong grip on your reason." He gave me a meaningful nod.

"I guess . . . we have no other choice," I conceded, my hands trembling in my lap. Never had I ever imagined myself journeying from heaven to the inferno in a single night.

Augustin swathed me in his outer cloak and propped me against the tree that had supported his back during much of our discussion. Looking into my eyes, he told me that he wished to bring me another dress and some food and wine from his cottage; for if we were to bargain with a demoness—and face whatever other perils existed in the fallen angels' dominion—my body needed to be as fortified as possible. I could not disagree, since I doubted I could manage to stand on my own.

"Promise me that I shall not find you dead upon my return," he said before setting out for his cabin. With an affectionate smile, I vowed to cling to life.

In his absence, I considered the matter further, unsure how our desperate measures could possibly portend a favorable outcome. Here I was—a Christian who had likely disappointed God when I chose a sinful man over paradise, now planning to negotiate my fate with one of His fallen angels.

This is madness, Swanie, I thought as I gazed toward the river, my ice sensing the ebb and flow of its currents. *Where exactly is the realm that demons call home? It can't be hell itself, since God cast them to earth when Satan rebelled. Is it in the earth's core or something? How does Augustin expect to take me, a living human, to a place like that?*

And what will Ashima require in return for my life? Will she demand to share Augustin with me until I leave the world for good? I'm not sure I could agree to that, although I guess it'd be similar to the relationship he had with Gisela. But I just got Augustin back, and Muniche desires him as much as I do. I don't want to share my Keyholder. I wonder if she has the authority to break the curse that binds Augustin to earth . . . then I'd have to convince him to turn from evil at the absolute last second. No different than his propensity for saving my life at death's door. This is truly insane.

By the time Augustin returned, I had resolved that no matter what horrors we must face, I would not accept a destiny apart from him. I would not allow his efforts to save me to prove ineffective. We would greet the dawn together, either on earth or in heaven. I believed that he loved me enough to put his fate in God's hands if eternity proved our only recourse.

He helped me change out of my wedding dress and into a clean frock that seemed to harbor an unusual weight. My fingers sensed magic of some sort woven into the fabric. Before I could ask Augustin about its purpose, he handed me a buttered roll. Beckoning me to sit upon his lap once more, he poured dark wine into a sturdy chalice.

Augustin fingered my pulse again as I sipped at the wine, washing away the stickiness coating my throat. He observed that my heartbeat was still too feeble for comfort, and concluded that he must perform a bit more blood control on me before we embarked on our mission. "Are you sure we have time for that sort of thing?" I asked, glancing toward the eastern sky as he drew a slender knife from the belt of his trousers.

"Sunrise is three hours away, my swan," he assured me. "Now give me your left hand, so I may open a channel between our bloodstreams. You should continue to eat and drink while I grant you my blood, for our combined efforts ought to invigorate the life in your system. I shall pump your heart myself, as far as I am able. Though it may not feel particularly pleasant, we must endeavor to accelerate your convalescence, or our adversaries shall seek to exploit your frailty."

It was *not* particularly pleasant to feel the strict hands of a dead man pumping the heart of my soul, forcing our united blood to course swiftly through my veins. My life gradually superseded his death, conquering my lingering weakness. Grimacing from the discomfort of his callous sorcery upon my blood, I nibbled at the bread, washing each bite down with a sip of wine.

"Did you accept the keys just because I'm the Lady of Muniche?" I asked after several minutes of eating. True warmth had returned to my blood at last.

Augustin chuckled. "I suppose that you were the main reason, though not in the manner you imply. I would have yanked you from that raft before your fatal leap had fantasies regarding my new responsibility not distracted me. It was an alien experience, to feel such purpose and loyalty engulfing my soul . . . realizing the gravity of the role I had just taken upon myself . . . believing that I would see our city prosper within a few centuries."

He chuckled again and sighed, our incomplete bond filling my heart with images of renewed triumph, hope, and allegiance reborn in a heart that had long renounced such things. "He did not lie, when he said that I may be the one to eradicate Muniche's curse," Augustin went on, our hands still locked together as his blood flowed into my veins. "He beguiled me into this by reminding me that I do indeed love my birthplace, for she is my mother and also my wife. He was quite a persuasive rascal, that brother of mine."

My eyes bulged, and I tried to tilt my head up to see Augustin's eyes. "That *brother* of yours?" Apparently more had passed between the two of them than simply the keys of Muniche. My thoughts traveled back to that night just one week ago when Otto, after heaving a sigh of resignation, had finally referenced the man he had cursed as his brother.

Humor rumbled in my Keyholder's chest. "He came to me while I wallowed in despair at my failure to bridge the gulf between you and me, offering an escape from centuries devoid of meaning. It took me a fair amount of time to hope that I may be able to save *you*, along with Muniche. Now that I feel you in my arms I can say truthfully that I forgive him completely, not just for cursing me . . . but for being the instrument of our mother's death."

The joy flowing into my heart through his hands surprised and thrilled me. I had never imagined that Augustin, the bitter outcast, could embrace the beauty of forgiveness so wholeheartedly. It would never have come about had Prince Otto not forgiven him first, after acknowledging that Augustin had radically changed over the years as a result of the love we shared.

The fact that this man—who had once scorned the responsibility of the Teuton city as a curse in and of itself—had taken Muniche's keys out of love for the city, out of a desire to restore her glory, delighted me. If that were true, solace would remain for him even if we failed to prolong my time on earth. And if anyone could break the curse Otto had laid upon our city, Augustin would manage it.

"I think she's happy with you," I murmured, closing my eyes to concentrate on my master's touch. "Marelda likely celebrates your appointment as Keyholder as we speak, welcoming your predecessor into her heavenly home."

After swallowing the last of the bread, I finished the wine and set the chalice upon the ground. Augustin's right hand slid away from my heart for a short moment to slip his iron keys into my grasp, closing my fingers securely around them. "*I* think that you have more right to these than I," he breathed in my ear, his hand traveling back to my heart, which pounded steadily now, rejuvenated by his touch. "We shall rule Muniche as equals, my swan. You embody her soul; thus you shall help direct her destiny."

Bliss churned through my veins at such a prospect, but I ordered myself not to hope too keenly for fear of disappointment. Frankly, we had no control over the time of my death. Whether I lived to see the daylight depended on divine mercy alone. These fantasies that raced through my mind now could never truly come to pass. Had our love not always been fraught with disillusionment, with separation, with indecency even? It seemed like the pleasantest of dreams to feel my love for Augustin uniting with Muniche's love, every beautiful memory we had shared coalescing into correctness—glorious, but no doubt as ephemeral as my fading life.

I kept my morose speculations bottled within, clasping Muniche's keys protectively in my right hand. Ironic that I had never held them before without my Keyholder's hand entwined with mine, a permanent reminder of his authority. *Augustin believes I wield the strongest power over our people's fortune.*

Soon enough, Augustin deemed me as healthy as I could be in our current situation. Sealing the wounds in my hand and his expertly, he wiped the excess blood on the hem of his priestly robe, which he had put on overtop of his basic tunic and trousers. An appropriate outfit for our forthcoming journey.

Then he pulled me to my feet and asked me to walk the short distance to the riverbank and back unaided, critically observing my movements. While I still felt a bit stiff, it astonished me to discover how completely my body had recovered from my attempted suicide. Vitality pulsed through my limbs as I walked to the Rhine and back, the odd slippers he had put on my feet granting me expert traction.

"You might as well continue to stretch your legs, even sing a song or two," Augustin suggested after I had paced to the riverbank for the third time. I turned away from the Rhine to look at him, seeing his firm gaze trained on the night sky. "I must fashion a fiery portal for our passage."

He vanished into the forest before I could question him on that, so I altered my course to follow the river's path. Fingering each of Muniche's keys, I took a deep breath before humming the opening lines of one of my favorite songs by Nightwish, "Beauty Of The Beast." Somehow it seemed too fitting as I prepared to confront a conclave of demons in hopes of reclaiming my long lost love.

Eventually, my master beckoned me to the fire, which he had built between the riverbank and the forest. Its flames roared skyward in freakish shapes and colors, black edging what appeared to be an empty portal. I halted a meter away, its heat already uncomfortable at that distance. But my Keyholder stepped to my side and took my hands in his, removing the keys from my grasp and placing them into a pocket beneath his outer robe.

His eyes burned seriously into mine as he intoned, "We must walk through that portal to reach the realm of fallen angels, physically and together, without apprehension."

I recoiled, looking from those devilish flames to Augustin's face. "Can I . . . *do* that . . . as a mortal human?" It did not seem possible. The flames clawed at the nothingness, a warning to anyone mad enough to attempt this passage. Did Teuton priests learn how to open this sort of gateway, or was this a sorcery granted only to the dead?

"You can, because you are with me." A brilliant blue sword appeared out of nowhere in Augustin's right hand, while he held his left out to me. "The flames of the entrance are unnatural, and I shall shield you from their impact. Come with me into the dominion of the accursed."

It can't be any worse than travelling the currents of time, I told myself. *I don't do this alone. Augustin's with me.* Gathering all of my courage, I clutched my Keyholder's hand and stepped with him into the fire.

Chapter Twenty-seven:
The Devious Dimension

God may not forgive how I've strayed this time, I thought as we passed through Augustin's fiery portal. Less than two weeks ago, I had told him rather righteously that I could not embark upon the dark path for the answer to all of my troubles. Yet here I was again—on my way, body and soul, to a place thronged with demons. *I'm as much of a hypocrite as Prince Otto,* I realized.

What could I offer a demoness in exchange for my life? Augustin believed that we could succeed, so Ashima must be far more obliging than Wuotan. He had insisted that he could close the deal himself, since as an undead human he held more sway than a mortal like me. But it distressed me that he would give and give again for me, when I could offer nothing but a deteriorating body subject to sickness and ultimate death.

Could Ashima render her youth spell permanent, so I could remain by my Keyholder's side until he left the world for good in 1493?

The fires of Augustin's portal cooked my soul from the inside out, my eyes squeezed shut as we stepped out of the only dimension I had truly known. My grip on his left hand did not waver. He guided me forward into a place where the air smelled of smoldering flames and ash. My nose scrunched at the atmosphere's innate tautness; I sensed no hint of fresh air, no breath of hope.

"Stay beside me, Swanhilde." My master's voice brought me out of a deep hopelessness that clung to me, inundating my brain with images of Freya's torture. Recognizing that my dark thoughts must be a natural result of this accursed realm, I shook myself and gripped Augustin's hand, as if it were my only connection to reality. *How could any entity, demon or not, subsist in a place like this?*

"Come. We must depart this anteroom and meet the messenger. The weight you bear now is a defense mechanism meant to keep mortals and celestial beings away." Augustin tugged me forward, his grip ever certain.

Cautiously, I opened my eyes a crack as my feet moved automatically. The portal had brought us to a shadowy chamber walled in molten rock dripping with liquid fire. Smoke swirled its way upward into darkness, toward an abyss overhead rather than beneath. Ashes crunched under our shoes, each step giving off odors that seemed appropriate to a killing floor. But the fires leaking from the walls . . . they glowed with colors hardly suitable to a place of destruction. Vibrant crimson, neon green, gold that rivaled heaven's brilliance . . . and was that hot pink? Really?

As we neared an archway of mirrored obsidian, its surface casting our dark reflections back at us, I realized that I gawked at the oozing flames far too intently. They seemed to call to me, beckoning a living human to offer her soul to a realm where she would find no escape. I cleared my throat and shut my eyes for a second, trying to reassert my strength of will. Remembering what Augustin had said before we struck out for the archway, I repeated, "The messenger?"

"The demonic domain is a land of hierarchies. Each fallen angel occupies a set role, unchanging throughout eternity," Augustin told me, his vigilant gaze fixed upon the landscape on the opposite side of the archway. All I could see at this point was an otherworldly glimmer of darkness and colors, similar to time's currents. He held his sword at the ready, a warning to any who dared challenge us.

"Demons who once claimed higher positions in heaven —Ashima, Wuotan, and Satan for example—have separate spheres within, although Ashima rarely spends time in hers. Those tend to be the personages primitive tribes will worship, while the lower-level demons bow to their overlords, perpetuating chaos."

That made sense, strangely enough. I recalled the stories I had read in the Bible about demonic activities. "Is it only the demon overlords who possess humans?" I asked, thinking of Zack, the foolish athlete who had stolen the Torstein from me in college—at Wuotan's bidding. Had Wuotan merely ordered one of his minions to occupy Zack's body while he watched and laughed?

Augustin gave a quiet growl; we had nearly reached the archway. "All fallen angels have that ability, but only some vacate this domain in order to do so. Groups of lower-level demons occasionally possess children as purveyors of chaos."

"That must be the type that possessed that one man in the Bible, and Christ exorcised them into the pigs that dove off the cliff."

"I would keep such musings to yourself until we are done here," Augustin said as we paused before the archway. He squeezed the fingers of my right hand, prompting me to look up at his face. "Swanhilde, allow me to present our case before Ashima, and do not leave my side. No matter what the inhabitants of this realm assay to offer you, *do not* accept any gifts without discussing it with me first. And *do not* take anyone else's hand. If you take a demon's proffered hand, it is considered permission and consent."

Augustin's eyes blazed with cerulean fire as they met mine, and I nodded, accepting his terms. "You're the only person here who wields my permission and consent," I murmured to him, winding my fingers firmly through his.

The landscape opened up on the other side of the portal, fires and igneous rocks the sole ornamentation. We had stepped onto a path that appeared to be of black glass, stretching off into the distance, with tongues of flame leaping upward on both sides. A sheen of sweat broke upon my face, but my footsteps dawdled as I looked around, catching hints of movement here and there amid the boulders. A humanoid entity approached us from farther down the path, but I could not yet make out its features in the hazy atmosphere.

"I've been here before." The words slipped out of me as I hesitated.

"That is not possible." Augustin pulled gently at my hand, trying to convince my feet to keep up with his. They did not want to comply. Glittering eyeballs peered at us from beyond the fires that framed our path.

"I was here in one of my dreams," I whispered, speaking Bayerisch this time for fear of being overheard. These devils were bound to the current timeline, so they should not be able to understand a dialect of the future. "I had a dream about this place on the night after Joel and I came to Eisenwald. I remember this glass, how it scorched my feet . . . and I remember your sword." I gestured at it.

"Meaningless visions," Augustin muttered, though I saw the fingers of his right hand clutch his sword's hilt more securely.

"Why isn't the glass scorching my feet?" I poked one of them out from under the scarlet dress I wore, checking for signs of damage. The black slipper appeared unharmed.

"Because I wove your current outfit with threads of my deadly magic, same as my outer robe. If you wore basic clothing here, the fires would consume it."

Augustin must have recognized that it would be no use to drag me forward. He stood still at my side, and I sensed his fire churning in a halo of cobalt around our entwined hands. I thought I heard a growl crawling through the fires to my left—my unprotected side—and I slid closer to my Keyholder. Sweat had begun to run down my back, but I sensed it evaporating within seconds. *This must be the core of the earth. Nowhere else could swelter with this type of heat.*

The messenger halted four paces away from us, and I turned my attention to him as he bowed at the waist, reddish eyes studying Augustin's visage beneath heavy black brows. He looked almost like a regular human, clad in a leather tunic and trousers that appeared to be a uniform, his hair falling to his shoulder blades in undulating waves. He was lean but muscular, standing about the same height as Augustin, his lips spreading apart in what might have been a welcoming smile.

But curved black claws grew from his bare toes and his fingers, which he clasped before him in a conciliatory fashion. His pearly teeth were fanged like those of a predator. In the multihued firelight, I judged his skin color as some type of copper, glittering like the precious metal.

"What brings you to the devious dimension, Cursed Destroyer?" The devil's tone sounded deceptively pleasant. He greeted Augustin in Teutonica, his eyes not acknowledging me in the slightest. The title he granted Augustin gave me pause—he used the traditional descriptor for *Cursed One* while appending it with an ancient term for *Destroyer.*

And if I was not completely mistaken, this messenger gave off an edgy vibe, as though he preferred to welcome anyone other than Augustin.

"We seek to confer with Ashima," my master responded, shifting his fiery sword so that it stood like a barrier between us and the leather-clad devil. He did not return the messenger's bow; his tone and body language exuded confidence.

The devil looked surprised, his reddish eyes shifting momentarily to me. "Ashima doesn't accept sacrifices of that—"

A snarl tore from Augustin's teeth, prompting the devil to scamper back a few steps, raising both hands. "I'll call her right away! Don't be angry! Give me just a moment." The messenger darted into the fires to my left, quickly disappearing.

Augustin sighed, irritation touching my heart through our tenuous bond. "As if you were a mere sacrifice. The nerve of that wretch!"

I raised my eyebrows at my master. "He seemed . . . kind of scared of you."

Augustin smirked. "Because my death works against the hearts of lower-level demons just as it works against the hearts of humans and animals."

"You mean . . . you can *kill* demons like that one with your death?" I gaped at him, respect welling within me.

"Their existence is not like that of the earth-dwelling beings. If I unleash my deadly anger upon the majority of the devils that occupy this realm, their bodies crumble into ash. The essence that gives them life must then be reborn within an enclosed furnace. Those who manage the furnace have a propensity for skinning its victims and fashioning the increase into the leather clothing you saw upon that wretch." He nodded toward where the messenger had vanished.

I felt sick. "Then these . . . creatures here . . . wear the *skins* of their fellow beings?" My stomach twisted, and I placed my free hand against it. I needed to look confident, so I could not throw up.

"This realm is laden with selfishness. There is no loyalty, no compassion."

I swallowed hard, blinking my eyes at a helix of light blue flames arching skyward at the edge of the path. *Think of something else. Anything else.* "Does . . . do the . . . demon overlords . . . wear skin too?"

"No, they clothe themselves in finery taken from the mortal realm. And my death gift does not work against former archangels, unfortunately."

So Wuotan had once been an archangel like Satan. That figured. My ears detected another hint of growls from beyond the fiery plumes to my left, along with what sounded like heavy sniffs. Some of the lower-level demons must appear more like monsters than human beings—just like in my dream.

"I keep hearing animal noises over there," I whispered, rising onto my tiptoes to speak directly into Augustin's left ear. "Why haven't any of them attacked us yet? Have you sliced them to bits with that sword before?"

Augustin chuckled and spun his sword in a circle. "They fear I might unleash my death indiscriminately, as my predecessor often did when something angered him. He was known for appearing at random and rending entire legions to ash."

I could not stifle a harsh laugh. "Have you ever done that?"

"Only once." Augustin eyed me in disapproval, and I struggled to contain my amusement. The majority of my fears about this place had dissipated, since my master had the power to keep these devils from harming me. *Now all I have to worry about is Ashima . . . and Wuotan, if he happens to notice I'm here.*

The messenger reappeared unexpectedly at my side, prompting Augustin to thrust himself in front of me, brandishing his sword as snarls spewed from his lips. The leather-clad devil held both palms outward, his entire body shaking. "Please forgive me, Cursed Destroyer, but the overlord of time and destiny is currently . . . occupied. She has no wish to delay her orgy at your—"

"Who is her current partner, and where are they?" Augustin interrupted, as the word *orgy* bounced around in my brain. "We are on a tight schedule."

"She is with the overlord of wisdom and war," the messenger answered, his reddish eyes abruptly fixated on the Gothic cross Augustin wore around his neck.

My lover spat out a curse. A second later, he tramped off down the glass pathway, pulling me along with him. "Perhaps we can work them against each other," he muttered under his breath.

"They have ringed his sphere with imps and sirens!" the messenger called after us in a distressed tone.

"So much the better," Augustin tossed over his shoulder. "This realm needs a strong reminder of who I am."

Scampering to keep up with him, my lungs began to pant at the stifling air. "He meant Wuotan . . . right? Ashima's in bed . . . with Wuotan."

"Not for long," Augustin growled. He changed course toward a break in the flames to our right, and we entered a rocky pathway that led toward a distant wall of solid golden fires. My eyes could barely make out an archway that must have been the entrance. Comprised of gleaming obsidian, black flames waved between the stones. A collection of writhing creatures gathered around the entrance, vicious growls and clashing teeth echoing along the path.

Terror returned to me as we pressed forward. I averted my eyes to my Keyholder's face, not wanting to study the demonic legion standing in our way. "Your death . . . can get rid of . . . those creatures . . . right?" I panted.

Augustin continued to stride forward without slowing. "The imps, yes. The sirens, no, for they have neither hearts nor blood. It appears that he has chosen four of them to guard rather than take part in the orgy. Fire, stone, wind, and light. I shall shield you from them as far as I am able, but beware of the light siren. Her element could permanently blind you."

I squinted toward the gathered fiends, my eyes picking out a naked female whose body shone as brilliantly as the sun. Looking away quickly, I blinked against the resultant blobs that clouded my vision. Augustin shoved something into my left hand—another flaming sword—and said, "Just in case the seductresses distract me before I can carve them to bits."

An instant later, I sensed black knives erupting from Augustin's inner self, his mien screwed up in fury as he glared toward the creatures blocking our path. We were about fifteen meters away now, and I noticed that the imps appeared to be hairless, four-footed beasts with slavering jowls and sizzling eyes. The largest among them—likely their pack leader, if that was a thing here in the devious dimension—let loose a howl and leaped toward us . . . .

And shattered into ash in the air above, just as its counterparts whined and crumbled to the stony ground.

Within seconds, silence fell, the stench of cindered decay wafting into my nostrils. Looking back at Augustin, I saw his lips curl into a sly smirk as he spoke to the only beings left standing—four voluptuous females, their blood-red eyes ogling my master in shock.

"Would you prefer to be torn to pieces, or will you let us pass in peace?"

Augustin pointed his sword menacingly toward our adversaries; but before he could make good on his threat, one of the sirens sailed forward, spreading her arms in an alluring gesture. Blue flames sparkled in her waist-length black hair as she purred, "Darling Wolfgang, what a pleasure to see you here! It has been far too long since our flames entangled so perfectly."

She stood directly before us and caressed Augustin's cheek with one finger.

So I jabbed my flaming sword into her back, breaking her flesh apart.

Chapter Twenty-eight:

A Terrible Verdict

I had not handled a sword with any level of proficiency in ages. Not since the late 1050s when Joel and I taught our eldest son, Max, how to fight using dulled blades. In the twenty-first century, I had no reason to wield any type of sword.

My reaction came completely out of nowhere, a spark of jealousy inflamed deep within at the possibility that Augustin had enjoyed elemental sex with that libidinous siren. Blue-fired. Black-haired. Ivory-skinned. No taller than me. Breasts that had to be at least a D cup, no trace of age or earlier pregnancies weighing them down. Wide hips and shapely ass.

Augustin could have taken her as my replacement, for the carnal aspects at least.

Without letting go of his hand, I thrust my fiery sword at her. I aimed for her neck and hit her somewhere midback, my non-dominant hand failing me.

But the blade cracked through her flesh, pieces of which shattered to the ground like tiny crystals. It occurred to me for a split second that the sword must have been made of more than just Augustin's fire, even though he had created it from naught but his magic. Something solid lurked within that blade, something strong enough to break the crystalline flesh of a siren.

She screeched as the blade sliced its way down to her right ass cheek. Before she or any of her sisters thought to retaliate, Augustin regained his acumen, his own sword slashing her head from her shoulders. Her scream cut off, and her skull cracked upon the ground and rolled a few meters to our right.

"Cut up her limbs while I eliminate the other three," Augustin said through gritted teeth, letting go of my hand and charging forward too swiftly for my mortal eyes to follow. The other sirens hissed at him, calling forth their elements in a vain attempt to impede his attack. His blade whirled invisibly, slicing off a head, two arms, a pair of breasts.

I shook myself, tearing my eyes away from my avenging mate to regard the headless siren upon the ground before me. Her body had started to crawl its way toward her severed head, which sat dented in a pile of embers, the lengthy strands of her hair smoking. I wrapped both hands around my sword's hilt and focused on hacking her gemlike body apart. *It's just like butchering an animal,* I told myself. *She has no soul; she's nothing but Wuotan's sex toy.*

After I had chopped the fire siren into at least a dozen pieces—watching them for a moment to ensure they had ceased moving—I turned for where Augustin stood over the other three. His immortal speed had already finished the job; limbs and heads of various skin colors lay scattered around the entrance to Wuotan's private sphere. I made my way around two ponderous boulders that had not been there before. I wondered if the stone siren had tried to chuck them at me, the frail human these creatures viewed as Augustin's liability.

I no longer felt weak at all. Adrenaline pumped through my veins along with a trace of my Keyholder's fire, reinforcing my ice to render me a viable opponent. "Will we have to fight any more of these bitches on the inside?" I asked in a casual tone as I stepped to Augustin's side, flexing my fingers around my weapon.

My master favored me with a fond grin. "Wuotan has twelve sirens total, so the other eight doubtless participate in his orgy with Ashima. I can hear four of them composing dulcet tunes within, so I advise you to tread cautiously despite our victory here. The sirens may try to allure you as they did to me. Their music alone can dull the senses."

I nodded, shifting my sword to my left hand and sliding the fingers of my right back through his. "I'll do my best to keep my head in the game. How long do we have until sunrise?"

"Less than two hours now, so we must disrupt the orgy without delay."

We crossed the threshold into Wuotan's sphere, an expansive domain aglow with radiant fires. The scents of death and destruction were less prominent here; in fact, I could smell enticing aromas that reminded me of flowers. Intricate statues of fire and stone adorned the landscape, some in shapes I could not identify, others representing angelic beings. Flaming pillars rose higher than my eyes could see, implying that this sanctuary boasted space as its ceiling, or perhaps the outer reaches of hell. Maybe this accursed realm was not in the earth's core after all.

"Do not allow yourself to be distracted," Augustin murmured in my ear as I inhaled deeply, trying to identify the source of that floral scent. It seemed to exude from a cluster of bright pink flames shaped like a bush.

I bit the inside of my cheek, silently ordering myself to maintain vigilance. Perhaps Wuotan infused some of his fires with lovely scents to lure unsuspecting women, those who wanted an escape from a purposeless life. Thinking of the sirens we had left in pieces at the threshold, I asked Augustin in soft Bayerisch, "Will he have to create fresh bodies for the four we destroyed?"

"He uses his fire and his sorcery to repair any damaged ones," he replied in the same language, his eyes narrowed toward an opening in what appeared to be a hedgerow of thick silver fires. The ground beneath our feet resembled black glass, similar to the pathway from the anteroom.

"At least they don't have to worry about being skinned for leather." My body shuddered at the thought, even though I spared no pity for the sirens. Gathering my nerve, I looked up at Augustin's face and asked the most pressing question. "Was the fire siren . . . the one you used to . . . have sex with . . . all the time?" I was not sure whether I really wanted to know.

"She was one of them, yes. But you should know I prefer ice. And love." My Keyholder raised an eyebrow at me significantly.

My ears caught the chords of the melodious song Augustin had mentioned earlier, drifting outward from the silver-fired chamber we approached. The tune thrummed deep inside my heart, beckoning me to lose myself in its harmonies. It sounded as if two sirens sang—one soprano and one contralto—while two others played instruments that might have been a flute and a harp. Though I could not understand the lyrics, voiced in a dialect different from the ones I knew, the words awakened deep-seated cravings within me, inciting my pelvic muscles to clench of their own accord.

My heart rate increased as we passed through the silver fires, the music pulsing around us in a manner that pushed a plaintive moan through my lips. I felt deliciously horny; I longed to strip Augustin's robe from him right this second and take him into my core. But the claws of his left hand pricked at my palm, his voice sharply urging me to control myself.

"We are here to save your life, Swanhilde, not to give these demons and their minions a peep show." He let go of my hand and sprang forward to decapitate the two sirens who stood behind a grand obsidian throne, their ruby lips trilling songs of eroticism. Their sultry words evaporated from my brain the moment their skulls smacked upon the glass floor.

Now my head was clearer, so I shifted my sword to my right hand again, my jaw dropping as I actually *looked* at the scene before me. The pitch black throne stood atop a marble platform at the center of the chamber, pillars of silver and gold flames rising along its base. Four diminutive cauldrons sat at the four corners of the throne, each belching out fires in the four colors of Teutonic magic— blue, red, yellow, and black. Augustin was in the process of chopping the singing sirens to pieces; their bloodless body parts fouled the platform's striking character.

A luminous male demon lounged upon the obsidian throne, his naked skin an entrancing shade of pale gold, each muscle curved in crisp perfection. Blond curls draped his head in a radiant aureole, his eyelids closed, his features smoothed into an expression of abject bliss. His sculpted thighs spread apart, the diamond-clawed fingers of his left hand cradled the silver curls of a woman's head, her soft lips closed around his cock.

At first glance, it appeared that the woman worshipped her demon lord through sex . . . but as my gaze fell to where she lay comfortably sprawled upon her back on a divan before the throne, I saw that she received pleasure beyond that of her current partner. Her skin gleamed like Wuotan's, but it was hued a pale silver rather than gold, her body appearing both sensual and strong. One siren sucked her clit, her sepia hands confining the demoness' pelvis in place. Two others lavished attention upon her pert breasts, kneading them and suckling the nipples.

A fourth siren venerated her demon lord's right foot, polishing its diamond claws and peppering its toes with kisses. My eyes drifted back toward Wuotan's waist, and I abruptly identified what he was doing with his right hand. He stroked the skin of the silver demoness' throat, fingering himself through her flesh. I heard her give a muted moan, and his clawed fingertips rested over her vocal cords, a sigh of satisfaction pealing from his lips.

Gross. The wine and bread churned uncomfortably in my stomach.

During the half-minute or so that it took me to observe what a demonic orgy entailed, Augustin had gotten into a tangle with the two sirens who had played instruments before we encroached upon their saturnalia. He scuffled with an olive-skinned siren who had wrapped a cocoon of energy around his body; her red-haired sister crouched upon his shoulders, her fangs and claws tearing into his neck. I saw blood running onto his cloak as blue fire blazed around him, fighting to overcome his adversary's energy. His elemental sword seemed to have vanished.

It took me a few seconds to react, my eyes blinking in perplexity at my mate's struggles. *Why is he having trouble with these two, when he ripped three apart earlier? Did these bitches have long enough to prepare or what?*

They could not kill him. I knew that, but I could not abide watching his blood leak onto his robe. That red-haired bitch gawked at all of our private moments right now. If I tried to slice through her with my sword, I might hit my master accidentally, so I needed to get rid of the energy siren first. Her elemental magic likely drained Augustin's vigor.

I summoned my ice to bolster my speed and strength, mouthing a silent prayer to God for aid, if my irreverence had not yet incited Him to forsake me. Then I zoomed around the front of the throne to attack the energy siren from behind, my sword gripped in both hands as I swung it at her legs. I felt the blade slice through her knees, causing her to pitch forward with a screech. The energy field around Augustin's body wavered, and out of the corner of my eye I saw him burst through it and take hold of the red-haired siren's throat.

Meanwhile, I drove the point of my sword into the energy siren's neck. Her crimson eyes glared up at me as I cracked her throat in two, and I felt her conjuring an elemental net around me. My braid rose a few centimeters as her magic prickled through my clothing . . . but she was far too late. Augustin's booted foot detached her head from her neck before she could achieve further mischief.

"If you could hand me that sword, I shall finish this," Augustin said, fatigue evident in his tone. I passed it to him and observed while he diced our latest opponents into pieces, breathing heavily as my own exhaustion mingled with what remained of my adrenaline. I sincerely hoped we would not have to spar with the four sirens engaged in the orgy—or the demons themselves.

Within moments, Augustin returned to my side and clapped his free hand upon my right shoulder. "I appreciate your help, Swanie. They caught me off guard while I finished with the songstresses. My imprudence put you in danger, and I greatly apologize."

"It's okay. Honestly, I'd rather butcher these fools than watch what's going on over there." I gestured toward the throne at our backs. Augustin pressed his lips into a firm line as he eyed Wuotan's throne, the red and yellow flames that occupied its posterior cauldrons crackling in an ominous manner.

"We have no time to waste. Remember, allow me to present our case."

Augustin passed the sword back to me, and I nodded my agreement, taking the hilt in my left hand and threading the fingers of my right through his left. As he guided me around to the front of the throne, I took a quick look at Wuotan and Ashima. Both still appeared wholly engrossed in their eroticism. Neither gave any sign of having noticed the melee behind them, or the fact that their musicians' melodies had ceased. Wuotan, his eyelids still blissfully closed, had begun to grind lithely into Ashima's throat, his fingers sliding along his length. She seemed not to breathe at all, though her pelvis bucked against the siren who lavished her pussy.

My stomach twisted again, and I narrowed my eyes at the smooth flesh of Wuotan's neck, arched backward in utter indifference. Could Augustin's elemental sword cut through a former archangel's neck? Had Wuotan ever experienced the torment of rebirth in the furnace, where demons skinned each other alive?

"Maybe I should just lop his head off and be done with this." The words fell from my lips in Teutonica for some reason. Augustin tensed at my side.

"I would not advise that . . . my child." The demon's voice surprised me, for it sounded exactly like it did in time's currents and when he invaded my thoughts. Dark and foreboding, hardly fitting for his glorious façade. His golden eyelids slid open to reveal irises of a striking azure, more vibrant than the Gulf of Mexico on a perfect summer's day. They seized me with their intensity. My ice trickled strangely through my blood as though lost.

Augustin planted himself between the demon and me, twisting his left arm in an awkward manner to keep hold of my right, blocking me from Wuotan's sight. "I would appreciate it if you could postpone this business," my master said, his Teutonica formal but stiff. "I have a case to present before Ashima, and it is time sensitive."

Wuotan chuckled, the sound grating at my spirit. "Pity. Unfortunately for you, I have finished but thrice thus far while Ashima has gained five releases." As he spoke the final word, I heard the demoness moan again and saw her body jerk beneath the dark fingers of the siren who drank from her core.

"Six now," Wuotan continued, his apathy so thick I suspected I could cut it with my fiery sword. "I fear it may take me days, weeks to match her. And I fear that your decision to mangle eight of my sirens renders me incredibly averse to heeding your whims. That you would offend me so greatly while carrying two mementos of the Almighty Tyrant . . . ah, what has become of you, Wolfgang?"

The demon's voice trailed off as he expelled a gratified groan, doubtless achieving his fourth orgasm. Augustin turned back to me and whispered, "Keep that sword at the ready," in Bayerisch. Then he let go of my hand and strode to where Ashima lay sprawled upon the divan, touching one claw to the silver flesh above her left breast, where I could see her throbbing heartbeat.

He bent over her and murmured something I could not translate, a trail of smoke rising from where his claw met her flesh. Her body shuddered, and her right hand reached up from where it hung listlessly to grasp Augustin's wrist. She detached herself from Wuotan's cock and sat up, her left hand lightly pushing the sirens away from her breasts as her eyes blinked nebulously at my Keyholder. I heard

Wuotan give a frustrated sigh, and then her irises shifted to where I stood several steps away from the throne, the flaming sword gripped in my strong hand.

Her irises were of a dazzling magenta, the silver curls of her hair a deeper shade than her skin, their tresses cascading upon her shoulders like blooming wisteria. She was beautiful, and her eyes shone with glee.

"You have brought your beloved here to fill her final hour with erotic delights! How wonderful!" she exclaimed. An instant later, she locked both arms around Augustin's neck as her pelvis convulsed beneath the sepia siren's hands, a rapturous groan spilling from her lips. "We shall teach her glories she has never known, my dearest," she purred in Augustin's ear. She took his earlobe into her mouth to suckle it as her body relaxed.

Anger boiled within me, and I took one step forward, weighing the sword in my right hand and silently wondering what would happen if I plunged it into that silver bitch's heart. I heard Wuotan chuckling again, and my master made a slicing motion in my direction, extracting himself from Ashima's hold and declaring that they had important matters to discuss. Ashima beamed at him beguilingly, and Augustin shoved the siren away from the demoness' pelvis, ordering her in a growl to occupy herself with her sisters.

The siren gave an incensed wail and fell at Wuotan's feet, crawling forward to bathe his left foot with her tears. Apparently she did not appreciate my mate ordering her about. The two who had caressed Ashima's breasts had begun to sift through the body parts scattered behind the throne, their expressions horrified. The fourth siren was in the process of polishing her master's right foot with a silken cloth, ignorant of what unfolded around her.

Do these sirens have brains at all? I wondered, *or did Wuotan steal those along with their hearts when he transformed their human bodies? Does he control their every move somehow? There were four standing guard outside his sphere, and then two of the musicians attacked Augustin after he cut their sisters apart. Did they do that at Wuotan's command or because they care about their sisters?*

My instincts told me that my questions would not be answered this night. Ashima had perched herself upon Wuotan's naked lap, her right arm draped across his shoulders while her left hand traced the curve of his pecs. Her magenta eyes remained riveted upon Augustin as he outlined our predicament, standing a few steps back from the throne and the divan. The blue-fired cauldron, positioned closest to him, glowed in a frantic manner, as if its flames reacted to Augustin's resolve.

Wuotan had fixed his gaze upon me again, a dangerous smile curling across his lips. I sensed a pointed scratching at my heart, and when I met the proud demon's eyes he grinned at me, displaying pearly teeth.

"I fear that you are slightly misinformed, dear Wolfgang," Ashima breathed when my Keyholder had paused in his discourse. Tragedy infused her tone as she went on. "There are some things in our reality that are inevitable, and the results of magic cannot be undone. You doomed your beloved with my youth spell, cast so hastily upon her without thought to the tides of destiny. You granted her but ten days of youth, and with the sunrise her life must fade forevermore."

"There must be some way to reverse the spell or to eliminate its fatal price," Augustin persisted. "Since you are the mistress of its witchcraft, you have the sway to alter it to suit our needs. As I stated earlier, I would grant you whatever desire you wish in exchange for my *Leitalra's* life."

"Ah, your temptation hurts my heart, dearest Wolfgang! How I wish that I could undo the entropy that creeps upon her even now." Ashima sighed and gave me a look of studied sadness. "Perhaps you ought to choose a partner of a state similar to your own, so destiny's tides do not drag her away from you."

"Swanhilde is my *Leitalra,* the embodiment of my soul. If I cannot have her, I shall annihilate this city bond, this false echo of *her.*"

Augustin spat the final phrase at Wuotan rather than Ashima, his right hand pulling the keys of Muniche from beneath his cloak. "You initiated this celebration the moment I accepted these keys, imagining that I would emerge from obscurity to lead the Teuton people away from the Almighty God. Prince Wolfgang, Muniche's infernal master guardian. But I advise you not to discredit the power of love and loyalty. If you refuse to permit Swanhilde to greet Muniche's future at my side, I shall ensure that the Teuton people forsake your ways. Is your authority not greater than Ashima's? Have you no power over a woman's inane spell, *master?*"

My lips parted in shock as Augustin tore into the golden demon with words hardly fit for an undead servant. And he tossed a hint of misogyny into the mix, which told me that must be a common degradation among demons, too. That was no surprise, since Wuotan had no male sirens. The two who stood amidst their sisters' remains sobbed and pulled at their hair, smoke and darkness hovering in a haze around their naked bodies.

"Cease your mockeries, Wolfgang," Wuotan ordered. His right hand had tightened into a fist upon the armrest of his throne, while his left held Ashima's waist in a possessive fashion. "Grumble all you like, but recognize that the man you should have killed to obtain those keys dug your slave's grave for her."

My eyebrows came together as I tried to follow the demon's implications. He clarified his point after a pause, his smirk aimed directly at me. "He sealed a bargain with me years ago that ended the Bayern line with him. Then he planted his seed into your slave's womb, engendering an infant marked for death."

"*What?*" Augustin and I spoke the word at the same time. He pivoted toward me, horror breaking across his face. My left hand crept hesitantly from my side to touch my womb, my brain doggedly counting backward. How many days before I had sex with Otto had my period ended? Why had Ashima's spell not nullified the potential for pregnancy? Otto's *child* grew within me now?

"Wuotan speaks the truth, dear Wolfgang," Ashima said. "The child's spirit resides deep within your beloved's. It is too young to have chosen a gender."

I was on my knees, though I could not recall sinking to the ground. Both of my hands rested upon my womb, the fiery sword forgotten. This was too much, too much to handle. Otto had given me a child. He had also apparently closed a deal that rendered my pregnancy nonviable. It did not matter; my life was to end with the dawn, no matter how much Augustin and I wished otherwise. Neither demon before us felt compelled to adjust the cruel hands of fate.

Augustin was saying something else to Ashima, his voice sounding broken, but I could not catch the words. My ice had retreated into my spirit, the scorching heat of this realm bearing down upon me as the gears turned in my mind, trying to find the solution that evaded us. Somehow, I sensed that it drifted just beyond my reach.

Dug your slave's grave for you . . . with the sunrise her life must fade . . . you should choose a partner of a state similar to your own . . . marked for death. Time and tide wait for none but the dead. Muniche's Keyholder and Lady were both dead. Marked for death. They were both . . . dead.

The answer hit me in an epiphany, and I raised my chin to meet Wuotan's gaze. He had referred to me as his child more than once since my return to this era. Did the demon hold the authority to make me Augustin's true equal?

Chapter Twenty-nine:
The One Promise
He Had to Break

"You know that I'm from the future, right?" I addressed Wuotan in a voice that sounded deceptively confident. I had to make sure that my epiphany was possible.

"Of course," Wuotan responded in a crass tone as Augustin swung to face me, his eyes bulging. He had asked me to let him present our case, but now I spoke to the demon of my own volition.

"You planted yourself in a time where you do not belong and proceeded to lure my servant away from me," Wuotan went on with a sneer. Augustin made a slicing gesture with his left hand, an attempt to silence me.

I held one finger out to him and looked Wuotan in the eyes when I spoke again. "You have called me your child several times since I arrived here. But you never once called me that in the future." I raised my eyebrows.

Wuotan waved his right hand dismissively. "Whenever a Teuton claims an extra point of mystical blood through the sorcery of my river, they become my child by default. Just as the Lady Freia became your blood-sister."

Rising to my feet, I shook my head once at Augustin, who looked as though he wished to slap a hand over my mouth. I sensed his agitation through our bond, and he sidled closer to me. But I had worked out my destiny at last—it was the only possibility that made sense. Lifting my head, I caught Ashima's gaze for an instant. She nodded at me, her magenta eyes sparkling as she grinned.

"I am currently unmarried by Teuton law," I said to Wuotan, "which grants you the highest authority over me—filial authority. I demand that you lay the filial curse upon me as it is the Lord's Day. The finality of such a death should override the effects of Ashima's spell, if your position is superior to hers."

"Yes! Do it!" Ashima crowed, reaching up to kiss Wuotan's jaw. "And when they are both dead, you can conduct their wedding. It would be so sweet!"

Wuotan appeared thoughtful, but suddenly a tall form of darkness blocked my view of him. Augustin towered over me with his hands upon his hips, his cobalt eyes burning with fury. "Swanhilde, *no,*" he interjected, his intensity prompting me to take an unconscious step backward.

He followed me, his black robe a mere centimeter from my chest. "You have no concept of what it means to be cursed, or what it would mean if that wretch cast it upon you. My deadly anger cannot kill him, but if he drives you to use it against him, you would become a true ghoul like Anubis. You could not associate with the living without putting them in mortal danger."

Augustin related his concerns in Bayerisch to close out our company. The two demons seemed to be discussing my proposal in soft voices behind Augustin's back. Disgruntlement rolled off of my Keyholder's body in waves of heat, melting the traces of ice that had returned to my blood. I had to help him understand that this was our only option, for we may be eternally separated if I did not take the black scar of the accursed onto my right forearm.

It also pained me to know that I could not bring Otto's child into the world. I wondered why he had not told me of the curse he allegedly laid on his family line. That had doubtless factored into his decision to exile Augustin—he had feared I would bear his children and bring Wuotan's reprisals down upon us.

"Actually, I *do* know what it means to be cursed, Augustin," I said quietly, holding his gaze with my own. "I know once I complete the curse, Otto's child must die. It wouldn't be possible for the child to survive anyway, with Ashima's hex upon me. It may be best for the infant to be spared the trials of the world . . . like our own daughter Marelda.

"As for the curse itself, Max shared a lot of his struggles with me while I stayed at the Black Castle, before I returned here. I know about the emptiness and the craving for life, the sense of inferiority among our people. I know that Wuotan will try to incite me to use my death gift against him, so I'll have to practice controlling my reactions even when I'm angry. And I know if I do this, I'll be trapped here with you until 1493. I'm willing to do it, to take you as my fated *Leitaeri* and chosen love. I want to be your Black Priestess."

Augustin rubbed his temple, his free hand clenching and unclenching. "You nearly entered heaven just hours ago," he reminded me, smoke rising from his sleek hair. The hood of his robe had fallen back while he fought the sirens, his blood still marring the fabric, although the wounds in his neck had long since healed. "To complete the filial curse, its victim must confront the gates of hell and accept Wuotan's offer of clemency. Your soul may not be *able* to descend to the abyss."

"I returned for you once, didn't I? I belong wherever you are."

"Ah, Swanhilde!" Augustin stomped away from me, ripping his claws through his hair as he stalked toward the far end of the platform. I watched him toss a few cerulean darts at one of the silver-flamed pillars, its colors shifting just a shade. *He knows we have no other choice, I realized, but he needs time to adjust his perspective. He might miss the privilege of drinking life from my veins and my lips. All I'll have to offer if I'm cursed is death.*

What would death mingled with ice smell like? For years now I had adored Augustin's natural scent of decaying campfire. Would I smell like Antarctica?

I could not suppress a giggle at the thought. Turning back toward where the two demons sat upon the obsidian throne, I fixed my gaze upon the one who had haunted me since I first found the Torstein. He raised his golden eyebrows at me, expectant, while Ashima lay against his chest with her eyes closed. Did this mean I had capitulated in our age-old conflict, if I allowed Wuotan to curse me?

Wuotan has wanted to separate Augustin and me all this time. If he curses me, he'll never be able to keep us apart. So I lifted my chin and asked him, "Will you do it?"

"It would seem as if I have no choice," Wuotan replied, his azure eyes taking note of the medallion I wore. "Have you not yet grasped that we have met before, in times long past, as you and your insolent *Leitaeri* subtly influenced the tides of history? You have failed me time and again, throughout the ages."

I reached up to touch the Torstein, its potential running a tingle through my blood. Both Freia and Beth had mused about a mutual destiny for Augustin and me. What had the *Eihalbe* in the twenty-first century once told me? *His course is murky, treacherous, and infinite.* Were the two of us destined to fade in and out of every era in Teuton history from the present to that day millennia ago, when our ancestors colluded with demons to obtain their enchanted blood?

There's more to Teuton history than meets the eye, and it's up to Augustin and me to unveil the whole of it.

One factor mired my brain in confusion as I looked from my medallion to the blond demon's face. "If what we've done in the past . . . what we have yet to do . . . bothers you so much . . . why don't you let Ashima's spell do its job? Eliminate me from the earthly timeline entirely?"

Wuotan pressed his lips together in an expression of aversion, while Ashima trilled with laughter. "Oh my dear girl, this one has no power to alter what history has already laid down. No one has that power, from heaven above to the abyss' depths. All of his efforts to sway your course have been hopeless cries for attention."

The male demon ground his teeth, his diamond claws leaving light grazes upon Ashima's silver hip. She gave a giddy squeal and murmured something in his ear. Wuotan rolled his eyes before squaring his shoulders and addressing me with a degree of esteem. "I shall cut your blood off from mine, *Leitalra*, and consume your mortal body with my torrid fires. Two of my sirens retrieve the necessary items as we speak."

The sirens' absence had escaped my notice, but now I saw that the two who had suckled Ashima's breasts were gathering their broken sisters' remains into a basin of green-hued flames. Augustin was on his way back to my side, his visage appearing resigned yet determined. He had come to grips with my choice; I sensed his acceptance through our unfinished bond. Ashima took Wuotan's lips in hers as my Keyholder resumed his place at my right side, his sturdy arm secure around my waist.

"Are you okay with what I have to do?" I whispered to him in Bayerisch, huddling close to his side. "Will you still love me after I have no life to offer?"

Augustin made a scornful noise and pressed a sultry kiss to the top of my head. "Swanhilde, do not be absurd. I love you for your mind, your personality, your sweet and gentle heart. I can relinquish your life to claim the entirety of *you* forever. Besides, our spirits shall always emit life in the *Gæstelort*."

"That's true!" I exclaimed, satisfaction propelling me onto cloud nine. So I would have to be cursed and lose my life. Big deal. I would give far more for the opportunity to share Augustin's exile.

The dark-skinned siren and her tanned sister returned to the platform, each one carrying the items necessary to level the filial curse—a strip of parchment, an iron pen, an unusually jewel-like knife, and a bowl that appeared to be made of the same obsidian as Wuotan's throne. Ashima slipped away from her erotic partner and perched herself upon the divan to watch the ritual, her magenta eyes gleaming with curiosity. Wuotan beckoned me forward as the tanned siren stepped to his left side, brandishing the bowl, her soulless eyes locked upon me. Moisture hovered around her body in a cloud of mist.

"Come, Swanhilde. Lay your hand in mine so that my death may shield you from Ashima's false youth." The demon held out his left palm toward me.

Something Augustin had told me before we entered this dominion provoked me to hesitate. "If I lay my hand in his, will he try to do more to me than just the curse?" I whispered to my master in Bayerisch.

"Not if you speak your intentions clearly beforehand," Augustin answered, "but I shall watch him closely as he invokes the curse. He knows it would be unwise to antagonize his Black Priestess' fated master."

I reached up to exchange a lingering kiss with Augustin, his lips so smooth upon mine. Then I stepped to the left side of the throne, the blue-fired cauldron to my right and the yellow to my left. I looked Wuotan straight in the eyes and said, "You have my permission to level the filial curse upon me, nothing more." Then I laid my right wrist upon his palm, taking a deep breath as I tried to center myself.

The tanned siren thrust the bowl beneath my arm, her hip nudging me rudely in the process. I sensed Augustin's presence at my right, one hand steadying my back. And I shut my eyes and envisioned my blood flow as Wuotan began to recite the spell for the filial curse, summoning my Teutonic magic to stem the tide as soon as his blade had done its duty.

It surprised me that Wuotan spoke the curse in the "Name of the Most Holy God," for I figured he might edit that part out. It sounded cynical issuing from the mouth of a demon, but perhaps he was as bound by tradition as the rest of us. I had heard the words of the curse twice before, but several of the phrases pierced my soul this time, as though they had been written just for me.

Due to the unpardonable sins you commit in excess. I had lost count of those. *Fate assigned to you with all of its sorrows.* There would doubtless be sorrows during four centuries on a wicked earth, bound to a sinful Keyholder. *Your desecrated name.* The countless mistakes I had made during my lifetime warranted a thousand curses. Maybe my legacy deserved to be burnt and forgotten . . . but which name was I to burn?

The blade slashed a stinging wound in my forearm, and I opened my eyes to see the dark blood bursting forth, then abating, raining into the bowl as Wuotan turned my wrist downward. The stench was sickening. I panted as weakness seized me with incredible force. Augustin wrapped both arms around me, and for a second I caught a glimpse of the knife's blade before the demon laid it down at his side. Was it made of *sapphire?* An actual jewel?

Suddenly Augustin's fingers closed around my forearm, drawing it to my chest, the mortal wound coalesced into a blackening scab. Someone began to applaud, and then Ashima's exuberant voice cut through the miasma in my brain. "Sign your name, sign your name! Your time is short!"

Augustin led me to the far end of the divan, where the bowl had been placed beside the sheet of vellum and the iron pen. It occurred to me to wonder, as I took up the pen in the hand that shook from excessive blood loss, whether the vellum was made of demon skin, too. Was that the only parchment available here in the devious dimension, as the messenger had labeled this place? *I have to finish this so we can go back home. This realm is wearing on my faith.*

I decided that only my maiden name deserved to be burnt. I had no desire for my curse to pass on to any of my three previous husbands. So I inscribed the name my mother and father had chosen for me onto the vellum with my own blood: *Swanhilde Rolande von Thaden.*

When I laid the pen down, Wuotan arose from his throne to snatch the vellum, his firm cock far too apparent as he strode forward in nude glory. Firelight reflected off of his diamond claws as he lifted the vellum, and I hid my face in my Keyholder's cloak in an attempt to quell the ridiculous cravings the sight of him ignited within me. *He's going to spend the entirety of your existence trying to compel you to turn your anger against him, so you'll lose control over the death gift you're about to gain. You can't succumb to any of his temptations.*

I lifted my head from Augustin's chest to watch the demon halt before his black-fired cauldron, his chiseled ass pointed directly at me. "May the name of Swanhilde Rolande von Thaden be burned"—Wuotan twisted his torso just enough so his eyes met mine—"and may it never be spoken again." The vellum, blotted with my own blood, fell into the cauldron, its flames snapping with freakish flecks of color while my legacy crumbled to ash.

Augustin's body sagged against mine, as though he despised witnessing this moment, even though we both knew it to be inevitable. His fingers still clutched my forearm, and I looked down at it while Ashima applauded anew, like the audience at a game show. The scab that ran along my radial artery from the base of my thumb had turned completely black . . . but the rune that symbolized Ashima's spell glimmered strangely beneath it.

Wuotan's deep tone penetrated my focus while I stared at the scab and rune upon my flesh. "Bring your slave to the sacrificial chamber, Wolfgang, and slay her quickly, before her youth fades away."

I did a double-take and lifted my gaze to Wuotan's. *"What?!"* Augustin roared, his arms crushing me against his chest.

The golden demon stood beside where Ashima lounged upon the divan, one of his hands rhythmically stroking her curls. "The curse cannot be consummated until her body has been sacrificed to me, and that is your task."

A strangled sound broke from Augustin's lips, and he buried his face against my neck. My forehead wrinkled as I stared blankly at the demons, confusion setting in.

"You're saying I have to complete the curse *now?* But what if . . . what if I wait until after my baby is born?" I placed my right hand upon my womb again. *What you're hoping now is probably impossible,* I told myself. *You can't bear a child once you've been cursed, even if you wait to finish it.*

"I fear that my spell shall shackle you into unceasing torment when dawn breaks over your earthly home," Ashima informed me softly, her eyes lidded as she met my gaze. "My sorcery shall seek to disintegrate your mortal body while Wuotan's shall restore it, refusing to grant you any death apart from sacrifice."

Her words struck me as undeniable, though I doubted any other Black Priestess in history—if any such entity existed—faced a similar dilemma. Otto's child was destined for heaven, and its mother was destined to die on the heathen altar . . . then be reborn in death. Resurrected in blood and locked out of eternity.

"I cannot do this, Swanhilde," Augustin groaned in my ear. "I promised you . . . years ago . . . after you saw me sacrifice . . . the Saxon woman . . . that I would never . . . kill you that way. It is sacrilege . . . and I would be required . . . required . . . to rape you first." His tears dampened my neck.

The idea of a repeat performance of what he had done to me when Wuotan possessed him that night so long ago instilled me with dread. Augustin had once told me that rape was a requirement anytime a human was offered to Wuotan. That was one reason I had begged him to sacrifice animals instead, after he fell under the curse—to abolish the sexual component of the rite. *And that meant . . . .*

I pulled away from my master's grip and took his hands in mine, invoking my ice to cool my blood and refresh his spirit. The obsidian locks of his hair hid his face from me as his body shuddered, as he sought to temper his grief. When he finally managed to meet my gaze, his eyes haunted with shadows, I asked him, "Did Anubis rape you . . . when he sacrificed you to Wuotan?"

Augustin grimaced, but did not look away. "He did."

Taking a deep breath, I said, "Am I to be less than you? I agreed to be cursed, and there's no point in lamenting my choice. We need to get this done, or Wuotan might order one of the lower-level demons to possess you. If I have to be raped and sacrificed, I'd rather you do it than anyone else."

Augustin sighed and bowed his head for a moment. "I suppose I must honor your choice. Come then. I shall try to finish this as painlessly as possible."

He took my right hand and guided me away from the marble platform. We passed through a separate partition in the silver fires and trod a lengthy corridor of black glass, encountering very few others on our way. Occasionally I saw leather-clad humanoid demons performing house-keeping duties, but overall it appeared that Wuotan valued his privacy. His sphere was vast and sparsely populated.

Eventually we descended toward a pit-like cloister absent of color. Jagged black jewels that stood at least five meters high ringed it, with black flames rising from the ground between them. At the center stood an altar of dark gray stone, its troths carved to collect a victim's blood, four flaming cauldrons positioned at each corner. The fires that leapt skyward from the cauldrons were pitch black. An eerie light shone upon the altar from above, yet when I looked up the atmosphere was shrouded in haze.

Fear had begun to eat at my resolve as Augustin paused a few steps from the ring of jewels and flames. "I must take that dress from you now, Swanhilde, for you must be sacrificed naked," he said in an emotionless tone.

My body quaked, but I understood the necessity of such preliminaries. So I nodded and shut my eyes as Augustin undressed me, removing the protective shroud of his magic and baring my body to the oppressive heat of this realm. Sweat broke out on my skin right away, and my Keyholder swept me into his arms before prying the slip-pers off of my feet. He cradled me like a precious treasure as he entered the ring. I thought I heard voices murmuring around us, speculating on my morbid fate.

Nice to know Wuotan had invited all of his minions to this event. Maybe I should keep my eyes closed the entire time, and concentrate solely on Augustin's voice and his touches, no matter how brutal they were to be.

I felt him lay me down upon the altar, the stone uncomfortable against my spine. Strange hues seemed to beat upon my eyelids, and I opened them a crack. Augustin's face came into view where he stood over me, so pale against the swarthy backdrop of his hair and robe, his jaw quivering with restrained emotion.

"You are not permitted to obtain release through this," he muttered in Bayerisch, repulsion evident in his grimace. His eyes strayed toward my pelvis.

"I understand," I whispered back, searching deep within for my last threads of willpower. "Do what you must. I'm waiting to die."

He gave a solemn nod and brushed my right cheek with a fleeting caress. "Swanhilde . . . forgive me for what I must do." The words that foretold the onset of torment.

I shut my eyes again and tried to relax, to remember my reasons for agreeing to this. *To be with Augustin forever. To guide him toward the path of light during his years of exile. To travel time with him and discover all of the secrets hidden from our people. To restore Muniche in power and glory.*

I heard Augustin recite the ritual phrases in Ælte Teutonica, dedicating my mortal body to his demon lord. Then he cast himself upon me without warning, his hands gripping my wrists in a vise, confining my element to my spirit as he jabbed his cock viciously into my core. I could not stifle whimpers of pain; his fire scorched me like it had the night Wuotan possessed him. Horrific memories bound me in their noose as he spilled inside of me and slid off the altar, leaving my naked body battered and chilled. It had taken less than a minute.

I can do this. I can do this.

My vaginal canal felt as though someone had planted live coals inside of it. My breaths had grown shallow, and uncomfortable twists ailed my abdomen. Had Augustin managed to incite a miscarriage? I was certain his fiery member had pounded my cervix repeatedly. Fresh pains arose in my left wrist and then my right. Instinctively, I reached for my element in an effort to soothe the burns that ravaged my insides.

But I could not grasp it at all. I felt the knife slash the bottoms of my feet, a firm hand adjusting them so that my blood ran into the troths. Cold had begun to creep toward my chest as my limbs bled out at Augustin's command. If I had thought to tap into my blood magic to stem the flow, I knew it would have proven futile. An undead priest controlled my fate as my frantic heartbeats counted down their concluding moments.

I opened my eyes one last time, my gaze fixing itself upon the love of my life. Cobalt flames blazed in Augustin's eyes as he raised the sapphire knife above my chest, pointing it downward to extract my heart. His visage contorted in passion, he voiced his final plea just before he drove the blade into my flesh.

"Come back to me!"

Chapter Thirty:
Glorious Saints

Come back to me . . . come back to me . . . come back . . . come back.

The phrase revolved inside my head as agony tore my soul from its earthly shell, death locking its immovable manacles upon a body that no longer had a physical heart. I might have seen it somehow—a vivid image of Augustin's fingers curling around my heart, its crimson life dribbling down the pale skin of his arm until a burst of devilish fire conquered it, those refulgent flames mirrored on his teeth, bared in what could have been interpreted as exultation.

But I knew better. And before I had the opportunity to fully process what had taken place and prepare myself for its effect, a new light broke upon my vision, a luminosity that would have taken my breath away, had I not left my mortal lungs behind. The resplendence that confronted me proved enough to make me pause in the mist for a moment of silent wonder. To this day, I have no words to express the glory of heaven's landscape; no human language or those of the fallen angels could do it justice.

I had seen this marvel once before, just hours ago, but I had already forgotten how inviting it appeared. Saints clad in white approached from the clouds as angelic beings and their loved ones came to greet them, to welcome them into an eternity none of us deserved. Grace had led me here, and perhaps this time I should seize this gift, relinquish the cares that bound me to earth.

Another saint stood directly beside me while I viewed heaven's grandeur, and at length I tore my eyes away from paradise to observe my companion. His face was unfamiliar to me, his light blue eyes ogling the scenery before him in what may have been wonder. Fascination permeated his aura, his black hair manifesting a short quiff cut, the shape of his nose reminding me oddly of Otto.

"Is this what beauty life entails?" The sound of his voice reminded me of my cursed son Max, the novice Keyholder I had left in the future. A slight chill ran over me when I realized *who* my companion had to be. My unborn child, Otto's son. Days old but already possessing a soul, an individual life.

I had killed us both.

"This is the beauty of God's kingdom," I responded, my voice sounding airy and abstruse. My son averted his gaze to me, his light blue eyes *exactly* like those of my chosen love. The man I had left behind. My murderer. Our murderer.

My son belonged here, but I did not. I could not fathom how to explain.

"You are my . . . mother?" My son appeared astounded, and he smiled. His smile looked a lot like how mine appeared in photographs.

"I am." I glanced toward the vibrant expanse beyond us again, trying to work out what to say. Apologies began to spill from my lips. "I'm so sorry. So sorry that I brought you here. That I didn't give you the chance . . . ." My voice trailed off as remorse swept over me. No matter what deals his father had made with Wuotan, this man deserved the chance to live, to make his own choices. I had stolen that from him for the privilege of perpetual death with Augustin.

I could not stay here, even though my lover's voice would not call me away from heaven this time. I had to return to the obscurity, to the darkness . . . to a demon lord who wanted to claim me as his own, resurrect me in fire and blood.

My son's visage appeared concerned, but I sensed that he had no concept of the motivations that compelled my choices. He was destined for perfection, spared the trials of a sin-cursed world. I had to prepare him to leave me, to hone his talents in a realm where no faults could taint them. Shutting my eyelids for a second, I silently begged God for wisdom . . . and forgiveness. Again.

Then I opened them and looked into my son's sky blue eyes. "God allowed me to come this far with you to grant you my love . . . and to promise you that one day we'll meet again. But I can't enter God's kingdom with you."

Surprise shot across my son's features. "Why not?" He sounded so innocent.

"Because love draws me back to earth . . . to a fortune of death and mystic studies . . . of an effort to lead others toward the light and truth."

"A numinous fortune," my son stated.

"That sounds about right." I smiled at him, then noticed a pair of saints headed our way from heaven's threshold. Two lovely maidens with black curls and eyes that matched my son's, both of the same height, their faces radiant with joy. One of them focused on my son, while the other beamed in my direction.

"Your grandmother and sister come to welcome you," I told him, my heart throbbing with gratitude for their hospitality. "Though we have to part ways here, you won't face your future alone."

My son's eyes widened. "We have to part ways?"

I sighed. "We do. You cannot return where I must go." I nodded toward the two Mareldas, who had halted side by side a few paces from where my son stood. Then I edged my soul backward, preparing to dive into the abyss to seek out that wretched demon who was bound to finish the spell and grant me infinite death.

"Please . . . wait!" my son cried out before I could get far. I continued to meet his gaze, attempting to convey peace and courage on his behalf. His eyes shone in heaven's glory as he whispered, "Mother, what is my name?"

That gave me pause. "Wouldn't you rather choose one yourself?"

My son's goodness touched my heart as he said, "I would rather claim the one you grant to me."

So I thought for a moment, my eyes drifting from his face to that of my first daughter, Marelda Swanhilde. The perfect name arose in my mind, one I had not yet given to any of my children. With a broad smile, I told my son, "Your name is Anton Ferdinand von Bayern. Your first name means 'beyond praise,' and it was the name of my dearest brother. Your middle name means 'peaceful journey,' a gift I know you'll seize in heaven. Your last name is that of your father and your grandmother."

"Thank you, Mother." Anton pressed his right hand to his chest as he said, "I'll cherish my name forever in honor of you. We will see each other again one day . . . won't we?"

"We certainly will. I promise."

My son turned away from me at last, and his grandmother opened her arms to receive him. As I paused one final time with the clouds obscuring the pristine robe that swathed my soul, I met my daughter's gaze. "Marelda, I love you so, so much," I whispered to her. "I wish we could have gotten to know each other."

"We'll have time for that. God never breaks His promises." The curly-haired maiden winked at me before taking a single step forward, her left hand stretched out. "Please tell my father . . . I love him so. And I can wait a little longer."

A rush of relief awakened my hopes anew, and I blew a kiss at my firstborn child before plunging back into the clouds, toward the place no light could pierce. Marelda's words implied that God knew we would be together in heaven one day . . . along with her father, my beloved Augustin. God would not forsake me despite the complex twists of my pathway. My faith would guide me in death, too.

It seemed as though supernatural forces swept me into the darkened mist, the sensation of otherworldly speed propelling my spirit along. The white of my robe dulled into the silvery blue of ice right before Wuotan's mental voice accosted me. *I had not expected you to reappear, nameless one.* A being ensconced in shadow hovered not far from me—the standard form my adversary took in spiritual realms.

My God still has a purpose for me on the earth, apparently. I found it ironic that Wuotan addressed me as 'nameless one' when Augustin had persisted in calling me 'Swanhilde' after the curse. Two Cursed Ones would refer to each other by their burnt names, it seemed, disregarding Teuton laws. I would have to figure out a new name for myself at some point. Maybe I should just go by '*Leitalra*' or 'Lady Muniche.'

Wuotan laughed contemptuously and stretched a cloaked hand toward me. *I intend to subvert that purpose with all that is in me. Come and see the domain where damned mortals suffer.*

I felt an urge to mock him in return, but I made no reply. Instead, I drifted forward to take his hand, forgetting Augustin's warning for the moment. But the demon snaked an arm around my spirit, his shade enveloping me, his sharp claws probing the heart of my soul. He still claimed sway over Muniche's essence; I felt her groan in response to Wuotan's groping.

That pain is with you still, Leitalra, *even in death,* he observed. *What a miserable destiny you have chosen.* Then we were falling rapidly, Wuotan's being seeming to squelch my spirit, dragging me into the depths of the earth.

Sounds of unspeakable torment encroached upon my ears, followed by an odor that I can describe only as mephitic. I longed to shut off my senses entirely, though I could not . . . and then, sepulchral gates rose from the smoke, encircled by solid flames of black. The heat must have been unbearable, judging from the howls of those inside—the moans of souls for whom hope had lost its meaning. A heavy shroud of melancholy eclipsed me, bringing tears to my spiritual eyes.

This was the prison of the damned, the place of outer darkness where those who rejected goodness were doomed to await the lake of fire. I did not fear for my own soul when I viewed hell's gates, but my yearning to persuade Augustin to repent intensified. I found myself thinking of people I had known in the eleventh century and the twenty-first, the ones who may have found themselves here due to malice, pride, apathy. Did Marga's soul rot inside? What of the semi-demon entities that had ravaged my people, the *Toteheri?* Were their essences confined in this awful place?

Quite impressive, is it not? Wuotan's thoughts seemed gruesomely content. *Unceasing torment—that is the fate of your Deity's basest creatures.*

I may have frowned, for I caught the demon's implication. Humans were God's basest creatures, in his opinion. A rather impish notion crossed my mind, and I said, *At least God offered His basest creatures an escape from this fate. Fascinating that He didn't present His rebellious angels with a similar opportunity.*

He knew we would not fall for His deceptions a second time, Wuotan rejoined, his arrogance echoed in the mockery of other demons drifting near the gates of hell. I could hear them, but their forms were all shrouded in blackness. I held my peace, suspecting that Wuotan was a moron, plain and simple. But there was no point in trying to reason with him, for his chance had been lost ages ago. He had chosen to rebel and must therefore shoulder the consequences.

Now he called me away from the gates of hell, away from the continuous screams and unbearable stench. He grumbled that it felt prosaic to offer someone like me a delay of eternity, an immortal body, and devilish gifts. *You are blinded by idyllic delusions and would not prostrate yourself before me, as is proper for a Cursed One.*

But you've met me in my immortal form before, in years past, I reminded him, in case he was having second thoughts about completing the curse.

The nameless one boasts an impressive memory. His mental chuckle agitated my brain, and he gouged his invisible fingers through my heart until I groaned. *But you will know your position before your ordeal is over. There is another place I would like you to see.*

A sensation of incredible speed enveloped me again as the demon's claws held me fast. *Shouldn't you take me back to your fiery realm and infuse me with the powers of death?* I inquired. Augustin and Max had confronted the gates of hell, but neither had mentioned visiting another place.

Wuotan laughed, a deep cackle that pricked my heart. *You have tampered with one of my devices on multiple occasions throughout your lifetime, and now that you have left mortality behind, you must learn to appreciate my perspective. Ashima is not the sole entity who polices this place.*

Abruptly, I found myself at the edge of what could have been a ravine. My eyes widened at the sight of tumultuous currents within, struggling madly against one another while ultimately flowing in one direction. These surging currents were not quite water, nor air, nor any of the other traditional elements. They constituted a vast expanse of darkness variegated with flecks of color and light.

Wuotan had placed me facing upstream, and the tide appeared nigh infinite looking that way, spanning to the far reaches of the horizon. I felt, as I took an unconscious step back from the whirling chasm, that I had seen this place before from a different perspective—from *inside* those turbulent tides. The demon behind me confirmed it just as I knew the truth myself: *Time.*

It seemed so unthinkable, to stand on the edge of this chaotic flood, viewing the interwoven strands of human existence and achievement, ever shifting, ever progressing, rushing toward an appointed end, an initiation of a perfect dimension. I shook my head without being entirely aware that I did so, lost in awe at the most indecipherable portion of creation—these knitted bonds of life, of purpose, of the *past*, all melding into the present, just beyond my feet.

Viewing the power with which those currents surged ahead, I could hardly comprehend how I had navigated them successfully on nine occasions. Three trips to the eleventh century, one to the late 1970s, one to 1985.

There's no way Wuotan or any other demon could safely propel a mortal backward through this torrent, I thought to myself, certainty grasping me deep inside. *It's physically impossible.*

Divine purpose brought me here after all, I realized, gazing pensively toward antiquity's horizon. Soon Augustin and I would journey to eras we had not yet visited, places where we could uncover the truth about our magic. We would have to speak to the Rhine's spirit again at some point, or perhaps to the Isar, and ask for some direction on which epochs we ought to explore. How long ago had the Teuton people obtained their mystical gifts?

On the contrary, it was by my *authority that you opened a gateway to this place,* Wuotan corrected me in a haughty manner, bringing my thoughts back to my present state. *I could have allowed the currents to smother you, had I wished it.*

What authority you claim here is given to you by God, for He maintains the final word on His creation, I riposted, still looking toward the far reaches of the past. I wondered absently how arduous it would be to struggle upstream until one reached the era of Biblical heroes like King David, Moses, or Noah.

Wuotan scoffed from somewhere behind me, then delved his claws into my spirit, shackling my heart in a tight grasp of darkness. I cried out in anguish as my heart rebelled at his ruthless touch, fingers that wrung it more cruelly each time it pulsed.

Look here, Leitalra, my adversary ordered, closing his free hand around my throat, *and see your lamentable fate. There is a reason why I retain some sway over your unruly heart, although I have cast your human soul out of my family. Throughout all of your protracted days and nights upon the earth, you will mourn whenever I handle your heart. You, nameless one, are inextricably linked to that city whose body and soul were consigned to* me.

I shuddered in his grasp, wishing that my heart would cease beating, so he could not torture me so maliciously. But that was impossible now, for I had turned away from heaven, had accepted a destiny of slavery, of pain. The swirling currents coalesced before my eyes, brightening into a replay of a time not long past, a time I desperately wanted to forget. I saw a burning city, walls and towers collapsing into rubble, dirty streets darkened with blood and the *Toteheri's* creeping death.

Weakness washed over my soul as that ruined city screamed inside of me, every scrape of her master's claws intensifying her agony. My hands rose to cover my eyes, their ethereality providing no shield, and I wailed aloud as another image supplanted the scenes of carnage. I stared into the solemn eyes of the Keyholder, Prince Otto von Bayern, seeing his sorrow, his regret . . . then his blood and that of his knights, dripping like rain onto my stones, ignited in crimson fire . . . then the Prince's lips forming those traitorous words: *Thus, I curse you to the one who has defeated me . . . as an atonement for my failure . . . may Wuotan guard your soul in death.*

You should have run to heaven's prison while you had the chance, Wuotan mocked me, his merciless fingers still sending waves of pain through my soul with each heartbeat. I sank to the ground on the precipice of time, closing my eyes in a pointless defense against those horrid images, against a demon's triumph.

You belong to me, desolate Muniche, and I shall subjugate you while you wallow in the land of men. You and your Keyholder will ultimately bow to my will regarding your city's fate. That ludicrous love to which you stubbornly cling will degenerate into repulsion, into lust, into enmity. There will be no escape for you unless your Keyholder kills you himself, and he is far too selfish to complete such an act. Wuotan laughed again, his hatred grating my spirit.

What if he's right, Swanie? I asked myself, as I moaned from the combined torment of terrible memories and a demon's sadism. *What if he compels you and Augustin to rebuild Muniche for his glory, silencing you forever on the subjects of goodness and love? What if he distorts your beliefs, blinds you to the truth, induces Augustin to treat you as his slave?* Dismal possibilities threatened to drag me into despair, my hopes crushed under a fallen angel's persecution.

But when I tore my eyes away from the replay of Muniche's destruction, I lifted them to the oblivion above me, opening my lips to plead with God to rescue me, to take me back to those resplendent gates of heaven, to allow me to forsake this suffering forever. I could not shoulder this alone. I was not strong enough.

Within seconds, a wondrous peace descended upon my heart, dissolving the demon's hold into complete insignificance. God would be with me always, and He would not have allowed me to abandon heaven if He had no plan for me on earth. My son and daughters would watch over me, along with all of Muniche's saints who had passed into paradise.

I circled deliberately away from the abyss of time, breaking Wuotan's grasp upon me and leveling my gaze on his shrouded form. *Muniche may have been consigned to you,* I conceded, *but that curse was created by man. If Muniche is truly united with my heart, she belongs to the light, and love will break your hold upon her.*

Sentiments like that can hardly protect one such as you, Wuotan rejoined, reaching one wraithlike hand forward to caress my cheek. *Remember the burden you will bear once you carry the weight of death. You must seek to please me or I shall use your anger as a scourge against you, transforming you into a true destroyer who slays the innocent.*

Cringing, I backed away from his touch, ordering myself to focus on goodness and light, on the glorious saints who would watch over me, on my beloved Black Priest who would teach me how to keep my anger on a short leash. I was not often prone to rage, anyway. As long as we avoided Wuotan as much as possible, I should not have to fear my deadly gift.

Turning back to the ravine before me, I directed my attention to the left, toward the future. My ears caught the wisps of a faint moan as I looked ahead, a hopeless dirge that sounded long forsaken.

Chapter Thirty-one:
Death

Uselessness greets those who look in that direction, nameless one. Wuotan's remark distracted me from those haunting moans, and I pivoted slightly to glance at him in confusion. *The future is beyond my jurisdiction, as Ashima said earlier. Ambiguity is all that can be seen when one peers downstream.*

It surprised and pleased me that I had finally hit on something outside of Wuotan's influence. The river of time stormed into the distance, churning in all sorts of hues from the deepest black to a vivid turquoise and a murky violet, ever-changing, ever-flowing, awe-inspiring—but far from ambiguous. *Time runs far into the distance, beyond what my eyes can see,* I noted. Unlike what Wuotan implied, I had no trouble discerning the sequence of eras to come.

The demon chuckled, stepping forward to run his claws leisurely down my back. *You have that advantage over me for the moment, since you come from a year that has not yet taken its place in history. The epoch of your birth lingers on the horizon, allowing you a diviner's foresight until your curse is completed.* I flinched at his words, and my eyes widened, superimposing every memory of the future onto those raging tides. I did not want to forget from whence I came, after the demon completed my curse.

Once you have reaped the reward of a timeless body, you shall never regain the opportunity to return to that century you forsook for the sake of a dying city and its spectral Keyholder. Your body and spirit will be bound to the present continuum, and even the song that wields my power shall prove unable to show you this vista again. It is part of the price you must pay. Wuotan gave a satisfied snicker.

My spirit sagged at the knowledge that I must soon relinquish one of the few advantages I could claim over my tormentor. I wondered absently what the river of time would look like once I could no longer gaze downstream. Then I wondered whether the phrase 'cursed for all of time' played a role in binding me permanently to the present, pushing the twenty-first century far beyond my reach.

Oh well, what does it matter, anyway? I thought to myself, favoring the inaccessible future with an apologetic half-smile. *The only thing left for me in the twenty-first century is my son, and he'd do better on his own, without my interference. Wuotan didn't say I'll lose my memories of the future, just the ability to walk there again.*

Nodding once in Wuotan's direction, I acknowledged, *I'll accept all of the consequences of my decision and leave the future in divine hands.*

Wuotan laughed again, placing a ghostlike arm around my shoulders and centering his own gaze toward what he saw as ambiguity. *So tell me, dear Muniche . . . is it infinite, that deluge of mortal suffering? Can you discern its conclusion, that marvelous establishment of a heavenly kingdom on earth?* His thoughts dripped with contempt.

I frowned and moved away from his arm, praying mutely for wisdom. *No, I can't see the end of time, for only God can know it,* I replied curtly. The river's tiny point on the horizon likely marked the year 2020, the very day I had played the Song of Time in the Black Castle.

Ah, your faith is so strong, so stubborn, and so irrational, Wuotan sighed, his spectral claws delicately grazing my heart. I felt no pain this time, just a vague distaste that a demon handled me so intimately. *If no one—not even the angels who remain in your Deity's prison—can lay eyes upon the culmination of time and the surety of a final judgment . . . I propose that the entire notion of an end is a lie.*

Wuotan's breath tickled my ear as he voiced his own beliefs in a seductive tone, answering many of the questions I would have wished to ask him, if I were a more daring person. *Perhaps the currents of time are infinite, and perhaps your Deity laughs at humanity's gullibility. So many hope for an end to sorrow, an end to suffering, a land of glory beyond the sky. They will ultimately learn that their eternity consists of slavery, of repression. Meanwhile, those of us who chose to rebel will continue to mock humanity, far above their stupidity, celebrating a perpetual delay of judgment.*

I turned completely away from the abyss of time to eye Wuotan in a mixture of disgust and pity. *One day you will bow to your Creator and admit your error, whether you like it or not,* I told him, filled with a voracious desire to witness that event for myself. Wuotan believed that the timelines were purposeless, that life and creation had no ultimate goal. My faith had convinced me otherwise years ago.

He cocked his shrouded head a little to one side as he responded scathingly, *That remains to be seen, nameless one. Come now, say farewell to the currents of your life and drink the wine of death!*

Wuotan snatched my soul away, carrying me back through the darkness, speeding toward a realm of rapturous fire. I barely had time to process the fact that we had returned to his personal dominion, that smoldering sphere where Augustin waited for me, likely scorned by lower-level demons, plagued by fears. I would have asked Wuotan to bear me swiftly to the sacrificial chamber so I could assure my Keyholder that he was not alone and never would be, that I planned to stay beside him until we could depart the earth together. But before I could form the words, Wuotan thrust my soul beneath a frothing liquid of scarlet, the blending of fire and blood—the river of deadly spells and blood-transfers.

"Drink, *Leitalra,* and welcome the incendiary force that consumes you."

Wuotan spoke to me out of the blood. A tiny portion of my brain found it odd that I actually *heard* his voice, when he had always seemed to communicate through spiritual telepathy during my past experiences with this place. I felt the boiling blood permeating the core of my soul, searing me from my head to my toes, inside and out, devouring every part of me. My instincts compelled me to struggle at first in a futile wish to avoid this cruel drowning. I quickly found that I could not even scream, let alone move. Thus I drifted inert beneath the blood, all of my humanity crumbling to ash under a demon's necromancy.

"Your feeble mortal body has returned to the dust from whence it came, aided by the scorching flames of your Keyholder's element . . . and your living blood has run dry, consumed by my infernal entropy."

Wuotan's ridicule resounded throughout my soul, amplifying the torment of his wizardry, for he spoke the truth—my living body was destroyed, sacrificed, forever lost. I felt his hands upon me in the same moment I felt my soul solidify, transforming into flesh infused with an unfamiliar strength, a vigor that seemed absurd to attain in death . . . for I felt the death within me, erasing all traces of life . . . inflaming me with desire, yearning, hunger for the one thing I could never have again, its absence casting a heavy net of emptiness upon me.

As his hands traced the curves of my saturated flesh, Wuotan intoned, "Thus, my flaming blood restores you, eliminating your weakness, granting you immortal beauty, boundless stamina, robust senses, faultless memory . . . and unceasing *lust.*"

His final word echoed in my mind, shivering along my skin, festering deep inside my heart—and then my body exploded from the bloody river, propelled onto its banks by some intangible force. It took me a few moments to make sense of my surroundings. Solid ground glittering with jewel-like facets, multi-hued fires rising toward the sky here and there in mesmerizing shapes, the viscous fluid from which I had emerged, its ripples sloshing at my feet without leaving residue.

But the unusual aspects of my location took a back seat to the speed with which my senses processed everything they experienced. My mental faculties felt shockingly augmented, as though my brain had grown to the size of the earth itself. Every memory from my entire life sizzled in an infinitesimal portion of my mind, the scenes as clear as what I saw before me. A patch of fires crackled three steps away from me in the shape of a perfect circle, their colors the exact hue of my love's irises.

Augustin. My memories of him burst like fireworks throughout every facet of my brain, bathing my body in delicious warmth. I put one hand to my forehead, surprised that it did not feel enormous like Brain's head in that old cartoon, *Pinky and the Brain.* Countless sensations distracted me as my mind replayed all of the glorious memories Augustin and I had shared.

That first kiss in the archives of Muniche, his ardent passion chasing away my frailty from blood loss. The erotic sensation of his fingers tracing the scabs from my blood-transfer with Freia, how they had widened my entrance so gently before he claimed my virginity so long ago. The way his eyes stared into mine in our world of dreams, his fiery spirit glimmering with devotion, with fidelity, with *need.*

I needed Augustin right now. Why the hell was I still standing here next to a river that stank of sweltering gore?

"Ah, *Leitalra.*" Wuotan's voice invaded my thoughts, and I spun to face him, the innate elegance of my body's movement distracting me for an instant. At last, I had the notion to look down at myself, to see what exactly death had done to my flesh. One gasp escaped my lips, prompting a strand of my brain to catalogue the scent of my breath

—the chill of ice mixed with something quite dreadful, a barren wasteland perhaps.

My skin appeared strikingly pale and flawless, though another speck of my mind wondered whether it would be possible for me to tan in the sun anymore. People would think I was a ghost if they saw this hue of skin against the midnight quality of my hair. My breasts seemed to have grown a cup size, standing pert and sensuous, the nipples a vibrant shade of reddish pink. I tilted my head to get a fair view of my hips—more rounded now, though my waist had tightened, my curves outshining the youth Ashima's spell had granted.

The absence of the familiar scars around my heart from my blood-transfer prompted me to frown. Lifting my left hand to touch the unmarked skin, I saw that my nails were tapered into sharp points that extended maybe three centimeters from my fingertips. My tongue worked its way across my teeth as I blinked my eyes at my claws . . . and I sensed the needlelike quality of my canines. I was dangerous now, a deadly destroyer.

But what had happened to the symbol of my gift to Freia?

"The scars from your blood-transfer have vanished with your life, since they marked your initial acceptance into my family." Wuotan's statement prompted me to look at him again. This time I noticed that he wore some sort of crimson robe belted in gold, its fabric swirling around his muscled body in a mysterious fashion, though my senses detected no trace of a breeze here beside his bloody river.

"I find it ironic that I disowned you and birthed you in the same hour," the demon went on, his azure eyes looking me up and down. His scrutiny incited me to cross my arms over my breasts; I did not appreciate the fact that I stood naked before my tormentor. Wuotan raised a blond eyebrow and smirked as he added, "Your lifeless body is my gift, as is your lifeless blood, so in a technical sense you shall always be my child."

I took a deep breath, my lungs pulling no hint of life from this dominion, although the floral scent of those bushy pink fires tantalized me again. I shook my head several times, trying to keep my thoughts focused on what was important. I had no wish to repartee with a demon while my one true love likely awaited me in the sacrificial chamber.

"Where is my Keyholder?" I asked, speaking for the first time since my body had erupted from Wuotan's river. My voice sounded rich and melodious, no hint of moisture impeding its course. Would I never need to clear my throat again?

"I would like to grant you a gown before you greet him in your impeccable form," the demon said, lifting one palm in a conciliatory gesture. "If you parade yourself among my minions now, some of them might fall prey to jealousy. Your loveliness surpasses that of my sirens, enhanced by that precious vulnerability in your eyes. Those womanly qualities that have not left you due to the persistence of your heart . . . faith . . . hope . . . *love*."

Wuotan's lips descended upon mine a tenth of a second after he finished speaking the word *love*. His strong arms tugged my nude body against his, groping their way down to my ass while his tongue imparted the savor of fallen glory into my mouth. My element sang within me, unwarranted elation humming along every nerve as my pristine body reveled in the gratification of the unceasing lust Wuotan had instilled deep inside of me. No mortal human could satisfy me now; my maddened hormones recognized that immediately. But my oppressor offered all that my undead body craved.

My brain had begun to question myself by the time Wuotan released me, my reason reasserting my willpower. *What are you doing, you idiot? You can't let this demon entice you or you'll hurt Augustin. This sort of ecstasy is empty; Augustin told you that before.*

Wuotan's luminous eyes scoured my own, doubtless reading each blazing emotion that passed through my system. "Would you like me to show you what erogenous triumphs your immortal body can achieve?" he crooned, the fingers of his right hand making their way between my legs. Their tips stroked my folds, and I shuddered.

"No, thank you. I would appreciate something to wear, and after that I'll be returning to my Keyholder." My body seemed to scream in protest as I forced myself to step away from Wuotan's seductive touch, but a quiet thrill pulsed through my veins when I recognized my power. *I can refuse him, no matter what urges he's planted in my new body.*

"I shall lure you into my bed soon enough, *Leitalra*," Wuotan informed me with a confident wink. Then he left me at the shore of his bloody river, my first opportunity to process my ordeal in private.

In his absence, I brought my arms down and took a second to study the only flaw in my alabaster skin—that black scar standing out so sharply on my right forearm. Tracing it with my left index finger, I discovered that it felt much tougher than the rest of my flesh, almost as if it were formed of stone. I would have to wear tight sleeves whenever I interacted with my people, for fear of revealing my status as a cursed witch. An aberration.

Okay, Swanie. So you've got a nigh perfect body and a brain that'll never forget anything ever again. Your vagina's nearly dripping thanks to that wretch's seduction; you need to get dressed and run to Augustin before Wuotan tries any further temptations. There's no life here in this realm . . . and none in your body . . . it's like there's a black hole at the core of your being, consuming your spirit but leaving your outer façade untouched.

My eyes shifted toward the river of burning blood, their hawk-like precision identifying each minute shade of crimson swirling within, each breath of smoke and steam rising toward the sky. Looking upward, I discerned the paths of smoke and dusky haze, each mote evaporating into a black sky without stars. Was this an entirely different planet than earth, or a different dimension? Where exactly had the fallen angels staked out territory in the vast universe?

Wuotan returned with a dark dress draped over his left arm as I crouched at the river's edge, sinking one claw into its sticky solution and bringing it to my lips in morbid curiosity. "Searching for life, are you?" he asked me. "You shall not find it there, I fear."

The rancid flavor of the blood prompted me to retch. I made to spit it out, but I sensed it dissipating at the back of my throat. *That's weird.* Rising to my feet, I raised an accusatory eyebrow at the demon and said, "Then whenever two people do the blood-transfer, this river infuses their veins with *death?*"

My adversary smirked and beckoned me toward him. "Come, *Leitalra.* Let me clothe you in finery for your murderous *Leitaeri* so you can both be on your way. I have eight sirens to restore this day, unfortunately."

His complaint brought memories of the Humpty Dumpty rhyme into the forefront of my expanded brain. I struggled to stifle laughter while I evaluated the dress Wuotan had chosen for me. The skirt was of wide and flowing layers of black, fringed with ice-blue trimming that sparkled as though inlaid with gems, possibly light blue zircon. The bodice matched the skirt and bore a square décolletage with flared sleeves, sky blue tassels garnishing the waistline. Six buttons of pure silver adorned the front of the bodice, and I saw that Wuotan also carried a veil of black and silver which he likely planned to attach to my hair.

"Didn't realize you were a connoisseur of fashion," I remarked as I tugged the skirt up to my waist.

"My kind appreciates art in all its forms," he said, securing the skirt in place and guiding my arms into the bodice's sleeves. "Your religious scholars have failed to teach you that there is intrinsic beauty in chaos."

I smoothed my expression into impassiveness as I buttoned the bodice and Wuotan turned his attention to my hair. Its tresses fell to the middle of my back, absent of the frizzy quality that had dogged me in my mortality. I felt the demon's fingers braiding it with inhuman celerity, attaching the veil to the top in seconds, letting it fall upon my shoulders in a diaphanous wave. He gave me no shoes, but while my feet detected the burning heat in the ground, it no longer impaired them. Ice enveloped my body in a potent shield, one no fire could penetrate.

Except perhaps for Augustin's cobalt flames.

The thought of him incited my thighs to clench beneath the skirt. "Where is my Keyholder?" I repeated the instant Wuotan finished with my veil.

The demon sniggered, and I shot him an expectant glare. "So insistent and brash, when I could assuage needs you have yet to comprehend." He sighed heavily and ran his tongue across his lips, one final invitation. I scowled, so he gave a single nod and said, "Later, then. Come with me, *Leitalra*. Your Keyholder awaits you a short distance from here."

I matched my pace to his, unwilling to follow him like a servant, and we left the infernal source of Teuton blood behind us. Curiosity smoldered within me about that river. I knew I ought to question the demon on its source, since Otto believed it to stem from somewhere purer than this place. Its cerise currents ran toward a point beyond where my perfected eyes could see, multihued fires lining its banks. But I had seen a mountainous obsidian boulder upstream when Wuotan went off to retrieve my dress, a crag that blocked my view of the river's source.

We passed through a partition of deep purple flames to reenter the corridor of black glass, the one that seemed to be the central passage to each section of Wuotan's sphere. Anticipation seized me as my eyes swept the landscape in search of the colorless pit with its jagged rocks and sable flames. My questions about the bloody river retreated onto a side burner in my brain, eclipsed by images of the man I loved most. I hardly noticed as my pace quickened, but the demon evinced no difficulty matching my stride.

Catching sight of the blade-like pillars in a valley to our right, I nearly broke into a sprint. But Wuotan caught hold of my right arm, forcibly turning my body to face him. "There is one question I ought to ask before you flee to your precious murderer, never to be seen again," the demon said, his azure eyes watching the reactions that doubtless sped across my visage. I wanted to pull away from him; his arrogance irritated me.

"Two other Christians have faced the filial curse in the past five centuries." Now Wuotan had my full attention. He let go of my arm, and I flexed my shoulder, surprise widening my eyes.

"You would not know of them, for they fled to heaven's prison when offered eternity, refusing to complete the curse. Anubis did not appreciate their cowardice, as he termed it. He was quite relieved when your dear Keyholder crumpled before me at the gates of perdition. But you, my dear Lady of Muniche, are the first Christian to return, to embrace death. Is your faith so puny that you would prefer earth to your Deity's kingdom?"

His tone mocked me, but his eyes remained inquisitive. My lips curled into a wavering smile as I replied, "My faith is strong and immovable. I embraced death because of that sentiment you so blatantly discredit. I love Augustin, and I would face anything, everything, to stay with him."

Wuotan shook his head at me, appearing exasperated. "He sacrificed you."

"My sin killed God's son," I responded, "and He loves me anyway, so if I'm to imitate Him, I must also love my murderer." And I did, with all of my heart, with a loyalty that spanned the universe.

The demon narrowed his eyes at me, measuring my face, my stance, likely testing the sincerity of my heart with that influence he claimed over Muniche. And at length he admitted, "Ours shall be an instructive relationship, I predict."

I darted away from him before he could sidetrack me further. My *Leitaeri* awaited me at the heathen altar, and as I approached I could hear the nasty voices of Wuotan's minions mocking his devotion to me. Scurrilous whispers and growls surrounded me as I blew through like a wintry wind, dashing between two of the obsidian stones a mere two seconds after I departed Wuotan's company.

And I saw Augustin on his knees with his forehead pressed against the rim of the altar, his hands gripping it as if he longed to tear it to pieces. I heard him weeping for me, blood stains forgotten on his fingers, the sapphire knife discarded on the ground. Ashima perched upon the altar at his side, clad in a dress that reminded me of the starry sky, her silver fingers stroking Augustin's hair with a lover's touch.

A menacing hiss spewed from my lips, and my fingernails extended into icy daggers as I sprang at her.

Chapter Thirty-two

A Marvelous Reunion

Knives of death hovered around my spirit as I leaped, yearning to find purchase upon the demoness' heart. Augustin had warned me that our deadly anger had no power to slay a former archangel—or to send one into the confines of the furnace. But primal instinct drove my reaction, though my rational brain began to question myself a twentieth of a second after my toes left the ground.

How dare that sleazy bitch soothe my Black Priest? That's my job, no one else's!

Maybe you should get a grip on your fury . . . in case Wuotan conveniently places himself in the path of your death.

It doesn't work that way. I can direct my anger, and all of it is aimed at Ashima right now.

All of those conflicting thoughts passed through my brain in the half-second it took for me to reach my goal . . . where Augustin caught me in midair, having leaped to his feet at the sound of my hiss. Ashima's giggles tickled my ears as my ire wilted in Augustin's grasp, his fingers digging into my shoulders, touching the skin beneath my veil, fiery tears welling in his light blue eyes. His familiar scent saturated my lungs as I inhaled, my spirit reaching out to bind with his in a realm no demon could reach.

"See, I told you she would return to you, Wolfgang!" Ashima exulted. "You mean more to her than an eternity in heaven."

Augustin's countenance crumpled; and if we had still been mortal, he would likely have fallen to his knees. As it was, he held me in a grip I had the strength to break, though I certainly had no notion to do so. My thoughts in a whirl, I clung to him for support as scalding tears spattered his cheeks. "*Why?*" he gasped, his visage contorted in pain, his hands somehow finding my hips through the silken skirt. "*Why,* Swanhilde?!"

I understood him immediately, for his expression spoke all of the words his voice could not. Blinking away my own frosty tears, I reached out to trap some of his in my fingertips, sensing their magic sizzling against my own. "Because I love you," I whispered passionately. "And I keep my promises."

Something between an animal's howl and an ecstatic cheer erupted from Augustin's lips, and his eyes blazed for a split second with euphoric madness. Then he kissed me with such fierceness that I feared he may never release my mouth. I did not *want* him to, for his powerful love sated my cravings, his heat rippling along my skin, sinking into my blood. The incomplete city bond throbbed between us with otherworldly energy as my heart murmured his title again and again . . . master . . . *master.*

When he finally pulled away enough to hold me at arm's length, Augustin shook me, his hands tracing their way up my arms. "You are *mad,* Swanhilde!" he shouted, waves of heat rising from his shoulders.

I grinned up at him as his hands locked my face in a vise, his vehemence causing no damage to my perfected body or my desire for him. The boundless love and celebration suffusing his aura nearly threw me into a mania. "You are *mad!*" he repeated through clenched teeth, all of the fires around us mirrored in his eyes.

"For you," I whispered, blinking away my tears, ordering my ice to retreat into my spirit so I could better appreciate the effects of my lover's fire. The entire landscape around us had come alive with a fresh cerulean glow. The sacrificial pit was no longer colorless.

Augustin shook his head at me, a victorious smile lighting up his face. He moved his hands downward to touch the smoothness of my neck, then the tassels of my bodice. "You are *so* beautiful," he said, his eyes appraising me in full.

"Wuotan gave me this outfit so his minions wouldn't be jealous of my body." A mischievous smirk spread across my face.

If it had been possible for Augustin's eyes to pop out of their sockets, they would have done so. A ravenous lust washed over me as both of his hands fondled my breasts through my bodice's fabric. My eyes closed in bliss, yet before I could find the words to beg him to ravish me here and now, Augustin growled.

"Has that wretch violated you?" I opened my eyes to see his burning into mine, his hands jealously clasping my arms.

His protectiveness warmed my heart. *At least I'm not the only one who wants to keep her mate all to herself,* I thought. A hint of a blush heated my cheeks as I admitted, "Before he gave me this gown, he groped me and kissed me. He had me under his sway before I could react . . . and my body . . . well . . . it kind of betrayed me." I bit my lip and shuddered.

Fury flared in Augustin's eyes. Winding an arm around my waist, he turned me away from where Wuotan stood at Ashima's side, leveling me with an evocative look. "The curse is completed, so we should go before he tries to entice you further," Augustin declared. I was all too ready to agree.

"Wait, my dearest!" Ashima crowed as my Keyholder raised his left palm toward the smoky expanse above, threads of fire magic winding around his fingers. "If you leave without holding the marriage ritual of your people, that silver cord between you will remain half-finished!"

Her remark gave me pause, but Augustin sneered. "We shall complete our marriage under the authority of a priest who believes in love, not under the likes of you," he answered, without offering either demon a glance.

I heard Ashima give an incensed cry, while Wuotan merely chuckled. An instant later, Augustin cast his black-fired magic into the air before us, where it solidified into a portal similar to the one through which we had entered the devilish realm hours before. "Farewell, overlords of the damned," Augustin said in parting.

When we stepped into the flames, our portal's essence invigorated my spirit, mimicking the touch of Augustin's hands, so tender and warm, stroking his innately wintry Lady with the aura of summer. Why it had never occurred to me earlier, I cannot say, but now I really began to ponder that intrinsic glory of fire and ice. A priest with the eyes of a sultry sky, a spirit of the hottest fire . . . a priestess with winter in her breath and the coldest ice in her blood. We complemented each other so perfectly in every way—body, soul, and mind—and now we were *together* after decades of forbidden love, of separation, of disjointed fates.

This good fortune could not be real, my rational mind told me, grasping at the pessimism that fueled my ever-present doubts. It could not be, this union in death, endless time to spend with my dearest love . . . for the cost had been so small in spite of everything.

I had surrendered my life—an undeniable truth, for I sensed the death festering inside my body, an unending emptiness, a longing for natural vigor, for blood. I had made bitter enemies of both Wuotan and his sirens; the demon would test me throughout my exile, incite me to rage against him and relinquish control of those black knives lurking within. I had renounced the future forever, closing my gateway to the time of my birth. I had turned away from heaven twice in one night, banishing myself to earth until our successor came in 1493.

But what did it matter, as long as Augustin stayed by my side? Death was nothing now, a specter that had no bearing on our fortune. As long as I clung to my faith, we could stand against Wuotan's schemes, remaining as one to deter that demon and his minions from beguiling us.

This slavery on earth seemed to be the highest price I had paid. I would likely rebuke myself repeatedly over the years for forsaking heaven, especially when times grew difficult, when my imperfect nature induced me to quarrel with my bonded mate. But had Augustin and I not always been at odds in one way or another, and had we not always forgiven each other, renewed our faithfulness, put the past behind us? We would have so many wonderful things to accomplish—a city to build, a people to heal, past eras to explore to learn the vast potentials of our magic.

All of those thoughts raced through my brain during the millisecond it took us to cross through the fiery portal. By the time we set our feet upon the grass at the banks of the Rhine, I was shaking my head and chortling like a child. "This has to be a dream," I insisted as my eyes swept over the river, noticing details that had been beyond my mortal capabilities—the currents surging beneath the surface, the sandy bottom strewn with rocks and leaves, the multifaceted hues of early dawn shining on the ripples.

Augustin let go of my hand and circled around to extinguish the fire with a mere gesture. Then he favored me with a worshipful smile, his eyes sweeping over my gown before locking with mine. Denial held me fast as I said, "It can't be true, this promise of centuries together, this suspension of the effects of time, this realization of every fantasy, the reconciliation of Muniche and Swan-hilde, of the dead city and the son she cast out."

Part me of believed it to be true, but those long years of fighting fate just to think on my love for Augustin stoked my lingering doubts. I shook my head again, setting my hands upon my hips as I glanced upstream toward the place where my former Keyholder had pushed our raft away from the shore. "I'll wake up in a second and find myself lying next to Otto."

A comforting smile appeared on Augustin's face as he stepped forward to take both of my hands in his. "Swanie, love, rend the doubt from your heart," he coaxed, awakening a memory of a time long past, a humid afternoon when I had met him during Muniche's final hours. He had spoken the same words then to assure me that he had not returned merely to watch our city fall—his heart desired Swanhilde first, always. He brought my fingers to his lips, kissing my knuckles.

"Do you remember the promises I wrote in my diary during that dreadful time, when I feared that our bond could never be reformed?" He pulled me close and leaned his forehead against mine as he recited, "'Another chance, yes . . . then I would hold her tightly, never loosen my grip on her heart, keep her, love her, be everything she needs, her master, her husband, her Keyholder. Anything.'"

His fingers touched my cheeks, brushing away the tears that his passionate vows drew from my eyes. I trembled in his grasp, my dead heart pounding wildly, my veins singing at his touch. And we finished the quote in unison, my Keyholder's eyes seeming to reveal that torn page, blotted and worn, the ink hardly expressing the fervor audible in our voices: "'Swanhilde, my love, how I long to recreate what we have forever lost . . . and if I can, darling, I would never forsake you, for our souls belong together. I love you. For all of eternity.'"

One wordless plea burst from my lips, and Augustin enfolded me fiercely in his arms. The heat of his mouth met my ice in faultless harmony, the fingers of one of his hands running gradually up my spine, their claws digging greedily into my hair, unfastening the veil, loosening my braid. When his lips moved away from mine to plant kisses upon my neck and cheeks, he crooned phrases that rendered me helpless in his grasp, their earnestness overwhelming me. *Never* had I ever heard a Keyholder speak such endearments to both Muniche and Swanhilde, the poetic quality of our ancient dialect resonating in my heart.

"Nothing . . . *nothing* has changed . . . my only love . . . my precious Lady . . . my deepest joy . . . my swan . . . my heart . . . my equal . . . my . . . *master*."

My body shuddered, echoing the ecstasy of my heart, and I thrust my hands into Augustin's luxurious hair, forcibly pulling his lips back to mine. It felt as if our spirits had melded entirely into one being in the realm beyond this world, our love painting colors of daybreak across the gray sky. When at last we parted, laughing and panting, our hands still intertwined, Augustin winked playfully at me, shaking his ebony hair down around his shoulders.

"You intend to be good to me, I hope?" he implored, looking deep into my eyes. "You see what sway you possess over my heart, a lonesome outcast who has just now found what glory can be attained in death. Darling Swanhilde . . . you must never leave me, never again."

His eyes beseeched me, brimming with steamy tears. I had never seen him look so vulnerable, so devoted to the woman who embodied his city, the place to which his loyalties had been forever cemented. Muniche's soul hummed inside of me, urging me to reassure my Keyholder, to vow my everlasting fidelity—and for Augustin, I could do no less. This was exactly what my heart had longed for since I first realized I loved this man some forty years ago, after he had bled my secrets from me and risked his life to spare me from death.

So I took his face in my hands and reached up to kiss him gently on the lips, holding his eyes with mine as I repeated the same pledge that he had spoken on a frigid night in 1044, when he had sealed my heart to his forever. "I will be good to you . . . I promise." Then I laid my head against his chest, taking hold of his right hand and placing it over my heart, the warmth of its fire seeping beneath the fabric of my bodice to penetrate my icy spirit.

We could have stood like that indefinitely, with my head resting upon my master's heart, his right hand instilling glorious adoration and peace into the core of my soul. The tolling of a distant bell aroused us from our reverie, my sharp ears catching the richness of its sound. It was the church bell at Eisenwald, some five kilometers from where we stood at the riverbank. My perfected ears could hear it so clearly that, for an instant, I believed we were somehow in the village itself.

Augustin stirred, and I drew back from his chest to look at him. His eyes were on the northern sky, lightening above the trees, and he murmured, "It is morning, yes, the dawning of a new day, Sunday, the 28th of June, *anno Domini* 1074 . . . and you are still with me." He smiled down at me, his light blue eyes glowing with rapture.

I shivered all over at the significance of that statement, that *truth*—and a white-gold ray of sunlight broke through the trees as I stared up at my husband, marveling at this magnificent turn of events. We had thwarted Ashima's spell; the runes that had marred my mortal flesh had been burnt to ash upon the heathen altar. Now I was an undead human, a Cursed One, possibly the only Black Priestess in Teuton history . . . and Augustin and I had centuries ahead of us to enjoy the pleasures of immortality, of each other's company.

All of my doubts and fears evaporated into the morning mist, and a smile that had the capacity to shatter a thousand mirrors stretched across my face. Skipping to the water's edge, I lifted my chin so the sun's rays could touch my skin. Birds chirped their whimsical melodies as the chimes for Lauds faded into stillness. The beauty of that extraordinary morning ousted the restraint from my spirit, prompting me to lift my skirt and frolic in the shallows.

I saw Augustin watching me while I danced, my ice-covered feet creating floes in the Rhine's waters. He pulled the medallion with the Torstein from one of his pockets, his light blue eyes shifting from my swishing body to the numinous stone and back again. "It appears that we have all of history before us, not just our magnificent future," he said, his smile breathtaking in the sunlight.

Chapter Thirty-three

The Perfect Day

Buoyancy invigorated my spirit as the prospect of sharing such adventures with Augustin filled my mind, prompting my body to move even more joyfully. I opened my lips to sing a triumphant song from my era, Paramore's "Hallelujah," spreading my arms to grasp at the threads of life in the atmosphere. I could sense the beating hearts of every creature that populated the forest and the river—from swimming fish, to warbling robins and doves, to the tiniest thrums of insects. I could not care less that decay gnawed at my insides; earth contained enough life to sustain me. Everything had finally fallen into place at long last.

Augustin caught me mid-whirl when I sang the chorus a second time, his strong arms pulling me onto solid ground. "My siren weaves a cheerful melody," he observed. Lifting me a half-meter off the ground, he spun me in circles.

I laughed with him, my hair swirling with the zephyrs his dance awakened. "I can't sing any mournful tunes today," I declared, "for this is the beginning of a wondrous death. We're together as *Leitaeri* and *Leitalra*, equals, devoted lovers . . . I can think of a few more love songs that reflect my mood perfectly." Beaming at Augustin, I kissed him softly, relishing his taste.

As he tightened his arms around me and I laid my cheek against his breast, one lingering frustration arose in a corner of my mind, tainting my delight. "This would be a perfect day," I murmured, "except for one thing." I shut my eyes to the morning's rebirth, images I wished to banish forever replaying before me.

"Tell me," my master coaxed, setting me upon the grass and brushing my hair back from my face. I bit my lip, abruptly unable to meet his eyes. Instead, I gazed at the earth beneath me, the grass and reeds, the sticks and pebbles. "Please, Swanie," Augustin urged, touching my chin to lift my head, though I kept my eyes turned downward. "You must not grieve today. Let me help you."

Tender fingers stroked my throat, and at last I raised my eyes to his, icy tears muddling my perfect vision at the sight of his concern. I sighed, forcing the tears back, then managed to whisper, "Four hundred years is nothing . . . nothing . . . if you still insist on walking in darkness . . . oh, master." I could not go on.

Augustin held his peace, letting go of my throat as my fears fragmented my joy, visions of hellish torment flaring within my mind. I buried my face in my hands, trying to contain my distress. My agnostic mate would consider my faith to be a vulnerability if I could not control myself. So I endeavored to ignore the horrific prospect of Augustin's soul sealed eternally in hell, separated from light, hope, and goodness.

We had gained enough this day to warrant a thousand celebrations. Beth had assured me that if Augustin refused to turn from evil after experiencing four centuries of death on earth, he was not the intelligent man I admired. Though he had sacrificed me to his demon lord today, he would spurn that wretched devil as our love deepened over the years. Ordering myself to believe it, I dried my tears, then raised my head to meet my Keyholder's gaze, intending to apologize for my emotional storm.

"Swanhilde." Augustin addressed me in a peculiar tone, his brow furrowed, though his lips seemed to be fighting a smirk. He opened his mouth to speak, then closed it; and I frowned, sensing his spirit's restlessness. At length he exhaled, contrition clouding his visage, and he stretched one hand out to trace the curve of my cheek.

"My dear swan, you need not fret over my destiny any longer," he told me, his expression guarded, assessing my reaction. I blinked at him in confusion as he confessed, "I repented of my sins six years ago."

My mouth practically hit the ground. "*What?!*" I interjected, jerking away from him to study his face, looking for some indication of bluff.

There was none. His blue-fired spirit radiated integrity, and that smirk had triumphed over his uncertainty. "I forsook Wuotan on the day that I broke our heart-bond." I gasped and Augustin shook his head at me, apparently amused by my surprise.

"You ought to know me well enough to realize that I would *never* accept an eternity without you, even if it demanded that I commit treason against my master. At the time, I had no inkling that I would one day accept our city's keys; so I assumed that if I found no way to free you, I had but one path before me." He chuckled, then added, "God is a far kinder Master than Wuotan, for He comforted me when I mourned you, while His fallen angel taunted my weakness."

I tried to speak, to somehow express my tumultuous emotions, a mad ecstasy mixed with utter astonishment. But my dead vocal cords seemed to have frozen. I simply gaped at Augustin, detecting the splendor of his faith brightening his fiery aura. He had turned away from evil of his own volition, and he had done it to keep his vow—for all of eternity.

Augustin snickered again and said, "How do you think I was able to stand so strong against Wuotan and Ashima in their own dominion? I called both of them by name and did not prostrate myself once, as the siren did after I shoved her away from Ashima's body. Divine protection covers me as it covers you. I must admit, Swanhilde, that you tend to be extremely unobservant at times."

That snide comment snapped me out of my daze. Placing my hands on my hips, I leveled a glare at my lover, this priest who seemed intent on fooling me at every turn. "Why didn't you tell me *before?*" I demanded, irritated at the roguish grin adorning his face. "You could have spared me a lot of grief."

"If I had told you *before*, you would not have come back," Augustin replied, folding his arms and looking quite pleased with himself.

It took a second for my brain to translate that, and then fury erupted in my veins. It was such an ignoble thing to do—to keep me uninformed just to be sure I would embrace death to stay at his side—and so typical of my chosen love. As soon as my body unfroze, I jumped forward and smacked him hard across the jaw. "You *jerk!*" I accused.

He staggered backward and put a hand to his jaw, then stared at the blood that stained his fingers. My claws had opened four slices in his flesh, the painful effects of his deception, and he grimaced, his flesh healing itself with supernatural precision. I shook my head at him, a grand relief superseding my anger, and Augustin favored me with a hurt expression. "I thought you wanted me to turn from evil, Swanie!" he complained, flinching as he fingered the vanishing scars lining his jaw.

Happiness pushed aside all other emotions, bolstered by the certainty of an eternity with Augustin—the realization of my greatest dream. So I leapt into his arms and took his face in my hands, kissing him more ardently than ever before. I felt his flaming spirit enclosing mine, claiming me for always; and the phenomenal truth of the matter replayed itself over and over in my mind as our lips drank the profoundness of love, of death, of a mutual fortune. Nothing could separate us now—not death, not Muniche, not demons, not time, not sickness or age. This was the fate I had yearned to seize since this man had claimed my heart decades ago.

When my Keyholder and I pulled apart, I directed my attention toward the sunrise, leaning my head against Augustin as I looked downstream at the sparkling rays dancing on the waters. "It *is* the perfect day," I whispered, relishing the touch of his hands massaging my back and shoulders.

"The perfect day in an imperfect world," my Keyholder mused, "and the commencement of a very long honeymoon."

I raised my head to give Augustin a curious look. "Four centuries?"

My husband grinned, touching the tip of my nose with the index finger of his left hand. "For all of eternity," he corrected, "with a few side projects. Building a castle, restoring a city, journeying to innumerable past eras. Simple, everyday tasks." He winked.

The suggestive quality of his voice reignited the fires of lust within me; they had smoldered in a back closet since I extracted myself from Wuotan's alluring hold. My ravenous instincts urged me to tear Augustin's clothing to shreds and position myself upon his mighty cock. I had sensed it prodding my abdomen during our embraces and knew that his cravings matched mine.

Since he had managed to handle me respectfully thus far, I searched my memories for the proper ways to charm a man. But my hormones had surged to the forefront of my mind, and I could not think straight. I needed to feel his bare muscles wrapped around my body, taste his blue flames weaving through my ice in sensual perfection.

I wound my arms casually around Augustin's neck and looked up at him though lidded eyes. "You know, I've been thinking about that mirror over your bed a lot, ever since you revealed it to me ten nights ago."

"Is that so?" Augustin questioned huskily, his hands encircling my waist.

"You had one of those in your cottage in Muniche," I recalled, my element casting my view of Augustin's face in an intriguing blue, "and apparently you felt the need to secure a larger one to your ceiling here, right after you built your attic. I wonder if that was the *real* reason you bothered to build an attic . . . just so you'd have somewhere to hang a suggestive mirror." I raised my eyebrows at him.

"I am a man, Swanhilde, though it appears you may have forgotten," he teased, his fingers having moved down to caress my bottom. "I enjoy admiring the magnificent positions a female body can achieve during the act of copulation. And I must say that my inquisitiveness about what *you* shall accomplish as an enhanced ice fairy has nearly overcome the remaining vestiges of my courtesy."

His flaming eyes had fixed themselves upon the pulse that beat so slowly at my neck, each throb of my immortal heart propelling my blood through my veins with incredible power. I could not drag our banter out much longer. I bowed my back so that I hung blithely from his shoulders, the swell of my breasts snagging his attention.

"Well, *I* am a woman," I reminded him, gliding my tongue across my top lip. "And I prefer to savor that sultry heat in your fingers, the fiery current your touch runs along every nerve in my body."

Augustin arched his head forward and nipped my jaw, his teeth pricking my flesh in a chastising manner. "Careful, my swan. If you keep this up, I may destroy that exquisite gown you wear."

"Your death works against clothing, too?" My breaths had quickened along with my heart rate, and I felt ice extending my pointed fingernails. "You'll need to teach me that one."

A snarl vibrated in his chest, and I could wait no longer. I took him by the back of his neck and charged onto the Rhine's waters, their verve uniting with mine to carry us to Augustin's cabin in less than a second. I paused just long enough to yank his front door open—it took all of my control to not simply splinter through its wood—and then I had my mate pressed against the door to his own bedroom. It was *our* bedroom now, and I ran my tongue over the pulse beneath his jaw.

"Teach me all I have not yet learned," I ordered him, the claws of my left hand snaking their way through his hair as my right undid the buttons of my bodice. Shrugging out of it without letting go of his neck, I commanded, "Fill me with your death, and subdue my yearnings beneath your sway."

Augustin's cloak had fallen to the floor, my eyes tracking each movement of his hands, which glowed an alluring blue. He undid his pants and stepped out of his boots, but he made no move to stop me when I ran my ice claws down his tunic, tearing it away from his chest. I had already yanked my skirt to the floor, and when his fingers pressed my damp folds my entire body collapsed upon him, the claws of my left hand sinking into his skull.

My master uttered a few crass words in Ælte Teutonica before casting me onto his bed, his fire plunging into my core, gratifying my every desire. I matched each movement of his hips as he ground against me, my legs winding around his thighs as my right hand traced its claws down his back. His muscles felt so perfect, so sculpted, so smooth beneath my icy fingertips . . . and then his teeth sank into my throat, the sting launching me over the edge. I cried out a jumble of syllables that might have been his name, his fiery claws gripping my ass firmly against him.

I groaned when I felt him finish, my eyes squeezed shut. This was euphoria.

My brain seemed to have gained the capacity to appreciate every sensation at a level I had never experienced before. If *this* was what sex felt like as a dead woman, I would have no cause to miss the life I had renounced. When I opened my eyes I noticed thin spirals of flame-flecked icicles decorating the windowsill. All of the candles in the chamber sported blazing blue flames, and a layer of ice coated the mirror above, Augustin's bare back glistening with frost. Our elements had melded in the room itself as well as in the spiritual realm.

It was so fulfilling, so incredibly enchanting . . . and I wanted more. I never wanted to detach my body or spirit from Augustin's. We belonged as one, not as separate entities.

We spent the entire day enjoying the beauty of love. The death inside of me drank Augustin's devotion as if its black hole could never be filled. My rational mind accepted that it could not, that an empty decay would cling to me throughout the remainder of my existence. But it was easy to ignore the hollowness when I lay in my Keyholder's arms, our magic shimmering around us in refreshing splendor.

As the lengthy summer day crept onward toward dusk, I began to muse about which Teuton priest would agree to perform the ritual wedding for us, so we could complete the city bond and mark our perfect wrists with the pink scars of marriage. Would we have to return to Bavaria or the Alps to seek out such a man? Would any Teuton priest agree to wed the dead, or should we keep that part of our fate under wraps?

"Swanhilde, darling." Augustin murmured in my ear, having taken a short break in his gentle draining of my blood. He had drunk from my neck often that day. Since the act no longer weakened me, I found it to be relaxing and sensuous. It heartened me that my master considered my dead blood just as appealing as when my heart had yet pulsed with life.

I breathed a quiet sigh as my lover trailed kisses down the length of my right ear. "This is truly the grandest day of my existence," he went on, his tone winding cords of bliss around my heart. "I have but one regret, one that refuses to grant me reprieve."

"I have no regrets." The words fell from my lips without restraint, for it was true. I lay upon my back on the sable blanket that adorned Augustin's bed, with my hands behind my head and my eyes upon our reflections. My master had such a sleek, elegant ass.

"Such a rebellious Christian," Augustin chided with a snicker, planting one final kiss upon my earlobe before rolling onto his back himself, meeting my gaze in the mirror overhead. "I regret that I could not enter heaven beside you."

"We'll do that one of these days," I assured him with a smile.

"If so, that means we shall have to kill each other at the exact same moment." Augustin raised his eyebrows at my reflection, anticipation seeming to dance in his light blue irises.

"We should be able to arrange that when Ritter shows up."

"Ritter." Augustin rolled his eyes and turned his head toward me. "Why any Cursed One would choose a title for himself rather than a name."

The term 'Ritter' meant 'knight' in German, so I saw Augustin's point. But I shrugged and reached my right hand over to stroke the tousled locks of his hair. "We don't yet know his circumstances, so it's not our place to judge. I'd expect you to be thrilled by the privilege of killing me twice. You spent the early years of our relationship insisting that you wanted to murder me yourself." I grinned.

"The high of murder has faded over the years," Augustin admitted, his left hand sliding over to stroke my hip. "It was not a victory at all, early this morning when I felt your mortal heart stop beating, when I saw your face crack in pain, your lovely gray eyes empty and cold. If I could erase that memory from my mind, I would. I saw your soul leave me as I begged you wordlessly to stay. I cannot handle that agony again, Swanhilde. You must stay with me now. You *must*."

The claws of his left hand began to sink into my flesh as his eyes flared with worry. I took his face in my hands and kissed him tenderly on the forehead, my own disbelief scratching its way to the surface in response to Augustin's anxiety. "I'll stay forever. Nothing can keep us apart," I promised.

We shared another round of lovemaking as the sky darkened, and then my husband noted that he needed to care for his animals. He had not milked his goats that morning nor allowed his chickens to forage, so we passed through his pantry into the yard behind his cottage, ready to repair his inattention. His two goats marched forward instantly and expressed their complaints, but Augustin soothed them both before crouching down to milk the older one first.

I collected three eggs from the chicken coop while he worked, surprised at how light each one felt in my hands. I wondered if there was any life left in them, after a day of abandonment in the coop. Probably not. The goats' milk might hold some possibility, though. I laid the eggs into an empty basket in the pantry, then returned to watch Augustin milk his goats as the stars appeared overhead.

"I spoke to our daughter briefly before I left Anton to heaven's glory," I said, perching myself atop a post of the wattle fence that sheltered Augustin's animals from predators. The night air felt delicious against my naked skin.

"Anton?"

Realizing that my Keyholder must not have looked for my experiences at the brink of paradise when he drank my blood that day, I rushed to explain. "The son Otto gave to me. We died at the same time and our souls approached heaven side by side. He asked me to name him before we parted ways, and your mother came to guide him alongside our daughter."

"Marelda." Augustin breathed the name reverently as he finished with the first goat. Her sister came immediately to take her place, and my master's hands cleaned her udders with warm water before initiating the process anew.

"She asked me to tell you that she loves you so much," I remembered, my heart swelling with emotion as that scene played through my brain. "She said God keeps all of His promises. And she looks forward to meeting us both once we've completed our destinies here."

"Destiny," Augustin corrected, a hint of amusement in his tone. "If you could retrieve a pair of wine glasses from the pantry, I would like to share this milk with you. Life lingers for a few hours once the milking is complete, and I can think of no better way to celebrate the first night of our unending union."

Thus we sat at the Rhine's bank not long afterward, our feet playing in the shallows as the starlight sparkled off of the water's ripples. The threads of life weaving through nature's tapestry thrummed against my skin, wordlessly assuring me that I had made the right choice. This was where I belonged—here in the eleventh century woodland with my cursed *Leitaeri*.

Augustin's cobalt eyes glittered when he touched his chalice to mine. "Eternal life."

"Eternal life," I repeated, raising the milk to my lips.

Chapter Thirty-four:
Onerous Trauma

During our intimate activities that day, I had begun to get used to the sensations that accompanied consuming anything as an undead woman. Whenever I drank from my husband's veins, the sanguine flavor of his blood lingered upon my taste buds as the liquid dissipated on its way down my esophagus. The dissolving sensation started somewhere at the back of my throat and finished before anything could hit my stomach.

That was doubtless the primary reason why Augustin argued that eating and drinking no longer offered gratification. No food or drink could even *reach* the black hole inside, so there was little point in attempting to feed it. Therefore, I cannot pretend I imagined drinking his goats' milk would prove any different. I had consumed a lot of it while I stayed at his cabin before Prince Otto arrived on the scene. It had a mild, creamy quality not incredibly dissimilar to cow's milk.

I was wholly unprepared for the experience of drinking life.

That creeping death eating away at my core simply vanished as my spirit erupted with elation. The savor raced from my tongue to the finite ends of each nerve, rapture fueling a transient instant of *completeness*. I had achieved true perfection; I lacked nothing. Ecstasy hummed through me from head to toe, my eyes widening in utter amazement.

I had thought I seized heaven on earth while entwined with Augustin's body and spirit hours earlier.

Wrong.

The creamy goodness in my chalice was the true source of Elysium.

Desperation conquered my reason as I sensed that emptiness seeking to nullify my body's newfound wholeness. Gasping, I tilted my head back to dump the rest of the milk down my gullet in one gigantic flood.

A strong hand grasped the back of my head and took the chalice away from me before I managed another swallow. My inner decay rose to the forefront of my awareness with the abruptness of throwing a switch, and a combined sob and hiss pealed from my lips. How could that wonder disappear so fast? It seemed like a cruel joke. This was not fair.

"Slowly, Swanhilde." Augustin's voice summoned my brain from its vat of maddened disappointment. I blinked my eyes a few times, recognizing that he had pulled me into his lap, his left hand secure upon the back of my head while his eyes watched my reason return. His expression revealed a hint of remorse.

"It is best to enjoy life's rush slowly, rather than consume it with ravenous hunger," he explained as my lungs drew short breaths of the night air. I tasted the wisps of life inherent in the atmosphere, but it seemed devoid after the glories the milk had granted.

Desolation washed over me. I quailed against Augustin's chest, foolish sobs tearing their way out of my throat. "Why," I croaked, shards of ice falling from my tear ducts, "why ... does it ... just ... *leave* ... me empty?"

Augustin tucked me against him, his blue-fired spirit offering comfort to my injured essence. "I know, Swanhilde. I know," he murmured, his lips planting reverent kisses upon my brow. "There is no shame in mourning our loss."

I know not how long I lay in my lover's arms, harsh reality shattering my perceptions of a blissful destiny with my chosen mate. Although I had felt the death lurking inside of me since Wuotan recreated my body deep within his bloody river, it had not troubled me so profoundly until I tasted life in the milk. The rush it had offered was too magnificent, too transitory. Even in my hysteria I understood that I could no longer experience life in my physical body any other way.

"If that is the aftermath of consuming life, why did you think it'd be a good idea to celebrate our union *this* way?" I asked Augustin at length, once my brain had siphoned the emptiness into its relegated corner. Raising my head from his chest, I observed his countenance. "Did you want me to experience that . . . so I can learn how to compartmentalize my lack of life?"

Augustin smiled, though his eyes still glimmered with regret. "Yes. Your control of your emotions and your cravings must be faultless before you emerge from our woodland hideaway. In the coming weeks, I shall teach you which sources of life offer the greatest succor, and how to reap them judiciously. We do not want to drain all life from our environment, you see. You also must learn how to use your death against the hearts of specific prey, like the point of an arrow."

My brain latched onto his first statement rather than the prospect of using my death gift to hunt—*your control must be faultless before you emerge*. "I have to tell Freia and Joel what I've done," I said, my eyebrows coming together. "And my children . . . and my grandchildren."

"More reasons for you to hone your emotional control." Augustin nodded at me, his expression serious. "Holda's child is due at the outset of August, if it does not come sooner. Helmut has asked me to attend to her birth. If you wish to come with me when I do so, that gives you five weeks to refine your destructive gifts."

Augustin retrieved my chalice from the grass and brought it to my lips, his left hand supporting my head as he strictly controlled the amount of milk I drank. Throughout the subsequent hour, he mollified the consuming maw inside of me with the sweet cream of his goats' milk, mandating that I must endure the fall along with the peak each time so my brain could grow accustomed to that experience. My taste buds detected the gradual decline of life within the milk as time passed.

Once the two of us had finished all that Augustin had taken from his goats, I observed, "I think I get why you suggested we use this milk to celebrate our union. I feel kind of languid and satisfied now, despite the emptiness. Never thought I'd gravitate toward *milk* for a party instead of alcohol." I chuckled.

"At dawn you shall bask in the burst of life expelled from a hen."

I laughed again, thinking of the eggs I had collected hours before. Those must be dead as a doornail by now. "I have to swallow it whole, right?"

Augustin winked. "It is not as difficult as you imply. Decay reaches up from our throats to initiate the consumption process. Technically, we can swallow anything that our teeth can tear apart."

"Even rocks?" I raised an eyebrow at my lover.

Augustin snorted. "Yes, but rocks hold a mere wisp of life, similar to what our lungs draw from the atmosphere. Fresh plants pack a stronger punch, as you would say."

"But blood from living creatures trumps all," I guessed.

"Yes, and that is why we must always tread cautiously and confine our decay in a sealed closet." Augustin rose to his feet and held his right hand out to me, our chalices balanced in the fingers of his left. "Come, my timeless swan. After we wash these glasses, we ought to retrieve the possessions you left behind when you joined my predecessor for your leap of suicide. Including his mare."

"He left the horse untied," I remarked as we strolled hand-in-hand toward his cottage. The cherry tree that bordered the path to the Rhine was bursting with crimson fruit, the scent of life emanating lusciously from its branches.

"An opportunity for you to identify her by her heartbeat alone," Augustin said, favoring me with a significant nod.

Augustin proved to be a patient instructor, as he had been in days of old when we studied languages together. He did not reprimand me when I struggled to narrow my knives of death into a fine point while we stalked prey of various sizes. I accidentally wiped out an entire den of beavers at one point and a swarm of gnats at another; both times, Augustin had asked me to slay a single creature. My failure with the beavers prompted me to withdraw for several days, my status as a destroyer saddling me with depression. How was I to coexist with the living when destruction draped me in its spectral net?

In response, my Keyholder tutored me on how to contain my death, even when my anger smoldered within. He assured me that I was no less of a Black Priestess if I preferred not to wield my death like an infernal blade. It was better for me to suppress my decay and concentrate on the beauty of life in nature, how it sang to my spirit as the breeze caressed my cheeks. As a cursed Teuton Lady, I could instruct the young on the nuances of their magic, imparting wisdom that no one else could share.

That idea stirred a peculiar mixture of anticipation and anxiety in my heart. At that point, the majority of the Teuton families in Eisenwald distrusted the Black Priest who inhabited the southern forest. If I wished to teach the children as Lady Muniche, like I did in the twenty-first century, I would have to convince each of their parents— my children and Freia's—that I was not dangerous. It would be hard enough to come clean about the fact that my one true love was not their beloved Daddy, Joel. I pondered how to handle that often during the month of July.

Wuotan's claws grazed the heart of my soul occasionally, but not nearly as often as he had tormented me before Otto's death. I mentioned it to Augustin each time I sensed the demon's persecution, and the third time it happened he flew into a dark rage and summoned Wuotan into his fire pit for a frank discussion. I stood beneath the grape vines as my Keyholder ordered the demon to cease his meddling, or else he would invoke the river spirits to witness against his role in the origin of Teutonic magic.

Augustin planned to petition the Rhine's spirit at some point to learn the river's insights on our people's heritage. He agreed that we ought to use the river spirits' gift—the Torstein—to solve such riddles, but to do so we needed direction on which eras we must visit. I argued that we should not embark on some grand journey until we figured out a more reliable method of bending time. If it behaved like it had during my initial trip to the eleventh century, the Torstein would likely vanish shortly after we arrived in some past epoch. I knew not whether instruments of antiquity could summon the gateway of time like Otto's song could on the pipe organ. His mystical tune demanded a very specific registration.

Augustin proposed that we could stop each other's hearts using our death gifts whenever we sought to exit a past timeline. I hesitated to commit to such a thing for fear that we could not manage the simultaneity such an act would require. But my master brought up a fair point. In the period of heathenry, many Teuton priests had achieved the second level of the priesthood; therefore, we could request the aid of our undead peers if the situation called for it.

I wanted to perfect my emotional control as well as my fighting skills before attempting any quests. I spent an entire day and night in late July endeavoring to conjure a workable elemental sword from the magic of my spirit alone. Augustin could create flaming blades out of what seemed like nothingness, though my enhanced eyes could see the magic building around his aura before a double-edged scimitar leaped into his right hand, threatening to temporarily mark my perfect skin.

Augustin suggested that we take a break an hour before dawn, when I finally managed to run a layer of cerulean fire along my icy dagger, reinforcing its energy rather than melting it into a heap of liquid. "I would like you to join me in the realm of the spirit for a private conversation," he told me as his current blade evaporated into smoke. "There are things I have not yet told you about my past and about this existence you now bear . . . things that must be passed from mind to mind."

I felt no qualms at such a prospect, for the life inherent in the spiritual realm had become something of an addiction for me in recent weeks. That was the only place I could go where my inner emptiness forsook me entirely, and it remained the only realm where we could speak without fearing that a demon may overhear. While they could impose on us in such a place—a pair of imps had done so just four days earlier—we could communicate in secret there, a safe haven to unveil our deepest burdens.

Recently, we had talked through the ache I felt in my chest at the memory of my lost daughter Freya. The fact that I would soon come clean to my children and hopefully nurture a relationship with each one weighed heavy upon me. Why had I been able to save my eleventh century children, while death had swallowed my dear ones from the future? Max had chosen to be cursed, but Freya's tragic fate haunted me still.

I suspected that I would never stop mourning her, as Augustin had never stopped mourning his beloved mother. There were some wounds that would never fully heal, their pains dulling and flaring at unexpected moments. My Keyholder promised that we could mend each other's broken pieces together, his presence a comfort my heart desperately desired.

The subject Augustin opened in the early hours of dawn was not one I had expected at all. We entered the spiritual realm with our hands intertwined, then drifted unhurriedly to the opposite bank of the Rhine, so we could watch the sun crest the eastern horizon. I sensed uncertainty radiating from my master's spirit, so I readied myself to listen, to offer whatever reassurance he needed.

You know of Lady Maria's failure to bear children, Augustin began, having perched his spirit on a sleek boulder that jutted about a half meter into the water.

I did a double-take, then attempted to stifle my surprise. *Otto mentioned it to me,* I responded, folding my spiritual legs beneath my icy robe, leaving enough space between Augustin and me so I could observe his countenance. *He said that he and his father sought the help of a forest witch around the time you were sent off for foreign schooling. The witch blamed demonic forces connected with you.*

Augustin gave the mental equivalent of a snort, his gaze focused on the stars, away from me. *I was not the only one in the Bayern household who communed with demons, though your predecessor preferred one that Wuotan tends to mock.* My eyes widened as Augustin clarified, *Lady Maria and her sisters often consorted with Frigg, a heathen goddess of lust and sex. She sought help from every deity to heal her barrenness . . . and . . . she sought help from me.*

Augustin hesitated for a long moment, the locks of his hair hiding most of his face from me. I held my peace and waited for him to continue, a sense of dread hardening the ice that fashioned my robe. *She called for me to bring a necklace for her and her sisters to admire. She often demanded that I run foolish errands such as that . . . as if I were a servant rather than a Prince. But that afternoon, when I brought the necklace into her private parlor . . . her oldest sister shut the door behind me . . . and blocked it.*

My lips had parted in horror, my spirit quaking as I waited to learn where this story led. Augustin confirmed the worst moments later, shame darkening his fires. *Lady Maria took me by the chin and said, 'Since the role of Keyholder falls to you next, perhaps you can give me what your father cannot.' I tried to fight her and her sisters . . . but they used their air against me . . . depriving me of the oxygen necessary to sustain my fire. The deficiency of air . . . caused my body to awaken, though I silently begged for it to sleep . . . and she took me into herself . . . her wintry wind chilling me to the bone.*

Augustin fell silent for a long while, his head buried between his knees, his shoulders bowed in disgrace. *Lady Maria raped you.* I gave words to the thought that swirled in both of our brains, the label Augustin felt too ashamed to accept.

I made certain that her womb expelled the child long before its time. And I begged my father to send me away, so I could access libraries and tutors beyond Muniche's archives. I did not tell him my true reasons. I was fourteen. She was thirty-two.

A groan escaped my thoughts, and I longed to take my mate's spirit into my arms. But I did not know if such contact would distress him now, so I simply told him, *Augustin, it wasn't your fault. You couldn't have known what she was going to do. Three witches wielding the power of air could stifle any fire.*

I vowed that it would never happen again. Augustin's mental voice carried a dark twinge as he continued the tale. *So I studied for the Teuton priesthood in Salzburg, in Vienna, and I learned of other demons, other sorceries.* He told me that he spent nearly a year studying under a scholar in a prominent Slavic city, but I shall not write the name here due to the graphic nature of the crimes its nobility hid.

Outside the city lay a revered monastery, a place where religious pilgrims traveled to venerate holy relics. The monk in charge of the monastery dabbled in sorcery on the side, a sorcery more heinous than the curses Augustin had wrought. Citizens of the city were required to deliver their firstborns to the monastery on their sixth birthday, to bring divine blessing upon the populace. Thus the monastery was filled with young boys and girls meant to devote their lives to religious rites.

I would not have known what really went on there had I not met Viktor. Augustin's posture had straightened, and his lips formed a reminiscent smile as my spiritual lungs gasped. I had not realized Augustin had known Viktor since his teen years; the Magyar had served my family faithfully for over a decade.

Apparently Viktor was a page at that point in his life, one who took messages to and from the monastery. He met Augustin while delivering a missive to his tutor and opened up to him over time, mainly because he caught him practicing with his fire magic in an empty corridor. Viktor eventually told Augustin that an insidious sorcery bound everyone in the city, rendering them willing and complacent about relinquishing their children to the monastery.

The monks there used the children for sex magic, Viktor told me. Children groomed and enslaved, taught to worship lustful demons, the grounds sealed tight so there could be no escape. I thought he exaggerated until I went in spirit form on the night of the full moon and witnessed a ritual. Five men brutalized a young maiden beneath the moonlight upon a stone labyrinth, her mouth and limbs bound as they caught blood from her armpits and groin.

I spoke to her several months later, after I had visited Vienna and passed the initiation into the Teutonic priesthood. I returned to the monastery in spirit form, and she believed me to be an avatar of Hadur, the Magyar god of fire and metal. She begged me to save her from her enslavement, to save her and all of her brothers and sisters. She was four months pregnant, and she did not want the monks to desecrate her baby. She begged me to save them both. Her name was Ilka. She was fourteen. But there was no way to save them in life; everyone in the city was complicit and ensorcelled. Her family would not have accepted her if she returned to them.

Augustin stared toward the distant treetops, his forehead creased in pain. I understood what must have come next before he found the words to describe it. *Ilka was your first sacrifice, wasn't she? You saved her and her child by offering them both to Wuotan.*

Yes, Augustin confessed, a multitude of emotions casting his robes in hues of every shade of blue. *I justified it in my heart, convinced myself that she wanted it, that the power I could obtain through such rites far outweighed whatever the monks worked upon their slaves. What they did was despicable, and it was my duty to end it. I set the monastery and its grounds on fire, calling on Wuotan's power along with Hadur's to turn it to ash.*

Viktor added a tonic to the slaves' drinking water that evening at my behest, so that they could sleep peacefully and wake to heaven's bliss. Only the sadists themselves were destined to scream as my fires consumed them, as my smoke stole the air from their lungs. I wove a spell over the entirety of the grounds that night, granting the lives of those inside to Wuotan and Hadur. Thirty-four children and twelve adults who claimed a false religion died that night. They were the largest sacrifice I ever offered.

Pink streaks had appeared upon the eastern sky by the time I fabricated a response to that tragic tale. *So the thirty-five children you sacrificed . . . all of them belonged to that monastery. And you raped only one of them, Ilka.*

Correct, Augustin answered.

If I had harbored any lingering doubts about my master's motivations when he walked in darkness, they completely evaporated at that moment. *Otto convinced me you'd assaulted little kids, when he recited the sins he saw in your blood memories. And when I asked you about it later, you didn't exactly disprove his accusations. But the children were raped by the monks, not by you. The only girl you raped was fourteen, and you were seventeen. Why didn't you tell me that?*

I was no saint then . . . and I am now by grace alone, Augustin reminded me, gazing pensively at the colors reflecting off of the river before us. *Though I used my gifts to preserve women in childbirth and spare children from the abuse and grief I suffered, I murdered so many and perpetuated the cycle of exploitation my stepmother began. I have hurt you brutally and offered your body to the demon I have long spurned.*

Augustin glanced at me out of the corner of his eye, then averted his gaze back to the waters. Just before I found the words to assuage the guilt I sensed permeating his aura, his thoughts entered my mind again, heavy with misery. *After the fire died down, I used Hadur's sorcery to create a batch of gold coins from a handful of pebbles. Viktor and I sojourned westward, parting ways at Innsbruck. I planned to travel through Italy and continue my studies, but I urged Viktor to go north to Muniche. I told him that I knew not when I would return there, but that once I did, he was guaranteed a place in my household.*

Wow, I thought when Augustin paused, fascinated by his history with the man who had worked for him before Otto leveled the curse.

Viktor liked you, Augustin noted, a wry smile playing upon his lips. *I told him that I loved you, one night after Gisela went on her way. It slipped out while I was drunk on wine and sex. I remember the warning Viktor spoke the following morning, while I sat studying your English dictionary. He told me, 'Beware that your master does not compel her to beg you for salvation.'*

I thought little of it at the time, but last month his warning came true. That wretched demon incited you to beg me to save you, the same way I saved Ilka and her unborn child. And I did it. Augustin gnawed on his bottom lip and met my gaze, his sizzling eyes revealing the depths of fate. *I saved you and Anton on the heathen altar, to spare you from a slavery far worse than death.*

Chapter Thirty-five

Coming Clean

He told me of his past experiences with demons to prepare me for what we might face, as Cursed Ones who followed the light rather than evil. Augustin decreed that he must train me to fight in every conceivable manner—with weapons, with magic, with intellect, and with elements far afield from my ice. He suspected that Wuotan might endeavor to unite his peers in an effort to thwart our plans. He did not want me vulnerable if demonic forces ever caught me alone. So my efforts to become a warrior goddess continued, my proficiency with my enhanced abilities gradually improving.

It was clear to me that Augustin struggled intensely with what Lady Maria had done to violate him. Speaking of his dark past took a lot out of him, and after I practiced conjuring and wielding ice blades that morning, I suggested we spend the afternoon lounging beneath the mulberry tree at the riverbank. He lay in my arms for hours as we watched nature's activity around us, at one point tracking the course of a merchant vessel headed upstream. I sensed the sailors' hearts pulsing with life, but my undead urge to drain the boat's occupants remained subdued.

I took portions of Augustin's blood that afternoon at his request. He found the process of bleeding as relaxing and binding as I did—something he had never known when he had no immortal partner to tend to his needs. He said it was a privilege to be vulnerable before me, to lay in my arms while I drank of his secrets without judgment. So I saw the fragmented emotions he kept hidden for so long, how they wove together the complex tapestry that embodied Augustin's soul.

The stories he had told of Lady Maria's assault and the infernal deliverance he granted to the Magyar slaves were as factual as they were deplorable. What was worse, Maria's sisters had gossiped about the *Leitalra's* triumph over the young man who would one day inherit the keys, spreading word among Muniche's nobility that Augustin was spineless and submissive. That was a major reason why he delved deeper into evil during his educational travels. He had never killed anything for a spell—human or animal—until he sacrificed Ilka. But the power he gained from murder was addictive, and he longed for more.

"Wuotan taught you to despise women, especially outsiders, to treat them like useless fools good for nothing but sex. He used your past experiences with Maria against you, convincing you that if you grew powerful enough, you'd never face that atrocity again," I murmured as the sun descended in the west.

My fingers fashioned a braid from several locks of hair that Augustin usually kept tucked behind his right ear, while his light blue eyes gazed up at my face in the peaceful stupor of bloodletting. "You didn't see Ilka as useless, or that Viennese prostitute who taught you how to please a woman. It wasn't until Wuotan mocked your actions at the monastery that you shifted your priorities."

Augustin blinked lethargically, his body passive in my lap. "Misogyny is a deep-seated sin, one that stems from the Garden of Eden. It gives men an excuse to not take responsibility for their faults. Blame the woman, punish the woman, seize the quick relief from guilt. Demons perpetuate it with a rod of iron."

"But you never wholly released your grip on goodness, even when I first met you in the depths of your darkness. You still saved women in childbirth and you respected Gisela and the other working women. Yet you presented yourself as an unrepentant murderer, a sinister Teuton priest I should fear."

A casual smile curled upon his lips as he said, "I tried my best to frighten you away from me . . . and look what came of that. I failed."

I giggled and leaned down to give his lips a gentle kiss. "Time travelers who have no death to fear but ritual suicide aren't bound to tread lightly."

"I love you, Swanhilde," Augustin murmured, closing his eyes as I finished with the braid, tucking it into his sleek black hair. "And thank you for this . . . you have put so much into words today . . . things I could never express."

On the last Thursday night in July, Augustin and I visited Eisenwald as unseen spirits. He wanted to check Holda's progress, while I recognized that I needed to stop avoiding what I must do. It was time to inform Joel and Freia that although Prince Otto had cast his body into the Rhine, I had chosen a far different death.

We arrived as the bells for Compline faded, when the village's inhabitants prepared for bed. He set out for the tanner's apartment right away, pledging to wait for me outside the Denlinger house once he had finished with Holda. Thus I stood alone in my best friend's front gardens, amid roses and lavender, my icy robe matching the nighttime hue of the Rhine along Eisenwald's western border. Which of my friends should I confront first? Freia or Joel? Or perhaps one of my children . . . Erika or Johann?

Gather some courage, Swanie, I ordered myself, expelling a mental sigh at the sight of the tip of the black scar visible above my right sleeve. *It's not like they can change what you've done. If your children don't want a relationship with you as a Black Priestess, that's their choice.*

Joel and I had raised our children to fear God, so it was highly possible that some of them might shun me as an accursed witch.

I envisioned myself in the spare bedroom Joel occupied at my last visit, and reality shifted around me as my spirit appeared in the center of the small chamber. A single candle glowed upon the bedside table, its wick woven with sage—my nose caught its woodsy fragrance. The window was open, and I noticed Joel's bow and quiver of arrows propped against the wardrobe.

Setting my spirit onto the dark blue woven blanket stretched across the bed, I prepared to wait for my ex-husband. My spiritual senses detected the elements of the Teutons in the house—Heinrich's metal, Freia's light, their children's metal, smoke, and fire, and my own children's air and snow. I sensed Joel's wind situated near a Teuton of earth toward the front of the house, and I smiled.

About time he got his head in the right place where Lorraine is concerned. They could run an apothecary shop in town once the old Rhenisch pharmacist has passed on. Pretty sure that dude's at least seventy.

I sat alone in the bedroom for another twenty minutes before my ice sensed Joel's wind approaching from the hallway. My spirit tensed as I readied myself to drop the bomb. The door creaked open, revealing Joel carrying a candlestick, clad in a new but dingy tunic and trousers. He must be working in the foundry with Heinrich, like he had intended; his biceps already appeared bulkier.

Closing the door behind him, Joel sighed and set his candle on the washing table, taking a moment to splash his face with water and towel it dry. His hair was longer now, his well-cropped beard more gray than blond. But he looked handsome enough for a man at forty.

After finishing with his face, he sat upon the stool before the washing table, yanking his tunic over his head and tossing it into the laundry basket beside the chamber pot. A moment later he grabbed a bar of soap, and I rushed to inform him of my presence, not wishing to be privy to my former husband's bathing rituals. *So I take it Lorraine has gotten used to the idea of you being a time traveler?*

"Holy *shit*, Swanie!" Joel leaped to his feet, knocking the stool over in the process, his bar of soap crashing to the floor. The gray of wind infused his irises as he blinked at me, where I sat casually upon his bed. "Don't Teutons have laws against barging into people's bedrooms?" He crossed his arms, appearing uncomfortable.

I chuckled and ran my fingers through my ethereal robe. *It's discouraged, of course, but I've always been the type to bend the rules.* I raised my eyebrows at Joel, waiting for him to ask the necessary questions.

He shook his head and shut his eyes for a second. "Looks like you didn't commit ritual suicide with Otto."

Looks like I didn't.

"Did *he* commit ritual suicide, or is he still skulking in the shadows like some freaky fated mate?" Joel met my gaze, his hands having fallen to his hips.

I burst out laughing, hardly remembering to contain my amusement to my companion's mind alone. *He committed ritual suicide, and so did I. Then Augustin showed up and called me away from heaven because Otto gave him Muniche's keys. And it was heaven, by the way, even though we committed suicide. You can tell Heinrich to let go of the ridiculous notions his religion taught him.*

Joel's eyes bulged. "Well that's . . . ."

Convenient? It would have been, had Augustin not put me under that weird youth spell that decreed I must die by morning's light. Grinning, I crossed my legs beneath my robe, enjoying the informality of this discussion.

Joel gawked at me and rubbed the bridge of his nose. "Freia told me about that. How did you manage to get out of that one?"

I died.

"O . . . kay?"

I bared my spiritual arm to reveal the cursed mark. *Turns out if you do the blood-transfer as a Teuton, Wuotan becomes your father by blood. That gave him the authority to cast the filial curse upon me, which means I'm going to be around a long time.*

Joel shuddered all over, bending down at last to set the stool back upon its legs. He retrieved the bar of soap from the floor and set it beside the basin before asking, "So that means you and Augustin are both Cursed Ones now? Immortal like your son Gust? Trapped on earth until . . . ?"

Until another Teuton survives the filial curse. And that's not set to happen until the late 1400s.

My ex-husband sat down upon the stool as we talked for a while about the possibilities such an existence held for me. I mentioned my role in creating the Torstein, as well as Otto's joy when he embraced Kezia for a shared eternity. Joel told me that he planned to continue working with Heinrich until he grew too old to do so, and he wanted to build his own house on the other side of the foundry, where Edwin and our daughter Erika would soon lay down their family's roots.

"It might work out between Lorraine and me," Joel admitted, a light blush playing upon his cheeks. "She was convinced she'd die an old maid since she's in her late twenties. I told her I don't mind raising a smaller family, if that's what she wants. Our kids see her as a sister already, and Max told me he won't be upset if I start a new family now that I'm staying here. He knows it's important to preserve Teutonic magic for future generations."

Relieved that our eldest son took his responsibility seriously, I hesitated for a moment before prying a little further. *And Cammie? Has she . . . .*

"If you're going to be honest with all our kids, you'd probably better start with her," Joel advised, his mouth twisting. "She hardly speaks a word every time I visit her family. I think she's convinced herself that you never loved her and that's why you didn't come back."

I needed to talk to her that very night, for my heart hurt at the thought of my dearest daughter wallowing in unnecessary grief. So I rose from the bed and wished Joel a long and happy life, promising to check in occasionally whenever Augustin and I returned to our cabin. We planned to embark on a honeymoon of sorts after Holda birthed her child, for Augustin wanted to take me to Italy to meet the scholars from whom he had learned medicine. I looked forward to relaxing on the beaches of the Mediterranean, marveling at the sea's perfect sapphire.

Augustin awaited me upon the roof of the Denlinger house, where he stood beside the primary chimney, his gaze toward the docks. *How's Holda doing?* I asked as I rose to meet him, the summer breeze filtering through my spirit.

Quite well. Her cervix has begun to dilate, so I expect her labor to begin within a day or two. She and Helmut can hardly wait to meet their child.

I smiled at the realization that I was about to have five grandchildren total. Taking Augustin's right hand in mine, I swung him into a brief dance in the sky, twirling my spirit beneath his arm. *The only person I've told so far is Joel. He's glad the two of us managed to unify our destinies. But I need to talk to Cammie, because apparently Joel's return has her grieving.*

Very well, Augustin agreed, snatching my waist and altering reality around us with a spare thought. Now we floated in Cammie's farmyard beside her well. *It appears that she is in bed with her husband. They sleep, but you should be able to wake her. Alger does not know the spell to create a heart-bond.*

You'll wait for me out here? I queried, wanting to be sure I had backup in case Cammie's husband noticed my spirit and raised an alarm.

I'll be on the roof, Augustin replied, his cerulean spirit darting up there in one bound. Gathering my courage anew, I headed into the house toward where I sensed two Teuton spirits in repose—an icy maiden and her whirlwind mate. Their home's logs rumbled my spirit on my way through the main wall, and I paused beside their bedroom window. Alger snored scratchily from the inside half of their bed, his mouth hanging open and his hair cropped short to reveal his damaged ear. Perhaps he was proud of his wound.

My eldest daughter lay on her side with her eyes closed, her wrinkled brows implying that she found no peace in slumber. I sent a soft curl of my ice forward to brush her face, hoping to wake her gently. Her body stirred, and her eyelids opened just a hair, revealing those gray irises that looked so much like mine.

Cammie . . . do you remember how to separate your spirit from your body? I sent the message softly to her mind, hoping that she would recognize my mental voice after such a long separation. Her eyes widened, blinking the sleep away. I saw her right hand tense against the blanket that covered her.

I crouched to where she could see me, and her lips parted as her irises glazed over with ice. *I'd like to speak with you, if you're willing. Can you meet me outside at your well?*

"Mutti?" she whispered in a voice so quiet that even my immortal ears could hardly catch the word. She stared at my spirit, frost encompassing her aura.

Come and see, I invited her with a wink, sending my spirit back outside. She had the capacity to follow me, for I had taught my three eldest children how to use their elements to set their spirits free the year before Muniche fell. But whether she had the desire remained to be seen. I set my spirit upon the stone rim of the well and waited, looking around at the plants she cultivated nearest to her house. Roses, pansies, and daisies grew in vibrant clusters along the path to her pantry.

My daughter's spirit wandered the path slowly, her expression hinting that she feared what my presence might mean. Her spirit looked the same as it had the last time I had frolicked with her beside the Meldorf stream, after the final blizzard of 1066 coated the landscape in white. Her blond hair shimmered with the argentine markings of ice, her figure that of an elegant dancer, her robe comprised of translucent azure.

She was gorgeous, but her essence hummed with sadness.

Daddy wouldn't tell me whether you would come here or not, she said to me after a lengthy silence, her spirit lingering beside a bush bursting with yellow roses. Her mind seemed to hesitate over the English words, as though she had not spoken our family's secret dialect in quite some time.

Your Daddy respects me enough to let me tell my story myself, I answered, unsure whether I ought to rise from the well to join her.

Cammie's eyebrows came together, her words infused with sorrow as she told me, *I believed you had ascended to heaven when Muniche fell. Even after Freia came home, I believed. Why did you lie to me?* Her countenance cracked in pain, her jaw quivering as her spirit began to sob.

Chapter Thirty-six:
Turbulent Waters

Numb with grief, I remained upon the stone lip of the well, remorse casting my spirit in a dismal hue. *Oh, Cammie. Your Daddy and I felt it would be best to shield you from the dangers of time travel, the dark forces—*

All of the children talked about Prince Otto's mystical song, my daughter interrupted me, her spirit shedding icy tears upon the roses. *Everyone knew that our Prince had seen the risen Christ, that our faith was not in vain. You knew that you'd travel to a faraway era when you died and that Daddy would do the same. But you led all of us to believe you were really and truly gone.*

Cammie stared at me, hurt evident upon her visage. I gazed back at her in silence, all of the excuses I could have given jumbling into ridiculousness. Joel and I should have been honest with our children instead of living a life of hypocrisy.

Erika kept seeing your ghost wandering amid the forest throughout our entire journey here and for months afterward. Max still has nightmares about the Saxons torturing you, taking you captive, starving you to death.

But you just played Prince Otto's song while the city burned and left us all behind.

I held my peace until she began to compose herself, knowing that I had no defense to offer. I had broken her trust. If she deemed herself unwilling to mend our relationship, I had no choice but to accept it. She turned her back upon me as her element calmed, frosty mist dampening the air around her.

If I could do it all over again, I would have told you the truth before I sent all of you here, I confessed, running my ghostly hands along the stones of the well. *My destiny drew me to the future, where Muniche's soul bound me to punish my transgressions. I couldn't have brought you with me, though I dearly wanted to, for the five of you are the foundation of the Thaden family. Without you, there'd be no future for any of us. I'm so sorry, Cammie.*

Did you come back here because your future family died, like Daddy did?

That question cut me like a knife as I envisioned how terribly that fact must have hurt our children. To learn that your parents led a double life, and reappeared only after their second family had passed away? That implied that our eleventh century children were meaningless in the grand scheme of things. I knew not how to quell Cammie's distress on that topic, but I gave an honest reply.

I returned because my destiny in the future had come to an end. According to Teuton records, I still have a few things to accomplish in your era. I'd be truly honored if you'd allow me to get to know you as a mature adult, as a wife and mother, as a manager of an impressive farm. I cherish the deep conversations we used to have on life and love, on family and God, on magic and Teuton history. I'd like to share that with you again, if you're able to forgive me.

Cammie's shoulders sagged, and she ran her hands through her golden hair, agitation still evident in her aura. *I don't know. I just don't know. There's so much.*

Take as long as you need, I urged her. *I won't be in town all the time, but I'll visit you, your siblings, and Freia's family as often as I can.*

Circling at last to face me, my daughter's eyes sliced into the core of my soul. *Daddy wants to build a life with Lorraine. Not you.*

I winced, my mind working quickly to compile the mildest explanation. *Your Daddy and I didn't get married in the future. Muniche took me as her Lady, and her essence draws me to her Keyholder. Something your Daddy could never be.*

Abrupt comprehension dawned in my daughter's frosty eyes. *You came here . . . to be with Prince Otto . . . as part of your destiny? The Prince was here in Eisenwald just a few weeks ago. I heard Heinrich talking about it with Daddy.* She cocked her head at me, her fingers playing with the icy flakes that surrounded her spirit.

We reconciled as Leitaeri *and* Leitalra, I told her, figuring that now was the time to come out with the whole truth. Preparing myself for a strong rebuff, I went on, *Prince Otto committed suicide in the Rhine River at the end of June.* Cammie recoiled with a gasp. *And he granted Muniche's keys to his eldest brother, the Black Priest who resides in the southern forest.*

Cammie looked stricken. *Then you . . . ?*

He's not cruel and evil like most Teutons believe. He avenged Muniche's blood—my blood—after Prince Otto cursed our city to Wuotan. He eliminated the half-demon force from the earth so they can't destroy the land anymore.

My daughter shook her head slowly, unable to meet my gaze. *Black Priests are servants of the devil, not God.*

That's true of most, but not all, I corrected her gently. *Remember, that man is the sole reason your younger brother wasn't forced to sully his future offspring. He'll tend to Holda's birth to ensure both she and the child thrive. And he saved Freia's life when she suffered the miscarriage early last year.*

Cammie stared at me, her expression bewildered. *The Black Priest . . . saved Freia's life? I . . . didn't know that.*

He is my partner and Keyholder now and forever, I told her with a solemn nod, rising from the well's stones to hover a few centimeters off the ground. *I know this is difficult for you to hear and accept, but I hope that one day we can be ice princesses together like we once were.* I smiled fondly at my daughter, reminiscing on her childhood, when we enjoyed carefree dances along the Meldorf stream.

Appearing pensive but not entirely unhappy, Cammie offered me a single nod. *I'll pray for you, Mutti. Thank you for telling me the truth.*

Her spirit evaporated as she returned to her body, and I rendezvoused with Augustin on the roof seconds later. *Hopefully that was the most difficult reunion,* I thought, reaching out to take his flaming hand in mine. *It's hard to know what to say, when I'm completely at fault for their gloom these past years.*

You did as well as can be expected, Augustin assured me as we drifted down to the street. *Helmut and Holda can't wait to meet you. I spared you the burden of opening that subject to them.* He grinned.

That was reassuring, although I had not worried that Helmut would judge my current path. He was creative and open-minded, willing to bend the rules when necessary. I told Augustin that I would wait until dawn to confront Freia, since she generally awoke at Lauds or shortly thereafter. I could ask her to bring my two youngest to speak with me before Johann headed into the forest for the day; then I could look for Max at the docks.

Augustin and I passed the night in spirit form, walking the streets of the towns on the Frankish side of the Rhine, villages where my lover often sold wines, cheeses, and produce. We would bring his goats and chickens to the Denlingers for safekeeping once we embarked on our journey to Salerno. Augustin paid Helmut and Holda to tend his gardens whenever he took an extended hiatus; and he noted that perhaps my presence would soften the local Teuton community's opinion of him over time. Some of the other youths would prove adept gardeners if they could get past their wariness of the Cursed One.

Morning brought the low clouds of impending rain, trapping sultry summer heat upon the Rhenisch village. I waited below her front porch as Freia kissed her husband and wished him a safe workday, standing at her threshold while three men of the house—Heinrich, Joel, and Edwin—struck out for the ironworks. Clad in a comfortable dress of light green linen with a matching head covering keeping stray hairs away from her face, my best friend smiled as she watched them go, then turned to reenter her home.

Freia. I called to her mind from where I waited amid the dandelions that ringed the foundations of her home. I heard her intake of breath, and I rose to meet her upon the porch, my hands clasped beneath my robe, my eyes shifting nervously around the landscape. Would she understand my choice?

Sunlight radiated from Freia's eyes when she turned to face me, shutting the front door behind her. "Swanie?" she whispered, surprise mingling with joy upon her world-weary countenance.

You were right all along. The words escaped my brain cautiously, my gaze darting from the gray clouds above to my best friend's face. *There's been hope for Augustin and me all this time. Otto offered Muniche's keys to him on the day we committed suicide . . . and now . . . well, you see what came of that. He called me back from heaven, just like he always called me back from time's gateway. I've taken his curse upon myself . . . so he won't have to spend four centuries alone.*

I managed to meet Freia's gaze as I finished the short version of my latest destiny, and a jubilant smile brightened her face. "Oh Swanie, I'm so, *so* happy for you both!" she exclaimed, stepping forward to take my ethereal hands in hers. My ice sensed her vibrant light and offered her a breath of cold in return. She closed her eyes for a moment as her spirit welcomed my ice, and then she murmured, "I've prayed for this for so long."

Apparently Augustin couldn't spurn his destiny as my Keyholder anymore, I intimated, prompting him to send a chiding snort to our brains from where his spirit perched upon the eaves, watching us. Freia squealed and waved at him good-naturedly. We spoke for a few more minutes before I asked Freia to send Johann and Erika out to the porch, so I could impart my news to them.

While I waited for my children to appear, I set my spirit upon the chair that faced the foundry, the same place I had sat when I first arrived in Eisenwald and learned what I had missed during my eight-year absence. Heinrich had been recovering from the pestilence, his body's robustness diminished, and Freia was in the process of mourning her youngest child's death. Now the shroud of sickness had lifted from the village, its families looking again toward the future.

Erika and Johann entered the porch together. Freia gestured them to the bench before the house, advising them to listen well. Both teens held pewter mugs of tea—I identified the scents of mint and rosemary arising from their cups. Erika's black hair was braided down her back, the wispy tinge of air enhancing her gray eyes as she sat down and looked over toward my spirit. She would turn seventeen next month, just days before she intended to wed Edwin Denlinger. She looked a lot like I had at that age; her bosom was snug and her hips rounded, implying that she should be able to handle the difficulties of childbirth.

My youngest son's hazel eyes looked exactly like Joel's before he summoned his snow to reveal my spirit to him. Johann's black hair was shaggy and casual, his deep green tunic and leather trousers appropriate attire for a woodsman. He was stockier than my daughter; his fingers, as they wrapped around his mug, appeared strong enough to nock many an arrow and butcher game. He crouched forward on the bench, his left leg restless as his eyes continued to depart from mine to study the trees beyond where I sat. He wanted to go hunting; my arrival delayed him.

I greeted them politely and inquired after their relationships with their resurrected father. Johann snickered at my terminology, while Erika's face brightened, some of the stories he had apparently told about his life in the future spilling from her lips. Johann sipped from his mug as his sister talked, his expression implying that although he tolerated her excitement, he had not yet decided if he believed Joel's tales or not.

Freia slipped back inside, and once Erika paused for breath, I broached the real subject. Meeting her gaze seriously, I told her that her mother, too, had returned to the future at Muniche's fall. *And now that her destiny in that era is complete, she—I—have returned here to build a better life for all of us.*

"Then you're . . . our Mutti?" Erika gasped, her eyes as round as a clock face. I nodded once—a motion Johann caught before he averted his gaze—and Erika cried out, "I *thought* that might be why your spirit looks like Cammie's! You're ice just like her! I remember. I remember!"

My daughter looked as though she longed to hug me, but such things were difficult for a mortal to achieve with a spirit. Instead, she gazed at me with wonder in her eyes as she drank her tea, and Johann gave me his full attention. "Mutti, did the future heal your feet?" he asked in English, his tone concerned.

His words brought back memories of a pleading five-year-old insisting that he could carry me to the Rhineland himself. *Darling Johann, my body is healed now in more ways that you can imagine,* I responded.

Erika began babbling about her upcoming wedding, and I waved for Johann to get going, a knowing grin on my face. He yearned for the forest to swallow him and obviously preferred not to spend the entire morning listening to his sister's chatter. So he departed the porch with an answering smile, and I allowed myself to marvel at my youngest daughter's zest for life. After she finished her tea, I mentioned her earlier promise to plant flowers for me, asking her to show me the colors of her labor.

Her gaiety bloomed while she led me throughout the entirety of the grounds, pointing out each flower and herb she had planted and tended on my behalf. Her silver oak tree grew at the edge of the forest, and Erika told me that Lorraine always whispered an offering of thanksgiving to its as-yet-unborn *Eihalbe* whenever she plucked its leaves for healing potions.

At the last bells for Sext, I caught my eldest son, Max, on his course back to the docks from the cottage he shared with Katchen and their children. He ate lunch with his family each day, any traders and mercenaries obliged to await his return as he dedicated the hour to his loved ones. It had started to rain by then, a light misting variety that glistened on my robe. Striding beside my son in spirit form, I greeted him with casual nonchalance and commended his success.

He halted at once, his blue eyes sparking with energy as he turned his head toward where I hovered, his bearded chin rising in acknowledgement of my praise. "I thought you'd come back one of these days, after Daddy told me the truth about the two of you," he said in English. "I've done my best to guide our family down the right path, to ensure that they never forget the magic of their blood."

You've done very well, and you should be proud of yourself, I told him, my eyes catching sight of Augustin's spirit drifting a few meters out upon the Rhine's waters. *I've made some rather permanent decisions since I came back here, and if you're willing to forgive me, I long to play at least a small part in your family's life.*

Max seemed more understanding of my choices than I had expected, and he admitted that he himself occasionally did business with Augustin. While he did not make a habit of conversing with the Cursed One, he agreed that his services had proven essential to the local Teuton community. "We'll all have to tread lightly and shun deadly sins, since Wuotan will seek to lead you and your Keyholder astray," he remarked. "I'll be sure to pray every night and before I come out here each day, so God can guide me away from greed and extortion."

Augustin and I returned to our physical bodies after I left Max to his work, for we needed to milk his goats and collect whatever eggs the hens had laid that morning. After we relished the fading life from the produce of his garden, we sat together at his kitchen table with the day's jug of milk. My master said we ought to enjoy life's glories before we continued with my combat training. Since decay's emptiness chewed at a larger portion of my awareness due to our extended interval in the spiritual realm, I wholeheartedly agreed.

We discussed plans for the month of August while we sipped from our usual chalices, the rain outside heavier now, beating firmly upon the cottage's roof. My master had intended for us to travel to Italy shortly after Holda bore her child, but Erika's anticipation for her upcoming wedding prompted me to suggest that we stay a little longer so we could celebrate with her and Edwin. Augustin was not too certain about such a prospect, since I had not yet told Erika about my curse. But I longed to witness at least one of my children's weddings, set to be held in the village church with a grand feast promised afterward at Cammie's farm. Her property held trellised gardens where everyone could picnic upon the grass.

"Helmut has already asked me to perform the Teutonic blood test upon his child on the christening day," Augustin mentioned, "and I believe Freia plans to hold a dinner for their family that same day. It would be polite for us to attend that event, if your control remains as strict as it has been." Augustin took a sip from his chalice and eyed me over its rim.

The thought of being in attendance while Augustin bled Helmut's child gave me pause; a baby's blood was certain to emanate a strong aura of life. Could I keep my decay locked within during such a rite? "Maybe we should milk your goats first and bring the creamy goodness along for the meal. That way we can enjoy life while the living enjoy their food," I mused.

"You must certainly learn to drain living blood with restraint at some point," Augustin stated, "but that is a task for another day. Come, Swanhilde. There is a place I have been meaning to show you. When Erika took you to her silver oak this morning, it brought the matter to the forefront of my mind."

I drained my chalice and leaped to my feet, clad in a summer frock of yellow linen. "You're going to show me where you planted your acorn, aren't you?" I asked as Augustin passed into the parlor and opened his front door for me. "I've thought about that oak from time to time. The fairy from the Thaden grounds told me you'd treated it well. Its *Eihalbe* should manifest itself in just two years, right?"

"Quite likely," Augustin replied, lifting the hood of his priestly robe to shield his head from the rain as we stepped outside. "We must hope that it deems the two of us worthy of its discourse. I have offered gratitude to its kin whenever I have harvested its leaves for use in rituals and potions, but I have not spoken to an *Eihalbe* directly since this curse fell upon me."

"The one from the Thaden grounds told me you treat your tree well," I mentioned, thinking back to that mystic fairy who had earned my respect and gratitude tenfold.

Augustin made a sound of acknowledgement before telling me, "I planted the silver acorn at the cove where I store my dinghy, a pristine inlet that I have hidden from the main portion of the river with a buffer of dark energy. It is a refreshing place to bathe, and other healing plants grow along the water's edge, wild chamomile and nettle along with a healthy batch of ground ivy."

The pool was about a five minute walk north of Augustin's cottage, the path one he had not yet shown to me. Several ponderous boulders concealed its entrance from the main trail to Eisenwald. The pool itself was lovely and clean, its bottom comprised of fine sand and pebbles, the dinghy roped to a small dock not far from the trail. I had a strong urge to cast off my dress and bathe then and there. I would have acted upon it, had Augustin not paced to a thick oak stretching toward the sky among its cousins of elm and linden. His fiery spirit radiated reverence as he knelt upon the earth before the tree.

With soft footfalls, I joined him, kneeling at his side as I noticed a marble marker set in a rock-lined circle beneath the silver oak's boughs. I did not recognize the name etched upon the marker. *Selig Rune.* But beneath the name I saw *MLV* carved into the stone—1055.

"I retrieved your child's body from the dust . . . after I left you at Lord Edwin's door . . . on that terrible morning," Augustin admitted in a grieved tone. "He was a son . . . perfectly formed . . . his hands clutched tightly . . . in an effort to live. I buried him here beside the water . . . then wrote that note to you . . . before I violently begged death to take me. I gave him that name . . . because it means 'blessed secret.' And I planted your silver gift here . . . as his guardian."

Chapter Thirty-seven:
Acceptance

"Oh . . . Augustin." I had no words for this. I had not known that he had gathered my miscarried child's remains and interred them with honor, after Wuotan incited him to torture me on that endless night. That he had taken the pains to do so before he initiated his vain attempts to destroy his undead body . . . that reinforced what I had recognized in him when he confessed his acts at the Magyar monastery.

Augustin cared deeply for children and would not permit them to suffer, as far as he wielded the power to prevent it.

"I know you would have seen this . . . in my blood eventually," my master went on, his palms pressed to the damp earth, his head bowed in remembrance. "I have wanted to bathe with you here, in this place secret to everyone but us. But I could not . . . discern . . . how to bring this before you . . . when I would rather you never think of that lurid night again."

"It wasn't you who tortured me that night," I reminded him. I had seen his remorse in his blood and in his records of that incident, and I knew that no matter how much I consoled him, his crimes that night would haunt him forever. "No demon can ever possess you again, since you've claimed divine protection over your soul. That means you'll never hurt me like that again."

"I hope . . . Selig Rune . . . can forgive me . . . for taking his life," Augustin whispered, his tears mingling with the raindrops.

"He and Anton Ferdinand have already become the best of friends," I said, laying my right hand gently upon my lover's back. "They've seized heaven's glory along with their sisters Marelda, Gloria, and Bethany. We've got an entire conclave of glorified Teutons watching over us. They know your heart."

We bathed together in the pool while the rain poured down, our devotion binding our spirits as we made love in tender fashion. We drank love from each other's lips and luxuriated our bodies in the water, my heartbeat yearning for that ultimate completion we would not know until we sealed our bond in a Teutonic wedding. Augustin had mentioned that we could get married at a waypoint along our journey to Italy. I could hardly wait to be his wife by Teutonic law.

Holda's labor began the following morning, a Saturday. We went to town together in our immortal bodies shortly after Helmut stopped by in spirit form to tell us of his wife's travail. Augustin assured him that it would doubtless take most of the day before the child would come, but he pledged to attend to her shortly and bring me along to help Helmut take his mind off of his wife's sufferings. I sat on the couch in our parlor reading the German half of my Bible while Augustin spoke to my son at the front door. I caught Helmut's eye for a second before he sent his spirit away, and I saw a curious grin play upon his lips.

Augustin clad himself in a plain tunic and trousers and packed his medical bag as I waited in the parlor, fighting a desire to sprint all the way to Eisenwald. But my Keyholder reminded me that we needed to appear like normal people whenever we mingled with the public. So we sped along the trail much faster than appropriate, but I obediently slowed my pace the moment my acute ears caught the sounds of human heartbeats.

"All that life inside them. They have no concept of their privilege," I said in cynical Teutonica as we neared the place where our path opened onto a street dominated by the village's woodworking industry.

My master chuckled darkly. "With any luck, you may get the privilege of bleeding Holda a bit while she labors."

I slowed my pace even further and stared up at Augustin. "What?"

"Some laboring women require that sort of release, depending on the flow of their blood. If they grow fevered or if the pressure rises, as your modern tomes proclaimed, steps must be taken to alleviate stress on the heart."

I eyed Augustin doubtfully. "Well, at least Holda didn't have to suppress her element, since she's mist. That might help the baby slide out more smoothly if she can direct her magic properly."

"Her Teutonic gifts are still incredibly new for her, but I shall do all that is in my power to ease her suffering and ensure that she and her child greet the dawn in strength and hope," Augustin assured me.

When we reached the tanner's, Holda's father met us in the yard out back. He and his wife were at work as usual, since they closed their business on Sundays and Mondays. Augustin introduced me to them both, and Holda's mother gestured for us to go upstairs to the garret where her daughter and son-in-law lived. Both parents were in the process of washing the remains of a cow carcass in their well, the stench of death and decay evident in the air. The tanning business was a dirty but necessary job; the leather-making process took over a year to complete.

I remembered what Augustin had said about the clothing the lower-level demons wore in the devious dimension, as we climbed the stairs to where my son and his wife resided. At least the hides here were taken from animals already butchered at the shop next door. The odor of blood permeated the atmosphere in this part of town, but my senses detected the death lingering in its fluid. No life to lure me, aside from what emanated from the workers themselves.

Upstairs, we found Holda in the process of washing a bundle of clothing and blankets meant for her baby. Helmut hovered in the background with a look of helplessness, likely wishing his wife would rest instead of giving in to the nesting instinct. I sailed to Holda's side in an instant to help her, and soon the two of us were chatting like old friends while completing tasks for her forthcoming treasure.

Augustin set his tools in their bedroom before invoking his magic to clear the entire apartment of dust and grime, the excess drifting out the windows that faced the street. Then he asked me to use my ice magic to fill several bowls of cold water, for the rains had moved on and the day was hot and still. I did as he asked after helping Holda hang her laundry out the front window, where the backyard's stench of decay should not wholly taint them. Augustin installed himself in the kitchen to prepare a stew for the young couple while I melted my ice into several wooden bowls, Holda's vibrant green eyes watching in fascination.

"I'm so happy you sent your children here to escape the Empire's forces," Holda told me at one point. "Your son is so respectful and kind, and I'm honored that he was willing to join my family. My father feared I would die an old maid, since nobody wants to deal with the tanning industry."

Holda broke off as a contraction struck, and I applied pressure to her back to counter it. After it had passed, she expelled a sigh and I said, "I don't see how Helmut could have resisted you, because I've heard you sing. Someday I'd love to weave melodies with you."

"Oh yes, we have to do that!" Holda exclaimed, beaming. "When Wolfgang told us you'd returned, Helmut was thrilled because he knew you'd have more songs to share."

"I most certainly do." I grinned, sensing a camaraderie I had missed.

We spent the afternoon trading stories, and I filled Helmut in on all that he had missed since we parted ways in 1066. Unlike my other children, he demanded to know of my experience with the filial curse, with Wuotan and his minions, with the sacrifice and the resurrection out of the devil's bloody river. Neither he nor Holda appeared disturbed by any of it, though Helmut admitted that he was grateful his marriage negated filial authority over him.

"I don't think I could handle the things Wuotan's done to you," my son said, respect obvious in his eyes. "Facing that burning river once was enough for me."

Offering him a sly smile, I answered, "Love is the greatest magic of them all. I could do no less for an eternity with my dearest *Leitaeri*."

Once Augustin ushered Holda into the bedroom to support her during the birthing experience, I invited Helmut to walk with me along the Rhine. Holda's mother had come upstairs by then, and I confessed to my son that I was not sure whether I could keep myself in check once she began to bleed. "The scent of life is doubled around her already, and I don't want to sink my teeth into your baby or start sucking blood off the floor," I told him.

My comment did not phase my son, for he admitted that he longed to get away for a while himself. "I have no clue what to expect or how to help her, and I'm starting to feel like I'm just in the way," he said. He retrieved his lute from a corner of the parlor before we descended the stairs and strolled to the riverbank.

We took the northern road out of the village and sang the many duets I had taught Helmut years ago, as dusk descended over the Rhine. He strummed several Nightwish melodies and sang the male parts in "Astral Romance" and "The Pharaoh Sails To Orion," as well as Haggard's "Lost" and Lacuna Coil's "Reverie." I taught him some newer tunes to share with Holda when we turned our steps back toward Eisenwald, songs by Amaranthe and Visions of Atlantis.

Night had fallen by the time we reached the edge of town, and my ice sensed Augustin's blue fire coming to meet us. Helmut froze at the sight of my Keyholder, his wintry wind swirling around his body, lightly plucking the strings of his lute. Augustin smiled at us and relieved my son's tensions without delay, announcing that Holda had borne a healthy baby girl with blond hair and lovely hazel eyes.

"Both your daughter and wife are doing well, though Holda is exhausted after working so hard to create life," Augustin said, as Helmut bubbled over with relief and fatherly pride. "I would advise you to help her as much as you can in the coming weeks and give her body time to heal."

"I'll do that. It's no problem at all. I can make a mean stew, myself." Helmut grinned at Augustin, not showing any evidence of mistrust at his status as a Black Priest. Augustin mirrored his grin and pledged to bring some produce and cheese to the christening, set to be held a week from Sunday.

We left Helmut to celebrate with his family at the tannery's door, and I slipped my right hand through Augustin's left as we pointed our feet toward the southern forest. I noted that he must wish to torture me, since he pledged to bring cheese to the christening; that meant we would be unable to drink his goats' milk ourselves this upcoming week. My Keyholder jostled my shoulder and said that I must learn to find contentment in the life our lungs drew from the air, for his goats needed to rest from their lactation for the winter months. He intended to ask the Denlingers to dry them off during our imminent excursion.

Helmut and Holda chose to name their daughter Dagna Idalina von Thaden. Augustin and I visited the Denlinger house for the feast, each of us bearing gifts for the new parents along with a flask of fresh milk for the two of us. We brought containers of ripe mulberries and bilberries, a bundle of carrots, three cabbages, and four salted cheeses. I had also spent several hours that week sewing a dress for the baby, tapping into the skills I had honed at the Meldorf estate so long ago.

It was truly a marvel to sit across from my Keyholder at the Denlinger's long dining table, taking part in a familial gathering. Freia and Joel included us both in conversation often, as did Helmut and Holda. Freia's daughter Anna scampered here and there, her round blue eyes peering at the infant Holda held to her breast. Johann sat beside his father and exchanged hunting stories, while Erika huddled as close to her fiancé as she could get, whispering in his ear and giggling about their own private jokes.

Augustin caught my eye occasionally, satisfaction veiling his expression in peace. Perhaps the dead could find belonging amongst the living after all, even if it took some time for my oldest daughter to accept my chosen destiny. When my Keyholder conjured a cerulean fireball above his right palm, weaving it nimbly between his fingers, Anna crowed with delight and climbed onto his lap, begging him to allow her to touch it. Augustin chuckled as he tossed his glowing ball from one hand to the other, dropping traces of its magic into Anna's tiny palms, which glowed the luminous orange of natural fire.

After the meal, we all went outside to the silver oak, where Augustin voiced a solemn request to harvest a small stem and leaf for the Teutonic blood test. Not long afterward, he pronounced the infant's blood to be ninety-seven percent, the same level as her mother and father. Their faces shone with pride as my master placed a hand to the baby's forehead and invoked the ritual blessing.

"May your gifts guide you down the path of light, and may your magic bloom for future generations, Dagna Idalina."

Chapter Thirty-eight:
Liberated

My Keyholder and I set out on our journey on the last day of August, a Monday. We toyed around with the possibility of riding horses all the way to Salerno, but since Otto's mare did not have the stamina of Augustin's stallion, we dropped both horses off with the Denlingers alongside the goats and chickens. We would travel using a method beyond my recently-mortal comfort zone: through the air on the power of our elements alone.

While I had no compunctions about floating far above the earth as a spirit, the idea of zooming across the sky in my physical body made me uneasy. Augustin had to talk me through it multiple times, reminding me that I had done it before in 1066—when he carried Freia, me, and our belongings from Muniche's town hall to the cathedral during the siege. A Teuton of fire could tap into similar elements to aid such a venture—light for speed and energy for endurance.

As an icy witch who had yet to fully master the concept of drawing dissimilar elements from her blood and spirit, I informed Augustin rather testily that it was up to him to guide me in the proper direction if we were to travel like

Iron Man. He rolled his eyes and assured me that even if I invoked my deadly energy to propel me to the exosphere and then permitted my body to fall unheeded to earth, I would survive relatively unscathed.

"You tried that when you attempted suicide after Wuotan possessed you," I translated. My master bowed his head and affirmed it. One could torture a Black Priest in countless ways, he said, but killing one was nigh impossible.

We packed two snug bundles to wear upon our backs while we traveled, and I had to stop myself time and again from adding things that were unnecessary for immortals. We needed no food nor drink nor bedding. Even soap was superfluous, since our bodies did not sweat. Augustin had learned long ago to clean grime from his skin and clothing by manipulating the air and earth particles if a water source proved unavailable. He washed with soap for the fragrance alone.

In the end, my pack contained three dresses, socks, underwear, an extra pair of shoes, a hairbrush and ties, my medallion with the Torstein, a sleek dagger, and a pouch of currency. Augustin packed changes of clothing, his own brush and clips, currency, several maps, and a double-edged sword for show more than use. Our claws, elemental magic, and deadly anger were weapons enough; but my master contended that in some places it was best to give off a strong impression.

We departed our cottage at Lauds, Augustin's left arm holding me against him as he rocketed us into the firmament. Turning southwest toward the Alps, his heat shielded us from the chill and the wind that tore at our clothing due to our speed. I wound my arms tightly around his waist, my nerves eating away at what vitality my element could have offered. Hopefully no one down below happened to be gazing at the sky. If so, they might imagine us to be fiery divinities.

Within a mere sixty-two seconds, Augustin set us both down upon a grassy mountaintop, fog cloaking the air below us in morning's mist. I took a deep breath and flexed my muscles, lifting my chin to meet my Keyholder's gaze. "Whew. That was a whirl," I commented. Thank goodness I had braided my hair and secured its deep blue covering with multiple pins.

Augustin chuckled, his own hair tied at the nape of his neck. "It is much easier to travel through the sky when I know the route to our destination. Once we continue on, we may have to rent horses occasionally or simply sprint. Elemental ventures like that one are best concealed from the milling populace."

I raised my eyebrows at him. "We could have left last night. Astronomers might think we're a shooting star if we do that in the dark."

"We departed at Lauds for a reason," my husband informed me, turning to face a stone wall about twelve strides from where we landed.

I had not yet bothered to take a thorough look at our location. Now I saw an edifice of gray stone to my right, winged angels sculpted on either side of its primary entrance. A smooth portico stretched several meters out from the door; sunflowers reached for the heavens from hefty pots marking each corner. A dirt roadway lined in brick wove away from the door, descending into the fog toward the tree line far below the peak. Clusters of edible flowers and herbs sprang from the grass around our feet, the scents of mint, lavender, and Edelweiss tantalizing my nostrils.

I heard the hearts of quite a few living humans occupying the alp. Most seemed to be congregating in the same area—religious pilgrims gathered to raise prayers at Lauds. This was the abbey Augustin and I had visited in spirit form when we sought a method to free me from Muniche's bonds. Standing at the stone wall, clad in a brown monk's robe with his pale hands clasped before him and his face pointed toward the sunrise, my ice recognized the element of a stocky Teuton I had met years ago. Smoke.

The robed man had not yet acknowledged our presence, though he likely heard us talking upon our arrival. Augustin—who wore his black priestly robe with the hood pushed back—stood watching the monk with an expression that implied they tested each other's intentions. Which would break first?

Confusion had shoved all other sentiments aside, for while my icy spirit felt certain it recognized that man's element, it truly could not be. The man I imagined in my memory was dead. But my brain had worked out one thing, at least.

"That's the chronicler who recognized you when we came here as spirits. Right?" I asked Augustin, speaking in quiet English. A corner of his mouth quirked into what may have been a grin. "The one who gave you that tome about Teuton cities and their Ladies. Is he the Teuton priest you said could officiate our wedding? Why is he dressed like a monk?"

Augustin's smile had grown wicked, and he said, "Come and see." Then he strode toward the man who watched the sunrise, what little I could see of his face—an ear and a portion of one cheek—awakening further memories of my years in Muniche. I crept forward myself, brushing my hands off on my dark blue skirt.

"I was correct." The monk spoke in a tenor voice as Augustin halted at his right side, leaning his hip against the stone wall and folding his arms. The clean-shaven man's lips formed a smile.

"On the contrary, it was Swanhilde who solved her destiny's enigma. You implied that my intellect alone could decipher this, but she relegated me to a mere wielder of the knife."

"You accepted Muniche's keys." The monk nodded toward where Augustin kept them hooked to his belt.

"So I did." Augustin's eyebrows slanted downward. I had stopped several steps away from where the two men faced off, my lips parted in shock as I *stared* at the monk's countenance. Could it be?

I saw the man's Adam's apple shift as he swallowed. "Are you here to bleed me, *Leitaeri?*" he inquired, raising his eyebrows at the Black Priest standing over him. The monk was at least six centimeters shorter than Augustin.

"I am here to request that you do as you did for my predecessor, in ancient times when he taught you the rites you spurn here. My *Leitalra* and I must finish our bond in blood marriage, a mystical rite blessed by the heavens."

"Father . . . *Paulus?*" The name burst from my lips unexpectedly.

The brown-robed man turned away from the sunrise to look at me. What little remained of his hair was more silver than brown, his mien creased from age and brutal tortures of years past. His smile crinkled his blue-gray eyes as he greeted me. "*Leitalra,* what a privilege it is to see you again. I owe my life to you." He put a hand to his chest and ducked his head.

"Excuse me?" I felt my forehead wrinkle as my brain tried to make sense of what I saw before me. This man had been captured by the Saxons in 1059, and all of Teuton history proclaimed he had died at their hands.

"Apparently we are fated to rescue this wretch from his captors during one of our eventual journeys through time," Augustin told me, an impish smirk gracing his face. "Because apparently this chronicler has a rather authoritative historical volume to write, and he had not yet started it when—"

"I have worked on it for over a decade now," Paulus interrupted, lifting one finger in Augustin's direction. "I intend to have it copied and distributed among every conclave of our people. *Der Weg Teutonisch*, I have titled it."

"'The Teutonic Way.' You could not devise a more striking title?" Augustin rolled his eyes at the monk and heaved a tolerant sigh.

Paulus turned back to respond, his expression evincing studied insolence. But as he opened his lips, I cried out, "Wait a minute. Wait. You're saying Augustin and I are going to travel time to rescue you from the Saxons? But you gave them Otto's song!" When we had last discussed Paulus, Augustin's ire at this man's cowardice remained deeply entrenched. Now I watched them banter like brothers. I was missing something.

"Our adversaries bled it from me, *Leitalra,*" Paulus explained, his gentle patience placating my agitation. "A deranged Teuton who worships the Emperor—Werner, I believe was his name—drew the song from my blood and vowed to use its sorcery against his own people. Hatred and contempt darken his heart."

"I have not yet hunted the traitors who betrayed their kin," Augustin noted, catching my eye with a determined look. "I have eliminated most of the *Toteheri,* but my vengeance on your behalf is not yet complete."

Fires smoldered in my blood at the thought of such sedition. So many silver oak fairies had fallen prey to the Teuton traitors, and now we had the name of one of them. "Werner," I repeated, fresh plans simmering in my mind. "Once we catch the rest of the *Toteheri,* we ought to go north to bleed the Emperor and those of his inner circle, learn where his Teuton henchmen hide."

"We ought to enjoy our honeymoon first, assuming this historian is willing to conduct our wedding." He nudged Paulus' left arm.

"I have performed that ritual but once," Paulus protested, his tone telling me that he intended to do it anyway.

"All it takes is a book and a bit of blood magic. I have full confidence in you. We simply need to scrounge the necessary materials." Augustin smirked.

"There is a lovely meadow and stream less than a half *Wegstunta* from this peak," Paulus ventured in an uncertain voice.

"Excellent." Augustin slapped him on the back, keeping his right arm upon his younger brother's shoulder as he directed him toward the abbey. "What about silver oak? Do any of our sacred trees grow upon this mountain, or must I make a quick detour to my home?"

I trailed after the two brothers as they gathered the items required for a Teutonic wedding, keeping silent and listening to their casual repartee. *Augustin must have come back here in spirit form to question Paulus after Otto and I went on our ten-day escapade,* I realized, shaking my head at how oddly everything had come together. *And he must respect his younger brother enough not to bleed him without permission. I'm surprised he didn't pin Paulus down on that final day, before Otto showed up and offered him the keys. He must have truly believed that we would solve this puzzle before I vanished into heaven.*

Because we're fated to save Paulus from the Saxons and lead him to this abbey, a peaceful place apart from the fray.

Because Paulus is fated to write Der Weg, *and I totally should have heard talk about that in Muniche if he'd started working on it then. Why didn't I realize this before? It all makes sense.*

And Augustin said . . . Paulus performed the Teutonic wedding once before, for his predecessor. Prince Otto. And that means . . . Otto must have given Kezia Teuton blood. Or did Paulus do the blood-transfer for her?

My intuition told me that I would get all the answers eventually, when the time was right. Today our focus was on the final consummation of the city bond, a renewal of the vows we spoke in Muniche's cathedral two nights before our hometown fell to the ravaging horde. Elation grew within me as Paulus introduced Augustin and me to the two other Teutons who resided at the abbey, a middle-aged man of earth and a reedy youth of water. They agreed to witness our wedding without reluctance, our status as Cursed Ones notwithstanding.

Before I knew it, Augustin and I walked hand-in-hand across a lush meadow to where our priest and witnesses awaited us. Our packs left at the base of the single silver oak tree upon the mountain, we paced forward as twin souls yearning to seize the most glorious union the Teuton people could achieve. Augustin had brought a small table down from the abbey and helped the others fill it with the instruments of the traditional Teutonic wedding—the braid of silver oak leaves, a crystal goblet filled with water from the trickling Alpine stream, a smaller flute of vinegar, the iron stirrer, the bowl, the wooden cup, a pyramid of dirt, a clump of bitter herbs, a sheet of parchment, an iron pen, a small inkwell, and the sapphire knife Wuotan had used to curse me. Augustin had imbued its blade with immortal fire to ensure that it could successfully slice the flesh of the dead without crumbling into ash.

Behind the table stood Paulus von Bayern, his monk's robe not quite the norm for such a rite, the aged book in his hands appearing as though it had lingered in some forgotten corner for the past five centuries. A collection of cerulean flames crackled upon the ground to Paulus' right, and to his left stood the wooden post that awaited the joining of our blood. The middle-aged Teuton and the youth stood side by side some distance from the post, their elemental-hued eyes watching us as we approached. The young man grinned from ear to ear.

When we halted before the table, Paulus eyed each of us in turn, solemnity evident in his blue-gray irises, which swirled with just a hint of smoke. Then he lowered his chin and read from the tome, his tenor voice speaking the ritual words in Ælte Teutonica rather than the current dialect. "We come together this morning in this sacred grove to bind two Teutons by blood, oath, and love, representing the incomparable union of the Keyholder of Muniche and his Lady."

A sense of arcane import seemed to descend upon me as Paulus' lips formed the phrases few but priests or scholars could translate. Where had he found that antique volume, anyway? He voiced the required query in the same language, the question to which neither Augustin nor I would react: "If either party wishes to renounce this binding, may he or she speak now, before these leaves meet the fire."

Augustin's fingers tightened around mine when his brother cast the braid of silver oak leaves into the blue flames, prompting them to snap as a breath of silvery magic rose toward the sky. That was something I had not seen before, a mystical event mortal eyes could not perceive. I glanced briefly at Augustin while Paulus stepped to where his peers stood to ask whether they accepted their duties as witnesses. My Keyholder's gaze shone with dedication and love, his smooth lips curling into a satisfied smile.

I sensed his fire reaching out to my ice, and I clenched my thighs as desire exploded along every nerve in my body. *We're going to have to find a private peak once we're done here,* I thought, taking measured breaths in an attempt to assuage my need. *Maybe one with some snow to enhance my vigor when we finalize our love. He'll be able to caress my heart again in just a few minutes.*

Squeezing my eyes shut for a moment, I tried to focus on Paulus describing the first rite of the Teutonic wedding, working to keep myself contained. Augustin's desire smoldered around me in a sultry swell, not helping my efforts. My breathing had quickened along with my sluggish heartrate. The pattering throbs of the three living hearts around me could not distract my raging hormones; my core had begun to leak upon my underwear. *Help.*

Augustin somehow retained a semblance of reason, for I felt him turn my left wrist upward and present it to Paulus. He placed his right arm securely around my waist as his brother took the sapphire blade to my wrist, the sting jolting my awareness out of its lustful pit. My gaze traveled downward to watch the blood well upon my pale skin, its color darker, its consistency more glutinous than it had ever been while I lived. I remembered to force a few drops out of my body and into the cup Paulus held before my flesh sealed itself; such things were not easy for the dead to accomplish. I saw that the blade's edge did not appear damaged as Paulus brought it down upon Augustin's left wrist. A mere five drops of his blood slipped out to fall into the wooden cup.

The sharp scent of our dead blood cleared my brain even more, and I paid attention while Paulus described the second rite—the acceptance and disposal of sorrows. His Ælte Teutonica laden with mystery, he asserted that bound partners must face their share of trials along with triumphs on this earth, his hands adding the stream's water into the wooden cup, then the dust, then the vinegar, and lastly the bitter herbs. During this recitation, I suddenly realized that Paulus edited the traditional phrases every time they mentioned *life*. I had never realized the middle Bayern brother had a sly streak.

Although the death inside of me consumed the bitter drink before it made its way down my throat, a loathsome aftertaste remained on my tongue once I took the sip from the cup. I did not bother to smother my repulsed expression as I turned to my left to hand the cup to Augustin. When our gazes locked for a split second, I detected hesitation in his before he knocked back more than a mere sip. He grimaced, scowling at the now-empty cup and igniting it before casting it over his left shoulder.

I watched the discarded cup crackle into blackened embers, hardly able to contain my amusement. But Augustin tugged on my left hand, which he held once more in his right, reminding me that I ought to listen as Paulus read the customary statements on the duties of husband and wife. Then our priest asked us to face each other and join hands. Augustin's gratitude and devotion poured into my spirit through our touch, his eyes gazing seriously into mine as he spoke his vows in Ælte Teutonica.

"On this day I pledge my body, heart, and soul forever to you, Swanhilde Rolande von Thaden und von Bayern, before these witnesses of earth, fire, air, water, and soul. I give you myself as your husband, with my faults and my strengths, and I take you to myself as my wife, with your faults and your strengths. May we be from this day forward a dedicated Keyholder and Lady, of one mind and blood, devoted solely to each other and our city. I pledge to stay with you and you alone, as your husband . . . for all of eternity."

Tears swam in my eyes at the alterations Augustin had made—*forever to you, for all of eternity*. Death could not part us, and neither could the powers of heaven or hell. Not only that, he had referred to me by the name I had inscribed upon our first marriage certificate . . . and over half of that name had been burnt in Wuotan's fires. I had not yet chosen a new name for myself, and thus far all of our acquaintances had simply called me *Leitalra* or Mutti. But Augustin had made his promise in defiance of Teuton law, granting me my cursed name forever. For my beloved master, I could do no less.

Drawing myself up straight, I held my Keyholder's gaze with my own as I repeated the vows back to him. "On this day I pledge my body, heart, and soul forever to you, Augustin Abelard Ulrich von Bayern." My love, hopes, longings, and joy spilled over like a fountain, wreaking havoc with my perfected voice, causing my fingers to tremble as they gripped my beloved's hands. When I reached the final phrase, it came out nearly as a sob. "I pledge to stay with you and you alone, as your wife, for all of eternity."

Augustin murmured, "I love you," in my ear when we walked to the post, his nearness chasing away the uncertainties that had haunted me since he had fished my body from the Rhine River and pleaded with me to stay. Our love surrounded us in a shield that no evil forces could break, and I knew—somehow I *knew*—that once the sapphire blade united our blood upon the post, Wuotan's sway over Muniche would dissolve. A Black Priest and Priestess—a *Leitaeri* and *Leitalra*—bound by blood and love, the profoundest magic of them all.

I laid my right hand atop the post without hesitation, my gaze still locked with my chosen mate's. His strong hand covered mine in fire and death, his free hand winding around my waist, pulling me to his bosom. He bent his head toward mine, his lips parted to receive my kiss, the aura of death expelled from his lungs luring me into an eternity I could never have fathomed. And Paulus recited the concluding words in a tone that seemed to pierce the depths: "May the couple seal their marriage with a kiss, and may the union be complete!"

We could have kissed until the earth perished in fire, the bonds of Muniche cemented forever with the thrust of the sapphire knife, recreating a oneness that had never really been lost, an intimacy that had long yearned to flourish anew. I felt my husband's blue fire coursing through my veins, pounding in my heart, our elements singing a symphony of happiness, a renewal of the equality we had shared since the night he offered me his fiery heart in the

Bayern gardens. It seemed like it had been meant to be all along. I had been irretrievably fated to be Augustin von Bayern's ageless wife, his *Leitalra* for centuries of traversing the timelines.

When Paulus withdrew the knife from our hands, a violent crack of thunder roared through the heavens, the sky above remaining cloudless and bright. I heard our two witnesses voice a few foul interjections, but Augustin raised an eyebrow at me, both of his hands resting upon my hips. "He can hurt you no longer," he said quietly in Teutonica, his spirit's fingers wrapping protectively around my heart. "Wuotan enjoys expressing his distaste using thunder and lightning."

"Love broke Otto's curse after all," I whispered back, leaning into my mate's embrace. I need not fear Wuotan's influence any longer.

Eventually Augustin led me back to the table, where Paulus smiled at us, his visage content. Our witnesses had signed our marriage certificate in ink already, and now I took up the iron pen and dipped it into our commingled blood, affixing my full name to the physical record of this victory: *Swanhilde Rolande von Thaden und von Bayern.*

Then I handed the pen to my Keyholder, wondering whether he had the courage to reclaim his own true name at this moment, before the very brother who had once written of his curse. Augustin met Paulus' gaze for a second, silent communication passing between them. Then he directed the iron pen across the parchment before us, spelling out that name in crimson calligraphy, the name that was and always would be his: *Augustin Abelard Ulrich von Bayern.*

Chapter Thirty-nine:
A Personal Journey

Two weeks later, while my husband and I vacationed on the northern shore of Sardinia, I presented a possibility that stirred my hopes. We had not yet taken any journeys using the Torstein or Otto's song, but lately I had reminisced on the two times I invoked the arcane gateway for personal reasons.

My first adventure, taken as a soon-to-be college student ignorant of the complex nuances of Teutonic magic—that version of me had witnessed my parents' church wedding, fulfilling my intrinsic longing to see my mother again. Then my second, taken at Hans' prodding but ultimately one I cherished—the privilege of sharing my heart with my mother, gaining her wisdom on my convoluted destiny.

"Before we got to know each other in 1044, the only person you truly loved was your mother, Marelda," I reminded Augustin, "and now we have the power to visit her, to get her insight on your ultimate fortune."

My husband appeared indecisive, averting his eyes from mine to the azure sea before us. "I do not know . . . if I could handle such a venture," Augustin said after a few moments of thought. "There is so much darkness in my past, I fear to stand before her as I am."

"You don't need to bring up your past mistakes. You've repented and changed your actions. Marelda wanted you to become the Keyholder of her city, a defender of her people. And you've done exactly that." I nodded at Augustin as he looked at me uncertainly.

"Honestly, I don't think you have a choice to *not* speak with her, if you don't want to alter history," I went on. "How else would she have known to tell you that she wouldn't survive Otto's birth? And how else would she have been able to paint that portrait of you as an adult, the one Maria hid away? You visited her as you are now, the eternal Prince of Muniche."

Augustin's eyebrows came together broodingly, and I suspected that he recognized my point. "If we do such a thing, we must take pains to circumvent my father, Prince Ulrich. The city bond may replicate itself as it did when you met with Camilla."

"That's true." I tapped my chin with my forefinger's claw as I considered. "Prince Ulrich unlocked the city gates each morning at Lauds, right? If so, we could catch Marelda while her Keyholder's doing his duty, then reopen the portal before he investigates. But he might not even notice our presence, because we'll both be there and our bond is complete. I think what disturbed Hans was that I had no *Leitaeri* when I visited my Mutti, but he suddenly had two *Leitalrae*—myself and Bertha Lohr." I tilted my head at Augustin, awaiting his comeback.

"And if the Torstein vanishes before we can reopen the portal, as it did when you first came to the eleventh century?" Augustin raised his eyebrows.

"Then we'll scurry away to the nearest pipe organ so I can summon the gates that way. Easy. But we should be fine if we make it a quick visit. The Torstein didn't vanish until after we'd escaped from the Gypsies, and we'd been there a good half hour by then. I can keep an eye on it while you talk to Marelda."

Augustin shook his head at me, looking somewhat put out. "You are a daring witch, darling swan princess."

"Time travelers don't tread lightly," I answered with a wink.

So we went, the subsequent morning when the sun's earliest rays sprinkled the sea with gold. Augustin spent the night restlessly walking the beach, praying for peace, for discernment about what to say. As I emerged from the brush, having clothed myself in my dark blue dress and braided hair beneath a matching net, my husband turned away from the waters to face me, his black cloak sweeping the sand, his hands flexing restively.

"If we are to do this, you must not leave my side, Swanhilde," he stated, his eyes shifting from mine to the medallion hanging from my neck.

I had no qualms with that. Giving him a reassuring smile, I stepped to his side, undoing the clasp of the medallion's chain and holding the amulet securely in my left hand. I felt the familiar solidity of the Torstein against my skin, the power it secreted addling my blood...so I reached my right hand out to Augustin, welcoming the warmth of his fingers linking with mine. Lifting my eyes to the sky, I recited the spell for the first time in all of history, focusing my thoughts on a day long ago, the hour of Lauds, just a month before a birth that would kill more than one soul.

"'I go to observe, not to interfere. To become a part of the past, not to change what is past. I go to see with my own eyes, to hear with my own ears, that which cannot be fully understood another way. I seek the past to learn, to return forever changed. May the gates of time take me, and restore me as I was, but new.'"

The space between us and the sea split open with a wretched crack, revealing the labradorite gates of time—the portal to innumerable raging currents, the unceasing endeavors of humanity, of life. I felt Augustin recoil at the sight of that mystical doorway. For an instant, I thought of my most recent encounter with the tides of history . . . on the precipice of fatality, accompanied by Wuotan himself, his scathing tongue informing me that I would never again see the future after I had died.

"A place of utter aloneness in a web of humankind," Augustin muttered in a caustic tone, clasping my hand more tightly. "It is rife with devils who imagine themselves to be divine, their claws marring the threads of history's tapestry."

I could not deny that, but I had no wish to abandon our plans. This trip was necessary; I felt it in my heart. It would help Augustin more than either of us could comprehend. Squeezing his hand, I nodded toward the eddying currents beyond the gateway. "I'll stay right beside you. I promise."

Augustin heaved a sigh and nodded at me, his spiritual hands surrounding my heart in an unbreakable grip. Then we jumped through the gates together, into the vortex of confusion and helplessness . . . but somehow the union of our souls seemed to persist although our physical senses became worthless. The certainty of Augustin's presence heartened me throughout the journey as I fought to ignore the sirens' ridicule, the eldritch moans that rose from the depths, the evil laughter of our greatest adversary. Wuotan scorned our audacity, our refusal to accept our place as his servants when we charged brazenly into the past.

The unpleasantness of that ordeal shrank into unimportance the moment we burst through the gates. My physical senses returned in a flash. I felt the heat of Augustin's fingers upon my skin, the sturdiness of stone beneath my feet. The musty scent of a castle's interior mixed with candle smoke arrested my nose; the familiar chimes of Lauds clanged from the cathedral's bell tower not far away. The chamber was dimly lit, natural flames decorating the candles atop a windowsill, a ledge, a table beside the grand bed against the far wall.

Upon that bed lay a young woman, her face flushed but beautiful, damp curls draping her forehead, her body bloated beneath an elaborate blanket. She groaned softly in her sleep, her hands clutching the blankets, the smell of weakness saturating her blood. I sensed the blue fire in her spirit—a faint glimmer shackled by illness and perhaps by the prejudice of her era, by guardians who believed that a woman should not exhibit her element even in private, in a bedchamber vacated by her Keyholder, a Prince who had gone to unlock the city gates.

I nearly forgot to close the portal of time, so absorbed was I by the sleeping Marelda, my mind pondering a thousand things at once about her life, about her fate as *Leitalra* of Muniche, the mother of three squabbling sons. As I turned to lift the Torstein in a silent command, I heard Augustin gasp, an anguished sound. His arms wrapped around my body, his immortal vitality diminished.

"Oh, Swanie," he moaned in a voice so low that even my sharp ears could hardly distinguish the words. "This is too much. I cannot do this . . . her frailty torments me." He sobbed soundlessly.

I extricated myself from his grip after a few moments and placed the chain with its medallion back around my neck. Then I took hold of my husband's face and said in no uncertain terms, "You *are* going to do this, Augustin. You must fulfill your purpose in coming here, to touch Marelda's life in a time when she desperately needs it."

His hands traveled upward to wind around my wrists, his sorrowful eyes searching mine, drawing some of my earnestness into his own spirit. His breathing gradually slowed and he shot a glance at the woman on the bed, lines of grief marring his visage. I clasped his hands in mine and pressed them supportively. "Go to her," I urged. "She loves you."

Augustin walked slowly toward her with the steps of a ghost, his left hand locked with my right, fingering the sapphire that united me with the woman on the bed. He had given the ring back to me on the day Paulus performed our Teutonic wedding, placing it upon my right ring finger, where it would remain eternally.

He stopped centimeters from the bed frame, his entire body shuddering while he stared down at the somnolent Marelda. His eyes shifted from her hands, slender and pale, to her clammy face, then to the table beside her bed. A pair of candles illuminated a basin of water and a cloth.

Augustin shared a long look with me and I smiled, extending my element to sprinkle upon the water in the bowl. It grew frigid in an instant, and Augustin released my hand to take up the cloth, dipping it into the water and wringing it out. He motioned for me to step back into the shadows of a violet drapery upon the wall, indicating that he needed to cross this bridge alone, that my nearness would be his strength.

I sank back against the tapestry, concealing myself in shadow, tracing my fingers around the Torstein where it lay in its medallion. Its magic addled my blood, as usual, and I glanced down at it for a second. *No disappearing this time, okay?* I thought.

I watched as Augustin wiped his mother's brow with the cloth he had dampened. She stirred, and he bathed her entire face before laying the cloth upon her forehead, his eyes glistening with tears. He ran his fingers carefully down her hand, as though he feared she may slip away before her time. Her hand twitched, and Augustin caught it in both of his, kneeling upon the floor and training his eyes on her face.

"*Leitalra*," he breathed in a tremulous voice. "My Lady . . . awake."

Marelda murmured indistinctly, her eyelids fluttering. Augustin raised her hand to his lips and she opened her eyes, blinking at the unfamiliar man who knelt at her bedside, caressing her hand. "Who is there?" she inquired in a hushed tone, her eyes shifting to her left, where her husband usually slept. "Uli?"

"Hush now," Augustin soothed, reaching forward to brush tangled curls away from her face. "He has gone to open the gates. Dawn has come."

Marelda's eyes, wide now with fear and bewilderment, focused on those of the man bending over her. She must have recognized something in those eyes—perhaps how similar they appeared to her own—for when she spoke again her voice remained low, not calling out for help. "Do I . . . know you?"

I saw Augustin's lips quivering as he answered, "I am the son you love. The son to whom you sang an extra lullaby every night, so he would not have to face the dark alone. The son who gathered flowers for you from the gardens. The son who sees you every time he looks in the mirror. The son who wept bitterly for you . . . when . . . when . . . you died." He broke off with a groan, his tears spilling over.

"Oh . . . Augustin." Marelda tugged him toward her. He buried his face in her breast, his shoulders quaking with sobs while her hands stroked his hair, his back.

"My darling boy . . . my sweet child . . . there, there . . . your Mutti loves you." She murmured softly to him, kissing his hair, her arms cradling him as though he were still a toddling boy who needed maternal comfort. Perhaps that child resided within him yet, for how long had it been since he had last felt his mother's love?

Presently, Augustin began to compose himself, lifting his head to stare into his mother's eyes. He blinked repeatedly, likely rallying his courage for the painful discussion he must have with the feeble woman before him. Marelda smiled at him, but I saw sadness in her eyes as she reached out to touch his cheek. "You do not bring joyful tidings, my son, or you would not have come to meddle with my dreams." In spite of her illness, she was perceptive.

Augustin wiped his tears away on the sleeve of his robe, then took hold of her hand. "It is true," he confirmed in a broken voice, his gaze drifting from Marelda's face to her swollen abdomen. "The birth of the child in your womb—a son—is destined to take you away from me." He pressed his mother's hand against his face, endeavoring to conceal his anguish, and then he went on.

"For years . . . for many years . . . I grieved bitterly. I hated the child . . . hated the woman who replaced you . . . hated God for allowing you to die . . . for placing me in a family so manipulated by the bonds of Muniche."

Augustin paused, his tears drenching both his hand and his mother's, his other hand grasping the fabric of her nightdress. I had a clear view of his expression from where

I hid. Never before had I seen him look so ashamed, so repentant. His eyes were squeezed shut, leaking steamy salt water, his lips curled back to reveal clenched teeth.

Marelda whispered something to him, her free hand gently smoothing his hair, and he continued his confession. "I forsook all of my responsibilities . . . allowed that child to assume my place as Keyholder, as Prince. I sought pleasure in sin . . . in blood . . . in power. And whenever I thought of you . . . it tortured me . . . for I knew . . . I knew that you saw my wickedness . . . that I had failed you . . . disregarded all that you had taught me. Oh . . . *Mutti!*"

Marelda pushed herself into a sitting position against the headboard, the damp cloth falling to the sheets as she folded her wayward son in her arms. "My poor boy," she crooned, kissing his forehead, holding him tightly to her breast. "My dear Augustin. Be still. I love you always, no matter what you have become, for you will always be my son. My Augustin. My little Prince."

She took his face in her hands and kissed him softly on the lips, an act which seemed to snap Augustin out of his misery. A look of gratitude appeared in his light blue eyes, and he reached up to clasp both of Marelda's hands in his, bringing them down to rest in his lap, where he sat at the edge of her bed.

"God should have given me permanently to Wuotan after my decades of irreverence," he admitted, "but He is merciful to an extent that amazes me. He sent me an angel, Mutti. A kind woman to love me in your place. To prove that grace and forgiveness exist even for the worst of men, even for priests who have cast their lot with Wuotan."

Augustin looked toward me, his eyes summoning me from the shadows. I touched the Torstein again before stepping away from the drapery, then hesitated. "Come," Augustin said, and his mother turned a little to look at me, though her hands remained imprisoned in her son's. Her eyes began to glow with happiness when I approached, and her lips parted into a brilliant smile. My husband wrapped his left arm around my waist as I reached the bedside.

"Mutti, this is my dear wife, Swanhilde, the woman who rescued me from the path to hell. She chose to love me when everyone else mocked me, and through her kindness she taught me that there is more in this world than sorrow, than cruelty, than death. I repented of my sins because of her and reclaimed the position that I had once rejected . . . for she is my *Leitalra*." He retrieved Muniche's keys from a pocket of his cloak and held them out for his mother to see.

Marelda sighed quietly, her smile accentuating her beauty. "So you are Muniche's Prince after all," she declared, "just as I had hoped. You are her master guardian, a priest who loves his Lady and walks the path of light. This is the greatest gift I could ever receive. Your tidings are not as tragic as I feared."

She chuckled, an airy laugh, then reached out to touch my left hand, giving it a friendly squeeze, her eyes remaining on those of her dearest son. "I began to look past the horror of your tale when you mentioned your reminisces of me during your years of iniquity. If you had not changed your ways, you would not have come here, for shame would have held you back."

She tilted her head rather impishly at Augustin, her smile evoking my own memories of a master who always seemed a step ahead of me. "Now I know where you got your intuition," I remarked while Augustin and Marelda shared a laugh—hers lighthearted, his subdued.

"My son is intuitive?" Marelda directed her smile toward me. Her light blue eyes sparkled with interest.

"He's the most intelligent person I know," I said with feeling, disregarding his grunt of rebuke. "He's a voracious learner, always seeking the truth. He records our history and knows more about Teutonic sorcery than any other priest. He knows twelve languages—"

"Fourteen," Augustin corrected, his fingers pinching my waist, an unspoken order to cease my accolades. His gaze was on the far wall, and his cheeks burned.

But I was hardly finished. "Fourteen languages," I repeated, enjoying the maternal pride that smoldered in

Marelda's eyes. "And he's a doctor, always using his skills to help those in need. He has saved countless women from meeting your fate in childbirth. He has defended Muniche from our enemies on more than one occasion, always striving for our people's good, our honor.

"He dances like a god of fire and captures the sunbeams in his hands. He is an artist like you; he uses pens and ink to sketch exquisite portraits of our love. And his love is more powerful than anything I've ever known. He is such a devoted master, the best husband anyone could ever find." I abruptly ran out of words, and Augustin drew me close, his adoration making me tremble in his arms.

"She exaggerates," I heard him say, as I shut my eyes to better appreciate the intimacy of our spirits' bond. "What good qualities I may possess are nothing compared with Swanhilde's. She is the kindest person I know, such a generous and compassionate woman, one who reawakened those characteristics within me when I believed myself incapable of goodness. She has been faithful to me for decades, even when I failed her time and again.

"She is educated and inquisitive, the perfect balance to my own personality. She reads and writes at least seven languages. She has an innate aptitude for beauty, both in nature and in the artwork of man; her talents at weaving clothing are unmatched. She manipulates her element, which is ice, with a precision that few can boast, and she sings with the voice of an angel. She is everything I could have desired in a wife: loving, loyal, forgiving . . . the greatest gift heaven has ever given to me."

I felt Augustin's warm lips upon my hair as I hid my face against his chest, loath to accept his praise, for it was so undeserved. But Marelda's light laughter coaxed me from my hiding place, and I turned my head to see her eyes smiling into mine. "Come here, my dear girl, let me embrace you. I have never been so happy in all of my life. This dream is a wonderful answer to prayer, for although I am not destined to see my son's future in this world, I know now that all will be well for him and for you, dear Swanhilde."

Her arms welcomed me into the fellowship of the Bayern family. When I rested my head upon her breast, I sensed the cobalt glow of her fire uniting with that of my husband, beckoning me—the child of ice—into a blissful realm that I had rarely experienced in life: the sphere of motherly love and acceptance.

Shivers ran down my spine as I realized that Marelda von Bayern approved of *me*. This saintly woman I had long respected hugged me as though I were her child, the daughter she never had. And we were the same, the Ladies of Muniche, our hearts indelibly bound to our city and our Keyholders—a lamentable fate but also one of possibility, of hope, of unique sisterhood.

Tears moistened my eyes by the time she released me, and my whispered "thank you" came out shakier than I liked. But she clasped my hands securely, her own eyes glistening with tears as we gazed at each other, our silence speaking the words we could never form.

"You must care for him attentively, dear Swanhilde," Marelda adjured, her gaze suddenly solemn. "His happiness is dependent on you and he is a stubborn boy. He needs a woman who will love him unconditionally and direct him always toward the path of virtue."

I marveled at her sagacity. The Augustin she knew well was only four years old, yet she already had a keen grasp on his personality. "I will care for him during all of our days as Keyholder and Lady," I assured her, "and afterward when we enter paradise. I promise."

Marelda leaned forward to kiss my forehead, then directed her attention to her son. I slid off of the bedclothes and stepped back to the corner of the bedside table, wanting to observe this final encounter as discreetly as possible. For a long time they simply gazed at each other, their hands and elements intertwined.

"Ah, Mutti," Augustin murmured in a passionate tone, "I have missed you so terribly."

"Of course you have," she responded with a touch of sadness. "I wish that I could live to see you grow into a man, into a great Keyholder and Prince. But the ways of

God are perfect, though we do not always understand." A tiny smile curled on her lips and she sighed a little.

"I have been learning that," Augustin said, a half-smirk adorning his face. He raised her hands to his lips, then reached out to smooth her curls. "You ought to lie down and rest before . . . before your *Leitaeri* returns." His eyes drifted toward the door to the hallway, shadowy in the candlelight.

She acknowledged the value of this, and he helped her recline, fluffing her pillows and retrieving the cloth from where it had fallen earlier. He dipped it into the basin of water and muttered something about Marelda's flushed complexion as he moistened her brow. I knew that he wanted to heal her, to ease her suffering and ensure that she would survive the birth of her child. But the horrid strictures of time travel tied his hands, and I saw in his eyes how much it cost him.

Marelda undoubtedly perceived his struggle, but she smiled at her son and urged, "You must cling to your faith, Augustin, in every trial, for God promises a brighter day."

"I know, Mutti," Augustin murmured, dabbing her face before returning the cloth to its place beside the basin. "I strive to follow goodness forevermore."

Marelda's smile widened, and she lifted one hand to tuck a lock of obsidian hair behind Augustin's ear. "Trust God . . . and be good to her."

Her eyes averted to mine briefly, then returned to her son's as she addressed him again. "Guard and protect her faithfully and love her always, for she and I are the same. We are Muniche, your mother, your wife, your divine destiny. Never forget who you are—the master guardian of Muniche, the mentor of our people."

"I will never forget, Mutti. I promise to be good to my Lady and to our city. And I do hope . . . that when we meet again . . . you shall have little reason to be ashamed of me . . . I hope." The pledge smoldered in his eyes, and he leaned down to kiss his mother's lips with the reverence of a lover.

She exhaled softly when he lifted his head. Her eyes shone with maternal affection as she whispered, "I love you, Augustin . . . my sweet son . . . my master."

"As I love you," he replied, "with the fidelity of my eternal soul." He kissed her eyes, then said, "Sleep now, my dear Lady, sleep . . . and dream of a better tomorrow."

He stroked her forehead rhythmically as her eyelids drooped; and then, to my astonishment, he began to sing a song I had never heard before, likely one of the lullabies his mother had once sung to him. My eyes bugged, and my mouth fell open. I had never expected to hear Augustin sing anything, let alone a lullaby, and in a quiet, flawless baritone. Marelda's visage grew peaceful while he sang, and by the time he finished she had slipped into a serene slumber, her chest rising and falling steadily with her breath.

We returned to our own era shortly thereafter, opening the necessary portal in an adjacent chamber. No servants nor errant Keyholder disturbed our passage, and the Torstein remained within its medallion, silently waiting for me to invoke its sorcery anew.

When we stepped back onto the shores of the Mediterranean, the early sunlight glistening off of the ripples, I closed the gates of time and swung to face my husband, placing my hands on my hips. "You can *sing*," I accused, frustrated at his reluctance. The entire time I had known him, he staunchly insisted that he claimed no musical talents, that the best he could do was growl along with the darker Gothic tunes from my era.

Augustin grinned, his posture quite at ease as he stood at the water's edge, his hands folded behind him, his gaze on the blue horizon. "My singing voice came back to me in the presence of my mother," he said, sounding as surprised as I felt. "Many other qualities returned to me. Tranquility . . . trust . . . belief in a blissful eternity . . . and the ambition to look after you as your Keyholder should." He raised an eyebrow at me and laughed, a sound of satisfaction.

I laughed with him, feeling his newfound joy enveloping my heart through the strength of our bond. "So . . . you used to be afraid of the dark?" I asked, remembering how he had identified himself to Marelda.

He smirked and grabbed my waist, pulling me onto the water for a dance. "The blue fire inside of me chased that fear away, for it is my most vivid memento of my mother, that saint who watches over us even now." And he lifted his face to the sun as we danced, our heartfelt tribute to *Leitalra* Marelda von Bayern.

Chapter Forty:
Final Muses

It seems I have reached a fair stopping point in this saga, for I initially agreed to write the story of my *life*, which ceased in June of 1074. I have rattled on for a good ten chapters about my death, so I ought to quit before this saga turns into a book series that never ends. Those sort of series used to annoy me in the twenty-first century, the tales that never seized any sort of resounding conclusion. At this point, any readers who have stuck with me throughout my journey should conclude that my fated master and I continued onward, defying Wuotan's machinations while guiding the Teuton people toward the light.

Augustin and I have experienced many adventures to date, and countless more loom on the horizon in the space of obscurity that Wuotan's sorcery barred from my sight. Sometimes the trials overshadow the victories, while at other times the opposite proves true. But even after one hundred and eight years of this exile—the calendar for May 1182 currently hangs on the wall of this writing chamber— I still do not regret that I chose death over paradise. It will always be a privilege to face the events of infinite timelines with Augustin faithfully beside me, my husband, lover, Keyholder, master . . . my equal . . . my fate.

With a sense of accomplishment, I paused in my scribbling to glance over my shoulder at Augustin. Perched upon the windowsill of our writing chamber, he scrutinized some book or other by the radiant sunlight of afternoon. A slight breeze ruffled his gorgeous hair, half of it pulled back from his face in the style I have always loved most. His expression suggested something like scornful amusement as he scoured the aged tome in his hands, and at length I could no longer handle the suspense.

"What *is* that book you're reading?" I demanded, whirling back around to face the desk. Snatching up the pen, I scrawled out a few sentences in an attempt to put forth the impression of indifference.

Augustin snickered darkly and snapped the tome closed. "This is the *Book of Asenath*, one of the artifacts I procured from the Crusaders," he informed me. "I have not yet deciphered whether the scribes who penned these writings wished to create phony histories or archaic novels."

I turned to face him and said, "The Crusaders passed through nearly twenty-five years ago, and you *still* haven't finished perusing their relics?"

He smirked and responded, "Other matters have occupied my time." His eyes burned pointedly into mine, and then he cocked his head at the window with its view toward the north. Far in the distance, between several mountain peaks and our castle, the spires of a resurrected city reached for the sky.

I smiled, recognizing the truth in his words. I leaned my right elbow against the desk and directed my gaze to the window, my thoughts drifting to that city of ours, that hub of trade that the Empire had never truly obliterated. A monastery rose upon the ashes of Muniche some time ago; and when an enterprising duke chose to span the Isar with a stone bridge in a place not ten meters from where a drawbridge once welcomed passers-by into the greatest Teuton city, people and business progressively returned. Augustin and I were in the process of building our fortress around the same time. Thus the reborn Muniche and the Black Castle of her cursed guardians claimed more common ground than her pious council members would deign to acknowledge.

"I'll have you know that I've reached the last chapter of my life story," I told Augustin, part of me marveling that it had taken just under two years to organize those tortuous memories.

My husband rose from the windowsill and wandered to my left side, his eyes running swiftly over the sentences that decked the pages before me. Tapping his tome on the edge of the desk, he queried, "And what 'final muses' do you intend to offer to your son?"

I had pondered that question for some time already; it was one reason I had included the chapter about our visit to Marelda. Over the years, I had become an expert at sidestepping compulsory tasks for as long as possible. Augustin, as always, ensured that I did not evade responsibility indefinitely. What lessons could my life story teach my son Max, the twenty-first century Keyholder who had taken death's chains upon himself?

"I'm not entirely sure," I confessed, sliding the pen between my fingers. "Part of me thinks the best advice I could offer stems from our recent experiences, not from those of my life."

"In that case, you must consider chronicling the significant events of your death as well," Augustin declared, his tone hinting that he had planned for this all along. Tossing the *Book of Asenath* onto an empty corner of the desk, he crossed his arms beneath his cloak and eyed me meaningfully.

"My darling swan, recall that while your primary audience is your son, he shall wield the authority to share your writings with others. The Teutons of the future would be far more receptive to *your* histories than those of the Black Priest Wolfgang. Our stories must see the light of day at some point, I aver." He pointed one finger at me, its claw catching the rays of sunlight. "Through you."

I considered his assertions, my thoughts leaping forward to an epoch when my cursed son would bear the responsibility for München and her people. An arduous task, certainly, and one that we would never fully understand, since the reestablished Muniche housed a new soul. But Max might face some of the trials we had already endured, and maybe general principles could be outlined for the Teutons who had once been my peers.

"I'm still a Cursed One," I said, thinking out loud. "If I leave my records in this castle, they'll be stigmatized."

"But your people remember Swanhilde Meissner von Thaden." I jerked in surprise at the sound of *that* name— the Lady of Muniche, 2000-2020. "Your son can present your writings however he deems appropriate. Perhaps the day may come when all writings of the accursed are freed."

Augustin took a step forward, his face suddenly fierce. "Our days are few in number, Swanhilde, though we imagine otherwise, and our influence in the Teuton community is limited. But our histories can reach much further. Our words can outlast the most ancient of the Cursed Ones. If our greatest goal is to effect change, both of us must write of this death and of the lives around us, if only to illustrate the power of goodness, the triumph of light over darkness!"

Blue flames erupted upon every candlestick in the chamber, decking those on the desk as well as the chandelier high above that we rarely used. I ogled my husband in silence for a moment, sensing his intensity through our bond, seeing it reflected in the fires, in his matching eyes. Desperation washed over me and I cried out, "But if I were to write everything—*everything*, as you say—it would take centuries, ages, all of eternity!" An impossible proposition.

"That it would, but imagine what we shall write in eternity when we record the events that are mere prophecies now. Think of the beauty, the perfection with which we shall create in paradise, when we reap our rewards at last." Augustin pivoted to face the window and raised his countenance to the sky. His fingers gripped the stone sill, his posture rigid, a thousand emotions sketching their art upon his mien.

The breeze caught his hair, obscuring his expression just a little, but I could see his eyes burning the heavens as he murmured, "Unhindered . . . untainted . . . by the curse." He lifted his right hand to brush his hair away from his face, and his sleeve slid downward to reveal a portion of that pitch black scar.

But I knew that he referred to a greater curse—the selfishness and evil that vexed humanity. Centuries must pass before we renounced that burden for good. I left the stool to drift to his side, and he placed his right arm around me, drawing me close. Sighing, I gazed at the firmament, my eyes imprinting its likeness onto my memory: hues of sapphire, puffs of purest white, golden fire mingling with the blue, fashioning luminosities that mortal vision could not discern. I imagined I could see heaven's boundary there, though I could not.

"Now I'm questioning my decision to turn back yet again, thank you very much," I chided my husband. "We still have over three hundred years of exile."

Augustin grimaced. "And to think that on that morning, I said that I did not fear the curse." His gaze seemed to pierce the fabric of the past, seeing a far cloudier day than this one, when we stood at the window of his bedroom in Muniche, young lovers knowing nothing of the ordeals to come.

A snort escaped my nostrils. "The things we feared that morning had little to do with reality. Love vanquished the specter of death, after all." I grinned beguilingly at my master, remembering how I had clung to our heart-bond then, elevating our devotion above customs, above reason.

"Love . . . or was it madness?" Augustin's teeth, so sharp and magnificent in death, glittered in the sunlight. He pressed his lips to the side of my neck, the heat of his fire prompting me to tremble with desire. As I closed my eyes to concentrate on the adoration enveloping our spirits, he whispered in my ear, "I trust, though, that most of the time you can forgive me for luring you back to this hell."

His breath warmed my skin when he spoke, and a smile crawled across my face despite the somberness of our discussion. "Most of the time, yeah, that sounds about right," I answered, turning my face to the left to wink at him.

Augustin shook his head and smirked, his eyes reflecting the numerous interpretations of my response. "Our day will come, Swanhilde," he said, giving me a final hug before releasing me and averting his gaze to the sky. "And it will be a glorious one at that."

I paced back to the stool and retook my seat, my thoughts returning to the Max of the future, the Cursed One who had named himself in honor of my husband. He had condemned himself to protect Muniche in death, a choice similar to ours, but plagued with aspects I feared to contemplate. How could I have any advice to offer to Max —I, the mother who had allowed him to be cursed when I knew the infernal cost?

"How can I possibly end this tale?" I murmured mostly to myself, my fingers clutching the pen with more force than necessary. "What instruction can I give him that he hasn't already learned?"

The single bell in the tower of our fortress' chapel pealed out a long, deep note signifying the hour of None, and Augustin's hand patted my left shoulder in the same instant. "Say what you wish, but do not overthink it," he advised, reaching out to retrieve the *Book of Asenath* from the corner of the desk. He strode away from me toward the door, but paused at the threshold when the bell rang a second time.

Favoring me with an expression somewhere between solemnity and inanity, Augustin said, "Tell him that he needs to create a metal band with the servants of his castle, like we have, and that he has a lot of ground to cover before he can claim to be anywhere near as talented as us."

I laughed out loud at the mental image of a twenty-first century metal band living at the Black Castle, complete with guitars, bass, drums, keyboards, violins, cellos, flutes, and— "He can't forget the organ."

I laughed again at the absurdity of some of our exploits in recent decades. Then I shook my head at Augustin and made a shooing motion. "If you don't get out of here, Vlad will finish ringing that bell and you'll be late for practice."

"The master of this castle is never late," he rejoined, opening the door to peer down the staircase beyond. I made a scoffing sound and prepared to turn back to my work, listening to the fading resonance of the third bell.

"You need to complete that book with haste," Augustin opined in parting, glancing back toward me from the foot of the stairwell. "Tristania is on the roster for today, and none of the servants can command those soprano lines with your splendor."

Flattered, I sang out a few bars in the strong voice the filial curse had granted me. "Faultless, my siren!" Augustin's praise echoed up the stairway as he caught the darkness in his robe and disappeared, his book in tow, while the fourth and final bell for None reverberated throughout the castle.

So from this, Max, you can see that beauty can be celebrated even in death, not merely in the forms of blood and sex, despite what some of your predecessors likely believed. Yes, we have built the Black Castle in the Alps with the help of some of the greatest masons and architects of the time; and yes, we have chosen all of our servants in light of their musical talents. We have commissioned tapestries, paintings, and statuaries to ornament our halls, and our servants care for a vast hidden garden abounding with flowers and fruits.

This castle need not be an anteroom to the grave, a melancholy into which many of our kind have forced our home to degenerate. While its location discourages all but the most desperate or dauntless of mortals from paying social calls, we need not shun all of humanity when we have walked the path of death and seized the wonders of redemption. Wuotan is *not* our master, though he prefers to envision otherwise.

The most grievous burden I have shouldered throughout this exile thus far is the necessity of coming to terms with life's brevity. I have not yet found peace with this and doubtless never will. Those who experienced the Empire's conquest have passed from the earth, and those of subsequent generations cannot fathom the nuances that drove our choices. Our loved ones have left us and our people believe Cursed Ones are incapable of goodness, hypocrisies of old entrenching themselves afresh.

I expect that you might face similar challenges, my son, as the years pass and those who trust you embark on their eternal journeys . . . Sango, Üwe, Stefan and Vreni, Jan, Matthias, Fonsi, Siggi and Lise. Unlike most Cursed Ones, though, you shall have Günter and Zorina at your side, although I would advise you to open a serious discussion with Günter about his intentions with Zorina. They are already married, as I recall, so it may be too late to adjust her destiny; but the two of them ought to consider the heartbreak their future will bring, after she has grown old and left her immortal husband behind. You might be obliged to kill Günter out of compassion when that day comes, Max.

As München's eternal *Leitaeri,* you will experience the irresistible pull of the city bond, how it will shape your heart to embrace the female personification of her collective soul. Under the influence of the bond, you will love many Ladies throughout the ages. When the day comes that you sense an abiding affection that stems from a seed more profound than Muniche's sway, I would plead that you do what must be done to unify your fortunes. To have no twin soul to walk beside me in this exile is a fate I would wish on no one.

I do not know how soon you will discover this story of my life; but we will see to it that you find and read it first, before all of the other writings we intend to preserve for your eyes alone. Perhaps you will find it quickly—shortly after I have vanished through the song into the era that claimed my life nearly one hundred and eight years from this day—and perhaps it will take you months, years, decades to find it. But when you do, I trust that you will disclose the tales of Augustin Abelard Ulrich von Bayern, the greatest Keyholder of the greatest Teuton city in Europe—and those of his wife, the Lady Swanhilde Rolande von Thaden und von Bayern, that madwoman who should not have loved him but chose to anyway, knowing that her choice would follow her down the ages.

While I could go on, I have no wish to shirk today's music practice. So in closing I remind you, Max, that while Wuotan's filial curse has grounded me in this current continuum, pushing your era beyond my reach . . . the same is not true of you. Time's currents would bend to your will, if you wish to make use of the river spirits' precious gift . . . and reunite with the family no curse can ever bar from you.

My son, Augustin and I await you here.

Finis

~*~

Can you believe we've finally made it to the end of Swanie's saga? It's been a long and twisted ride, and it looks like there's more to come . . . at some future point!

If you haven't grabbed *Veiled Magic,* the free short story you can get in eBook form by signing up for my newsletter, now's the time to do it. It's a sweet story set during the events of *Arcane Gateway* that details how Swanie and Vreni became friends.

Turn the page for a sneak peek at the first chapter.

Veiled Magic excerpt
© C.L. Carhart 2022

Chapter One:
Swanie von Thaden

My heart pounded as I slipped through the train's doors seconds before they shut. I had run straight to the station without looking back. Feeling as though all eyes followed me—judging everything from the sweat beading upon my forehead to my jostled pair of glasses to the loose laces on one of my shoes—I made my way to a single seat at the back of the car. *Please, God, don't let anyone pay attention to the schoolgirl who just got on this train,* I prayed.

Rush hour had ended over an hour ago, so locals about their errands comprised the majority of passengers. I clutched my schoolbag to my chest as the train began to glide along the tracks, the conductor's voice blandly announcing the next stop. Summoning my nerve, I peeked at the passengers just long enough to confirm that no official-looking adults occupied the car. I sighed in relief, a miniscule amount of my tension dissipating. *So I won't get in trouble for skipping school. At least there's that.*

I was not the type of student to play truant without good reason. Something awful had happened not twenty minutes before, and I needed to get away to think. To process the implications of what I had done.

At first I considered taking the train north to my mentor's apartment. The grandmotherly Lady of Muniche had taught me so much about my magic ever since I discovered it last year, in October of 1992. Seven months later and I could conjure ice from my otherworldly spirit and my blood—the two eternal sources of Teutonic mysticism. My people kept their elemental gifts hidden from the outside world, to protect both humanity and ourselves. Today I had broken that rule spectacularly.

My intuition told me Lady Muniche would understand, but she might also order me to return to school. And I was too afraid to do that. Too afraid to see the face of the bullied girl in my class, to confront the questions in her eyes.

I just wanted to help her. It upset me to see her cornered by those seniors, brutes who treated her like a salted slug. Their harassment was immoral. What was the point of having ice magic if I could not use it to help people?

The train halted at my stop, and I slung my schoolbag over one shoulder as I headed for the exit. Very few people remained in the car, and no one else got off here. I realized belatedly that I had not tightened my shoelace, so I paused to do so before setting my course for the sidewalk. A single taxi idled at the curb, but I ignored its driver. I would walk home—an activity that some of my more affluent classmates would scorn. Morgen and Ava would guffaw if they learned I had taken the train to my neighborhood like a peasant.

The situation called for unusual methods. I could not have stepped into the office to call my father's chauffeur first, not unless I faked illness. Morgen had a talent for that, but I was a pitiful liar. And now I was about to step onto Thaden property in the middle of the morning, when I should be in school.

I'll have to sneak in through the side gate, I told myself, quickening my pace while trying to put forth the impression of nonchalance. *Pappi should be at work, but I'm going to have to evade Lise. And then I'll have to decide what to tell Hans.*

The thought of Hans brought heat to my cheeks. Despite my efforts to stifle my attraction to the man who ran the Thaden household—a Teuton priest of black fire who played a pivotal role in awakening my magic—my muses returned to him more often than they should. Over the past few months, he had instructed me on how to hone my ice to the point where I could separate my spirit from my body. That was the type of magic I used to help the bullied girl.

I should have managed it without detection. Regular people could not see a Teuton spirit . . . but I had not expected the girl to find my ice-coated body in the bathroom stall.

Hans will be mad at me when he finds out what happened. But I have to tell him, find out if I need to go into hiding now that an outsider saw my magic. That was not a pleasant prospect. Although my father was a Teuton just like me, he had shunned the very idea of magic ever since my mother passed away. He was the reason I never knew about my ice until age thirteen—long after most Teuton children first discovered their elements.

I did not fault my father's distrust of sorcery. Blood magic had killed my mother, whom he dearly loved. He could mourn in whatever way he saw fit.

But if I had to go into hiding because Vreni saw my magic, he would be hurt. Betrayed. Disappointed.

Hans will know some way around this.

When I reached the curving stone wall that surrounded Thaden property, I unlocked the aged door that opened onto the side street, out of sight of the house. That was the door I always slipped through when Hans took me to study with Lady Muniche, because my father would have a fit if he knew I was learning all about our people's traditions courtesy of a crone. He wished to envision a world with no magic of any type, no spirits that embodied the rivers, no tree fairies, no demons lurking in the shadows.

That world had left me behind.

In the back gardens, I took a circuitous route to the house, trying to hide behind hedgerows whenever I could.

At this hour Lise might be cleaning, and hopefully she would not feel inspired to glance out any of the back windows.

Just as I skirted the deck en route to the side door, I ran smack into Lise's husband Siggi. The head groundskeeper carried a rake over his shoulder, the brim of his hat shading his face from the late spring sunlight. "Whoa there!" he cried out in an easy voice as I knocked into his long legs. "What brings you here at this time of day?"

I nearly swallowed my heart. I had not expected to encounter anyone in my quest for the house, for my family's property was large. "I . . . uh . . . I . . . ." Words failed me, and I stared down at Siggi's dirt-caked boots.

"Has somebody hurt you?" he inquired gently, his tone holding no rebuke.

Gathering my courage, I lifted my chin to meet his warm brown eyes. "I'm looking for Hans," I admitted, keeping my voice down in case any other workers lingered in the vicinity. "Is he in his office?"

Siggi raised an auburn eyebrow at me before looking toward the house. "I think so. He's usually checking your Pappi's investments at this hour."

"Okay." I breathed a sigh of relief and took one step forward before halting. "Siggi, *please* don't tell your wife I'm home!" I begged, not wanting to face Lise's reprimands. I did not need both her and Hans angry at me.

Siggi gave me a casual salute and said, "As you wish." He winked and then turned away, sauntering toward a patch of blooming peonies.

At least he had no conniptions about me skipping school. Hesitation slowed my steps as I headed for the side door. I felt certain Hans would not be pleased to be pulled away from his accounting duties, but I needed someone's guidance. As a Teuton priest, maybe he could advocate for me if Vreni squealed about my magic. Maybe.

I made it into the house unseen and crept up the back staircase, a tingling sensation running along every nerve. My brain replayed what had prompted me to run home, and I tried to work out just how much I should tell Hans.

He needed to know the main problem—that an outsider had not only seen my frozen body, but also the moment my spirit returned to it, breaking it out of its icy coating.

If nothing else, I certainly hoped those brainless seniors were spooked enough to never bother Vreni again. I had sliced my spiritual hands through their chests, enshrouding them in ice's cold, and sent a pointed message to their minds to stop intimidating girls. When in spirit form, a Teuton could project thoughts to a person's mind, akin to telepathy. Hans once told me that my spiritual voice had similarities to my actual voice; therefore, I had attempted to lower it when I spoke to the bullies, trying to imitate the principal's sharp tone.

The three had exchanged a few curse words and worried phrases before the largest one said, "This place is haunted! I'm getting out of here." Seconds after they scattered, Vreni scurried off to the restroom. Where she came upon me.

I had never really spoken to her except in passing. Vreni was new to my private school this year, and the rest of us had formed cliques long ago. That was likely why those awful guys had zeroed in on her. Had she stayed in school after I ran from her like a chicken? How many people had she told? Did anyone believe that she had found a classmate literally frozen in a bathroom stall?

I stood now before the door to Hans' office. Sounds of typing seeped through the wood, so I knew he was in there. Dropping my schoolbag to the floor, I placed a hand to my chest and forced my lungs to take a deep breath. At least I had not felt smothered, even in the midst of panic. Could I maintain my poise while relating the story to my secret crush—an adult I feared, respected, and adored in equal measure?

It was time to find out.

To be continued . . . .

Curious about where my writerly muses
will lead readers next?

Order *Cursed Escape,* the first book in the
next Teutonic fantasy saga, from your
preferred platform!

I would be delighted if you would leave a review for this
book. Reviews help other readers find the stories they long
to enjoy, and this indie author appreciates your feedback!

If you'd like to read the short story about how Swanie
became friends with Vreni, subscribe to my newsletter to
download your eBook copy of *Veiled Magic.* Stick around
for giveaways, photos of locales that inspire my books,
ARC opportunities, and snippets of my current works-in-
progress.
https://dl.bookfunnel.com/jp1vp51i52

Numinous Fortune is available on library platforms. Ask
your local library to order it in eBook or paperback so
Swanie's story can reach more readers!

Follow me on social media:
https://www.facebook.com/CLCarhartAuthor
https://www.instagram.com/c.l.carhart.author
https://www.minds.com/clcarhart/
https://www.bookbub.com/profile/c-l-carhart

Acknowledgements

It's about time for me to offer a heartfelt thanks to the many friends, family, and random acquaintances who've made an impact—no matter how small—on Swanie's saga.

Carter – The fantasy-romance-loving husband who has been a gracious sounding board for fifteen years. Some of his input includes Wuotan's throne of black stone, Freya's death by dismemberment, Swanie & Joel visiting their children while in spirit form, Camilla's name, Ubel's element, the "Dead End" sign at the trailhead to the Black Castle, and the fact that Swanie's dad Max studied for the Teuton priesthood. This saga would have been boring—and possibly never finished—without you.

Daddy — The man who pricked my conscience about Teutonic magic and its devilish roots. I look forward to exploring the nuances of that issue in future series! Your advice has shaped many a book, and I truly appreciate the fact that you've never questioned my faith despite the complex themes I tackle.

Mommy – I'll never forget that you apologized for judging this series so harshly after you first read *Numinous Fortune*. Few people have the courage to do such a thing. FYI whenever you get around to writing your book of observations, I can totally get that thing formatted, uploaded, and published.

Liz — Never imagined that one day you'd be editing my "wicked" books when we first met in a far different place. Thanks for your keen eye and sensible feedback, and for recognizing that being a Christian doesn't mean you can't enjoy darker-themed novels.

Catherine — Thank you so much for faithfully beta reading and giving me insight on a survivor's life. I admire you.

Sarah — Another gracious beta reader who corrected my missteps on childbirth, C-sections, and chickens. I hope you keep hanging around.

Uncle Phil — The beta reader who reminded me not to mention any real-life entities in a negative way in my fiction. I've been looking out for that ever since.

Phil — Family obligations notwithstanding, I appreciate your input on *Arcane Gateway*.

Becca — For telling me that you bought *Arcane Gateway* to support me as a friend, but by the end you were reading it because you liked the story! Thanks for buying and reviewing every book since.

Jenny — For giving me a much-needed boost mid-series when you read *Arcane Gateway* and liked it so much you had to buy signed copies of every book!

Mark & Alice — For taking a chance on my series when I had barely stuck my neck out in the public sphere, and for reviewing each book fairly. I'm truly grateful for your support.

Nessa — For the lovely character sketches you created for the first two books in this series. I hope your art career takes off as you mature and gain experience.

Mr. Smith — Your character made it all the way to the final version of this series. Thanks for forcing me out into the real world; you made sure this series would reach the public.

Mr. Grinstead — The frog at the bottom of the well.

Andrew — For having a hand in Augustin's epigraph, and for informing me of the term, "Excursus." Now all of my readers know it exists, too.

Elena — For pointing me to Jenna Moreci's channel, which was an essential guide on my indie author journey. Thanks for your stalwart support of the creative community.

Each successful author in the *Wide for the Win* Facebook group — For convincing me not to publish my books in only one place.

And for all of you readers who have made your way through Swanie's entire saga—keep being awesome!

Teutonica Translations

Aelte Teutonica – old Teutonica, used in the B.C.E. years
Der Weg Teutonisch – The Teutonic Way
Eihalbe/Eihalbae – singular/plural, fairy of silver oak
Gaestelort – spiritual realm
Gaestelort Troumerae – spiritual dream world
Leitaeri – Prince/Keyholder of a Teuton city
Leitalra/Leitalrae – singular/plural, Lady of a Teuton city
Teutonica – old Teuton dialect
Torstein – stone of the gate
Toteheri – dead army
Truhtein – master
Wegstunta – an hour's walk, about 2.3 miles
Wuotan – demon lord of the Teuton people

Medieval Hours of Eisenwald

Vigils – midnight
Matins – 2 a.m.
Lauds – sunrise
Terce – 9 a.m.
Sext – 12 noon
None – 3 p.m.
Vespers – lighting of lamps/dusk
Compline – before bed/dark

Pronunciation Guide
(for names and commonly used words)

Abelard – AB-uh-lard
Augustin – Au-GUS-tin
Bayerisch – BEYE-rish (eye is pronounced like eyeball)
Bayern – BEYE-urn (eye is pronounced like eyeball)
Dane – DAH-nuh
Der Weg – Dare Veg
Eihalbe – EYE-hahl-buh (eye is pronounced like eyeball)
Eisenwald – EYE-zen-vald (eye is pronounced like eyeball)
Fonsi – FON-zee
Freia/Freya – FREYE-yuh (eye is pronounced like eyeball)
Ina – EE-nuh
Isar – EE-zahr
Jan – Yahn
Jarvis – YAR-viss
Leitaeri – Leye-TARE-ee (eye is pronounced like eyeball)
Leitalra – Leye-TAHL-rah (eye is pronounced like eyeball)
Lise – LEEZ-uh
Matthias – Muh-TEE-uhs
Muniche – MYOO-nih-khuh
None – Nohn
Swanhilde – Swan-HIL-duh
Thaden – TODD-n
Torstein – TOR-stein (stein is pronounced like a beer stein)
Toteheri – TOH-tuh-hare-ee
Teutonica – Too-TAHN-ih-kuh
Üwe – EW-vuh
Vreni – FRAY-nee
Wuotan – VOH-tahn

About the Author

C.L. Carhart has been writing since the age of 4, dabbling in everything from children's books, to fantasy, to historical fiction. Eventually, her lifelong interest in European history inspired her to create a paranormal fantasy realm based on the Teutonic people groups. The *His Name Was Augustin* series provides a first glimpse at this other-world—a place rife with ancient mysteries and dark magic.

Born and raised in southern New Jersey, C.L. spends her free time hiking with her husband, enjoying metal music, snuggling her feline familiars, and dreaming of the wonders of Germany.